Sin Eaters:

Retribution,

Devotion Book Two

Sin Eaters:

Retribution,

Devotion Book Two

Kai Leakes

www.urbanbooks.net

Urban Books, LLC
97 N18th Street
Wyandanch, NY 11798

Sin Eaters: Retribution, Devotion Book Two

ISBN 13: 978-1-60162-417-8
ISBN 10: 1-60162-417-4

First Trade Paperback Printing July 2014
Printed in the United States of America

10 9 8 7 6 5 4 3 2 1

Distributed by Kensington Publishing Corp.
Submit Wholesale Orders to:
Kensington Publishing Corp.
C/O Penguin Group (USA) Inc.
Attention: Order Processing
405 Murray Hill Parkway
East Rutherford, NJ 07073-2316
Phone: 1-800-526-0275
Fax: 1-800-227-9604

Sin Eaters:

Retribution,

Devotion Book Two

by

Kai Leakes

Acknowledgments

We have come to the end and I have gone through so much to get these wonderful characters out and share their voices with the world. This has been a fun learning experience and I thank everyone who has supported me in this and waited on this release. A big thank you to actress Kimberly Hill for being my kick-butt looking cover model & photographer Kris Mayeshiro for an incredible image. You both were a godsend!

To my support system and muses: My mom (Sakina): you were the first to help me grow my library. The first to help me fall in love with the fantasy stories and romance I adored. Before book clubs it was us discussing the various books we shared. You instilled in me my love for books and reading as well as supported my bookstore habit. I love you and appreciated the hand you had in the creation of my imagination. To my little brother "T": for asking about that novel. To Grams, all of my uncles (Skip, George, Petie), my cousins (Aisha, Felice, Breiona), and the rest of my family: for embracing me in everything I've done and continue to do. (Uncle Shannon, I miss you.)

To Liz, Ashely, Paulette: for being true to me in this life and supporting me in this all. To Nikki-Michelle: for pushing me to send this story, loving my characters, and helping me through this writing process by kicking my procrastinating butt. Love you, sis. To Ms. B (Brenda Hampton): you saw something in this story, stood by me and my work then took a chance on a newbie. I'll always

Acknowledgments

be thankful for what you've done and to L.A. Banks (Momma Banks) for having inspired me in this journey and leaving your words as a marker of wisdom for me.

Finally but not last, to my supporters (Zansheree, Natasha, Lawrence, and others): Thank you. To those I've forgotten and you the reader: Thank you for trusting in my work and for diligently asking for more. We are on this journey until we ride it to the end and hopefully you all will love this series as I have. #TeamSineaters, I appreciate you all and let's hope for more stories to come.

Dear #Teamsineaters, it was requested to add an index for the fans to reference the terms and sayings in the series. This can now be found in the back of the book.

Welcome back to the world of the *Sin Eaters* and Cursed. When the Light and Dark are at war, sometimes the Grey can only be your salvation.

~Kai L.

Prelude

The past . . .

"Where are you going to go, boy? You're surrounded!"
Like hell, woulda ever let ya take me down, boss,
rushed into his mind as he ran. More like sprinted
through the thick, grasping trees that surrounded him.
Rigged branches reached out to him as if they had a
mind of their own. Their thick almost-black rooted stems
twisted in their uprooting from the bowels of the earth
to make him trip, but he was smarter than the trees. He
leaped and veered out of their menacing way and his
arms jolted outward to part through bushes.

With all of the trees that surrounded him, he would not
have believed that he was back in Harlem, had he known
any better; but for those who don't know it by that name,
New York was where he was. The bustling city lights
covered the sky like fireflies splashed across the sky's
black canvas. The noisy zipping of various buckets and
hacks driving carelessly pass tourists and city folk gave
him a sense of how close he exactly was to civilization. It
also gave him a sense of purpose.

Twigs snapped suddenly and the rustling of leaves
tussling against each other let him know they were still
hot on his trail. His mind was racing as he looked for an
out. All of this was too familiar to him. Beady red eyes
flickered at him in the darkness of the wilderness—no, of
the park. He was in Central Park. He should have realized

that. Those piercing eyes stared at him in delight, ready to seize the opportunity to hogtie him so that he could be their little plaything but he would not give them that satisfaction. Not yet.

Beads of midnight dew kissed his face the moment he stepped through the thicket. His wingtip shoes abruptly skidded as they made contact with wet, slick grass. He jumped. Then he lifted in the air, almost floating for a mere second. Both of his large feet clacked against pebbled stone the moment they met the ground.

He could hear the enemy. He could feel them breathing against the back of his neck. Each hair on his body stood in salute, coming alive in electric awareness. In this life at least, he knew he could die on his terms and die giving them a fight. In seven minutes, his time would be up soon anyway, so what could he really do about not being bumped off?

Seven . . .

A whizzing sound sizzled past his ear and he felt the hot trickle of blood mixing with his sweat and the quick pop of the gun after the fact. They wanted to play dirty. They wanted to make him appear to be a patsy and a hood. He had to laugh; he was better than a hood. Sure, at one time, he had to fill that slot but now he was his own man, a bruno to a well-known trouble boy who protected the meek of Harlem. They worked together with his gang to find those who were kidnapped or were bumping gums to the wrong people. They worked to regain money lost in predatory loans and schemes and wrongful repositions. They worked to build up their people and to protect all who walked the streets of Harlem from the highbinders that made it their mission to tear down the community. But these men who were after him, the very scum and thugs themselves, were no normal men.

Corrupted monsters in the flesh of coppers more like it. Oh, what he wouldn't give to go out between the gams of a looker for a change.

Six . . .

The menacing snarl of dogs in the distance made him grimly chuckle before closing his eyes with the feel of his body vibrating with his gift. His gift allowed him to use the sound waves around him to channel it into music. With a slight part of his lips, he let out a low hum. Whistling, he changed the pitched and dropped into a low crouch. Both hands extended outward and he observed his skin lighting up in swirling patterns against its burnished surface. That was his clue to project that vibrating power out in waves toward the hunting dogs. A change in his vision instantly allowed him to see through their glittering eyes. He then knew where to run next. With a quick shift of the pitch of his song, he caused the dogs to halt their barks, whimper, and then stopped in their tracks to turn. *Attack,* was his simple mental command and he watched the dogs attack their owners before sprinting away in retreat.

His sweat dripped down his face like rain on the ground before him. His ragged breath came out in sharp bursts and he pushed up to start his run again. They wouldn't get what he had been given a vision to find. That he was sure he had hidden well; he had taken something priceless, something rare, and something they wanted destroyed but couldn't. Something they had to hide from his people because he had learned it could kill the leader of their kind.

Five . . .

This was a once-in-a-lifetime win for their side and he had to make sure they would never get their hands on it. He knew the enemy had Warlocks and Witches who could work into his mind. Luckily, for him, his Mystic gifts were too strong for them to break through, so he inwardly laughed and stopped once he met the end of a pond. *Shit.* He could hear them and he knew he was at his rope's end. The jig was up. He felt himself snagged by the ankles and thrown to the ground. The heckling and putrid nostril-burning plumes of a Dark Gargoyle let him know that the enemy had him. Yep, there was nothing for him to do but practice constraint, settled in his mind.

Four . . .

"Boy gave us a good show, but tonight we will feast on your filthy Light-filled body," a voice sounded around him, causing him to glare toward the thicket then narrow his glowing jade eyes.

Two Anarchy Snatchers stood before him, something that was very rare for him to meet. A blonde with a finger-wave bob and curves that clearly whispered she was lethal stepped forward. She wore a form-fitting ruby gown that fit the current times and her movie-star looks, with a tiny dot near the corner of her blood-red plump lips that dripped that "it" factor. Sure, he was familiar with her from where he worked. She was new at the Phoenix Club. Her ambiguous race made her the bees knees with the patrons at the club. But it was her ass and those lips and sultry voice that always told those she so wanted to join her true birth. He had to laugh because as he watched her, black currents dripped from her fingertips like squid ink and snaked its way toward him while forming a slick black rope. Yup, this broad's true birth was nothing her meat bag of a shell perpetrated.

"What a shame, what a shame. I would have loved to keep you around a little longer my dear sap," the woman cooed. She gave off a chilling light laugh then sashayed forward.

At that same moment, her companion, who was what the women would call a "beefcake," strolled near her side. He flipped his lighter and lit a white cigarette with an impassionate sneer across his chiseled face. The tall, jet-black-haired Rudolph Valentino doppelganger whistled and more coppers appeared from behind the trees to surround them on all sides.

"You took from us, boy. Do you have anything you want to say before I make you my bitch and give you to our master?" His captor snapped his fingers and flashed his pearly whites, staring down at him, his leather shoe pressed against his windpipe cutting off his air. "Nothing to say? Stand him up, darling. I can't hear him."

Three . . .

It felt good to get off the wet grass. He felt his body being snatched up by his feet to stand upright. The pair had moxie, which amused him. But they were as stupid as rocks for not frisking him. Working his wrist, his blade snaked from his hands and he gave a raspy reply: "Hey. *C'est si bon,* mista, right?"

It was simple for him to drop the blade around his ankles and use his power to cut his ankles free. His fists landed into the first copper who jumped him. An elbow connected into the ribs of another. A quick neck grab then lunge over his broad shoulder had him light a third minion aflame in holy Mystic power.

"My name ain't boy and screw your torpedo scum squad. You may have caught me this time but it is only because I let ya. By the way, spiffy shoes, cat, but mine are much better." His jubilant brawl with the enemy had him blindsided and shackled by black ropes from the female Anarchy Snatcher.

Sparking trusses of power snaked around him. She pulled, which had him falling backward hard on the ground. The hussy's demonic strength allowed her to hoist him into the air; another thick rope tightened around his throat. He knew what was about to occur before it even happened and that familiar sound of rope snapping against a tree limb made him close his eyes in acceptance.

Two . . .

"What a pitiful shame," he heard the blonde mocked. The cords she controlled tightened around his throat, painfully cutting into his flesh at the same time.

"He has nothing to snitch about so end this because this is nothing but a vacation for him." His captor yawned exasperatedly. He turned on his heel to light up another ciggy then coolly walked away. "Until we meet again, boy."

It was time. He bore his teeth in a triumphant grin and his eyes blazed their familiar jade iridescence. *Never break your cool,* he told himself. He connected to his birthright and power blazed around his body causing the mob around him to back up in fear of being touched by the light. They were going to burn tonight, like all those innocents, those demons snatched from their homes or cars; and as they blazed, he was going to have his moment of peace.

Yes, he'd get to see that glimpse of his family at the gates before coming back to exact his vengeance but he hoped that maybe this time he'd get to see her. He fought for her. His true love. The one they had kidnapped long ago and with his every return entry into the divine plane, it let him know that she could still be out there, reborn somewhere. Whenever he couldn't find her. This gave him hope to save her, as he should have before. But now he had something that would give his side the advantage over this never-ending war and soon he would start this cycle all over again.

So with a happy birthday to him, he focused on his spirit. Willing it to remember all he had ever done. With a brazen shout, he spit at his enemies feet, "My name is Calvin . . . never 'boy.'"

The taut snap of a rope and crack of a tree's limb sounded in the night. The image of a man in a long, sweeping black coat with a billy club in his hand and a blade in his other hand flashed across his faltering gaze. Piercing, icy blue eyes surrounded by long black curling hair stared back at him in grief. The male aggressively cut at his enemies before his remorseful eyes made Calvin solemnly smile one last time. A whoosh with a flash of dimming light and the sound of a gong signaled . . . and then he was gone.

One . . .

Chapter 1

It was the jarring sound of his Glocks going off, a piercing, soul-gripping scream, a tearing pain at his heart and soul chakra—with that of the intercepting clanging of metal scraping against concrete—that drew his attention away from pushing his power to a lethal level. Calvin Freeman-Tem knew without even seeing what exactly was going on behind him. It was a no-brainer for him that today was a game changer. Game changers in his world were no idle thing for him. They were like being given an anointing message in church, or getting a specific message penned to you in a horoscope or palm reading. They were like little bursts of sage advice given by a loving Nana, which was helping him now. The battle they were in was mounting into an epic warfare that was going to change not only his ragtag group of warriors, his House, and position, but also all of the Nephilim, both Light and Dark, and humans' world.

His cousin was cut down. The Oracle was gone. He knew this by their familial blood bond. He could feel the stopping of her heart. She had been hit by a Cursed blade. Only such weapons could cut down, maim, and kill a Nephilim; human weapons took longer to harm, but that wasn't the case with special-class Nephilim weapons, both Light and Dark. She had been hit hard, and because she was still awakening, he knew she was done for; she was still just human, even though she was coming into her power. His heart was breaking.

Today in the life of an Immortal Mystic warrior as himself, all hell was about to let loose. It wasn't due to the fact that the sudden rain that was falling around them had fallen at an eerie, slow pace. Or that the woman, who was his god cousin, wailed on her hands and knees in half-Dragon form causing the building to shake with her power. Even as the beauty of the Dragon's iridescent wings overtaking the sky memorized him while she pounded onto the concrete roof of the high-rise they were currently located wasn't the reason for his sharp awareness. The same could be said with the fact that the Dragon was between his cousin Sanna and a guy, he had formed a relatively close friendship protecting them both with a power sigil that etched into the concrete surface. That pretty dope show of new power from the Dragon wasn't why he looked on in frozen awareness where he was.

No, it was the fact that he stood watching in painful shock, tucking his winning prize against the lining of his jacket, covering it in Mystic power to keep it there, as the atmosphere around them began to pulse with a life of its own. He was familiar with it. He was very familiar with the exchange of power that was connecting with the life in every molecule in the area. The Reaper was coming to life and his homeboy was turned all the way up.

Calvin glanced over his shoulder checking for the two bitches who caused all the chaos and disarray around them. There was no sign of them, but his Mystic Locus Tracer was leaving a trail for him in the darkness of the night. He turned at that moment to see his friend, Khamun, once known as the Attacker, an unknown aggressive and manic killer, running through the streets of Chicago, Illinois, and St. Louis, Missouri taking down any being or entity that was either Cursed or touched by the Cursed, bulking in size. Calvin knew shit was getting real the longer Khamun stood dumbstruck. He stared down at the body of his cousin's fallen body and the stream of ruby blood that stained the rooftop.

Khamun's ropy locks sparked with silver currents of power, flowing over the cord-tight surface of his constricted biceps, forearms, and surging around his clenched fist as an energy ball. Dude looked like something out of an anime series to Calvin. His usually warm brown eyes were pitch-black. The typically Hershey chocolate tone of his skin began to radiate in a fiery cadence. His already cresting fangs were now at animalistic lengths and his boy just kept getting bigger in size.

Calvin remembered in his Mystic classes that only Archangels, warrior-class entities, could get to sizes as Khamun, and right now, dude was on some WWE proportions. Hulking up was an understatement. The moment the Reaper's silver-black wings overshadowed his god cousin's Kyo's wings, and shifted from being soft feathers to that of steel and "cut you hard as a diamond" mode, Calvin knew to step back. He saw everyone—Marco, Lenox, his baby sister Kali, the new kids on the team, everyone—step back as Khamun propelled in the air at sonic force, and hovering over them for a millisecond.

Calvin heard one of his crew say the guy he knew as R.J. was the Key, but in that moment, he didn't give a damn; his family and R.J. lay gutted. Chumps were about to get their heads busted in. Yet again, as was his right, he was about to take that familiar role he always did. All while Khamun, no, as the Reaper, who his boy officially learned was his true nature, began his holy wrathful binge on the two women who set him off: the Dark Lady and her bitch of a pet, the Medusa. Sweat ran down his face and he wiped it away while catching his breath.

Calvin popped a Qua Gum stick in his mouth to replenish himself. He wiped his brow, made sure all his Mystic-blessed bullets in his Glocks were replenished, and he glanced at his other team members and followed his boy. Both Lenox and Marco gave him an understanding nod. He wanted to stay by his cousin's side, but he knew he had to do his job, and by doing that, he was still honoring his cousin. It was his turn to be the anchor, since he was the Mystic of the group.

It was his duty to cover the Reaper in charging healing spells as a means of keeping him in the game of hunting after the enemy. Even though he was getting tired from using all of his magic, he had to do this. Even at risk of his own health, he had to do this, because he was trained to do so, family was everything to him, and he wanted to get his vengeance out on the broads who just took from him. Eye for a damn eye. Crooked tooth for a jagged grill.

So, he jumped from the roof using his power to buffer his fall, and he landed Timbs first in a full run in the narrow alleyways before him as he tracked the Reaper in the night sky. This was for family and this was for his blood. Today was going to be a good day for hunting the Cursed. Welcome to the life of a Guardian Team, especially the life of an Immortal Mystic Class Disciple, such as Calvin was.

The Reaper slowly stood while everything surrounding him gradually faded behind him in a tunnel of sound waves and light. He wasn't done. They were not done. His fiancée lay crumbled and in critical danger. Bright red blood drained from her stomach wound. The man who took the brunt of it lay beside her, lifeless, as something like screeching shrieks, which he identified in the back of his mind, came from Kyo.

Something had snapped within his lethal mind causing him to deliberately roll his broad shoulders. The Reaper instantly came alive and his amber irises flickered in the moonlight before darkening to coal black. With every breath he took, his metallic silver ebon wings rose up and down in his fury. His locks lifted from his muscular shoulders. His muscles tightened and constricted to the point where his veins seemed ready to burst. This couldn't be happening.

A snarl flashed across his handsomely defined features and his incisors dropped to deathly lengths, marking him ready for the hunt. This was his fault. With his fists clenched to the point of his nails almost cutting into his palms, a sonic current surrounded him. The wave of energy covered him in a cloak and he disappeared, using a transition spell, which landed him near where his enemy had fallen beside the building. Nostrils flaring, he inhaled deeply, instantly catching their scent like a rabid dog.

She should have stayed in the compound as he tried to make her. *She should have listened!* Before she had come into this life, his soul mate, Sanna, the woman in his arms, was just an extraordinary female human. Sanna had been attempting to make a name for herself as a chef and restaurateur in the St. Louis, Missouri area with her best friend. Life was good for her, as he recalled. It was his duty to watch her, to protect her as all Guardian Angels did. However, that changed with the onset of her returning migraines and her first face-to-face meeting with a demon sent out to harm her.

After that, his role changed. He ignored the rules of his people, the Nephilim Society, by breaking his code of never interacting with humans in the flesh. It wasn't hard to do for him, because the day he was assigned Sanna's case, he had fallen in love with her vibrant soul. It was only later, once her life became threatened, that he learned she was not just an ordinary human, but also one that carried Nephilim DNA. This was when things changed.

He and his team of protectors, Nephilim and Immortal humans who had come together to work in Society to protect innocents from the Dark, came to Sanna's aid. As special beings, they could blend into the human population without anyone knowing if they were angels or other worldly entities. This was how he, her cousins Calvin and Kali, and his cousin Marco and Lenox, were all able to surround her in protection after the demon attacks became worse. To human's eyes, even demons appeared human, only if they were possessing a corrupted human, which to Sanna's eyes at that time any demon attacked, they appeared human, until they shifted to reveal the monsters they were. This introduced Sanna and her best friend Kyo to his world: a world where if a person was not a full-blooded angel, then that person may be ostracized, while being used. His world was full of hypocrites who believed that the only role of an angel was to protect and ignore the human condition. By breaking those bigot codes, he and his team, his close comrades discovered generations of hidden secrets. They learned that not only was Sanna half Nephilim but that Kyo was a Gargoyle.

It was revealed that Sanna was also a powerful force called the Oracle. Through her, they found an old book of Nephilim codes, laws, lost biblical truths, and journal entries labeled a devotion book, which had other lost companion books. In the book, he discovered that he was no ordinary Guardian Angel. That the fangs he bore, were no genetic anomaly placed on them from generations prior of the first Fallen Angels lying with humans.

No, he was a creation meant to hunt down demons and feast on the souls they craved to make dark through their demonic blood. He was a Reaper, from a line of Sin Eaters meant to destroy the Cursed. Both women in his care were special. It was their destiny to make the Nephilim Society, mainly the Council, realize that they were dying in the war against Light and Dark, and all because of their prejudices and staunch beliefs. Their ignorance was aiding the Cursed.

The Cursed were dark Nephilim who made his people almost extinct on earth all on the orders of their evil King, his daughter the Dark Lady and her Dark Gargoyle pet, the Medusa. They were a part of a kingdom of demonic entities who hunted, ravished, and possessed their prey. With just a touch or bite, they tainted, to kill and pillage any human they wanted and destroy any angels they could find. Those key things continued the ancient battle between the Cursed and the Light. This with the attack against the Oracle and his family was why he now was in full Reaper mode.

His prey's spicy feminine scent had him propel himself in the air. At the same time, he wiped blood from his face with his cocoa-tatted forearm. The blood fresh from his battle smeared into his mouth making him lick his plump lips with the taste of both his cousin's and her demon Protector's dark marker. He flattened his tongue to the roof of his mouth then slowly curled it, moving it around to savor it like wine. This allowed him to implant their tracker into his body. Air quickly became his friend. It caressed him as a familiar lover would which allowed him to leap up and surge through the darkness. Darkness caused his sight to switch into night vision, helping in his hunt to locate the Dark Lady's pumping pulse easier.

He saw that both she and her Dark Gargoyle stumbled through back alleys trying to make it back to their head-quarters. Their escape was not about to go down tonight. He let out a low growl. He knew they heard him, which made this ever more satisfying for him. Retribution was only his and he could taste their anger at losing the battle before it turned into sour fear. This was a fear he was

familiar with. See for him, this was the true, purest form
of fear, fear not created and owned by the Dark.

The Dark was known to feed on fear from humans and
they never feared anything themselves except their Dark
Lord. But this was a dread new to them and the Reaper
laughed knowing this was perplexing for them. The terror
they were experiencing was based in the knowledge and
rooted in the reality that he could snuff them out and lay
them at the feet of their Dark Lord for their failure, all
before showing them what true divine punishment was.
Mortal fear was what it was, a flaw in their eyes with
mixing with humans. This was that irritating fear that
maybe they had made the wrong choice in accepting the
Dark and the Reaper loved it. You reap what you sow
meant oh so much when dealing with him. However now
he knew that his cousin was coming to that realization.

Unbeknownst to Khamun, this was the reason why his
line was wiped out long ago: his power was a threat. The
true Dark Lord himself had to be careful in how he killed
the Most High's most revered weapons. If he killed off too
many, he threatened to destroy the delicate good-versus-
evil balance and ending his reign in hell. There were rules
to this game and the Reaper was slowly learning that. He
had to check how he killed his enemy. If he allowed his
spirit to truly fall by killing his prey out of darkness and
not light, then his birthright was over.

The sound of a slight scraping of metal caused him to
take in his surroundings. A miniscule glint in the dark
had his instant attention. They were near. Hurriedly he
flew in the sky to drop upon a rooftop's edge to watch
his prey. The Dark Lady stood below holding her side
while resting her shoulder against a brick wall. Her long
mahogany dark hair was matted to her ruddy sepia face.
Her back heaved up and down. Her downcast face let him
know that she was watching her pet pale and sway from
loss of blood.

Khamun quietly stared into the darkness. He could swear that he saw sparks of light, only known with his kind, surrounding the pair in spurts, mainly around the Dark Gargoyle. *Interesting. There was some change in that one.* He could taste it in her blood. Something airy and sweet mixing in the typically pungent acidic taste of their Cursed kind. There was something about it that forced him to store that awareness to memory, but for now he couldn't care less. They took from him and now their putrid husks of a heart were slated to be his.

With a quick shift upward to stand again, the Reaper paced back and forth on the rooftop's ledge, listening to the pair argue with each other. He observed as the Dark Lady slapped her Protector, and then laughed in crazed delight while she gestured with her hands. *That bitch is clearly crazy.* She limped around the tight alleyway, circling her protector, yelling about her faults in the battle. The woman was berating her about her lost arm, telling her that she was useless as a Protector. The scene was comical to him. Like a dramatic screenplay or something on reality TV. He watched his crazed cousin turn back around and kiss her Protector on the mouth, her tongue snaking out to part her bloody lips. Battle lust could amplify a lot, but this crap was insane. He had to spit in disgust over the disrespect the Dark Lady put on the Medusa.

A part of him felt conflicted. That holy part of him that knew that if she were an innocent he would fight for her behalf, but this was the Medusa. She was a beast known for her incredulous tracking skills and a renowned kidnapper and murderer of innocents and Nephilims alike. She was indiscriminative in her pursuits and ruthless. Any pain she felt or disrespect she felt, he was sure that the Medusa enjoyed it too, in her own sick way. Therefore, he watched them and narrowed his eyes.

He would be just as indiscriminative and divinely ruthless in his pursuit of the pair. A quiet reprieve made him chuckle deeply while his locks flew around his stern and handsome features. Eyes glowed like amber jewels sitting in the sun. The sun itself represented the gold ring circling his iris, which pulsed with his power. He licked his lush lips and ran a khemetic-angelic tattooed inked hand over his crisp-cut goatee that only lined his jaw. The Reaper swore he saw, as quickly as a wink, the Medusa's hatred for her Mistress. He swore he saw a razor's edge of Light flicker behind her irises. Ready to slice the other in pieces, but as quickly as he observed it, was as quick as it had disappeared.

Again, that was something stored to the dome. He really didn't care what he just witnessed because he also saw that sick love and devotion for her Mistress at the same time. He remembered the satisfying look in that bitch's eyes before she sliced at his beloved. And for that, an eye for an eye was, yet again, his right. So he quietly watched. His wings rested against his back; his blades slid from his gloved hands. The darkness and the kiss of the moon acted as his invisible cloak, shielding him from their view before he dropped behind the bickering women. The sound of his Timbs hitting wet puddle-lined pavement was his entrance. Its echo had the women turn his way in a hiss. Their wide-eyed shock amused him as he dropped his invisible shield. The moment they turned to run, the rush of the hunt had his blood rising causing him to sprint after them to their dismay.

A husky laugh projected out from him. They pushed a garbage bin his way. It scraped against the asphalt of the alleyway leaving a caulk outline against its surface. Rushing him as if it were a living body or a team of linebackers, he jumped over it. He lifted in the air then landed behind the gliding bin with ease. Sweat sprinkled his brow. Both women, his prey, ran faster, having heard him and sensed him behind them. Their blood dripped wherever they moved and he traced it as if it were a neon paint trail. The blood sung to him and made him thirst, made him crave.

He knew they only ran because they were severely weakened. It wasn't rocket science that the closer they got to their home, the more support they could have in protecting themselves. This was why he leaped over them and made them run in another direction. Not because he assumed he couldn't handle their army on his own, but because he wanted to hunt and this was fun for him.

"Hey. Hey! Yeah, we are not done, cousin, and you know it!" the Reaper taunted in a boast to let them know he was still stalking them.

Not knowing where he was, he could see that they were clueless and that they were off track. He noticed that they took to another alleyway in the streets of Chicago. They climbed over fences and threw poison-tipped daggers while shooting off rounds his way. The need to survive caused one to make erratic choices and the wasting of ammunition was one of them, in his opinion; but again, whatever worked for his advantage was a plus for him. He dropped low like that of a panther in order to scan his surroundings then lunge forward in a run.

"I smell you both and I am so hungry; let me get a taste," he cajoled with a toying smirk. He then briefly rubbed his hands together in taunt. Thumb pressed against his nose, he flicked it in cocky amusement then propelled his body into the wind again. His dark wings innately expanded into the night, almost swallowing the alley before dropping down in front of the two stunned women. His locks fell over his handsome face, accenting the danger lurking beneath the surface of what he was. Muddled tension filled his surroundings and he enjoyed it. He used it to his advantage, connecting to the very air around them, manipulating it to become thicker, so that it became harder for his prey to breathe while his eyes shined in the moonlight.

"You and your kind have taken from us for the last time. The balance has been broken for eons and for coming after what you had no right to try to take from me. You and your bitch are mine. Fair exchange is no robbery, so say your prayers."

He watched the reality of who and what he was resonate within their eyes, before it quickly was replaced by cold malice and pride. As he stepped forward, they stepped back.

Now this was interesting to him; it caused the Reaper in him to maliciously give a fang-dropping grin. He saw the one called the Medusa hold her bloody, dripping stump. She clearly was in pain. Sweat dripped down her face. Her pupils were dilated. Her breathing erratic in between the reptilian clicking of her tongue. However, through it all, her instinct to fight was right there on the surface of her being. Her nails lengthened and, as if on cue, the smell of pungent poison saturated the darkness.

"Now I wonder where that part of you went, baby? Come give me your other arm, I'll cauterize it for you." In a manner of seconds, he was in her face, reaching out for her.

Her poison-filled nails swiped at him and her blade-heeled foot sent him sliding backward. Her legs moved as twin windmills while she struck out with one hand. Droplets of her blood kissed the pavement. It came out so fast that he noticed that she had to step back to gain her energy. He gave a throaty laugh again then ducked from a blow to his head by the Dark Lady.

Both women moved in sync to help each other. One was behind him. The other in the front of him. Their hisses and grunts made him think of the Williams sisters playing tennis while they swiped, kicked, and punched at him. Pipes burst from their places bolted on the side of random buildings. Their metal shafts flew at him, seeking to impale him.

Slick move, cousin. A brush of the Medusa's nails cutting across his chest, seeking out flesh she could not get to made him turn. He moved up and down, ducking and deflecting while he heard his cousin give a gleeful laugh and clap of her hands in joy, watching.

"*Dios, diablo.* Gosh, devil, it looks as if we have you in a bind, primo cousin. *Escucha!* Listen, your precious Oracle looked as beautiful as a living doll when she lay dead by my hands. I wanted to take her precious body then and there and make her mine; you know, eat her plum and tongue screw her until I cum, but you interrupted that, primo." The Dark Lady brazenly sulked using her fingers and tongue to illustrate what she wanted to do. Her voice turned into a sickening whine, sauntering toward him.

Her silky hair curved around her body as if it were a curtain to enhance her deep-set curves and ample attributes. A jewel-covered hand with its stiletto-shaped nails seductively ran over her sweat and blood-covered bare bronze stomach. She licked her ruby-dusted lips, her own steel-colored eyes glinting in the moonlight. "And now I want my fair exchange."

She swung toward him. Her asp ring seemingly came alive then tried to bite at him. A blow from her razor-sharp nails gashed at the side of his face. The sting of it caused him to curse with the taste of his own blood.

He wiped at his cheek and sidestepped each of her weakening moves. Sometimes she'd make contact against him, causing him aching blows. Other times, her hits came in exhausted blows. He knew she was battle worn so he decided to hurry this up with a punch to her solar plexus. The blow made her pitch a black charge that cut across his side before it disappeared. He glanced down in astonishment and slight amusement at his torn shirt. Blood spilled in a thin trail over his toasted-nutmeg skin.

Both foes stood panting waiting for the other to move. The Reaper's eyes focused on a gye nyame symbol necklace that suddenly appeared resting against his cousin's heart before fading away. He had no idea why that appeared to him as it did, but he slowly flashed a knowing smile. He was very familiar with that necklace. He wondered if she remembered that her brother still wore his, too.

An opening of a side door caused music to spill in the alley. The atmosphere filled with static, making both women pant faster for air then quickly clutch their chests at the same time. Pain centered in their torsos and a deep jerk resonated around their hearts. The Dark Lady glanced at the Medusa and she glanced at her mistress. Both women clearly understood that they were now staring their deaths in the face. That survival to eliminate a man they had underestimated was now on the back burner.

"Try something different to use as a play against my mental next time, cousin," the Reaper coolly replied. He clutched both fists at his sides then reached deep within his spirit. What he collected from within himself was then casted outward at both women. As if time had slowed down, he sent both women flying into a brick wall in front them. Pulsing lights spilled into the dark alley, the drifting singsong voice of Azealia Banks rhyming about the "212" drew his attention. A public domain, he needed to be careful.

The Reaper stepped over strewn bricks and debris with a smirk, cracking his knuckles. Both women lay unconscious against a booth in the building. Bricks, debris, and dust covered them. As he made his descent into what seemed to be a club, clueless humans, random

Nephilim civilians, and Cursed entities danced while the music pumped. The Reaper made note of the many humans and Nephilim who were not of the fighting castes as was evident by their auras and insignias glowing on various parts of their flesh.

Back in his past, he had once wished he were just a civilian Nephilim, one whose only concern was the general Society meetings and keeping an eye out for mundane vices. Not hunting down hardcore sinners or demons, as he was doing now. But, that was then and this was now. He accepted what he was born to do now and right now. Music made him bob to the beat and pull out his sword. Everything would be done on the low but to a soundtrack, he could dig.

While he scanned the club, a deep voice interrupted his musings behind him, to tell him that whoever it was had his flank covered. Dr. Eammon Toure stepped from the cloud of soot. The elder stepped over crumbled bricks with a gun in his left hand and his right clapped on the Reaper's broad shoulder. That look in the man's eyes matched his own. Wrongs were about to be settled tonight and both men moved as one. They separated to flank a set of stairways that led to the waking women. The music seemed to feed the Reaper by giving him energy. That signature vibe let him know his boy Calvin was there, fusing the music into his team and innocents within the club. *Much respect,* filtered through his mind.

The Reaper lifted his blade, ready to battle. He rammed it down onto the Dark Lady hitting nothing but the club floor. *Bullshit!* He let out a roar of frustration. Had he been totally blinded by his rage, he would not have noticed his target's unconscious form sliding across the floor by an invisible rope. A tether, which ended up connected to the now–red haired Winter, the Dark Lady's personal Witch. She stood with a sad expression in her gaze that let him know she was sorry. However, for good measure, he guessed, she thought by sending the urgently psychic plead over the music, *"You can't!"* would help matters.

Pillars and equipment began to shake. He was furious and that was an understatement. The Reaper was over the games. A blast of power flew toward the Dark Lady and Winter. He saw the shock in Winter's eyes and then the feel of a boot slamming into his temple, knocking him to the floor. Pain echoed through him. Then the quick flash of a female's shadow passed by his peripheral. He knew who it was before she opened her mouth. His own nails scraped at the dance floor under his chest. He glared upward at the Medusa.

"Touch my mistress and you die. You understand?" the Medusa snarled.

Spitting out blood, the Reaper, astonished, bobbed his head, and then pushed up on both hands. *Chick has to be out of her damn mind.* All he could do was study her from the side of his face, ready to battle. "Yes. I understand. Touch your mistress, then you die."

Swift with purpose, he tiger-clutched the Medusa's chest and dropped her to her knees in astonishment. The sound of her scream in terror made him laugh. A flicker of calm scurried over her features, almost softening them the moment her gaze fell on Calvin, who now stood behind a DJ booth watching them closely.

Calvin had taken over for a DJ he had persuaded into going on a break. A huge smile flashed across his face. He gripped the sides of his jacket, pulled it forward, and then whipped it backward as if he were Michael Jackson performing "Smooth Criminal." One hand lifted in the air, cueing a bass-thumping interlude to his next track. Adjusting his Beat by Dre headphones on his head, Cal used his own Mystic power to jolt it into the Medusa all while pumping up the crowd to keep her off balance.

The Reaper used that moment to do what he always did best. He reached out to twist her heart cavity. A pumping activated against his palm causing him to flinch in angry perplexity. The feel of that unnatural pulse, suddenly coming from a creature such as her, made him push her away. An odd sensation hit him.

Strange crap was going on, because her body instantly lit up in thousands of tiny airy lights before fading away.

"Now that is interesting. It should be a husk in there and light should not be within you. Hmm. *Shit!*" Another blast of Witch fire hit him hard, causing him to turn his back to cover himself.

In that same moment, the Reaper felt Lenox come to his side. His brother-in-arms hunkered down near where he stood bent over coughing. His brother-in-arms locked his ice-blue gaze on him in concern. No words were needed between them. Nox's eyes glowed with an ethereal wisdom. His boy turned slightly to the side pointing his favorite silver Glocks. Two rounds let off toward Winter without breaking eye contact with the Reaper.

"Marco and Kali are with Sanna. Bro, she's breathing but barely and she needs you," Nox said in warmth and concern.

"Do you see me working, man? I have shit to do here, bro. Let me handle mine. Let me get holy retribution!" the Reaper yelled in blind anger.

Lenox curtly nodded, then let his twin silver fighting sticks slide from the sleeves of his black leather jacket and hoodie. "A thousand shall fall at thy side, and ten thousand at thy right hand; but it shall not come nigh thee, this is our Templar creed. As you wish, bro, but remember, I'm here to oversee and keep your objective. All right?"

The Reaper gave a curt nod in response.

"Indeed. Time to take down a witch. I'll catch you on the other side," Nox said with a salute.

Khamun hated that he had to blast his boy like that, but he was in battle and he was working the Witch fire off him. The Reaper turned to observe a man whom he called his "Conscious" disappear in the dancing crowd to go after Winter.

Nox moved as if he were lighter than a feather. He flipped his fighting sticks in both hands and made contact with his prey. Each stick swung inward then impaled a demon through its chest. Appealingly satisfied with the sizzling and popping of its charring flesh, he regarded the area around him and saw a tall stereo amp. Climbing it, Nox kicked another demon that suddenly showed its true nature from its guise as a drunken college clubgoer and he tucked his sticks back within the sleeves of his hoodie.

A smile played around his chiseled face, one that had many women in the club gazing his way. He regarded Calvin and signaled with a tilt of his chin to repeat the track so that he could dance to the music. Nox moved his feet to the music and the tempo pumped faster. His footwork and hand movements distracted the demon. He bent low and lifted his body in the air on one hand. Lenox suavely balanced his muscled frame and used his other hand to pull out a gun from his harness. Blasts of a round of bullets ricocheted into the skull of the watching and reaching demon. Dropping into a back flip off the amp, the Reaper saw Nox run forward and chase after Winter while unaware that she shook the Dark Lady awake.

Simultaneously, Winter's head tilted to the side catching Lenox in her view. Her hand flung forward releasing several ebon currents Lenox's way. Her movements appeared calculated but Khamun soon realized it was erratic as to not hurt Nox. The woman, the Reaper knew to be the Dark Lady's personal healer and crafter of any form of dark mystic power pressed her well-manicured nails together and threw up a wall that flew toward Lenox.

Forever the skilled warrior Nox dodged each charge. Effectively he dropped into a roll, whipping out ninja stars. Winter averted each one with a dropping windmill. Quick as a sprite, she ducked behind a nearby bar, pushing a clueless human to the side. She lifted a hand and bottles went flying. While the music, persistently droned in the background, to the human eye, what Winter casted into the air seemed to be nothing but moving rave lights. But, Khamun and his team knew better.

Behind him, Calvin mixed and spun tunes that connected via an illuminating airwave to demons. The swirling illuminating threads ripped them in half, sending the demons' dark matter toward the Reaper's so that he may have fed and retched from his body. Prior, he had felt his body tiring out from the previous battle and his current chase. Now, the delectable taste of his enemy filled his palate and fueled his body. He was definitely thankful for the food. Movement made him cast an eye around the club. The Medusa, who now stood dazed, rested her good hand over her vibrating chest. The Reaper noticed that the Dark Lady now had a human attached to her mouth. Her plush lips were ruddy with blood and her steel irises glared at him before she threw the casualty to the side at the Medusa.

He knew she had grabbed the mortal, not just to feed, but to break the cloaking barrier that Calvin was crafting through his music to keep the people clueless. Now that she had brought the battle into the human world and to the attention of civilian Nephilim, he knew the club was going to erupt in chaos. As if on cue, chaos was exactly what occurred. Humans went running. Those civilian Nephilim, who could see everyone, before the humans could, tried to help however they could, but they were also too scared to be of any true help.

Random humans began to twist and contort into demons at the will of the Dark Lady. They moved in his team's ways as opponents and obstacles to distract them, but where there is Dark there is Light. He and his team saw a few brave humans step up, climbing over strewn tables, chairs, and debris to fight against the possessed zombie-like humans. Their auras and pupils shone bright with white Light, making them gifted with small strains of Nephilim DNA. They worked with the civilian Nephilims and pushed back whoever they could who got in Khamun and his team's way, making an opening for them to get through.

The Medusa venomously dropped down over the human to rip the heart out from the male's concaved chest with her tail. She gluttonously fed on it herself before casting a panicky glance his way. Yes, she knew he wasn't done with her or her mistress but while he pushed his way through the crowd it was Dr. Toure who caught his attention. The man calmly walked behind the Dark Lady and gripped her by her neck, bringing her down on his knee. The elder then stooped down to hover over her, whispering against her ear.

Whatever it was Dr. Toure whispered had the Dark Lady thrashing and screaming in the old tongue. The elder's eyes appeared to emit a source of potency that took the Reaper back. He could smell and taste old magic. No. The Reaper felt as if he was in the presence of an Old one and his father was the only Old one he knew, so he had to be tripping. Shockingly, when the Dark Lady went flying across the club without Dr. Toure laying a hand on her, the Reaper knew something was under the surface of the man he had once assumed was only a Guardian Disciple. Guardian Disciples were a group of immortal humans with no power, but who carried the angelic DNA strains of the Nephilim race.

"Your father ended my light but you will never have my child. Not in this life or the next. Now it's your turn to die," the Reaper swore he heard the good doctor's accented booming voice say.

Those words and the conviction behind them had the Reaper thinking before it disappeared from his mind. It wasn't time to get invested into something else. Several long strides then a leap in the air had him chasing after the Dark Lady again. The Medusa battled to get to her mistress and Winter threw herself over the bar to kick Lenox to the side all while she slid across the bar surface.

The Reaper heard Winter whisper on a coded psychic link that she was sorry. She hopped off the bar, ran, and grabbed the Medusa by her uninjured hand. Both women sprinted in their heeled boots seeking out their Mistress and trying to catch up to her before he did.

The Reaper enjoyed that. "Run faster," he purred, appearing at their side during their run. He then shifted to move behind them just to toy with them.

Winter pleaded with her eyes before pressing her wrists together. Her red hair returned to its dark hue, a jewel around her neck hummed then pulsed outward to cover the women in a shield. She dropped her head back chanting in the old dark tongue with various dialects fused into it.

The Reaper noticed her look his way while she pleaded. Her café au lait skin glowed like honey before paling into a ghostly sheen with her valor. Her words floated over him in a psychic mist: *"You can't, please understand. This is not just because she is my mistress. It's more to this then her being who she is. I can't explain yet and ears are listening, I must go; forgive me, but I play the game to survive for you all."*

With that, he watched her dissolve into a miasmic mist leaving the club empty of all demons while humans stood shocked and Nephilim civilians appeared just as confused. One gaze at Dr. Toure made the Reaper uncertain again. The man was glancing around as if he didn't know why he was there. The doctor stepped over strewn equipment, bricks, and other items in the club then pulled out his medic bag to help those who were hurt in the fight. "I'm a doctor, please let me help."

The Reaper didn't understand it and he didn't have time to question his Elder about what was really going on with the man. For now, he was pissed from this loss. Heads needed to be chopped off. Not only did his team suffer loss, but now some innocent human and Nephilim corpses lay strewn around the club floor. Their blood mixed with that of demon ash still floating in the wind. Fist connecting into a nearby wall had the Reaper sending a blast throughout the club making lights flicker off and on.

"Two shots to the head and a Hail Mary, then poof, bitch, you're dust! Next time, I got you!" the Reaper roared, pacing in a circle. His balled fist created a crater on its smooth surface. He stepped back then ran both of his large hands down his face with a deep exhale.

Lenox's presence at his side and deep mutter for him to remember that the fight wasn't over had him slightly annoyed but grateful. He gave his brother-in-arms a warrior's clasp before walking off frustrated. Too much information just happened in such a short span but, most importantly, his prey had gotten away. The Reaper clasped his hands over the back of his neck then inwardly cursed, "Wipe the innocents' minds and call in the cleaning crew to fix this bullshit. I'm out."

Shit is cray, flicked in the Reaper's mind. Exiting the club through the back alleyway, he took to the sky and sought out a place of solace within to ease his mind. His massive dark wings lifted him into the sky. He headed back to the rooftop for his soul mate whom he knew lay in a comatose state. He needed her to be okay, to be alive.

Chapter 2

Her dreams were tormenting her. She remembered an incident back in college with a student whose death devastated the campus community and her. His name was Lance. No one could understand how he had been attacked, but now she knew the truth of it. Her beloved Khamun had been around her always, even that far back with Lance.

However, her spirit whispered that there was something more to that memory, whatever it was. Spasms of piercing agony ricocheted throughout her body. Each crescendo of pain pulsed, and slashed through her. She then saw sparked flickers of golden white light behind her closed eyelids that guided her to a new dream, a past life, and memory. Triggered impressions so crisp, so real, that if she reached out then she could feel, smell, and taste each action. It all played for her as if she were in a movie. Burning tightness clutched at her lungs and throat, causing her to seize. The sensory world she was in swallowed her with hits, making her recall how bad her migraines used to be. But this was more. This was pain from her mind, soul, heart, and body. This was knowledge and she rent the air with a scream as she saw her family fall around her.

Fury filled her spirit. It claimed her in its own righteous indignation when she saw the man who came to her only months before as her protector then later as her soul mate die in front of her.

This is not going down on my watch, her mind screamed. But what could she really do?

Yes, she was still new to her role in all of this of understanding exactly what she could do. But from her time with her mate, the man she would go to the bowels of hell for, she innately knew that the power within her could feed him and vice versa. So she reached out pushing at the blinding pain. She cried in dismay at the images before her, shifting under her feet like quicksand.

What gave the impression of her standing in WWIII now shifted to an ancient battle reminiscent of Desert Storm but only in the deserts of Egypt. Men dressed in robes and women adorned in caftans flew in the air. Illuminating wings of various hues shined with a radiance so magnificent that it sparked calmness within her. A calmness that let her know they were on her side the moment they threw flames of holy fire at approaching monsters. Each monster resembled men and women with deteriorating dark wings of innumerable hues. Putrid entities that seemed to step out of the newest horror film fought back, throwing bolts of currents, willing shadows to shallow whatever got in their way.

Granules rained around her. Blasts of sand cloaked her while she watched in amazement. She noticed in that moment that she was dressed in rich burgundy red linen that draped around her in a robe caftan. Her feet were covered in soft yet durable sandals and her hair fell around her face in two strand braids, each roped braid adorned with jewelry. A throbbing marred her spine, causing her to press a hand against the small of her back. She had to figure out what it was, so she shifted to the side. When she moved, she noticed an idle plush soft iridescent feather that glittered like millions of diamond crystals laced together, resting at her feet. *No way.*

"You are awakening to your original form."

She turned in shock then found herself staring into the face of a man so striking, yet graced with a rugged strength that it made her blink in astonishment. A small part of her mind noticed that he spoke to her without moving his mouth. In fact, she instinctively knew who he was, which was strange. Every book she read was wrong. He was not what she had been taught him to be. He was tall, dressed in white linen, was graced with a thin muscular build. The currents from his hands wrapped around each finger as if it were a glove, glowing and forming into the shape of twin blades of fire. This man with dark wooly dreaded hair, burnished oak-colored skin, and soul-knowing golden brown eyes cast an illuminating warm and welcoming smile upon her that made her fall in supplication onto her knees. Her tears cascaded down her face. A mound of sand was her friend because she sat lost for words staring at his brown sandaled feet.

There was a gentle touch of his hand on the crown of her head. It sent a surge of vivid clarity, healing balm, and vitality throughout every nerve, mitochondrion, and follicle of her body. This man was the true Sin Eater.

"Do not be troubled, you now understand why you and your blood are needed," she heard. It made her glance up then notice a male angel who flew over their head. He was cloaked in darkness, dressed as an Egyptian or Nubian King, but his menacing wings and eyes shined with holy righteousness. Something in her felt as if she knew him but her attention was drawn back to the radiant man before her. Her misting eyes averted to the ground in respect.

He spoke to her spirit again: *"Awaken my brother-in-spirit. He has been asleep for far too long, as have you. Sister, heal the discord in my children. The Houses were born with reason. The battle is nigh and as you young people say, everything has happened for a reason. Go with peace and remember, as it was before, so shall it be again. I am pleased to see you awaken again."*

She had to try to memorize this all. She had to study his face one last time in honor but rubble suddenly spilled around them. Land quaked and angels fell from the skies like confetti. The words, *as it was before, so shall it be again,* echoed in her mind. Every syllable wrapped around her spirit covering her in protective covering. Armored gladiators and indigenous men and women came across her vision. Some of them were dressed in red, gold, and white robes and caftans with crosses linked together with other various religious symbols embroidered upon their armored garb. Those mighty men and women went head to head with similarly dressed humans, whose eyes flashed red, while others' faces revealed them to be demons in the flesh.

"Yes, remember this. See there is no separation, we worked hard to unite a whole from all around but this is the last of my teachings that have been lost. Watch, those mighty warriors are not the same as you were taught, but more. We protect the innocent, our spiritual link."

A man flew past her dressed in the same garb, his armor illuminated with holy indignation. A large battle-axe was nestled within his large hand. The silver glint of a second blade attached to his forearm made her mind click in déjà vu. Others ran past her with various advanced weapons, using gifts similar to the ones her new family had and she understood the history around her.

This was the founding of the Nephilim Society. This was the beginning. The second war. A woman with flowing two-strand braided midnight hair and wings that matched the feather Sanna held in her hands glanced her way. The magnificent woman clapped both of her hands to bury a pair of demons in the hot, arid sand. Determined, the angel jolted a surge of holy power into the earth illuminating it. Familiarity smashed through Sanna's body then jettisoned her back to her flickering reality.

Blood seeped from her lips. Pain raked through her making her clutch her stomach. She saw her spirit guide holding out several nails in his hands. Each rusted thimble looked to her like railroad nails but smaller and tinted in red blood, iridescent with power.

"You are holding on too long. Go with blessings, wisdom, and strength, stubborn one. We will meet again," he whispered.

She felt the gentle brush of his lips on the crown of her head. The gentle anointing sent a jolt of immaculate clarity and knowledge through her, this time grounding her. She was one. Her soul had been blocked for so long and it was so good to be awakened. A blessing to remember the truth of it all. Even it if took awhile to understand it.

It was good to know who she was again. Having been reborn into Nephilim flesh often complicated things. First off, it was always guaranteed that with each rebirth, the memories of the past life and original life would be blocked until the Priming came. However often it was, that didn't guarantee full past life knowledge in itself and many didn't gain vessel knowledge until they lived millennia. Therefore, she guessed that the fact that she was privy to some of her full memories at such a young age was a blessing and a warning that something was going to go down.

"Sanna!" bellowed from an unknown place close to her.

Searing agony had her convulse upward making her sharply inhale with its pounding force. The sharp electric shout of her name had Sanna retch forward again. A scream tore from her; then she emptied her stomach. Her distress ripped through the air. She felt her vocal cords rattle and she clutched her stomach in tears. She was back in Chicago. Back on the high-rise of that, damn roof. *Oh my God, I'm back.*

"Sanna! I'm here. Baby, I'm here," she heard.

She almost asked, "Who?" as the last fragments of her once-blocked mind healed together with awaking awareness.

Warmth encompassed her. It surrounded her in the form of comforting, straining muscles. She tried to see his comforting cocoa rich face. The rugged, strong jaw of his that was home to a crisp, cut goatee. Lips plump and firm that always spread into a dazzling grin when she was near. Long, dark lashes the housed eyes the color of warm honey in the sun. With locks that fell in ropy, crinkled veils whenever he held her close. She wanted to see the man she dreamed about over a lifetime, but all she could do was feel her eyelids fight against opening.

The rich scent of her sweetheart helped steady her erratic breathing, as tears streamed down her face. In that particular moment, her body sucker-punched her again, making her flinch in pain. *Crap!* She felt like a piece of meat being ground into sausage and once again, her head throbbed but in a different way. It was something akin to a normal headache, something she could actually welcome.

"I still want that broad's head!" crashed into her cerebrum. There was the congested sound of cars, rain, and city life clamoring around her. She seriously wanted to shake everyone and tell them all to give her a moment of peace, to stop shouting incessantly; but then that voice thick with a familiar New Yorker/New Orleans-fused deep timbre ricocheted around her, "I'm sorry, brah, but she fucked up when she went after my family! No harm but she committed a foul, ya feel me?"

Sure, she could feel him. It was so strong that she could feel him pulling at her skull just like everything around her. Silence was what she wanted to feel. Everyone around her was going on in varied conversations she could only listen to. Their hushed, worried, and sometimes heated words had her recoiling into her mind to try to figure out what was going on with her. However, what she did figure out was that soul awakenings were hard for her kind. In combination of almost being run through with a Cursed blade, her body was going through the seven levels of hell.

"I'm here, baby. I had to handle something but I'm back," he called to her. Her mind registered the soul-deep octave of her mate Khamun. Droplets of rain kissed her forehead and she remembered why she was on the roof of a high-rise in Chicago. She had just gone to war. Her blood seeped from her body and she flinched then looked around with clear vision. Flashes of the battle played across her muddled vision. That crazy heifer was running a blade at her again. She needed to get away. So, she shoved as hard as she could trying to get away, suddenly realizing that she was pushing at Khamun instead and not at the Dark Lady. Relief made her slump her shoulders in gratitude and love had her pull him toward her in a tight embrace.

His pain was palpable and it had her fearful. She knew he had just gone through the gates of hell in watching her die. *I should have just listened and stayed out of the way. I was so stupid,* ran in her mind while her lips pressed against his jaw, neck, then lips. She deeply inhaled his comforting spicy scent. Her fingertips raked across his embracing wings while she slid back. *Savior, he is fine.*

His brown skin was slick with sweat. Flecks of what appeared to be blood and dirt let her know he had killed some more. His crinkly locks covered her own face, spilling as if they were rain and his rich, warm power-charged scent made her stomach clench in need. Her love for this man was beyond words. Loving him helped her now understand what he meant when he told her months ago that he was created for her. Because angels knew their soul mates usually within the first meeting, it finally dawned on her that she was always his. He was her soul mate and she was created for him.

His healing embrace was intoxication. It felt as if he always knew how to make her feel good, even when she felt like crap. The simplicity of his support and love gave her the desire to lose herself against his mouth. She wished he was offering his dimpled smile but she understood that right now was not the time for smiling. Right now, she didn't want to think about how she almost died. She had to focus on the welfare of her family.

"He needs healing. You all do," she concernedly stated. Khamun's embrace held like a vise grip the moment she tried to sit up.

His exhausted voice waned and she heard, "San . . ."

Leaning forward to cradle Khamun's concerned face in the palms of her hands she stared into his gorgeous eyes. Twin pools of golden amber melted with every emotion known to man. *Calm him, San; it's about him, not about you,* she reminded herself. She leaned in to kiss him deeply, drawing his lower lip into her mouth, tasting his weariness and love.

"It is my job to heal you, heal you all. Please let me do so. This body is healed . . . I mean my body is healed," she pleaded.

How Khamun slid back on his haunches to study her face, his locks spilling over his broad slowly rising and descending shoulders, made her check her mental state. So much knowledge from her dream was pumping through her that she couldn't sort it all.

"Who are you, beauty?" he muttered. He slowly ran the pad of his thumb over her, tilting her face up.

Needing to feel his touch made her turn her face to kiss his palm; then she attempted to stand, wavering until she gained her balance.

"Who are you, Oracle?" he asked again, his voice constricted with emotions held back while his amber eyes reflected his devotion.

Sanna placed a hand against his shoulder to stay upright while musing, *what a darn good question.* Her hands slowly ran over the tight-coiled muscled swell of his arms to reach up to adoringly cup his face. She ignored his question knowing it wasn't the time for that, although a part of her wanted to ask him the very same question back. Instead she inwardly sighed and resorted to just saying, "I have to help."

She listened to Khamun's exasperated exhale. Understanding settled into his eyes and he nodded. His large, strong hands ran down her sore body to trace her now-healed stomach. She had to assume the movement of the many warriors around her, had covered her in healing proprieties. But an inner voice inside of her reassured her that it was all her own power that kick-started her ability to heal. Khamun's head bowed forward to rest his forehead against Sanna's head. She could tell he had a lot on his mind as he spoke. "I thought I had lost you. That can never happen, ever. Now go heal."

"I am always with you, Khamun. I have to be; you're my Guardian, silly," she gently coaxed hugging him tightly. She was relieved when the fear in his eyes disappeared, which allowed her to slide off his lap and quickly go to work.

Her best friend, her Protector, sat prostrate on her knees. Her hands rested on the young man who had turned into a live Dragon to protect them all. Devastation covered her face, which made Sanna feel her sister's pain. Kyo appeared haggard from the battle and broken. Her mismatched jade slanted eyes were a dimming green and hazel. Tiny, thin cuts were on her temple, cheek, and plump bottom lip. Her shaggy, short bob was adorned by specks of dust and blood. Sanna could understand the pain by placing herself into Kyo's shoes. Having witnessed the death of her best friend and the man from her dreams fall in front of her would break anyone. Kyo glanced back and forth in a daze before realizing her best friend lived.

"Sanna!" Kyo pushed up fast, barreling into Sanna in joy, gratitude, and sadness. Her soft face was tear-streaked, her body tense with emotion. In the moment, all it took was an embrace and Kyo broke down again, tears sliding down Sanna's neck.

Oh, sis, wisped in Sanna's mind. She could feel the heartache, devastation, and confusion from her best friend with the piercing dig from Kyo's fingernails in her spine.

"I felt my soul split in threes. To feel that is insane. Don't you ever, ever walk into enemy fire without me; you hear me, sis?" Kyo pleaded.

"I know, sis. I wasn't prepared but . . . Khamun said the same. I'm so sorry. I'll make sure to not do it again. I promise you, but let me heal him please, for you," Sanna whispered softly. Kyo gave a slight flinch that Sanna noticed. It was a soul resuscitation. The gravity and reality of it all hit hard. In silence, Kyo hurriedly turned to drop to her knees to cradle the young man's face.

To Sanna they appeared like long-lost lovers. Twin dragons, locked in a sensual and deeply loving embrace via their auras. It inspired her to expand her own gifts to heal him with every last bit of her being for the woman who was more than a best friend, who was like a second sister.

"He's the one from my dreams, sis, remember? The park and the tree? Anyway, I . . . I stanched the bleeding as much as I could and I can't find a pulse. I'm scared," she explained in a rush.

Khamun's deep tenor, interjected into Kyo's frantic speech, hoping to keep her grounded, Sanna could tell.

"His name is Ryo, little sis," Khamun muttered stepping to their side quietly watching, "and don't let fear keep you from your gift. You helped him a lot; his breathing is slowing into a meditative state."

Game was on. Sanna nibbled on her lower lip while she felt for a pulse. Fingers pressed light yet firm against his wrists and she waited patiently. *Goodness, I wish I knew what I was doing,* ran across her mind. Nervousness made her want to stand and walk away. Nevertheless, the comforting touch and the masculine warmth from Khamun surrounded her to help her connect to her core power.

Definitely, she was thankful for him. A surge of energy quickened her heart and pulse, sending it into the male named Ryo as if she were a jumper cord and he was the drained battery. Her eyes fluttered slowly then closed the moment the verses for a prayer of healing emerged from her suppressed memory. Each word spilled from her lips like second nature, covering the dying male in front of her in a cloak of healing balm. It amazed and shocked her that she was gifted with this ability, one that she was still learning. The rain around her slowed then froze in the air. Each glistening bead of water lit up like floating fireflies as the quick thump of a pulse found her fingertips and she beamed.

"Give me your hands, sis. I can heal him only so much, but he is touching death and only another Dragon can bring his soul from that gate, or . . ." She let out a soft, nervous laugh then she glanced at Khamun who was kneeling with one arm resting on his knee. His head was bowed in deep contemplation, which made her feel trusted by him in this. That alpha strength he projected had Sanna quickly glancing toward the people who surrounded her. It hit her that everyone around her was in her earlier comatose dream as she slowly put the pieces together. Knowledge was power and dang if it didn't trip her out that she didn't connect Khamun to that mysterious angel that was flying over her within the awakening vision she had.

Khamun's essence flowed around the three of them then connected and shunted Ryo's spirit. Yeah, she was instantly blown away. Now this was a professional in her view. Her baby was working his magic and she knew he was innately keeping Ryo's spirit in his body. Khamun's ropy hair flowed with sparking currents of his Guardian powers.

His body was still bulky from battle, his muscles tight in power. His sparks of electricity changed various colors with each calm breath he took. His long fingers opened and closed in rhythm with his beating heart and rising and descending broad shoulders. She could see that even though his eyes were closed, through his thick lashes, she could see a slight glow illuminated from him. By doing whatever it was he was doing, San could sense that it would help to move him; otherwise, Ryo may be lost.

Stress from Kyo hit San's psyche instantly, causing her to work toward amplifying her own healing balm. Quiet footsteps from behind her alerted her to the presence of her brothers Dare and Take, and her cousin Calvin, who held something wrapped in a coat. Her other cousin, Kali, appeared by her side as well to crouch down near her, laying a hand on Kyo's back. This team was her family. One family and Sanna's heart strengthened in that understanding.

Not many families were able to hold on to each other in such a rich bond. Yet, one chance meeting from a man who was once her Guardian angel and who was now her fiancé changed all of that. She felt blessed while she glimpsed the loving faces that looked to her in faith. Common sense told her that each one of them was going to tear her a new one later, due to running head-on into battle. Even the quietly fuming Amit, who stood cross-armed next to her equally fuming brothers. But that only let her know how much they loved her and she loved them just as much.

Tears rimmed her eyes. She inwardly thanked the Most High for saving her mother and for Dr. Toure fighting fiercely for her mother's safety. Both of them stood side by side near her and she blinked for a moment, taken aback. The scene of the pair almost reminded her of an old family picture of her mother and father taken in their youth. San had to shake her head as something clicked within her but it quickly faded. Her spirit whispered to her that something was there but now was not the time to inquire about it. Later for darn sure she intended on finding out what that spark was. Her spirit continued its calming whisper of immaculate wisdom, telling her that this family's love was strengthened and cleansed, and that she needed all of it to bring him back.

Kyo's hands rested over Ryo's heart then entwined with his own hands. Sanna gripped their hands while the knowledge within her mind made her absentmindedly nod as if talking to herself. Her soul was guiding her. Sanna watched her god sister lock eyes with her in amazement, then lifted her own glowing palms in the air. Swirls of yellow light danced over her creamy, tan skin and circled around Kyo's extended painted stiletto-tipped nails.

"Wow," stumbled from Kyo's lips. She closed her eyes and whispered her own prayer of thanks. She then leaned forward cautiously to lift the makeshift gauze that covered the man she had desired in her dreams. Her fingertips lightly ran over the provisional stitches she had sewn into Ryo's smooth, muscled, and lightly scaled skin. Each stitch lit up with Kyo's warm touch. Ryo gave a slight sigh then shifted into the power, his body returning to its human state. Kyo felt her god sister connect to cover him.

A quick glance down, Sanna traced the improvised stitches Kyo had sewn over her own healing flesh. Her god sister was a true medic and had learned a hell of a lot when she was in medical school. Maybe Kyo's short time in medical school really was for a reason. That reason being right now. As the old saying goes, everything happens for a reason. Sanna was just grateful for that, that reason was today. Lost in her thoughts, a surge of healing currents exited from her body, then attached with Kali's, melding with Kyo.

Kyo's eyes flashed that of a Dragon's and her golden wings unfurled from her back in sync. Her growl ripped through the air and filled the spirits of everyone around her. Her power fueled them with righteousness while she bowed forward, pressed her forehead against Ryo's and kept her fingers flat against his wound. Her lips and shimmering tears traced his face. She found his dry and slightly parted lips then kissed him softly.

Sanna could tell that Kyo suddenly and innately knew that he needed her. He needed whatever the growing power she now held within her. That desire had Kyo caved into submission and love for him. Kyo parted his lips with her tongue, wetting each dried edge. Her jade-painted metal-hard nails lovingly traced the chiseled sides of Ryo's goatee-lined jaw as she inhaled him deeply. Sanna could see Kyo's heart felt afire. It was so alive that it fluttered in a blaze. Kyo gasped then exhaled releasing a faint iridescent mist, which passed from her and into Ryo. The intensity of it, from what Sanna could tell, caused Kyo's eyes to water with glowing, healing tears.

Ancient prayers in Japanese, then Tibetan, flowed from Kyo's lips. In that moment Ryo's heart jumpstarted with a clutch from Kyo's hands, making him jerk up and scream.

His 'no' surrounded everyone and jettisoned outward to blaze any dark entity within close proximity into ash. Sanna stared in awe. His body collapsed back on the cold, cement room with the return of his breath. Sanna noticed Kyo narrowed her twinkling eyes then tilted her head from side to side with a light smile on her pretty face. Sanna knew her god sister was also blown away. Ryo's wound was now completely healed. His caked-on and dripping blood washed away in the rain revealing slick, creamy, tattooed tan skin and clean, dark, low-cropped hair.

Kyo's mismatched jade and hazel eyes glanced around her family then up to the skies as she thanked the Most High for restoring life.

"Dying is crazy! Damn. But knowledge is power." Ryo coughed in the middle of a dry heave. Kyo gave a slight tired laugh and helped him sit up, her fingers running down his tattooed, toned back then up over the side of his dragon-tattooed neck.

Sanna was delighted. Ryo was now sluggishly breathing, staring at everyone, dismayed. His searching oak slanted eyes intently settled on Kyo again while flickers of a million emotions made his irises glow varied colors of the spectrum.

"I told you I'd find you, baby. Sorry it took being kidnapped to make it happen though." With a flash of a tired, lopsided smile Ryo's eyes fluttered in exhaustion then rested on the skies. His muttered thanks brought reality to the present.

The sun was rising, which meant for Sanna that the Dragons would soon be stone. It was time to go. Besides, she was blacking out from exhaustion. The team quickly parted to scope the perimeter and she felt herself hoisted into Khamun's arms.

Chapter 3

Khamun muttered commands to his tired team. Pacing back and forth, he dropped to one knee to reach down to pick Sanna up with ease. Though she was thick in all the right places, as he liked her vivacious body to be, she was not heavy at all. For him, she felt like a pile of pillows. He noticed how her buttery skin seemed to command the attention of the rising sun's rays. Each beam appeared to caress her skin. As if on cue, there went his mind, distracting him from what had happened on the roof and dictating that he focus on where he should kiss her next time they were alone. It made his body tighten in need, desire, and love, regardless of the fatigue that was taking over his own senses. He needed to get everyone out of here ASAP, before his and San's Protectors were vulnerable to attack from Cursed stragglers.

"Sun is about to rise, we need to get our Gargoyles to safety. Do a quick body check over the whole team for me, Nox, bro," Khamun casually reminded everyone.

Lenox tapped his Bluetooth ear bud. Several long strides had him moving across the rooftop, speaking with various Nephilim team members who had come to help. The man paced back and forth with a frown forming across his face while he also gave orders and initiated a quick extraction. Khamun could appreciate that. His brother was about business, no need to question a thing.

Dr. Eammon, who had come to act as an extra hand with his street team, was adjacent to Khamun. He additionally was taking the time to pull out his iPad in sync, showing everyone the streets of Chicago. "Streets are clear and the Chicago team's sweep was a success. Whatever demons were still lurking have been disposed of and any pedestrians who were around were hit with the Slayer Runes. Clearing out is authorized, young man."

In his Nephilim culture, Elders deserved the utmost respect, especially seasoned warriors such as Dr. Eammon. While his Elder spoke, Khamun noticed the seriousness in the male's dark eyes. The minimal gray sprinkled at his temple, full goatee, and low-dreaded afro seemed to have spread after the battle. From what the good doctor explained, he understood that his team and every Nephilim solider who was securing the block needed to depart before the human population became alert to their presence. This had to happen before any protection runes depleted themselves.

Dr. Eammon held an iPad out for him to check out. Khamun studied the many different street cameras on display for him. The pads of his long fingers were his mouse, sliding them across the screen to see different angles of the city. Maps displayed before him, outlining human sectors, Nephilim sectors, known demon dens, and blended sectors of the city.

Images before him had him frowning, and then idly scratching the side of his beard-covered jaw. Various exit routes in his mind helped him decide which would work better. In confidence, his amber-honey eyes naturally fell upon Sanna. He watched in concern, steadily observing her breathing and slight occasional movements to see if she was okay. Her usually naturally thick-coiled hair was now a wet messy and curly mass that spilled over his arms. Some of it splayed over her shoulders and breasts as well as covered half of her face. This woman had taken him from hell and back to the light in one swift move of her almost death.

He still wasn't prepared with how deeply she had changed his life. From only watching her as he matured in life, to interjecting occasionally to protect her from the demons that seemed attracted to her like a moth to a flame, to later learning that she was the key to the future of the Nephilim race, he was forever grateful to the Most High for inserting her into his life. A part of him echoed in his mind, whispering, *again, and you will protect her from those who will always want her for being who she is.* His people were always trained to listen to that inner voice. The echo of the spirit was usually associated with residual memories of past lives that a Nephilim had lived. Accepting, he held that information to heart and noticed that blood stained Sanna's clothes. He had some choice words to give her but, right now, all he could do was watch her.

Sanna turned her face upward to look at him with droopy, hooded eyes. She made his heart stop with a glance. His spirit and heart spoke to her. He could tell she wanted to soothe him from his worry, but right now, she could not; she was too weak. Lashes fluttered slowly before him, fighting to stay open, allowing him to perceive that her body was shutting down on her again. Tonight was a long, soul-wrenching event. Plain and simple, everyone needed a moment to digest what just went down and rest.

"Let's roll out," Khamun ordered. Wings unfurled from his back to levitate him in the air. The team's mental link opened. He utilized the Bluetooth to address other Nephilim fighters. Exit routes were ushered but he quickly changed them for a faster departure plan.

His body felt electrified causing his wings to span out to cloak the sky. The feel of his locks lifting in the night air, his aura illuminating, projected a spark of the divine for hope in dark times. Tongue flicking over his lips,

Khamun used one hand to pull his torn black hood over his head with his power. He bowed his head. His eyes flickered in their incandescent honey hue and he whispered a Transition spell. He used the last bit of energy to send everyone home instead of using the cars. A simple rooftop that was home to a secret battle was now empty with the rising sun.

Anger took a grip of his body. His abs constricted. His hands shook. They fisted by his side and he closed his eyes trying to calm his simmering fury. She was reckless, too new to be in the middle of a battle.

Listen to your gut was what his father always taught him. Did he? No.

He should have forced her to stay at the compound, but no, the Oracle in her called to him, voiced to him that it was time, so he obliged. He was an idiot. His eyes grazed over the women in his arms, his soul mate. She lay quiet sleeping against him, lashes fluttering from time to time with dreams. He wanted to reach out and shake her, literally. Just stand her up on her feet, rest his hands on her shoulders, and shake her until sense slammed into her mind. Then he wanted to kiss her. Tongue her down so intensely that the sweet, intoxicating scent of her arousal would make them both fall back into their bed into a heated mating.

The idea of losing her literally tore a piece from his core. He had underestimated how battle-wounded she was. As they all shifted through the Transition spell, Khamun saw how her body lit up with beacons that outlined her every wound she was trying to naturally heal. Because of it, he was now seconds away in going to pay his dear cousin another visit and finish what was started. His love for his cousin Marco wasn't going to stop her death by his hands this time, had he lost Sanna.

Wrath bubbled within Khamun's spirit as he prayed on it. He remembered and old proverb that was ingrained in his mind from his past training in Italy with a true Moorish Disciple that, *"to him who watches, everything is revealed."* Thinking about everything that had recently happened, he definitely knew that was truth. He had watched and he had learned hell of a lot, so much so that it had changed his life.

Khamun quietly continued studying Sanna's resting face. Her gentle face made his memories take him to the moment when she was just a Guide, and he her Guardian Angel. Back then, he would talk to her through her sleep. Connecting to her spirit to calm her fears, anxiety, and sadness, or to let her share the treasures of her life with him through talking in her sleep, it brought him peace. It made him fall in love with her.

His fingertips brushed over her temples. The subtle movement of him bowing his head to murmur softly to her spirit, connecting to her, caused his locks to spill onto her shoulder. Sparks of soft light danced behind his closed eyelids, intensifying with each breath he took and causing him to shudder. This was different. Before it was a gentle binding, but now it was fierce, strong, and passionate. Kinetic. Muscled cords in his back suddenly tightened. A familiar tension in his spinal column made his shoulders bow forward then ripple in response. He knew his wings were threatening to unfurl, even as his incisors descended.

"Damn you were reckless, my heart," he huskily responded while her body curled into his warmth. A drowsy smile played across her soft features in her rest, he noticed.

"For you, I will be reckless. For my family I will risk all," she breathed, more like moaned, while shifting in her sleep. The delicate curve of her knee slid between his own solid thighs causing his mind to waver into erotic desire. Even though she was asleep, *she is wrong for that,* he thought. His lover was seducing him and shit was throwing him off task. He leaned in against her temple with a gentle press of his lips. His light brush had him experiencing her silky skin as if it were the first time.

"For you I would do the same. For my family I would sacrifice my all but you lie in my arms battered and bruised. I praise the Most High for covering you in protection and healing you before I got the chance to see the stomach wound because, Sanna, you were reckless," he sensually whispered against her neck.

He felt himself grip her tight in constrained frustration and protection, shifting her into his body. A slight twitch of the corners of her mouth dropping into a frown while she slept caused him to shake his head in amusement. Her flawless almond skin furrowed in upset against her brow. Khamun could not stop himself from softly chuckling at the sight of her. To him she was the classic epitome of beauty and traces of "around the way" girl. With that of Dorothy Dandridge and Jill Scott, he had heard his mother say. However, to him, she was simply Sanna Steele and his. The pad of his thumb softly brushed over her plush lower lip, until he used his own mouth to trace them with another soft kiss. She tasted like whipped cream, honey, and strawberries entwined into her familiar sparking essence.

They were soul connected. He knew this without a doubt, especially with that kiss. The Guardian bonding should not have been this intense, yet it was. It was humbly intoxicating.

"You were, baby. Why even deny it." Khamun continued to observe her from beneath his hooded lashes. He felt her try to wake but she only shifted against him to slip deeper into the calming, healing slumber he gave off.

"Protect you . . . I was . . ." She yawned then snuggled closer. Her slim fingers slid through the strains of his locks to lace against each ropy lock.

"Trying to protect . . ." she sleepily exhaled.

He gave up. She didn't understand his worry about it, so he had to let it go, but he knew she could not do that again ever. It was time to move up training, so she could learn from him and defend herself better if she was to run headlong into battle.

He slowly dissolved his mental link, instantly feeling it reinforce while she shifted up against his body, cupping his face. He watched her head tilt to the side. Soft black crinkled curls fell around her oval face. A curling lone black strand caressed her perfectly plump lips while her long lashes fluttered slowly awake. White sheets slid away from her body in a fluid motion. He could not keep his eyes from trailing down to glimpse her buttery breasts in his shirt. Her typically chocolate rich eyes were now an opulent amber hue with their luminance.

"If I lose you, I would sacrifice my all to save you. That is why I did what I did. For you. For them. You know what this feels like, so I know how you are feeling. I'll be careful. For you. I promise," he heard her lightheartedly say.

Her hands reached up briefly to cup his hard jaw before dropping while she fell back into her sleeping position.

The simple intimacy. The power in that touch made Khamun blink in slight awe and appraisal before muttering, "Shit."

With just a touch, he felt ready to peel away from his mortal flesh to settle into her body within his angelic form. Sweat slightly brushed his brow from the desire that was flushed throughout his body. A cooling calm settled over him once his beloved's link dissolved. Leaving him in a state of comfort and fading embrace from her psyche. He shakily exhaled slowly, lost in his mental reflections. She was powerful, his woman, his soon-to-be wife, and the Oracle. *Damn she is powerful.* Their connection alone made his semi-relaxed shaft harder than diamonds.

Khamun's Adam's apple worked up and down with each swallow he tried to take in, fighting to gain some control over his aching body. He needed to chill out. As a result, he shifted out of the bed, and adjusted himself. Thoughts of his love were combating his logic. He turned to observe her beautiful, plush body outline the sheets of his bed. Sensual hunger had him never getting enough of drinking up her image. *Maybe I could just kiss her thighs and get a slight taste of her while she rests. Take my time to just give her a little pleasure and let me feed a little from her caramel essence. Maybe?*

Ever since the first time he had laid his eyes on her, he could never stop watching her, wanting her; however, right now he wanted her badly in the most carnal way. However, in the same breath, he needed her to heal and rest. He could smell the fresh application of healing salves his mother had made for the few open wounds she had. The intense sweet aroma had his mouth watering. He could almost taste the blood that seeped into the bandages that covered her.

Tiny cuts marked different parts of her body with dark bruises against her Shea butter–smooth skin. He'd have to take care of them later when she was up.

Flashes of his mouth with his tongue lapping at each wound, healing them, commanded his attention while his fingers caressed her covered softness between her supple thighs until his mouth connected to the sweetness he desired. Every image played across his mind causing him to cast an inwardly smile. That type of healing he could make worth the while of obtaining those battle scars.

Pulling his locks back into a ponytail, he stretched. Both of his large hands ran over his scruffy face before he stepped out of their room to walk down the hall. He needed to shave, but he'd take care of that later. Pictures of his house family over the years, as well as his parents, passed by his massive frame making him furrow his brow briefly lost in thought. San was definitely in his mind. Like her, he'd do everything in his power to protect the people who came into his once-fledging House, people who chose to dedicate themselves to his mission and who opened their arms to him as family. These people, his family, all of them deserved the Most High's praises with his own for their selflessness. Due to that, he knew it would be nothing for him to sacrifice himself for them. If it meant life and death to protect them from harm, he'd do it without hesitation, regardless of the cost.

Khamun stopped near the edge of the indoor veranda in the compound. With a leap over the banister railing, he landed in the middle of the living room in a low crouch. The compound was quiet. Usually after a battle, even though healing, he could find Calvin sitting with Nox watching basketball or football. Kali would be in the kitchen making the place smell good with the usage of the spices of her nation and various dishes like aloo ki puri with coconut curry chicken. But today was different.

His family was drained. What they had witnessed had taken a lot out of them all, which he understood deeply. The scent of faded sage let him know that Kali had gone through the compound and blessed the rooms. Kali was the House's spiritual security. Her Mystic gift allowed her to feel whenever a threat was on the land or in the compound before the general security cameras or alarms did. So, while he walked, he could feel the urgency of her prayers in the air with that of another thread of energy connecting to him. The weak tug had him following it as it led him to the healing rooms.

The b-boy he had hooked Calvin up with to work on some tracks lay resting and healing. It was an interesting sight. Though he was on one of the healing beds covered in medicinal drenched white clothes, his body was fully stone. Next to him was Kyo who sat by him on her knees. Her head rested upon his granite shoulder, her lips pressed in a frozen kiss. Khamun rested his shoulder on the doorway observing the screen. Kyo's hand was entwined with Ryo's as her eyes seemed to be carved closed in her quiet statue rest.

He noticed that Take sat behind his sister with his wings expanded. His hand lay on her shoulder in a protective hold. His posture displayed that he was watching over the pair in his mimicking statue state. Fangs appeared carved by Michelangelo's touch on the trio's mouths while their dragon nails occasionally casted shards of light in the room. The scene was magnificent. It reminded Khamun of something he could see in the Sistine Chapel. Definitely, he wanted to paint what he observed.

Khamun could not believe that this dude was his Protector. He had lived a long time and was reborn many times, none of which he could remember, but he could feel it in his soul that this Ryo aka RJ was his bodyguard of sorts. Him having a Protector felt right and incredulous at the same time, only because Khamun was accustomed to having his family act as surrogate Protectors. For a long time it was just him and Marco busting heads in the streets. Then Lenox was next, then Calvin right after him. Everything seemed to be set in place for him at that time when he was younger and then Kali eventually moved in without his permission.

He literally walked into the abandoned building they had taken over for their first compound and, like magic, there she was with her bags on the floor. He had always known her because she worked with Calvin and was his adopted sister. He had seen the potential she held when he first saw them taking down demons. But before he would allow her back in the family he had demanded that she find out her Mystic roots. He did it protect her, but the day he walked into his compound and saw her bags, he knew immediately that there was no holding Kali back from her destiny. She was quickly an extension of him, the little sister he had always wanted.

They were his first family, the ones who accepted him in all his changes. Marco, Lenox, Calvin, and Kali watched his back. They were his only Protectors even when he did not want them to be. That thought made him idyllically think back to Kali giving him San's blood. Damn, he wanted to shake her for that but was damn grateful for it at the same time. But, like he remembered when they first came into his life, it had to happen; otherwise, he would have been left in the darkness alone. Now, more humans and Nephilim needed him and his House. It gave him a sense that his House was going to continue to grow, so, as they say, with change there's growth, which he could respect.

He had a Dragon, a real deal living Dragon. A mythical lethal fighter he had grown up reading about from his mother. Homie was something dangerous, not only when he transformed into his full dragon form, but also in his natural state, which he was witness to. The Most High definitely knew what he was doing since dude matched Khamun's own unique style. It was natural law to have a Protector in the old days, he learned from his book, and now history was being reborn through them.

Quietly moving through the multilevel underground compound, he let his mind continue its wondering. Hell, from what he saw back when Ryo helped Take and Dare out at the house party they had attended, Khamun saw how much of a master of mixed martial arts and a killer with his hands the guy was. The House now had its second sensei, Lenox being the first, and Khamun really could appreciate the Most High's plan even more. Dude definitely was going to be an acceptable addition to the household, as would Amit.

Amit had held his own in the battle although he was still learning how to adapt to his new gifts as a demon den tracker. Now it was time to see how he was going to cope with his own change from surviving being a Cursed captive to now being part of an elite group of Nephilim fighters who were considered rogue. Everything was falling into place, even with the onset of more change. Rubbing his chin in recognition and reverence, Khamun headed to the kitchen thinking of his next game plan with that of Sanna's sleeping lush form.

Chapter 4

"Shit! Shit. Shit. Shit. *Shittt!*"

The Medusa had to duck from the shards of glass that flew her way in the dilapidated factory she stood in on Chicago's South Side after making it out of battle, all thanks to their lethal Witch, Winter. Every time she slid down an inch or two, she was forced to sidestep the pieces of crumbling wall that seemed to want to follow her. Pain had her recoiling in conflict of pleasure and newfound discomfort. It had her gripping her seeping wounds in a slow exhale. Lingering thoughts resulted in a hidden smirk across her pretty face. He was magnificent. The very image of what a warrior was to her. The only difference was that he was not in her dreams. He wasn't in Ghana, fighting by her side while they slashed at pale monsters with red eyes in the dark, cloaking jungles. No, this time, he was in her reality. In her face, going head to head with her, protecting his new family, which was disrespectful because that act alone pissed her off. She felt betrayed.

He should be with her. On her side. Fighting in unison with her. Protecting her family. He should be standing near her. His large hands running down her body. Cloaking her in healing Witch light, not darkness. Not standing there, doing those most intimate warrior things with some other broad on his team. The injustice of it all left a sour, acid taste in her mouth, which was not acceptable.

Inwardly chuckling at herself, she shook her head. The Dark Lady roared behind her, yet again, "*Hijo de puta!*"

The Medusa couldn't help from letting "Ya heard me" slip from her own mouth in agreement with the Dark Lady. She fleetingly felt the Dark Lady's cold, blazing stare etch unto her back before they shifted away. More items shattered then flew around them in a rage. *That damn man and his phrase.* Every time he uttered that drawl, it made her eye twitch and now it almost just got her in trouble.

Something about that phrase with its application to every sentence he had to utter annoyed and turned her on at the same time. His emerald glowing eyes with his rumbling molasses-thick blended New Orleans and Brooklyn accents did things to her that had her hungry to get a taste of his sweetness. *Damn, Mystic! Damn, human Immortal bastard. Calvin!*

He should be ready and engorged for her. Eager to impale the adrenaline rush that was currently keeping her heady and hungry for sex, but no. That sexy, glorious bastard had to be her enemy. He had to be the one to give her strange dreams of hunting in Africa, of fighting for her safety. Of roaring in indignant fury at being kidnapped by dark shadows with glowing eyes and putrid scents; but where were they taking her? She had no idea. She understood in her dreams that she didn't want to go and would die trying. But, she always woke up in sweating discomfort. Sheets shredded, and shameful tears falling down her cocoa-dusted skin confused and pissed at the dreams.

She hated the feelings he invoked, hated how much she needed him, but besides that, that fucker tried to kill her!

How dare he! ran through her mind. She didn't know why she wanted him so bad. Since the first time she saw him back in St. Louis. They had gone toe-to-toe.

She kicked his Mystic ass and pumped her poison into his leader, the Reaper. In that fight between her and her green-eyed prey, it was as if her biology whispered, "Mate." He was the polar opposite of her. He also fucked up the rotation and stopped her from her objective: ending that Oracle chick and capturing the key.

She ran a hand over her side, and the raw, regenerating, fleshy nub of her missing right hand. Blood seeped over her fingers as she ducked yet again from a flying brick. Pain made her grit her teeth. Not just an ache from the fight but that familiar searing, slashing, ripping, and jarring hurt that burned hot down her spinal cord. The pain was intense.

Its touch seemed to pull at the nape of her neck where the spinal protrusions began and spilled down the curves of her exposed vertebrae. It was comparable to burning acid that stopped at the lower base of her back then tapered off into her rear. Ragged breaths escaped from her lips. Her nails dug into the flesh of her palm. Her scaly skin began to become taut and it almost felt as if it were going to rip while she braced herself against a nearby brick wall. She needed to channel the pain away.

Shit! She couldn't move or walk away when she was like this. She had to get her mind elsewhere so she focused on the loss today. She had to admire the anger that the Oracle . . . no, she heard her name being screamed. Ah, yes, it was Sanna. She could admire that woman's skills in how she smoothly came at her and removed her limb. The woman's movements were ancient and worthy of a warrior such as herself, albeit the broad was on the wrong side.

"No, you are," echoed in the back of her mind. The Medusa ignored it in favor of keeping her mind on her objective: the Oracle.

The Oracle bitch's backing was fierce. The pain she inflicted would make any Cursed noble heady in pleasure, if it were projected toward the Light Nephilims. Therefore, it was a shame to her that she had to hunt Sanna down and end her Light. It would be interesting to see exactly what she could be if she was given the Bite.

"Like you or worse," echoed again in her mind. The scattered odd thought made the Medusa bite the inside of her cheek in restrained fury. Once again ignoring that strange, pesky voice that seemed to appear out of nowhere after that Reaper touched her. She hissed to herself returning to her thoughts.

How interesting it would be to see those beautiful fangs and wings of hers contort into absolute malice. But of course, a part of her didn't want to think of the repercussions of what that meant, if she had caught her.

In winning that big prize and turning her, it would mean the constant hunt of the Reaper. The man whose very fiery eyes put the fear of God in any and every Cursed he ever encountered and she could vouch for it. For some reason it amused her to see him rip her kind apart. His tactics were very dark, very much her style. But she refused to have her dark soul ended. Only the "True" death by hands of the Light kept her on her toes, ready for battles. However, it was the "True" death by the hands of the Reaper, that meant pain, torture, and forever living in the everlasting fires of Hades, which made her always watch her back.

Every fiber in her declared that he need not come after her. She enjoyed breathing. She would rather take a bullet from a mortal and not die than be ripped apart by the Reaper as she had witnessed in the club today. She shuddered to think about the light from his very touch being forced to infuse into her malicious DNA. To relive every dark sin she had ever committed gave the Medusa the type of nightmares only her kind were known to give. Although, the idea of going head to head with him still toyed with her interest and kept her curious, slightly. She had watched him well. She had felt what he could do with his touch and knew to definitely battle him with caution and awareness and never let him touch her again.

Her eyes were becoming glossy like oil over water, which drew her away from her thoughts. Her vision was starting to waver causing her hiss out in agony. All aspects of pleasure were gone. Intense pain made her sharply inhale while her head felt as if it were splitting in two. Each jab of discomfort made her reflect. When they went flying off the roof, she had no idea what the extent of the wounds inflicted on her.

Everything seemed to run in a fluid seamlessness. Her focus was on making sure everyone she encountered either A: died; or B: were left with gashing, life-threatening wounds. Each objective, outside of killing the Oracle, or the Dark Lady's future toy, she successfully achieved. She loved marking her targets in such a way; unfortunately, it seemed circumstances were reversed. That broad's touch had changed something within her, which made her feel this pain; it was the only explanation. Her body was now seamlessly burning with jarring heat. She needed to sit with their healer and she needed to fast.

Winter saved them in that club. Had she not tracked them and then gone head to head with those bastards, who would have known what would have happened? She herself had failed her Mistress by not protecting her as best as she could have, but something in her echoed that it was a shame that the Reaper hadn't shredded the Dark Lady apart.

"My lady, shall we visit Winter? I believe she has the healing properties ready; and you seemed to have a dislocated shoulder and open wounds down your back, Princess."

The Medusa knew she was risking confronting the Dark Lady in her fit of rage but fuck it. She had her own self to worry about and, currently, the bleeding in her side. Her slowly reforming fleshy nub of a hand and the fact that her hip was dislocated was not helping anyone, including herself.

The Dark Lady's edgy and heated voice flowed over her in icy tension as she squeezed her eyes shut from the searing throbbing. Leaking fluid appeared to seep through her grasping fingers and she was taken aback by it.

"Pain is what feeds us, Nydia, or do you forget that in your own needs? What we need to do is get what is ours and coat our hands in their blood," her Mistress patronized.

Nydia had to keep herself from slapping the Dark Lady, opting instead to give a curt nod in submission. The Dark Lady's irrational traits could be so damn annoying. Did they not just go head to head with the enemy? Did they not just barely escape from being eaten by the Reaper? The bitch was insane.

Carefully she kept her stance while her vision threatened to flicker in and out. "Yes, Princess, we do need to coat our hands in their blood. Their attack was an affront and of course we have the right to defend ourselves; but our healer is calling us and you know the rules of war."

The Dark Lady cringed then exhaled. Blood dripped from her Mistress's plush lips while her wavy mahogany hair draped her face in wet tendrils. "Father would not be amused by this . . . affront. *Sí*, you are right. Let us be about this damn healing and then payback will be had."

"This is an unfortunate failure on our behalf, daughter. You do know this disgraces our efforts of winning this war, hmm?"

The Medusa slowly uncrossed then crossed her well-honed, voluptuous legs while she sat at the Cursed kingdom council table. She listened to the low Cuban-accented voice of the Mad King callously address her Mistress. Today Nydia noticed that her Mistress chose to wear her jeweled silver crown upon her cascading hair. Mystery was decadence to the Dark Lady, which was why Nydia knew that she chose to wear that specific crown. Jeweled beads spilled down her mistress's face to cloak her features and leave only her kohl-lined eyes peering through its veil.

Millions upon millions of what appeared to be painted handprints adorned the council chamber walls. They added to the sinister coldness in the massive room. These were the difficult ones. Victims, or hostages, so the Cursed loved to called them. Fools who were taken from the human world and Nephilim hunting grounds by either Nydia's own hands or other Cursed entities' touch. Each soul that was trapped was to be used for later games or to be given the Bite, which would taint their weak bodies and make them Cursed.

Like an elaborate crown, the prints framed the Mad King's haunting visage. Tapping her nail against her temple with her good hand, Nydia couldn't help but watch in feigned respect. Dressed in a gray Italian suit that fit his broad, muscular frame, it accented his tanned walnut-toned skin, allowing the Mad King to project an old world suave allure. His goatee caressed his face in a salt-and-pepper hug while the dimples in his cheeks reminded Nydia of her mistress twin. If the King once smiled, it was always in sinister pleasure. *He could be the toned twin of Antonio Banderas with Afro characteristics, but only taller, at six feet nine inches,* Nydia considered.

The Mad King aka Caius Primus de M'ylce was the first and only created Fallen Elder. She had learned from Reina that he was created by taking the dark soul of the Original Fallen Arch Bernael. While the evil old one lay on the battlefield dying by the hands of the extinct co-angel of death Gabriel, he was fused into the Cursed bitten Vessel named Caius Grete, a cruel human who bartered with the Dark for more power to become a general in the Roman army because he knew he carried the Nephilim DNA strain. He was accepted into the Cursed fold with the sole purpose to be created as a test to see if the Dark were able to create life and extend their ranks.

Being the first and only created Dark Nephilim, procreation was a gift lost to them in the Fall unlike with their enemy. In order to make Dark Nephilim, the Bite had to be given or humans had to submit to the Dark through handing their souls over. This was the case of Caius Grete. He willingly did both for his own gain. He dropped Grete and became Caius Primus de M'ylce of the House of Deception. As the King of the Curse Society, he had earned his transition into the Curse and ruled it with malevolent power.

King Caius watched her mistress with a cool expression. His ebon eyes were rimmed in ruby rings that glinted in the light while studying his daughter. He calmly strummed his fingers on the glossy midnight surface of the council table in contrived attentiveness. Observing the Royal House ring that adorned his right pinky, Nydia let her anger simmer through her body to fuse with the pain running down her spinal cord.

The Medusa knew her King; she knew him very well. Pulsing veins at each bronze temple displayed his quiet fury. Nydia could almost breathe her mistress's equally agitated fury, which amused her. Reina was ready to shred someone or something apart, again. The bloody slurry of black-red intestines and bowels that currently lay at Reina's feet had Nydia staring in delight with a malicious smile. The lax councilmember didn't see it coming when her mistress snatched him up in her quiet angst and ended his darkness.

His death meant nothing to her as she casually took her seat at the societal table before the meeting started. The council member was the usual casualty of Reina's tantrums and considering her mistress was still angry about recently losing the battle with the deceased Oracle, he made a great punching bag. Everyone in the royal council was used to this, considering everyone of lower standing was easy prey.

"The more souls we pollute, the more humans who succumb to our darkness, adds to our garrison; and if we allow them to take from the numerous vessels we have already obtained . . ." The King paused. His nails persistently drummed on the arm of his chair until he continued. "The fact that my son is alive and on their side . . ."

The chambers rumbled with mutters. Currents of dark light surged then cackled while plumes of fire lit around the Mad King's eyes. "We will move on from that. Disgrace and betrayal from within . . . as I was stating, reiterating only pisses me off, daughter, but you clearly know that don't you?"

Nydia watched the Dark Princess swallow deeply due to frustration and rage. The fact that Marco was living was a shock to her as well, but she knew for her mistress that his appearance was a bigger disappointment. It also was a clear insult, as well as at the fact that she was just disrespected and blamed for something Nydia knew Reina had no control over. Had Reina been a random councilmember who just gave the Mad King the type of contempt he had just spit out, her tongue would have been ripped from her body, all the while as he took his joy in taking out his fury on the rest of her body. Fortunately, Reina was the Princess and she was needed. However, on another note, what he had explained before was true.

The true King, the Dark Lord Luc would take it upon himself to wipe out his Dark Nephilims and bring about the end of days without them for failing. While they all burned into cinders for eternity, his beasts and the First Fallen would reap the benefits of soul and blood feeding. Clearly, this was not acceptable and could never occur.

They all had worked long and hard for this right to aid in the war. The Fall served a purpose and the many dark seeds they planted through the Bite and soul pollutions helped keep their side well fed. It also kept the Dark Lord very satisfied in his plans for the massive end. So, no, they could not afford to lose even one battle or the scales would tip forever in the favor of the Light and right now, with how the Earth plane appeared, chaos ruled and all was good for the Cursed.

Nydia leaned into the table to comment for her mistress but was immediately interrupted by the pitter-patter of small feet and a sinister light giggle. Her oak-colored eyes narrowed in contempt. *He has brought in additional reinforcements, the bastard!* Digging her nails into the hard surface of the table with another on the blade hidden against her inner thigh, she kept her eyes on her Mistress, who also was seething in fury.

The quick shift of the energy in the air had the council becoming stoic in their demeanor due to the chortle that danced around the chambers.

"Valac, come from the shadows, child," the King amusingly replied, his eyes gleaming with malicious gratification.

The jovial, pleased snicker continued. The persisting pitter-patter of small feet in a shattering pattern echoed around them until they halted at the entry of an ebon shadow emerging next to the Mad King's chair. Lord Valac, also known as Brandon, was a package of immaculate evil, born in the body of a five-year-old. The slight tilt of his little face made Nydia notice how his buttery toffee skin casted an unnatural ethereal radiance. His soft, plump cheeks and black low-cut hair accented his almond-shaped pitiless, ominous eyes. He was the epitome of cuteness cloaked in sinister evil. A little Damien from *The Omen*.

Brandon was the fallen incarnate of Valac: a Nephilim child meant to be a vessel for the Light due to being gifted with the ability to control Dragons and heal, but who was now turned by the Dark Bite to do the Mad King's bidding. Nydia had heard from her soldiers that he had traveled to the child's birth home of Oakland, then to Tibet, where the boy and a strange book were being hidden by relatives.

The Mad King's will was supreme. He simply plucked the boy-child from his parents' blood-drained Light-desecrated lifeless hands with ease. He had destroyed all to get to the child and personally ordered the Cursed Bite to be given by his right hand, Jacques Fur'I, one of the mid-ranking Original Fallen who was chosen to watch over the Cursed Society as the Mad King's liaison. Nydia couldn't stand that bastard. Disdain coated her tongue, made her nails cut into the flesh of her palms, drawing blood, and soured her belly.

"Brandon, have you been wicked, my boy?" the Mad King asked.

Brandon's soft sneer made the Mad King pick him up in amusement to rest him upon his lap. Nydia watched him tilt the boy's chin up to stare him in his ebon dark chocolate eyes.

"Yes, Unkie. Yes. Yes. Yes. See! Blood." Shifting suddenly, Brandon pulled out a half blood-spattered ashen white wing from the shadows.

Ruby drippings decorated the floor while he and the King laughed. "A Nephilim scribe wing. This is satisfactory. Very satisfactory. Where is your father, child?"

Brandon's soul-snatching chocolate eyes flashed a reptilian red with a glance toward her Mistress; well, behind her actually. The familiar rich, spicy scent of malevolence and the hint of something else she could never make out made her watch in contempt.

"My King." The silky bass of Jacques's voice washed over everyone.

Nydia glanced at her mistress and only she could see the sensual effect it was having on the Dark Princess. Reina's knuckles were subtly brushing against the lush lips of the man Nydia wanted to rip to shreds. She sat silent locked in an old memory while he held Reina's hand to his mouth in a courteous kiss.

He was a lowlife bastard. The incarnate of the word erogenous and Fallen wrapped up in a prick demeanor. She had her dealings with him numerous times as she grew up, training to be the killing protector she was. It began as a simple stalk and study. While Reina honed her own lethal skills, the Medusa would act as Reina's shadow. They watched him to learn all they could, so that Reina could outshine him and garner her father's respect. Later it changed when Reina let him educate her in the history of their kind, extended fighting, and then some.

As they got older and Reina demanded she get her way, Nydia watched Reina fall prey to her curiosity by allowing Jacques to enact every dirty act of fornication created by the Emperor of Hell himself. Nights of ravaging, sweat-dripping sex, threesomes that included herself, orgies with the Dark Princess's new pets, BDSM, every known nasty, dirty position of sex humans couldn't even fathom were done in the fire-lit chambers of Reina's room. Since then, Nydia distasted the bastard for being so educated in his style of controlling Reina in subtle ways.

She used to believe it was a lie that this man had been around for so long and that he would know anything about what cardinal satisfaction really meant, but of course, he proved her wrong. After a while, Nydia began to notice how it really pissed Reina off that he also was a better hunter and fighter than she was at the time, so everything Reina did had her mistress studying from him, until she found ways to outdo him.

Unfortunately, how do you outdo an Original Fallen, especially when it is their gift to know all things? This of course, not only ticked Reina off but also, that shit pissed Nydia off to no end as well. *Prick!*

"Princess . . ." Casually moving his hand, Jacques flashed a casual, lopsided grin before stepping in front of her.

Through a furious haze, Nydia watched him smoothly reach out to kiss the bare knuckles of her partially newly regenerated hand, muttering as he contemptuously dropped it, "Harpy . . ."

He addressed her in such dripping loathing that it made her nipples hard in pleasure of having the honor of gaining his hate. Admiration and hate was their relationship. The sound of Brandon's loud, interjecting call, "Papa!" stopped the swift jugular slash of her blade making contact with his pestilent flesh while she sat in her chair. Her pupils turned ruby red in hatred.

The knowing look he gave Nydia kept her in her chair while she gave him a constrained grin of condescension. "Limp dick mother . . . my Lord, what a pleasure."

Rising smoothly from his chair, the King placed Brandon near him motioning with his hand. "Samael . . . I do mean Brother Jacques. Your arrival pleases me. Take your place."

Nydia watched him casually stride in moving to his seat at the right hand of the King. Brandon quickly bounced up and down in place, misting onto Jacques's lap with a disjointed giggle. The man was dressed in all black except for a touch of red. Slacks hugged a cord-tight formed backside made for gripping. Leather black loafers, and a red button-down shirt with a black vest accented his muscular, running back body.

He stood at six feet seven inches with creamy, golden, butterscotch skin, and a black goatee that lined his jaw and formed sideburns, which accented his bald head. A small line tattoo written in the old language from before his Fall swirled from the temple to the nape of his neck. Nydia noticed his brown dark-rimmed eyes watched Reina. His plush lips formed a smile as if he knew what she was thinking and Nydia saw dark currents spark over each ring-covered finger.

Mentally linking with her mistress, Nydia hissed softly, *"Say the word, my lady. I'm eager to pump his trite arse with venom."* Her nails lengthen in response.

Reina only flashed a brief sneer, inwardly musing then locking eyes with her. *"Oh, if only, my pet."*

"As it pleases me to be requested to aid in the war. As you are aware you know how busy we Originals are." Jacques's voice drew Nydia back to reality.

"Of course, dear friend, of course," the Mad King crooned.

His eyes flashed over Reina. Nydia could instantly feel her throat briefly close shut by invisible hands. The link that she and Reina shared allowed her to know that it was the Mad King whose fury was aimed at her mistress. The sound of Jacques clearing his throat quickly made their link wane.

"It is my understanding through the gargoyle missives that the Oracle has awakened and now is unable to be brought to our side?" Jacques quizzically indicated. He tented his fingers to tap his lower lip with the tip of his fingers while he observed the council nod their heads.

"And not only that she has awakened but that the one called the Attacker is a Sin Eater, a Reaper. Also known as the Angel of Death himself?" he continued.

Heat, then the sizzling inferno of flames overtook the chambers at the Mad King's booming voice. "What! This is but lies! We ended that line in the second war!"

Nydia was dumbstruck while she stared at the Original Fallen. She knew her mistress didn't even know about that, nor did she! He was the Angel of Death? Why did is seem that that bastard always knew too damn much for his own good?

"You would think that, my dear friend, but you are sadly uninformed. The one and only is back and from what I read from the reports, and read between the lines"—Jacques winked while he glanced at Nydia and Reina before continuing—"the Oracle is being protected by Dragons and by the Sin Eater."

Tenting his fingers to his mouth, Jacques narrowed his eyes in concentration. "As you just mentioned, is it not true, that your generation was under the creed to wipe these three lines out?"

The Mad King fumed. When he swallowed, his light sepia face turned ruddy with a curt nod. "This is true. After the first war it was decreed that in order for our line to stay strong and cause chaos on the earthly plane to not only soul pollute but to also wipe out our dear cousins' main pawns, the Sin Eater line, the Dragons, and lastly the Oracles. We were told to take them out. Which we were under the impression we did. We severely weakened their defenses and we gained more souls to pollute."

Dropping his hands, Jacques traced a circle on the surface of the ink-black wooden table. In that same moment,

Brandon slid out of his lap to sit on the floor to play with the bloody scribe wing. Sucking the bloody, fleshy spinal blade, he taunted the shadows playfully. "Baddd. You did not do as Grandpapa asked and now the Bright Lady has big dogs to protect her and the Bright Lady has her Tree-add."

Jacques gave an amused rumble, rustling a hand over Brandon's low fade. "Brandon, it is called Triad, smart boy, and yes. He in the Light has flipped the tables and created the Triad. Do you recall what that means, Caius?"

King Caius flattened his hands on the surface of the table then tilted his head to the side assessing the room. The sharp slamming of his fist drew everyone's attention. Currents of dark energy sparked to land on a council dignitary imploding him into nothing but visceral matter that rained in the chamber. "It means the beginnings of the final war have been decreed and in my foolishness of the past, we of the second line did not dilute and exterminate the lines as well as we believed, unless . . ."

Stretching, Jacques flashed a satisfied smile and glanced her way. A glass of ruby blood wine materialized within his large hand.

"Today we ended the life of the Oracle. My blade pierced her gut and she lay dead in her own blood, with that of her dragon protector. My Pet sealed it with a venom swipe as we won that victory, my lord Elder," Reina replied in brazen regard, spilling her half-truth with her chilly demeanor.

Nydia gave a slight smirk at her mistress's purposeful jab. She glanced to see Jacques swirl his chalice of fresh blood around in circles. He bloomed it while inspecting Reina with contentment, which appeared to reflect that he knew she wasn't sure if the death was verified. Jacques reached out slowly. Sipping from his cup he abruptly cast it aside in a roar. Platinum glinting fangs descended in his ire.

The beauty of it was so strong that the Medusa almost clapped when she noticed the Mad King suddenly gripping his own throat upon his throne. His dry, husky gasps echoed in the shocked and silent chamber.

"Remember where to point your anger, dear friend, when carelessness is founded in the root of this house. Your daughter is the only one who followed our laws," Jacques hissed in constrained anger.

With that simple sentence, Nydia watched him push back from the council table then stand, disappearing his cup and bowing his head. His lips parted to smile before giving an exasperated sigh. She watched the man brush his hands down his attire and straighten his tie. He ran a calm hand over his bald head then held his hand out for a yawning Brandon. "We are pleased that you requested our services. We will debrief with the Princess and her team about her victory, as well as your insurgent Mr. Mer'ce about the intel he has gathered. We will work through deciphering the rest of that . . . tome you successfully found with my son, my King. We will also correct the errors, on which you failed to educate your daughter. Do remember to keep building the ranks for the One Battle. The horns have sounded and our time to play is now."

Calmly moving around the room, Jacques slid his hand in his pocket. Addressing the King over his shoulder, he strolled to the door. "Now please continue with your meeting; it was quite educational."

Brandon wrapped his arms around his father's ankle, gleaming with a giggle, "Byeeeee, naughty Unkie! Papa, will we play with his head soon?"

The pair disappeared in the shadows and Nydia was impressed. This was one of those moments that made her actually like the bastard. Leaning back in her chair, the Medusa crossed her legs, inwardly gloatingly grinning. *Did Jacques just challenge the Mad King and win?*

Nydia often forgot that, although he was King and was a Fallen Elder, he was not an Original Fallen. He was created, unlike her mistress who was born a Cursed half breed. Her mother, the former Queen, was Light bred but given the Dark Bite. Because of this, it meant that King Caius still had to report to higher authorities and if he lapsed at any time, those authorities could do away with him at any time. In Cursed society, they had a King, but like in the earthly realm, Parliament could be a motherfucker.

Chapter 5

Lloyd Price soulfully crooned, *"C'est si bon,* it's so good."* The music connected to the Mystic energy in the room.

Calvin ran his lesion-covered hands over his blades, tracing each carved insignia. The curling filigree breathed with illuminating life upon the blessed steel as he whispered to it, warming the surface with Slayer rune songs his Nana used to sing him as a child. Songs passed down through his family reaching back to the creation of the heavens. His green pupils darkened. Before him lay the hand of the Medusa. Preserved in gauze blessed by Elders and doused in a combination of various oils and holy water, the hand looked harmless. But he knew it was still as lethal as it was when attached to its owner. Inhaling, he smelled the poison within, nestled in the blade-sharp nails. He now had an agent to use to make more healing salves against her lethal poisons, but really, it didn't matter. He had a feeling she would change the chemistry of the poison anyway.

Reaching out to touch the preserved hand, he paused over it. His fingertips almost grazed its resting surface before he opted to reach for the bottle of anointing oils resting near it instead. His eyes never left the hand while he tucked the clear vial in his jeans and closed the glass case that held his prized possession. She had a beautiful hand. A line of raised scales adorned her skin as if it were a jeweled hand glove. The end of the shimmering metallic scales formed a point at her middle finger, the rest of her cocoa smooth skin seemingly warm with life.

He couldn't help but think with the flex of his own arms back and forth trying to relieve the tension in his arms. Each cord tightened then constricted causing him to grind his teeth together. Man, his body ached from the battle. Every ligament screamed multitudes of curses due to the work he put in on the battlefield. It relieved him that his blood had survived but not without loss.

The Medusa had almost ended his blood's life. She had almost taken from him what he had vowed in his past lives never to lose: those he loved; and though he didn't lose them this time, his heart muttered something different. Glancing at the pictures on his wall, of Ghanaian war masks, weapons, pictures of the Harlem Renaissance, of 'Nam, his heirlooms, pieces of his past he once had locked away in Society archives to inherit in his next life, lost in his memories he ran the palm of his hand over the scalp of his low Mohawk fade. His mind was shifting over everything that went down these past months and days.

He pulled off his white A-line tank shirt. His fingers traced over the bloody gauze wrapped around his chest and waist. Four reddened gashes rested along his ribcage. His gift with healing always paid off, especially with battling the Medusa and her poison nails. But this time something different happened, something he hadn't expected.

Walking past his calendar, red slashed through days past, counting down the months left to his thirty-second birthday, his dog tags from his past life in 'Nam swung against his chest. He paused to run his hand over a black mahogany carved box sitting on a shelf in his built-in bookshelf. He had made this intricately designed box with his own hands in Ghana. It was his coming into his Guardian transitioning box and his dowry gift. Turning it in his large hands, the carvings gave him comfort while his mind drifted. He had planned to give it to her, which was custom in Society, whoever she was.

A bride gift to his mystery woman with the flowing braided hair decorated in tiny conch shells and a lilting light laugh. He could never see her face. He could only remember holding her and fighting off the Cursed bitten warriors for the neighboring tribe who used to be their allies. He could remember how they flooded his home, kidnapping whom they could then killing the rest. He had centuries to think about why it happened. He had eras to learn that it was due to his tribe being Nephilim and Guardian wealthy. Large numbers of oracles, healers, and slayers made up the village. The land they lived on was blessed by the Most High's own hand and rich in mighty spirits.

His Gran was the High Eldress of the Ashanti village and his Granpops was the Elder over the slayers and guardians. The day his village was destroyed was the day of his transitioning and mate bonding with his mystery love from the neighboring Nephilim village. He remembered holding her hand while they linked souls, given the union soul mark tattooed on his front right shoulder and hers on the side of her ribcage under the curve of her plush breast.

He could remember the proud sensually aroused feelings of seeing her presented to him, but he could never see her face. They were a soul and love match, freely picked for each other and no one else. He remembered his Gran having a flash after weeks of oracles and seers being blocked, her words telling him that she would see him again in a strange land and that he would get his lives back with the awakening of the One Oracle, his own blood.

Calvin's shoulders rolled with the flood of memories. Her Denotation vision paused the wedding. When she opened her electric white bleached eyes, they returned to their amber-green radiance. Later their consummation was interrupted by war. Debris rained around them, bodies went flying. Every Warrior, female and male, took to their weapons. Hand-to-hand combat was his strong point then and his blades, his trusty scythe blades were still in his hands even then. Pure blood demons faced him, as he cut monstrosity after monstrosity apart. Black-red blood covered the sky while it rained down purified by the mystics in the village.

People he loved died around him while he fought until his hands bled. He tried to protect his loved ones and his new bride, who he saw fighting in the beautiful style of a seasoned warrior. He remembered her method of fighting. Strangely she preferred her hands as well, using blades that locked between her fingers as if claws. Her tribe was known for the jaguar claws in fighting he recalled. Her mahogany pupils flash pure white, marking her, a Guardian oracle. She was coming into her maturity. Tradition stated that they would have been linked as one and matured in power together but now it was different, now their world was ending.

His mystery woman sliced and heart snatched demons. Each touch she laid on them caused them to implode into cinders due to her anointing touch. Rain fell then thunder sliced the graying skies as she hurled psalms against the demons that grouped around her. In harmony with her, he dropped down to finish a kill, fangs descending; then they stood back to back.

Briefly glancing over her shoulder at him, her light brown sugar eyes locked with his in love, as they fought side by side. That was all he could see of her were her eyes, her braids, her beautiful syrupy sweat covered coffee bean skin. As for that fight, he couldn't remember it all. He remembered watching his bride being taken, then given the Dark Bite before his eyes. Her blood splayed over his face, while he was bound then taken from her by strange men with pale skin and demon eyes. Men he later learned to be Cursed demons from the Europe nations. Men who took him from his homeland to Louisiana then took his name, replacing it with "boy." To this day, he hated being addressed as such and he hated the name Cuff. He was only seventeen then.

Thinking back he smirked slowly unwrapping his bloodied dressings, that name, "Boy" and what he had found was the reason he lost his life in the 1920s; well, one reason. His love for music, drinking, food, hunting demons, women, and his anger with the discrimination he lived in the enclave of the Harlem Renaissance were the other reasons he had been caught up. It was also the reason he had died protecting, yet again, his family, this time his great-aunt and uncle. They survived and waited for his rebirth to tell him all he missed, even as he prepared to fight in 'Nam. They begged for him not to, knowing his curse. He loved them and even though he was reborn in the eighties, their natural death still hurt to the point that he missed them to this day.

With a rub of his wrists, he reached to rub at the back of his neck, standing before his mirror in the bathroom. The steam of his shower slowly fogged the glass. The warm healing oils glistening against his skin absorbed into his body with a glow. Memories of the chains that kept him from his mystery woman flashed in his mind. The echoing words from his spirit whispered, *As it was before, so shall it be again.* He closed his eyes then clenched his jaw at the painful memories. That was then. This was now. For now, he had to get his business in order. The anniversary of his death was coming and soon, his light would be over again.

The fact that he always died before his thirty-second birthday was his curse, each time fighting to protect his family and loved ones. He died in Louisiana in the swamps, fighting Cursed who tracked him down and wanted his pregnant wife. Another oracle he had found and loved in those dark times. He lost both her and his life, but not before he sacrificed his light as a Guardian and burned everything around him in the swamps. His self-sacrifice garnered him his rebirth as an Immortal: a downgrade for those Society snobs who'd never set foot on a battlefield, but for him, an honor to get another chance at life. Running his thick tongue over his blunt teeth, he smiled; he did miss his fangs and Guardian ways.

Stepping naked into the shower, his skin sparked with Mystic currents as he turned the shower into a healing rain. Glowing water kissed his cocoa rich skin. Silky currents sank into his wounds, washing away the aches while it sloshed down his back, caressing the hard curve of his rear, then taut, muscled thighs and feet. Running his hands down his face, he lathered with cocoa, Shea butter, aloe, and sandalwood soap. His rough, large, cut-up hands slid over the plains of his flat abs. It felt good to wash away everything. The battle had him still amped. He went in head-on, ready to meet his end to only hit a rebuff. He was sure of it, that this was his battle, yet everything felt surreal. He was protecting his loved ones, fighting for their safety, for the protection of his cousin Sanna but it didn't happen.

At the end of it all, he stood watching the Medusa fall, her eyes locking on his. Something sparked in his awareness, connected to his spirit's memories. He was going crazy, he knew it. Maybe this death would be at the hands of insanity because as the bitch fell, he swore he knew her as surely as he knew himself. She was the woman from his dreams, his lost bride. He also knew something else. While he watched her fall, satisfaction hit him, only to trigger that soul link and instinctively provide a bond of protection to cushion her fall. He couldn't believe that shit. It was eating at him as he thought. He saved her, and in rescuing her, he knew The Dark Lady was protected too and all of it by his hands. Yeah, he was going insane; he had to be. This was nothing but battle weariness, wasn't it?

Stepping out of the shower, he wrapped his towel around his waist then exhaled. He knew he had to talk with Sanna. After witnessing her power, he knew she would be able to help her big cousin for a change. In their Society, the rare order of Oracles—or House of A'lor, Valor in human tongue—had levels, from zero to four. Though Seers and Mystics were never called oracles, their kind still either came from an oracle lineage or would produce a future oracle, which was why the Cursed typically targeted them first. Seers and mystics were level four. Level three belonged to Virtue oracles; these were typically oracles with a stronger gift and were also Guardians, like his lost love.

Level two was what Khamun's mother, oracle Neffer, controlled as Eldress and formally the last of their region's oracles, Dominion. Dominions, if strong enough, could read one's soul. Tell you who your past life was and sometimes awaken your memories. It was restricted to do so, but in emergency cases, Eldress Neffer had done such. It was no secret that Dominions were the regulators and the ears of the Most High so they were very much revered. They were the only stable link to the Most High, the only ones who could hear him with a strong clarity and obtain orders.

Now with the revelation of his cousin Sanna being the Oracle, a being within Nephilim Society so powerful, it made him think of the founding tales of the First Ones he learned as a child. He knew everything was definitely about to change. Calvin had recently just learned from his aunt that there was a level none in history had ever obtained or surpassed. A level that belonged to the First Ones and that was level one, Throne. They could do everything oracles, Mystics, and Slayers could do, but the only differences was they could directly speak to the Most High, receive direct orders and were the breathing Holy Spirit with the power of the divine . . . so it was believed.

This gave Sanna her title as the Oracle. To have a Throne-born always meant a war or something major was going to happen, like the Armageddon. This was why Thrones were so rare. Thinking on it all, Calvin wasn't sure if Sanna was able to work all of the powers that came with her position, but he was curious to find out just how bad ass his little San was.

Quietly chuckling in his massive room, he switched his playlist over. The Roots thumped on his Bose stereo system while he mentally processed. It seemed that his cousin San was definitely history in the living flesh and now linked up with the baddest Guardian Angel in the game. He figured both his cousin San and Khamun would most definitely be forces to be reckoned with. *C'est si bon.*

Calvin made his way through the compound, passing various pictures of the team through the years to seek out Sanna. From the corner of his peripheral, he saw his boy Nox painted in his Templar uniform, an old world painting his boy had found when traveling in Scotland seeking out knowledge about his past life. Nox's history tripped him out. When it was taught that there were African Mansas in his past, the truth of it always greeted him when Calvin walked down the great hall of their past lives.

Calvin paused for a moment to see the past lives that his family and team were able to remember. He saw Marco, a general in Cuba, standing near a black stallion, holding his general's hat with his sword at his side. Marco stared at him with the same steel-colored warrior eyes he held today. His boy was a huge factor in Cuba's independence and it was interesting that he still carried the warrior's name in reference. He remembered when Eldress Neffer presented Marco with the knowledge that he came from a line of Light always. The familiar haunted glaze in his brother-in-arms' eyes changed from that moment on, which was a blessing. The crap his boy went through was nowhere like what he had gone through, nope. Homie's shit was worse, so Calvin could get with understanding that darkness that lived with him. He carried his own scars himself.

Passing by his little sister Kali's portraits, he grinned then stopped at the empty canvases. Khamun. He never knew what his best friend's past was. It was on lock. Everyone in the house was able to remember a good part of their past lives if not all of it, except for their leader. Was kind of messed up in some way. He knew his boy was feeling the same in some sense. Tucking his hands in his jeans, he walked on. Soon, more paintings were going to be put up with the growth of their team. Life was changing big time.

Time to seek out his cousin. His DNA sang to him that she was resting. So, he hoped that she was in the process of waking up. He needed to spend alone time with his blood. He needed to see with his own eyes that she was healing.

Away from the hall of the past, he made a sharp right. His long strides shortened his time in landing in Khamun's and now his cousin's wing of the underground compound. Anyone not familiar with the layout of the spacious dwellings could get lost quickly. If there was a threat, who or whatever it was would die before ever reaching the living quarters and main living parts of the compound thanks to his little sister Kali's additional power.

Khamun had designed the compound well. He had opted to follow the reinforcement builds from the past and present. It was a smart move, done to make sure everyone who lived here was safe from dangers of any kind, and that included the end of the world. Calvin slid a hand over the wooden wall panels of the corridor and appraised his work. Each team member had brought their past experiences with building, designing, and other techniques creating their home. Calvin loved it. It breathed them all. Just like this house, the home back in STL breathed them and astounded the new team that was living there as well.

He remembered how long it took to transfer their DOBs, personal intel, SSNs, and Nephilim SSN codes into the house database. They had to develop additional employment records for them, such as with himself. Calvin's record showed that he was a retired lieutenant for the Army. Another file showed that he also worked with the FBI and prior as a cop, which he was via the Nephilim circuit. In the human circuit, he could walk into the branches and sit with human superiors if he so chose but because he also had a tie into the CIA, he was able to work like a ghost. His record also showed that he worked in occasional freelance, which also covered his broad background. His music was a side thing. It allowed him to act as a cover for cases.

Life was good as an Angel. Every occupation in the world had specific Nephilim positions to keep such functions going. Everyone in the house had such identities. Each cover reflected what they needed to have when functioning in the global sphere of protecting innocents, human and Nephilim alike, and it could change anytime depending on the situation. They also reflected their individual personalities.

Khamun owned Protection Corp., an architecture and restoration firm, which everyone in the house had a partnership in. His man Khamun also had a background linked with the CIA as a retired captain in the Air Force. He owned two community outreach programs, a center in St. Louis and in Chicago. Outside of running the law branch of Protection Corp, Lenox owned Temple & Co., which he was working to make international as well as being a partner in Khamun's corporation and an inactive major in the Air Force.

Every Guardian had a vice in protecting certain humans. With Khamun and Marco, theirs were children, who went through situations as they once did. Marco enjoyed keeping his affairs private. Therefore, the brother's record showed that he owned his own mechanic shop, was co-owner of Protection Corp with Khamun and worked as a freelance PI. It also showed that freelanced for the CIA. Marco also had a hand in opening the community centers with Khamun. Marco was as much of a ghost as they all were, thanks to the lady of their house, his baby sis Kali.

She was gifted with transcribing the tech world, locking down any information about their domain, hiding it, and finding rare information. Her Mystic power also allowed for extra ground protection. Baby girl furthermore had a tie to the Army. Kali owned her own nonprofit organization dedicated to educating women back in India and Africa. She also worked with women in the US who'd been labeled inferior due to class. Music and owning her own international tech firm were her other covers. This was why they had to update the newer extended house member's info. How Society had it set up, shit was stale. It had Guardians taking on mundane occupations that reflected their class status or how they passed their occupation comps. It was the equivalent to being told to take a test that made you go to a trade school, community college, your standard colleges, and Ivy Leagues.

These Nephilims were the ones who looked up to his House. Once they had learned that there were other underground teams forming because of word getting out about their House, and discovered that they wanted to link up with their house, everything changed. Kali began creating a global network. Its purpose was to be prepared so that next time they went to Society for the grand meeting, once the big reveal about Sanna happened, Society would see just how big the House of Dusk and Templar really was.

As for the newest members of the extended House in St. Louis, he and his fam had to explain that the perk of being part of a Royal house that was rogue was that they could do what they wanted. This only worked if their House abided Society rules, which they did in their own way. Watching how the newbies' eyes lit up with the new way they would live always amused him. It also was fun showing them every secret cavern and winding corridor connected to the upper STL city connecting to their compound.

The rookies had to learn that there were corridors that were flooded due to the Mississippi River, but they had turned those areas into diving zones. They had to learn that the city was home to so much mystic power from Native Americans, freed/runaway slaves, and immigrants who passed through the gates, that it was a charging zone, something the new team wasn't used to. Schooling the new breed, he assumed, would take a little longer than it did. However, the more his House supervised them after handpicking them, the more they knew they had chosen right. The new extended members to their House were going to be good, just like the new members resting under his roof now. Inwardly smiling, Calvin lifted a hand to knock on the double mahogany and steel-enforced doors, but heard his cousin before he could even rap his knuckles on its surface.

"Calvin! Come in," Sanna's soft, earnest voice yelled from behind the closed door.

Chuckling, he stepped in with a pause. Sanna sat bowed forward. Her dressings wrapped around her body with her wings rested against her back in the middle of her bed. Sunlight bounced off her iridescent wings sparkling like diamonds, which made him proud. Those very wings were harder than steel. They could slice through tendon and bone.

"Sup, shawty. I didn't want to wake you, love." Calvin moved around the spacious room to sit in a lounge chair, pulling it in front of his cousin.

San modestly held a sheet over her nightshirt-clad body; her crinkly braided-out hair rested in tendrils past her shoulders. He swore her golden dark skin was glowing like jars of honey in the sun causing him to smile in respect.

"No, you didn't wake me. I so slept enough and I think I heard you calling to me, anyway," she said to him with a soft sigh. Her hands rested on her lap. She appeared exhausted.

Calvin watched his cousin delicately flex her shoulders before she jadedly muttered, "These wings hurt."

He could remember when he gained his wings at his Immortal maturity, when he was a full-blooded Guardian, so he could understand where she was coming from. If he had to explain it in layman terms, he could describe it as going to a dentist, having your tooth pulled, then getting braces and having your teeth adjusted. Combine all of that with having a pulled muscle that muddles with your nerves that is centralized around your shoulder blades, your neck, and spine, then you still wouldn't be able to understand the first level of pain in gaining your wings. He was glad his cousin had slept through that bout of it because now she just had to deal with your typical spinal tenderness, burning, and pain.

"Yeah, shawty, it's part of the transitioning. You'll be able to unfurl them soon, naw what I mean?" He watched Sanna's toffee smooth skin flush red possibly in embarrassment, which delighted him. "I'm proud of you, San, and I did call to you, *cher*."

San flashed a shy, lopsided smile. Her crinkly, curly hair fell over her shoulder while she locked eyes with him. Drawing her knees up to her chest, she patted the mattress beside her, signaling him to sit. She was even more beautiful to him like this. Fam or not, his blood was in her element now and it fit her righteously. This meant a happy Oracle, a blessed house, and a blessed team. She was truly a Queen. He felt honored.

"What's wrong, Cal? I usually talk your ear off but what's wrong? Are you mad at me for last night?" she apprehensively asked.

Rising from his chair, two long strides had him dropping down on the bed beside her, shaking it. He scoffed with a chuckle to look into her worried chocolate eyes then dropped back to rest his hands under his head while casting his eyes upward to the ceiling. She always was able to tell what was on his mind with just a sweeping glance and now was no different.

"No, baby girl. Wasn't mad at all. On some straight truth, you scared me, but I knew you were doing what came innate. I just had to make sure you were safe and that no one touched my fam, momma."

Shifting in the bed, Sanna quizzically looked down at him. She arched her eyebrow then playfully shook him with her feet. "Oh, so, um, really? Man, what is wrong with you, punk! I'm still learning what this whole Oracle business is, but don't make me try to read you."

"A'ight check it, read me, shawty. I need you too. I have questions that only Oracle can answer." He needed her support. Hoped she would do what he needed without any extra questions.

Unfortunately, he watched his cousin blink, appearing confused, then sat back with a quiet resolve. "Oh. Well. Khamun's mom woke me to tell that me she was coming shortly. Maybe she can help?"

Calvin flashed a dimpled smile then thumbed his nose, "Man, now who's the punk, wodie? Naw, this I need you to do this, my blood. Not that I don't trust our oracle, I think of her as family, like another mother. Yeah. But I need your help." Calvin's mind went back to his own mother. A woman he never gained the right to meet in this life due to his difficult birth, yet a woman he knew was the same mother he had in his past first life.

He had felt her love and protecting hands guide him to be born even as her light faded. With that same thread of recollection, it also brought with it the dysfunctional memory of his father, Calvin Sr., or Walter as he called him. A man who, although he was the same spiritual father he had in his first life, was now blocked from that connection due to grief. His father, who he never called dad, was forever changed at the death of his life/soul mate. He forever blamed Calvin for the loss. However, that was then and this was now.

Calvin shook his head. His experience in all of that continued to push him to honor family above his own life. Clearing his throat, he went back to his conversation. "But you are here now and you are our Oracle. Not only that but you are the Oracle and you need to learn how to work your gifts, shawty. I take it you know a lot of things but don't know how to control or call on your gifts?"

Sanna huffed then rolled her eyes. She crossed her arms around her chest with a slight shrug. "Yeah. Why must you always know me so well? I'm trying but what you want . . . I don't know if I can do that, Cal."

Reaching up to tussle with Sanna's hair, he pulled her into his arms with a playful headlock. They both laughed, falling into a lighthearted fight before they let go. Taking several deep breaths, Calvin's chest rose up and down in a pant. He reached forward to hold Sanna's hand in support. "Look, baby, you know you can do this. Our blood is strong. You've always been strong of spirit. So get over it. Come on now. Help your confused, broken cousin. I need your help with this. Need you to tell me how I should proceed because, right now, I'm feeling crazy, shawty."

Sanna stared at him like a deer in headlights. As if she was ready to run at any moment. Calvin patiently waited for her to process what he had just disclosed. When Sanna didn't reply, he briskly sat up. Pain dug into the skin of his forearm with San's sudden vise grip. Her beautiful eyes were frosted over, turning silver before returning to their cocoa brown hue. Her head dropped backward then forward with a soft sigh. What he just witnessed was some powerful stuff.

His concern for her kicked into overdrive. Her breathing was erratic. Tears slowly fell down her face. He knew knowledge had hit her and he suddenly realized maybe he shouldn't have asked for her help because it looked to be encumbering. Both of his hands reached out to cradle her face while glancing deep into her eyes as they glowed golden. He spoke her name but it was clear that she was ready to talk, not as Oracle alone but also as San.

Lessening her grip, Sanna gently pulled Calvin's hand up to her lips to kiss his wrists. He guessed that she could see the old scars his lower-level Mystic gifts didn't heal all of the way. Scars that were not healed from the past lives always seemed to come back in new lives.

"Cal. I see your time ending, but I see it beginning, too. I don't know what that means just yet. I mean, I clearly see it but I can't tell you yet. This is something you have to experience without my interference. But thank you because you helped me understand something." He was shocked. He watched those scars disappear with her touch while she spoke.

Swallowing hard, respect and sadness reflected in his voice. "But, San, did I save her out there on the roof? Did I really do that shit? And why did she look . . . damn this crap is *beaucoup crasseux,* very dirty, cuz."

Sanna placed his hand against her heart then laced their fingers together. "Cousin, yes, you did. You did not betray us. I can clearly tell you that. What you did had to happen for all of this to work in our benefit. You worked His command well and now you are on your path."

He watched his cousin give a soft sigh then squeeze his hand. Her soft, brandy-colored eyes illuminated in wisdom and an almost motherly smile spread across her pretty, caramel features. "You know I'm learning from you all that when the Light and Dark are at war, sometimes the Gray can be your only salvation. You all taught me that well, especially Khamun, so don't worry please. I won't let you die, our Light will always prevail, but we have to move fast in order to answer all of your questions. We need Khamun's book. Can you bring that to me? Tell Ryo and Amit to come here with everyone else. Leave Marco and Khamun to themselves for now. They need to talk something out. I will get them later."

San carefully gave him commands. He gave a respectful nod to let her know he had heard her while she continued, "I love you, Cal; you've been like a big brother to me, not just a cousin. We all love you and we will not let you fall. You did no wrong, Cal. And you're not going insane."

She lunged forward to wrap her arms around him tight. Tears spilled down her cheeks. He felt her touch give him strength to work to heal the old hurts and confusion in his heart, "Oh, Calvin, your life . . . oh my goodness. Calvin."

Kissing her temple, he muttered an old rhyme, a spirit song. Sanna's father, Unk Bishop, had taught him the simple poem as a kid. A song he now learned was actually a spirit-anchoring binding psalm. Old habits never died and he knew this psalm always calmed him and his cousins:

Thus, blood to blood, ashes to ashes.
To keep you safe, I will entwine.
Two tears, a kiss, our souls divide.
To blend as one, and ever more.
I part with you, but never, gone.
Rebirth is balance, protected and sealed.
To reawaken, your strength abloom.
Eternity's grace, your armored shield.
To cloak us in His Light Divine, no Darkness ever,
will find.
So say, shall it be, blessed is His vow.
My love for you, my soul will bind.
As it was before, so shall it be again.

He felt her lean up to kiss his jaw with a soft, playful pat against his cheek. "Your reward will be great, cousin, and she . . ."

As San made way to tell him more, each word—Cal knew to listen closely, to Sanna, like keys to a clue—a knock at the door interrupted her. Dare walked in with Take following right behind him. Calvin couldn't lie to himself and say that he didn't feel disappointed in the moment. He was close to finding out more information about his past, about everything, but just as quick as it was coming, was as quick as it was interrupted.

"San, what were you going to say, baby?" Calvin had to ask.

His cousin just lovingly rubbed his hand, gently slid out of his hold then headed to a dresser, which had the book they had found weeks ago. Their unlikely ally, the Dark Lady's own Witch, gave the archaic, mechanical book to them thankfully. It previously only held blank pages, but thanks to Khamun's blood, a history about the lives of past Elders and Society was scribbled out for them to read or view through detailed drawings and ancient script.

Disappointment hit Calvin hard but he knew they would have a private chat again. Hopefully she would share more but until then it was time for work. It was now time to start getting the new team members in line with the rest of the team and come up with plans on how to protect innocents in Chicago and Nephilim Society.

He stood ready to go get the others but Sanna shook her head and held out her hand to stop him. "No, never mind; they are coming. I . . . I guess I called them on a mental link. Guess I'm figuring out this whole mind-syncing thing, I think?"

Dare chuckled then leaned back against the wall with his arms crossed. "Yelling in my head like a banshee, big sis, is not figuring that out. Was taking a leak then you made me blow up the bathroom in a Mystic charge, no joke. Like you all might want to buy a new toilet and sink, and paint some things. Yeah, my bad?"

Calvin saw Sanna rolled her eyes then sit down with a laughing huff at her baby brother. She tilted her head to the side to glance Calvin's way with a playful wink. Her voice lilted to give a New Orleans twang while she spoke, "Bae-bayyyy, when I tell you . . ."

Calvin gave a heartfelt laugh at his cousin's playfulness. He glanced up at the arrival of Kyo and Ryo who seemed to be holding a private conversation walking through the door. Traces of remaining dust touched their hair and shoulders with that of a soft glow to their skin. Calvin could tell that Kyo and Ryo had just woken up from their slumber. He noticed Kyo shift to head straight away toward Sanna, plopping down to sit right next to her with a bright smile. Both women gave a quick giggle with a playful shove before hugging tightly then holding each other's hand.

He noticed that San was studying both Ryo's and Kyo's body language with a quiet, sensual reserve. Calvin also noticed Ryo's eyes seem to catch Kyo's in a private, inaudible conversation. A quick playful smile appeared across his face; then he rigidly moved while gripping his waist in pain next to the woman he loved, Kyo.

Young dude is lost in love, Calvin mused in happiness for his god cousin.

Calvin could tell that Sanna was about to complain about Ryo's moving around with an open wound. But she was quickly distracted once Dare pushed his way through the room from his place against the wall. Her brother took two strides to drop down on the edge of San's bed with Take following suit but pausing to kiss the top of both Sanna's and Kyo's heads.

Good save, Calvin inwardly mused. He smiled while processing the full scene before him. The newbies were fitting into the unit already, naturally, like breathing, he felt while Kali and Amit strolled in. Calvin scrutinized his little sister unlacing her fingers from Amit's then plopped down to sit on the other side of Sanna and Kyo.

Damn, the women are already taking sides, Calvin regarded, before he felt a slap aside his head. He swiftly cradled his dome. Sucker stung and he swallowed hard with a turn to glare at San.

Lenox walked in next, dressed in a double-breasted pinstriped gray suit. He strolled in casually holding the arm of Eldress Neffer who was dressed in a royal purple wraparound sweater dress. Every male in the room stood in accordance. Both Dare and Take mimicked the others the moment they felt her strong aura.

Lenox glanced toward Sanna to give her a slight bow of respect with his head. He placed his fist over his heart before standing near the Eldress, acting as her shield while he announced her. "As protocol dictates, I present her Eminence Region Queen Eldress Neffer V'ance y A'lor of the Eastern, Southern, and Central Societies as well as the Co-ambassador to the African Continent."

Eldress Neffer held her hands up with a light laugh at the joking tone in Lenox's voice. "Gentlemen, please sit. I came at the right time, I see."

Her plush lips parted in a motherly smile. The power emitting from her five foot six inch curvy athletic frame commanded both respect and attention within the room as it softened into a mother's loving warmth. In her usual casual elegance, Neffer moved around the room in ease; her long burgundy-red locks swayed against her back. Stopping in front of his cousin, Eldress Neffer did something no one in Society had ever witnessed in generations, at least nothing he had ever witnessed. With flourished honor, she placed a natural manicured hand over her heart then gave the royal decree. In Society, this was a motion of grandeur, which consisted of a low curtsy to the floor.

Calvin noticed that the hem of her purple dress pooled around the Nephilim Queen while she addressed her future daughter-in-law, Sanna. "Oracle Steele, it gives me honor to be in the presences of a living Throne. You bring us glorious honor and we have waited centuries for your rebirth and the return of our oracle line. On behalf of the House of A'lor forgive us for our line diminishing."

Confusion flickered across his cousin's face. She rushed from the bed, her blanket flying everywhere. She urgently reached for Neffer, pulling her up with a hug. Locked in a tight embrace both women's eyes frosted over with power before returning to normal. San humbly responded, "Mrs. Cross, please stand, that's okay, you don't have to do that. I'm just me. Sanna. Please and it wasn't anyone's fault but the Dark for the orac . . . I mean our line, coming close to extinction. You did everything you could to hide those oracles you could find and you have kept everything in order. I should be bowing to you. I'm nothing special."

San was wrong in Calvin's opinion, but he figured she'd learn that soon enough.

Chapter 6

His mind was flickering over the events from the first time he ever laid eyes on the woman he loved. The woman who was his spiritual equal. A woman who was his spiritual wife and the foundation for his ragtag team of Nephilim Warriors. Deeply smiling, musing in his thoughts, Khamun scrambled eggs, chopped organic vegetables, found some smoked turkey, and sliced it while whispering prayers of cleansing over the food, and various cheeses. He never assumed that his birthright to watch her and act as her Guardian would turn into discovering that she was his mate. That she was an Oracle, a vessel with knowledge and power so deep that she would be the link of resurrecting a dying line within Nephilim Society.

He had his own role but he was still learning what that exactly was. From what he learned from her, he was a Sin Eater, an entity with the ability to take the sins from the Cursed, tainted humans, or any dark agent as his prey, feeding on them to return what was dark back to the light. That was where his fangs came into play as well as his need of Dark blood. He learned from her that he was a being as powerful as she was and that he, with his team, had a destiny to fulfill in saving Nephilim society as she, her siblings, and her Dragon gargoyle did. It was incredible. It was crazy as fuck but incredible. From all of this, his connection to Sanna was growing intense. Which made him wonder, exactly how linked was he to Sanna?

Talking with his mother was a must since she was no
longer the last Oracle, but something in him screamed to
read the book and talk with his father.

"Sup, man, how is she?" Marco inquired while lazily
walking in. His eyes were red from lack of sleep and from
the lit Trinity rolling between his fingers.

Trinities were cigarillos blended by three spices used
by the Three Wise Men to heal, anoint, and calm others
who needed benediction or when in prayer. Trinities were
well known to be an immunity and vitality booster. It also
calmed agitated gargoyles. However, the small brown
cigarillo was still shunned in Nephilim Society by the
pompous elitist houses who viewed them as drugs. Like it
or not, Trinities could be found throughout Society and it
was going nowhere.

Reaching for the offered smoke, Khamun studied his
cousin. Marco was rigid with battle stress and withheld
emotions. His hands kept opening then closing in constrained fury, hurt, and self-blame. His eyes held the
silent question of if Sanna was okay.

Shit was hard to watch, so Khamun tried to ease his
cousin's pain while he waited for him to open up and talk.
It usually went like this when either of them was upset
or needed to talk. The other always coaxed one to say
whatever and speak their mind.

Passing the cigarillo back, he offered a lighthearted
punch against Marco's shoulder. "She's resting, bat-
tle-worn and healing up fast."

"Okay, primo, bro, I just wanted to make sure." Marco
paused. Silent questions of remorse flicked in his eyes.

"It's good. We did what we could, you know, on some
real truth." Khamun's voice softened in understanding
and concern. "It's hard seeing your sister like that and not
react how we did."

"Man, forget that broad. Ella is my twin but fuck her
life right now," Marco retaliated.

There it was. Just that fast, anger and hurt lit into his cousin's eyes. Khamun knew why he was here; it was time for another talk, another rehash, more healing, and he was game. He saved the man who stood in front him. A guy he felt was a brother before a cousin as Marco felt the same for him. Saved him and kept his secret from the enemy and Nephilim Society.

Thinking back, Khamun inwardly recalled their very first meeting. He was a month away from being ten when he found his cousin: cold, wet, teeth clattering as if someone had a card attached to a bicycle wheel and was riding down a hill. Marco sat balled up, rocking, scared, dirty, wearing nothing but a pair of jeans. Various scars and burn marks marred his skin while his body convulsed with a frosty vapor misting around him. His wide, frightened eyes flashed between silver then black every time he coughed.

Khamun had been with his father, learning the city as was necessary of a young Region Prince and future warrior. They were walking the streets when blood recognized blood due to Marco's blood singing to him like a beacon in the wind. The closer he got to him, the stronger Khamun's need to help him rang within his spirit, as well as the kick-start to his thirst, which scared him. His father had expressed to never leave his side while on the prowl. To alert him of anything felt dangerous during their tour of the city. But, the pull was too intense of a cry to ignore. Besides, the first law of his people every child learned was to "*do unto others, as thou would have done unto thyself*," as the saying goes. So, he had to help however dangerous it was.

Evading his father was simple. He had learned early in life that he was good at blending into shadows, using the peripheral as a cloak. So, as his father spoke to a Nephilim family living in the Bronzeville area, Khamun simply stepped back into the peripheral, stalled his breath, and searched for the call. He knew it was wrong. Knew it was dangerous to be alone as a child running the streets of South Side Chicago, but he didn't care because he could hide himself well. He could make others forget he was even there and he would do so now if it meant helping whoever painfully called to him.

Inching closer, the hairs on his arms stood. Goose bumps traveled down his spine. It began to feel constricted around him, as if the alley were a living entity with its own life as it undulated around him. Legend had it that those born to be warriors in Society were born without fear or that they could mask it very well even at birth. For him, if suddenly felt that this task of his officially had kick-started that trait. Though his body sent him warnings, Khamun walked through unscathed, devoid of fear. Every wall in the alley seemed to reach out at him to claw at him while he cautiously moved forward. Sweat trickled down his burnished skin with the touch of a nearby wall before it snapped back, becoming saturated with fear of him.

A quiet smirk formed on his young face with his snicker. He didn't know why he laughed at the darkness becoming afraid of him; he was just a child but amused he was and he instantly wanted the darkness to run.

"Who are you?" Khamun unobtrusively questioned the cold darkness and the kid sputtered.

"Not you, dude." He looked at the darkness while his nostrils flared.

"Who are you?" Khamun repeated, instinctively knowing what was surrounding him. The rancid stench of the darkness made his stomach clench at its metallic sour smell. "Cursed," he muttered then looked at the kid. He noticed that the kid now stood from his fetal position. Then swiftly ran into him full on. The kid's pupils blazed dark. Blunt, small fangs descended, letting Khamun know that he was close to puberty and Khamun stepped out of the kid's way.

A sharp, jeweled blade appeared in the kid's hand slashing at the air. Trying to attack Khamun with a running leap against a wall, he used the wall for an advantage to hit Khamun with an air kick.

Laughing with merriment, Khamun sideswiped the kid with his hands behind his back. He moved left then right in that same stance before ducking, his short locks flying into his face. Khamun blocked each hit smoothly just like his father had taught him. He watched the kid use various types of martial arts that left him very impressed. This kid was expertly trained to kill but so was he.

"Dope," Khamun replied. Respect briefly sparked in his amber eyes. He enjoyed a sparring partner almost as good as him, but something was off about this kid; he seemed sick, battered, and hurt. Sliding backward he frowned. His opponent surprised him by landing a front kick to his chest. With a strained grunt, he held his position waiting for the kid to get close to him again, which he did trying to move past him. Spiraling in a sharp turn, Khamun kneeled to overtake the kid's space in order to knock him off-balance. With a loud crack, Khamun glared down at the kid, flipping the dagger he had taken from the Cursed kid in his hand. His face contorted into a grimace then he flinched with a glance to ground.

Throwing the dagger into the darkness with horror, Khamun hissed, "Cursed blade!"

Suddenly wiping his hands frantically on his pants, he fumed then made ready to kick the kid in a tantrum but stopped in curiosity. This was his first time being truly alone, face to face with a Cursed Nephilim. He had studied them since birth as all children in his Society did and his father had left him in a room with a Cursed, bloodied, physically broken, and held down. He had to stay in that room all night while his father watched, just to become familiar with their presence. But a Cursed child he had never ever witnessed. He was told they couldn't procreate but here a Cursed child stood, which was crazy to him.

"Prince Marco?" a lenient yet hard edge voice wisped in the air. Startled the kid looked his way quickly, then at his own self as if reality was coming back. The kid's name was repeated in the air making Khamun notice that he flinched at being called again.

In that same moment, Khamun felt the alleyway tremble in agony. The strength of it caused him to almost fall backward when the kid zipped forward slicing at him then running past him again, this time pulling at the darkness. All Khamun could do was watch in earnest. Khamun had a strange feeling that the kid was being followed. Unknowingly, had he paid closer attention, he would have also seen a dead Cursed minion slowly turning into frozen intestinal slush behind the Dumpster the boy was nestled by.

Chasing on foot, Khamun trailed the boy while they both climbed over fences, moving like jaguar cubs in hunt. The neighborhood swallowed them the deeper they ran into the city. Khamun believed that he wasn't going to be able to catch up, but something powerful in him seemed to spark with the darkening skies, guiding him on. Skidding to a halt near an abandoned building, he caught his breath noticing the boy named Marco pausing, cautiously casting a glance. Marco pulled out a pair of fresh clothes, quickly slinking into them then straightened his walk. That woman's voice echoed again and he saw a magnificent lady step from the darkness.

She stood dressed in glowing barebacked golden draping. Gold asp bracelets adorned her toned arms. Gold twisted hoop earrings that rested on her shoulder gave off a glint due to a streetlight. The heels she wore let off a scent that it carried a poison that could kill his kind in a blink. Nevertheless, there was something about her appearance, something about her that seemed familiar. The way her thick dark wavy hair with a couple of twisted braids fell down her regal back, kissing her ample, firm, and plush rear made his young mind twist in confusion. The candy dark chocolate skin of hers, the sinewy way she moved, drew his attention. She was definitely Cursed, but . . .

The woman turned to gather Marco in her arms, his hand resting on her swollen belly and Khamun gasped. The moment the sound escaped his lips, he knew he had messed up. The woman swiftly turned glancing past him as if she could see him. Her kohl-lined irises glowed a liquid golden-saffron hue that matched his own golden like a panther in the night shrouded in awareness. Yet he sensed that she couldn't see his position.

Rigidly keeping his own eyes locked on her, Khamun couldn't believe what he saw for a moment. A shimmering tattoo swirled down the side of her neck, which was familiar to him. That insignia made him unconsciously began to step forward when the woman's pupils pulsed with a power that held him back in force. He sharply heard her urgently speak to him without words within his mind: *"Step back, nephew. Do not breach the line. You hid yourself well but your sound let, me track you."*

For the first and only time in his young life fear locked on to him. This Cursed woman called him nephew, knew he was there, and could mind sync with him.

"Listen fast and listen closely. My son and I are no threat. These words you are never to repeat to anyone or death will come for us all. You did well in finding my son. Blood recognizes blood. You should know this saying, yes?"

Khamun acknowledged her in a trance. He couldn't stop himself. It seemed that the world had stopped and it was only them. The phrase she uttered he had learned only from his father and this woman knew it?

"Yes, and one day you will know my story but for now, you have found my son. He will need you now and you know where to find him. In a fortnight, I will die and no longer be able to hide what my son is and I need you to take him from here.

"My daughter, his sister, is too close to her father and I cannot bring her to you but my death will give her a protection she will later learn. Remember these words and tell them. I did not succumb to the darkness. I was strong in my torture and descent. I was the Light in the darkness. Tell them I love them and that they will bring me honor when they are adults. Tell your father, his sister was strong," she pleaded.

Khamun's mouth dropped. The woman moved her locks to the side and showed him the family mark. He never knew he had an aunt. This had to be some Cursed lies. It had to be and he had failed, failed in this test.

"No! You are awake for the first time in your young life. You have a duty. Listen to your heart, child. Listen to your soul. Listen to our blood. You and I are alike. You and I share the same gift. Please know you are not a danger to your kind when your gift fully grows.

"I believed it, and then I ran. That was my error for not trusting in my family. My weakness, due to our Society's inability to accept change and indifference, became my fall. When I ran they abducted me. Violated me with the Dark Bite, and then took me to Miami. But I made up for my mistake for allowing them to make me think differently of myself. Don't you ever run! Honor us, and fight for us," she urgently demanded.

Her striking regal face flashed in his mind. Her inner tears shone like diamond waterfalls against her beautiful bourbon skin. Her tears and the truth of her spirit were the start of his armor and his anger against the constructs of Society. He listened intently while she continued. *"I could not take them all down but I did my best. I created allies and more within the Dark Society, which will stay strong, past my death. Tell your father, my dear big brother, of me and he will understand why my children exist and he will know what they are doing. Now stay hidden; dark eyes are watching."*

A sound like a clicking of a reptile suddenly rang in his ears in that moment distracting him. A girl no more than thirteen years old with waist-length black hair, which held sapphire jewels, was dressed in a matching pale gold dress. She came forth holding the hand of two younger girls, both whom looked like the kid's age. The elder woman who claimed to be his blood muttered a phrase he had heard his mother use in prayer. The young girl with the long, dark hair flinched as sudden warmth radiating off her as if peace had hit her.

The same occurred for the two girls dressed in white dresses. One had amber doe eyes, braids, white bandages that wrapped around her limbs and silver nails. The other had an auburn ponytail that ran to the small of her back, a gye nyame necklace and an asp ring nestled on her middle finger. Her colorful fingernails sparkled in the shadows. He knew they were important but he didn't understand why.

As he inched closer, quick as a pinch, the putrid metallic scent and dark feeling returned covering the others. It alerted him to the fact that he was watching a gathering of Cursed. The woman he had briefly spoken with turned deathly cold. The familiar sinister feel of the Curse flowed around them and they stepped through an abandoned transit terminal. He noticed that the woman dropped the key she had just used. She had utilized a quick sleight of hand to pull out a copy while they walked away.

He learned that day that he had extended family. Khamun had also learned that the Cursed had somehow gotten to his family. In that moment, he vowed to help his blood by any means necessary. Anger simmered in his young body. He swiftly ran forward, picked up the key then headed back to the shadows. He had never told his father at that time the full story because he was too confused. But he made sure to learn all he could before that fortnight because he knew he had to get that kid out of that place. It sang in his soul to do so and his kind, Angels, never ignored the commands of their soul.

"Khamun . . ."

Mind lost in his mental rehashing, Marco's voice seemed to ring in his mind like that of his younger self. His voice turned into that of a battle-satisfied youth, enjoying his kills and watching his back. "Khamun, behind you!"

Blood of his enemies manifested before him and he felt the first rip of his maturing fangs descend from his gums. A strength he had no idea he possessed pumped through him. The smells of darkness once making him sick now made him hungry, thirsty to feed. He was so hungry. He was famished. He needed that essence. He needed . . .

He jumped at the touch of Marco's hand on his shoulder. Instinct almost had him flipping his brother, the man who was his dark cousin, behind him to protect him from phantoms of the past before remembering where he was. Damn, he had almost lost it. His hands ran through his locks. He glanced around realizing that he still clutched his knife in his hand. Coming back to reality, he saw Marco standing before him palms up. His pupils dilated in anxiety, and then melting into a golden-silver-rimmed hazel shade before flickering back to their icy gray hue.

"Sup, bro." Setting down the knife, Khamun realized sparks of his power danced on its silver surface and his clutched fists.

"You okay, primo?" Marco carefully questioned.

Trying to get his bearings and remember what he was doing prior, Khamun acknowledged Marco with a reassuring smile. He wiped his hands on his apron, and quickly reached out for a warrior clasp with Marco.

He then took another hit off his Trinity. "Never been better, fam. Tell me what you want to do, man; what can I do in your opinion?"

Tossing an apple back and forth between his hands, Marco rolled his shoulders. The white button-down shirt he wore seemed to tighten slightly with the swelling pressure of his bulking muscles while he processed his thoughts. "I have this feeling that you know, man. That you were thinking on it already."

Going back to the memory of the past, Khamun's stare locked onto his cousin with a curt nod. "We go in like phantoms, and we extract. Covert ops like before."

"Naw, hermano. You can say it. After what I saw last night, there's no saving her. You have my word as your brother and as your Shield. I release you from the vow you made to me and my mother."

Wow. He wasn't expecting that. A weight like a boulder surreally released from his shoulders as he felt that vow lift away. He noticed the truth in his cousin and he had much respect for that. The day was finally here and he was sorry about it all. Over the years, they had tried all they could to get word if Reina was alive and if she was okay. Over the years they had also run into the minions of Reina, the Dark Lady, never realizing she was Marco's twin until several years ago.

Through her malicious hands many Nephilim and humans disappeared or died. Blood soaked the streets wherever the Dark Lady landed and the Nephilim Council wanted her head. Unfortunately, Khamun had made his vow to his aunt after he watched her fall to her death at the hands of Marco's father, her words of thanks and other secrets echoing in his young mind. When she died, he had later heard rumors by Cursed minions that it was due to childbirth, but this was not the case and only he, Lenox, and Marco shared that truth.

Processing everything, he inwardly sighed. He never realized until now that Marco knew of the vow, which made him silently assessed his solemn brother before asking, "This is your wish, my man?"

Marco bowed his head in contemplation, his fist clutching by his side. The rolled-up sleeves of his button-down showed his many insignias against his smooth sepia dark skin and they glowed while his mind shifted in deliberation.

"Yeah, man. Been thinking about this for a long-ass time. When she went after our Oracle, the future of our kind, I knew she could not be allowed to continue, so you have the right to end her. There is no saving what is beyond gone. And if any light is still within her, ending her now saves that slither my mother left behind within her. ¿Comprende?" he simply stated.

Khamun understood too damn well. This was not a decision that was being made lightly, but he knew that for Marco's sake, that vow would always be a part of him. No, he would not be foolish enough to think they could save her. But, when the time came, he would let the Most High be the judge, and he the tool in either saving her light or ending it.

"Yeah, bro. Then the plan is changed. We go in, we extract those who have not been tainted yet, and we exterminate those of the Dark," Khamun proposed.

Both men gave a silent nod of understanding then froze staring at the figure in the entryway to the kitchen. Pressing a fist to their heart, they bowed their heads and both men waited for reprieve.

"My sons, that is not necessary," Eldress Neffer warmly interjected, walking through the kitchen then grabbing a pomegranate.

"Sauté this then add this into her omelet. Sanna needs as much energy as possible my heart," she instructed.

Khamun reached for a sauté pan then added the pomegranate seeds. His mother was dressed in her deep purple Eldress robes, which signaled an official meeting. In such a case, protocol dictated etiquette supersede family law, which was why both he and Marco had given her the royal respect she deserved.

"There is something I wish to discuss before we go into officially introducing Sanna to her training and soon, Society. Since meeting her and syncing with her, my visions have cleared up, though I am no way as powerful as she, I am still considering myself your House's head oracle."

Both men raised their eyebrows and Khamun chose to step forward. "Eldress. Mom, now that Sanna has come into her Awakening, I understand the need for you to act as a stand-in while you train her but she is Oracle. I am confused as to why you would take her rank?"

Khamun dropped his head during which his mother rested her hand against his jaw. The touch of his mother brought a comfort only a mother could while she softly spoke up.

"Because, my son, she is a Throne and His mouthpiece, the Oracle. Since she wasn't able to go into her Awakening naturally, her Oracle gifts seem to be diminutive. From just touching her, and from what she divulged, she sees a lot, knows so much, but she is not able to speak on it. Her visions are linear but as she tries to speak it, half of what she knows only verbally relays. The past mixes with the present visions. This can be a problem for your House and Society could use it to twist it and call her broken."

"Eldress . . ." Marco stepped forward but Eldress Neffer held her other hand out and cupped his face. Motherly concern shined in her gaze and he continued. "Tia, if they register her as a broken oracle, they may try to submit her to an asylum and banish her, regardless of her being the Oracle. The same was almost done to me. We have to do something, *sí?* I don't understand how her gift could be this way; she spoke in clarity before."

Khamun pushed the skillet away in frustration. He stepped out of his mother's touch with a shake of his head. "Marco is correct, Momma. As Oracle she spoke clearly how—"

Neffer sternly stepped forward to reach out and grab Khamun by his bicep gently gaining his attention. "But as Sanna, she does not know how to control her gifts yet, which is why I am here and why I will teach her until her mind works out the kinks. I will help with not only what she tells us when not speaking as Oracle, but also when her visions are skewed. I will help because she also will still have her migraines, son. I'm sorry, my sweetheart. She told me not to tell you because she didn't feel as if she could yet. She told me when Oracle used her up and Darren in the fight, she had a migraine. It was nothing as it used to be but she still has them and I wanted you to know."

Painful frustration filled Khamun. "Shit! I guess even Oracle has her limitations."

Neffer slowly nodded, hugging her son then turning to hug Marco. "I'm sorry, my boys. We came a long way today. We achieved something many Houses and teams around the world have not. We have a living and surviving oracle and not just any oracle, the Oracle. You cannot know how proud I am of you all."

The soft rustles of her robes kissed the marble floor with her movement around the kitchen fixing Sanna's plate while watching him and Marco. He could tell in his mother's eyes what she thought. Grown men though they were, Neffer would always see the two young boys who came to her, covered in blood, ash, dirt, sweat, and water after pulling off an elaborate heist that seasoned adults haven't been able to. That was the day his mother had learned that her son was something more and that was the day she met her Cursed nephew, who immediately claimed as her own, a boy who should not have existed.

"Yes, we did well, Momma, but what about Sanna, what about this House? She is ours to protect, which . . . damn it! We can't let Society know Oracle's true identity. Tell me what do we do then, Mom? Marco, what you think? Because my mind is not clear right now," Khamun urgently asked pacing the kitchen thinking about everything.

Crossing his arms over his chest, Marco reached to rub the back of his neck, thinking. "Hey, I know you know, primo. You said it. We have to protect her, and like you have to do every day in the streets, it's time she does the same: hide. We hide that she is Oracle. We can't hide that Oracle is back because of the spies but—"

Khamun interjected, beaming with a quiet understanding. "Like the Attacker. Well, the Reaper is a myth, so will Oracle be and if they think she is back but they don't know who she is; then we use this as a diversion until she is strong and we find more books. That's what's up."

"*Exactamente, acere.* Exactly, homie." Marco laughed. Both men knocked knuckles giving each other dap during which Eldress Neffer watched on smiling.

Pushing her dark red locks to the side, she continued to clean the kitchen before finding a tray. Speaking in motion, she cleared her throat. "Ahem, I have one more thing to say. I had a vision, which Sanna lead me to clearly see. Marco, sometime soon, you need to go back to St. Louis and check the team. While you are there, you will find a Guide who you must watch and remove from her current working environment. She will lead us to something associated with Ryo, and there is a third thread I'm not clear about, but it will lead us to someone who was lost. My sons, it's all related to the books, and Ryo let us know that one of the books was already taken awhile ago."

"By who? The Cursed?" Khamun asked.

Marco shook his head then reached out to help his aunt, as he shrugged. "Wouldn't even surprise me, primo."

Neffer placed an empty glass on a tray with a pitcher of ice water and the plate of food Khamun had cooked earlier. She walked ahead then paused, looking back at her two overwhelmed sons. "He explained it was them. We need to dig into that book more, sons. Come, let's get Sanna her food so she can help us look the books over. I am hoping Oracle speaks to help us clearly to gain a better footing because apparently these books are needed for our livelihood; and with the Cursed having one and we having one—"

"Whoever gets the next book will out trump the other," Khamun interjected. He took the tray out of his mother's hands and let her walk out.

Chapter 7

The brief meeting with Sanna, the Royal Eldress, and the rest of the house, minus Khamun and Marco, was still playing in his mind. He jettisoned one hand in the air and watched as he hit his goal. It was a clean sweep. Ball met net. It glided smoothly into the basket then bounced back to him only to end up taken by the newest member of the team. Lenox rolled his broad shoulders. His chest heaved in and out. His pectorals and well-defined abs constricted in exhaustion. Sweat ran down his broad bronze back, which accented the Polynesian tribal tattoos and Celtic weaving angel wings inked into his flesh.

Down the middle of his spine were biblical verse numbers and the Templar's creed: "A thousand shall fall at thy side, and ten thousand at thy right hand; but it shall not come nigh thee." The script was written in Celtic, Kemetian, and Polynesian script, and was indicative of his past cultures and his current heritage. A large hand ran over his close fresh low-cropped hair. It used to be thick, curling black hair that fell around his shoulders but once he, Khamun, and Marco decided to walk away from Society to start their own thing he had cut it in a symbolic release and eventually grew it back to where it curled around his neck. Now with this second transition, he decided to cut it again. Thanks to this beating heat, he was thankful for the decision. He tugged at his oversized basketball shorts, which hung low on his hips, revealing his defined hip lines while crouching low.

Behind him were his teammates flanking him and slick talking while he watched his opposing players.

"Hey, bruv, you're always spitting that splange but you need to worry about your wack defense."

Lenox inwardly chuckled at the bass-dropping Barbadian and slight British-fused accent behind him. He didn't have time for the slick talking around him, though he was laughing his ass off about it. His concern was about keeping the ball in his hands. His icy gaze could read every move his opponent was about to make, from the way his opponent shifted left then right on his feet, repeating the motion again. Yeah, young blood was about to try to take him. A flash of a smile had Lenox move to the side then turn to dogged Take, who tried to block him from heading after Darren. Amit slipped by. Nox passed him the ball.

"Make the hit, my man, I have you! They won't foul you up trust me!" Lenox roared, ducking under reaching hands. He moved his feet quickly to make it back on his side of the court.

The new blood in the house was uplifting. It meant that their team was growing and could establish a strong base within Society. He needed this. Needed this change and needed these people to focus on. He had worked hard to provide his best friends and Region Princes of Society a place they could comfortably maintain. He had done it for himself to honor not only his family but also all of the outcasts of Society.

At thirty-three and the eldest of the House, he had ended up doing that and more. It blew his mind at all that he and his family had created in such a short time span. What was short in the Nephilim world was almost eons in the human world. Sadly for him, his Prophet-gifted human parents, with whom he had traveled the world to collect the history of the Nephilim race, hadn't lived long enough to see what their only son had done. But, that was another story saved for another time.

This new generation of Disciples would come to understand the way the house worked. They would learn exactly what it took to establish what his brothers and he had almost missed out on creating. Lenox's mind returned to the present. He leaped in the air to snatch the ball Amit had thrown him, allowing him to turn and make a jump shot, a clean win, and victory. Now he could relax and stop showing the new blood what he could bring to the table on the court. They had other things to focus on. It was time for them to head to the training center to learn more about their new culture, while he had to get back to the office and return to his routine life.

"Now that we beat your asses, you both need to hit up the training simulations back at the compound," he joked, heading to the side of the court to pick up his water bottle.

They were outside in the sizzling heat of Chicago on the South Side, which demons always frequented. It was a great place to train newbies whose minds were now open to seeing who were humans, verses humans living with Cursed demons within them. The same went for humans who were Gargoyle-class entities, like Kyo and Ryo. The streets were thick with both breeds. Where they were playing, bullets were known to fly and demons loved to hunt.

"Beat our asses? Hey, Take, he said that they beat our asses. Did they beat our asses, bro?"

Take grabbed a towel with a deep laugh. His head shook left and right, sweat flying like rain around them. "Naw. I don't recall it that way. Almost beat our ass, maybe. But actually put a foot in it? Nope, never."

Dare flashed a dimpled smirk. His amber skin, now a toffee brown from the sun's caress upon his body, gave a hint of an ethereal glow while he tugged at his Nike shorts. Dare dropped into a squat. His forearms rested on his knees although his large hands moved in the air as he continued slick talking.

Sweat dripped onto the concrete near his feet with his laughter. "That's what I thought. I do believe the brotha is trying to persuade the court in falseness and punk-ass hating label-ism, am I wrong, my man?"

"Label-ism?" Amit questioned. His gray-green pupils were lit up by the sunlight. His Nike-clad feet were planted on the court's ground as he sat with his wrists on his knees. A wet towel flew in the air from his hands, landing against Dare back as he gripped his side laughing hard.

"What, damn? Fa'sho, man, label-ism. I made it up. Sounds good, roll with me damn," Dare joked.

Take's voice bellowed out in a rich laugh filtering around the fellow men. He ran a hand down his wet face. "You would be correct, bro. This poor man suffers from delusions of grandeur."

Lenox pushed up from his place near the bleachers and held his own laughter in while he held up his iPad. Images flashed on the screen showing the men, playing ball. Each shot, some dunks from Lenox paying homage to Jordan, flashed by with frozen screenshots of Take, Amit, and Dare standing baffled, played for both men.

"Like I said, I beat that ass. If you were pretty enough and born women, I'd say I rearranged that ass, and owned that ass. Tatted my name on that ass," Lenox mocked.

He gave his new brother-in-arms a chuckle with a casual shrug. "But because you both are family now, I think I'll say that anyway. This old man learned you today. Ball is my sport, had a full ride for being so good, thought you two knew that."

"Damn!" Amit yelled out instigating. His shoulders shook within his contained laugh.

Bag thrown over his shirt-clad shoulder, Lenox leaned forward to clap hands with Amit, shaking their hands up and down then separating with a fist bump. He coolly strolled to the other two men who watched him in appreciation to give them quick fist bumps. "Speak with you both back at the compound; hit up your twin, Dare, and I will set up sending her here ASAP."

"Okay, man, I appreciate that. We both do," Dare said.

Lenox heard Take grumble at Dare's joke. "Damn, I forgot to ask about how this mind syncing shit works. Yo, I'm not trying to be connected to my sis while she and Khamun . . . you know. But everyone else's females, besides fam, are fair game if you feel me. I'm competitive."

Nox chuckled. Taking out a bright red apple, he flipped in the air then took a bite as he disappeared in the sunlight. In his mind, he hoped that one day the House would bring Englewood back to its safe and former magnificence. Until then his team and the other Houses would continue to watch the streets.

An hour later, he sat at his office combing through case files over several clients he was working with. Various encoded messages from the cold bitch he had not one ounce of trust in his heart for, Winter, detailed where Cursed enclaves were located in the city and around the world. It also detailed whatever information about the Mad King, as she called him, she decided to share. The Dark Witch being their liaison was something he did not approve of. Not with the fact that at anytime she could use the lie that she only killed Light Nephilim to protect her mistresses for the greater good. It left a bad taste in his mouth. He was still riled up over the fact that she used that very same line again and had attacked Khamun.

He was sorry, but old school rules needed to apply in his opinion. "Know thy enemy and dispose of them the first damn chance you can get" was his own mantra and Winter's time was ticking away. Lenox exhaled glancing down at the papers. Yes, her work was impeccable; the detailed descriptions always came through. But, the fact that she lined each paper in light made him weary nonetheless; protecting his House and those true people dedicated to healing Society was what made it hard for him to silence his judgment about her. *Hell, she is the second right hand to the Dark Lady, the Princess of Hell!*

The smooth jazz of Thelonious Monk softly filtered through the room, coaxing him to calm down and gain a level head again. He was into his emotions again, something he did not have time to indulge in. Templars always stayed focused and assessed all aspects of a war plan. He would deal with Winter later on his own time. The dark silver ring, representing his house/rank, nestled on his pinkie finger glinted in the light of his office as he pushed the missives to the side of his desk. Various degrees representing his levels of higher education with that of various plaques of his accolades in his career lay in perfect lines on the mahogany panel wall behind him.

Upon his massive handcrafted dark oak desk sat his nameplate with a picture of his parents in Hawaii. Next to it was an array of paperwork neatly piled before him, his computer monitor, and a potted olive branch. Beneath his desk were nestled his several arrays of guns, hand blades, an adjustable steel staff, and other tidbits. Not that he ever needed them unless a client was a traitorous phantom and he rarely exchanged business with them. All lay attached to his desk.

He leaned to the side to pull out his Society case files just to glance and double check the work he'd done for other Houses in Chicago and elsewhere in the country.

He had just obtained a call about a rogue Disciple group hiding out in Chicago and living on the streets in Englewood with no leader or guidance. Luckily, for them, they were seeking the safety of his House and had not gone to Society for help. They were young and had heard about other rogue houses using the House of Dusk name, so to alert the Rouge Prince and his team of their existence they had decided to use the name as well.

Another smart move and another reason I need to get this firm international, he concluded. Tapping his pen against his desk, his icy blue pupils narrowed while thinking about what to do with the kids outside of immediately putting them in a safe house. Lenox ran a hand over his scalp, borderline exasperated. Too much was on his plate. Not that he did not like it that way; he just had to think strategically about certain things right now. The main being the Oracle's rebirth, and Winter's pleas for future sanctuary.

Finances needed to be switched into royal audits, now that Sanna was going to marry his best friend soon. She would be a Region Princess, but to Society she would be this stranger, this fresh-blood newbie who wasn't even born full blooded. To them, she would be this nuisance, a threat to the many full-blooded daughters who wanted their hand at the rogue prince. A prince they hoped to make return to his rightful place, so that they may live off the perks. These "women," and he used that term loosely, would taunt her. Then they would try to destroy her newly forming House, not realizing that she was Royal on principle of her Awakening.

Lenox gave an inward amused chuckle. He would love to be privy to seeing one of the many loathing socialites or their parents confront Sanna and truly find out who they were speaking with. The image of the crème de la crème of Society falling to their feet in shame for allowing pettiness, vindictive and greed-based behaviors to consume their so-called divine pedigree, amused him greatly. Especially since in actuality, they were acting worse than the "degenerate" half-breeds and full-blooded humans they shunned themselves. Of course, he would make sure to lay those facts out as officially and professionally as he could, with a smirk on his face the whole time, loving how their highbred faces shattered then cracked, falling to the floor to reveal the darkness that seeped within their shallow personage.

However, until then, he would be content doing what he did best, building up his practice and Society Houses around the globe. He could not deny that there was always a plan. Shifting his mind from his own demons, he pulled out a map and made a quick call. Atlanta didn't have a strong House presence down there. As of now, the houses supposedly taking care of the state were lost in their own dalliance of decadence and ostentation, as was becoming typical with many in Society now.

The Atlanta Society was too busy living out their lavish lives, sequestered in their segregated high-society communities, playing the philanthropists and trying to find ways to rub elbows with the rich, famous, and human old bloods. Their minds were nowhere thinking about the sudden reemergence of old world Cursed in the whole state, especially Atlanta. Khamun had requested him to set up a house down there years ago. He asked Lenox after getting a Denotation about Atlanta but various situations happened that kept pushing it back until it almost was forgotten.

"Time to get that ball rolling especially with the Oracle's baby sister living there," Lenox murmured to himself.

His fingertips scrolled over a roster of names from a copy of Khamun's book. They had both had a private conversation about what it could mean and they both concluded that there were lost Elders roaming around the globe. Elders who may be able to help rebuild Society with Sanna before it became lost. Circling his finger around a smudged name that he couldn't make out, he waited for his contact to answer but a deep cough grabbed his attention. Quickly standing, he hung up his phone.

"My Lord Elder . . . King." Resting a fisted hand over his gray vest-covered heart, Lenox bowed, his back erect, before dropping to one knee in his matching slacks. "How may I be of service, sir?"

Elder Omri Region King of the Eastern and Central Nephilim Society appeared before him with his hands in his black slacks and smile in his amber eyes. He stood dressed in black slacks with black casual shoes. His massive broad form seeped with power, casting a familiar vigilant shadow in the room as his all-white dashiki sleeveless cut cotton shirt displayed his muscled arms, arms Lenox was familiar going up against in training. The Elder was as hard as a steel door, nothing could take him down, so he once assumed, but that idea had to stay where it was.

"It damn very shall, young man." Elder Omri moved comfortably the office reading Nox's mind. His tied-back ebon locks swayed down his back while his large hands stayed in their pockets. "Please don't stand, my son, you don't have to be cavalier. You and I have a relationship that dictates otherwise in private."

Lenox quickly stood at the deep, commanding, accented voice of his Elder then sat. High King Omri was correct, as he trained Khamun to be the next de facto King of Society and appointed High Elder, he also spent time training second in line to the Royals, Marco and himself, to be the right hands/royal armament to the Prince. It was a task meant as a means for them to take their place as future high council members.

"I came to speak of my son and not the fact that he took me down on the training field so many years ago."

Years ago? No, more like three years ago. "Of course, High King." Lenox quickly corrected himself in remembrance that he was given the right to address him by his birth name, his true name. Something Lenox was forbidden by laws of the first Nephilim to ever reveal to anyone, let alone his own brothers. He was bound by a blood and spirit oath to let the King reveal the truth in his own time. He had to respect it or suffer a demotion in his power worse than death.

"In nothing but respect, and honor, what may I share with you about your son, Archangel Gabriel?" Lenox watched as the King sat and reclined in a chair.

The Elder's pointer finger and thumb rested in an L-shape against his salt-and-pepper temple and goatee. His wisdom-etched lines accented his regal and intense looks, making him appear older at times then younger as if he were in his mid-thirties. Elders aged well and often did not look as old as they portrayed or were. Piercing concerned golden irises locked on to Lenox, commanding his respect and attention. A question appeared to form in the Elder's mind and made him straighten in his seat while Lenox waited patiently.

"My son still does not know his true identity, nor does his wife . . . I mean fiancée?"

That question! It drove Lenox crazy that he could not share any of this with his brother or his future wife. But Templar's Creed and the blood oath always came before blood when dealing with the protection of that mentioned blood. It was not in his right, or power to share this, something he was only introduced into knowing once Sanna awakened just recently. So he quietly moved to his desk setting two cups of coffee down. That crap pissed him off, which made him rub his own temples then set his wire-rimmed reading glasses down.

"No, sir. He doesn't know but I believe Sanna may know more then she is sharing right now, which is understandable. She is dealing with a sensory overload of information," Lenox offered, gauging the Elder King's posture.

Upon his rich brown skin lay ancient tattoos on his hands which appeared to move with every sip of his fresh cup of coffee. Each various interweaving patterns and dots upon his hands represented the tribes of man. From what Lenox had learned Gabriel had chosen to be born into a tribe of men he was asked to oversee and protect in Africa. A row of inked black dots rested near his temple and traveled in a curve that followed his eye, something that made Lenox think of the eye of Horus. This man was the flesh and blood metaphysical body of the living tree of life and knowledge. Lenox was honored to be educated by him.

"Of course, this has always been the way of the true Oracle. Every life she has been in, the rare moments that He allowed her to take corporal form has always been this way for her. It saddens me every time and each time I pray for a graceful rebirth for her, one where she must not suffer in life," Gabriel matter-of-factly responded.

Damn. Lenox was still blown away by the knowledge that was just shared with him. Before him sat a man older than anyone he had ever met in his past life during the second war of the fallen. Older than even his own 9,012–plus-year-old soul and yet no one knew but him, the Queen, and the council of scribes, the First Guardians. A fresh tingling over his heart made him sit back in his chair and rest his ankle on his knee. The infinity branding with that of four lines resting against its looping helix. It reminded him that he was the newest member of an ancient order, one he used to belong to in his past life as the first Templar.

Several photocopied pages of Khamun's book slid
toward the Arch. Lenox stood in shock the moment his
office was washed in light, because before him sat the King
in his Arch form. Wings of iridescent gold shone bright as
if breathing light but cast a lethal hardness that warned
prey that they could slice through the hardest substance on
earth. He appeared the same age as Khamun in this form;
all signs of aging vanished without a trace. Burnished
toffee skin reflected the true divinity, the true mark of a
full-blooded angel, something the elite of Society would
never have, no matter how closely and selectively they bred
with each other.

This was a light only a select few in Society had.
Something he and his house members all had, a direct
line of divinity from the first Nephilims and the One Son.
This link also was found throughout the human world in
few humans. It was the divine Nephilim link and book
one of three documented this, which now rested in the
King's large hands. That book was the living tome of the
true history of the Nephilim. Lost and hidden, purposely
to be found by later generations.

"You came in time. I needed help understanding what
you wrote. The smudge I circled is undecipherable. I also
have more intel from . . ." Lenox quickly explained. He
cleared his throat, as he tasted the familiar bitter resignation that always crept in his mouth when he thought
of her. "Winter. I would like clearance to explain how the
book came into her hands. I mean better understanding.
Maybe it is something I can use to give to Khamun for
backup. I will also wish to have clearance to explain his
role as the new Angel of Death and how his vampiric
feeding on souls came about."

The Elder King sat in silence. His brows furrowed and
his eyes seemed to illuminate with old memories while he
scanned the pages in his hand. "No. All you need to know

is that the book was hidden on my behalf. My son will know nothing from me until he discovers that for himself on both regards."

The King glanced up briefly assessing Lenox before continuing. "I am pleased that he obtained my private diary and history of Society, the Devotion books, scribed by the first Archangels who landed on earth on their own. Through these set chosen keepers, the books were hidden at both my and my sister's request. But, he will not know that tale yet."

Lenox quickly locked down his open mind. This was bullshit. Utter prideful bullshit. Whoever assumed that Angels could not succumb to the very emotions that affected humans naturally were a lie.

Clearly, this Arch had been mortal for far too long to see how unjust this was. "Sir, I mean this in respect and I only know only a touch of the truth, but it would help our house and your son and nephew greatly if you told them how Marco's mother was taken. How she ran with your book to hide it in safekeeping because she had that gift of sight. How she—"

"No!" The reverberation of that one word shook the office with such an enigmatic force that Lenox had to step back from the desk and gain his bearings.

His skin began to feel as if it were ready to melt away. His soul ready to burst into flames and leave for the heavens as he sat and he swallowed hard at the force of it all.

"I . . . I'm sorry, sir," he began.

Elder King—no, Archangel Gabriel—stood hands fisted in constrained frustration. The proportion of his body mass index began to top beyond the scientific levels in his muscle mass. His chest began to heave up and down as he panted in old pains. The whites of his eyes were bloodshot with unshed tears of hurt. Had he been like Khamun, Lenox was sure he would have seen fangs dropping to killer mode. Therefore, in that moment the man who was Elder King of the Nephilim took a deep breath and bowed his head in silence. His hands lay stretched out in front of him as if they were stained or held lashed with scratches and lacerations upon them before he fisted them then dropped them near his sides.

"I am sorry, but no. That is not something they need to know right now. That my blood, my sister, took to running from her own kind because of the sacrifice she made before the first war to protect the One son. They do not need to know that she took on the plight of being the first Sin Eater. Picked by my brother-in-arms, the first Angel of Death himself to infuse the rest of his spirit. As you know, he had split off to give the Nephilim fangs so that they may inject darkness with light into corporal form with her."

Gabriel's eyes filled with eons of emotions that gave him the aging appearance of his many years and he continued, "He does not need to know that once our angelic brothers and sisters peacefully chose to stay on the earthly realm, that they would shun their own newly bounded thread of Sin Eater DNA within them. In addition, shun the selected full-blooded Sin Eaters Generals and her. That their prejudice would have them calling her a monstrosity because she accepted the last important piece of Death's gift: his heart.

"Listen as I school you, Lenox; this gift gave her dark wings and fangs that matched the first Vampires of human lore. Vampires, who, you know, were truly Cursed demons that killed and fed from humans in evil glee. She accepted this task to combat them, Lenox. Letting Death give her his gift with that of her chosen brothers and sisters to create full-blooded Sin Eaters for the wars and play emissaries within the Cursed ranks," Gabriel explained.

Lenox wanted to speak up. He wanted to say that he understood, that he now realized how Winter got her hands on the book. But out of respect, he listened to the lesson pouring from his Elder King.

"You younglings with the locked memories have no idea what it was like then and what I've been privy to see in my life on this realm! Her own Angelic brothers and sisters shunned all who valiantly took her new form and embraced it. They chose to hide from their true purpose: to take the sins of this world and wash it clean, by protecting and guarding the innocent from the Cursed. We are the *Sin Eaters*! We feed from our enemy, by fangs or touch. We drain them of their darkness and end them by returning the good to the Light. Those scared fools ignored the gift the Most High ordained us to undertake and became lost to the truth due to their own folly!"

Tears of disgust appeared to fall down the Angel's face, leaving streams of gold in its path and it was powerfully regal.

It was said by humans that these tears were the true source of holy water and Lenox knew it to be factual as Gabriel continued. "Why? Because those bigots themselves believed that they were pure because they took only a small piece of Death giving those judgmental fools fangs, but none of the full-blooded Sin Eater's true feeding power. Aoelon, Sariel, I am so sorry, sister! I am ashamed of their dishonor! I'm sorry you lost your true mate, my brother with his own sacrifice he gave you, only to be taken by our enemies when you ran. I . . . am . . . sorry."

Lenox could feel the depth of anguish in the Elder. It made him furious at Society to learn how Society did not have the Elder's or his sister's backs, how this was the start of the darkness that easily crept into the Society. It was frustrating and deplorable.

Lenox agitatedly ran a hand over his dark, fresh close-cropped hair. He stepped forward, seeking some way to help his Elder in his pain. His icy stare continued to take in the King and he opened his mouth to give some words of understanding, of support, but could only keep silent in respect as Gabriel spoke up again.

"They do not need to know that this is how she was taken. Used as a mule to birth a race that was not able to breed until finding her and the One son's shed blood. It is my fault. I did not fight for her enough but this is why you stand where you are now! Understand that! All things will be told in due time. That tale told in the books that you all are finding. I am proud of my progeny. Very proud of you all."

Taking a moment, Gabriel turned his back to compose himself. "That is something I will tell them both soon. Tell you all soon, but for now" —Gabriel shifted back to his mortal form then pulled out a pair of rimless glasses—"we will focus on something else and you will respect the insurgents my sister placed on the Cursed side. You will teach the team how to accept any more that may need sanctuary for they are ours and not the Cursed, now."

The pages that Lenox handed the Elder King earlier but were now on his desk flew into King Omri's hands, shifting while he glanced over the rim of his glasses. "Ah, let me see, forgive me for before, son. You are correct. This fleshly form has been on earth for too long and now it catching up to me; it had me in my emotions."

The Elder King tapped the paper with his finger as if jarring his memory. His intense gaze lit up behind his rimmed glasses and he gave a warming smile. "Ah yes, Michael. My dear brother. The Arch who left too soon with his sacrifice. His name is written in the true tongue of the Most High, which is why you cannot read it yet. His name is on the list of angels that died in the first war."

Say what? ran in Lenox mind. *The Most High's leading angel, the rumored Angel of Death not only sacrificed his gift creating the Sin Eaters but he died!*

He shook his head in disbelief while pinching the bridge of his nose. "I'm sorry, but I do not understand."

Gabriel shook his head. Creases formed around his slight almond-shaped golden eyes as he looked through the pages in fondness. "He'll tell you that story once you find him with the help of the books. I myself only learned later in my years mourning that his and my fellow brothers and sisters whose lives were lost were not dead, as you know well. After my journal was hidden, Michael gave his journal to his dragons gifted by our younger brother. The other, the final book, was also given to Michael by my sister; it lay in his hands lost when I saw him fall to his death, but I assumed wrong."

"But . . ."

Holding his hand up, the High King cut Lenox off. "I know all of this now because I know. Again, I am proud of what you all are doing, that is why I am here. It is time for you to find Michael. I was given the word to bring him back out of hiding, him and the others, stay abreast of that goal. As the First Guardians, we watch, we never are allowed to intervene unless to fix the scales of the war; we protect the history and correct it without intervening with free will. We are the gatekeepers; as we play our role, so does the rest of the world as was foreseen. Stay in the background; that is an order. Now, we will speak again, son. Before I go, know that the Cursed are planning a gathering in the coming months. This is our time to train the Oracle and her Sin Eater. Do tell my son and remember, Nox, respect that divine witch. Keep your enemies close and love thy neighbor."

With that, the King left Lenox high and dry and confused as hell. *Love thy neighbor and stay hidden?* "Damn, I hate when he does that."

Chapter 8

Several months later . . .

It was cold. Goosebumps formed on the back of her arms. Sanna Steele shivered, wrapping her arms around herself. Chicago, when it was becoming cold, was not fun, especially downtown near the lake. She couldn't believe he had dropped her out here like this. Told her it was time for a real world experience in training.

Thinking back, although she had survived her first battle, Khamun had promptly explained that she almost had died, too, which resulted in months of endless butt kicking by everyone in the House, but mainly by Lenox and Khamun with Kyo in tow. Now not only had she been starting from scratch and learning how to be a Slayer and a Mystic the past couple of months, but she had been sitting with younger Nephilim children and latent Nephilims learning about Society. She also had been having private lessons about the oracle principles with Eldress Neffer and practicing the oracle levels. Both she and Kyo felt as if they were in school again. This was not her cup of tea.

During her studies, it had astounded her that she was hustling and fighting as if the training was second nature to her. Heck, it was according to their teachings about spiritual rebirths. But, this was still unfair. All of the hard crap falling on her shoulders felt stressful, only because this was all new to her. Yes, she had been here before as

Khamun's mother had told her, and San could contest to that fact already.

However, she also felt it in her blood. It was just interesting to her that this all had come the way it had. Definitely, with the year her life had changed full circle from the sickly girl of her youth to the plus-size chef that old men only wanted. Then later becoming an entity of power and respect who was wanted by a man who happened to be a myth. An angel. It was still crazy to her.

She bet her old peers in North County wouldn't recognize her now since this change. She hardly recognized herself now. To say a woman of her size was unhealthy and couldn't run even a mile in situations of danger made her laugh. She was moving with the best of them and she was proud of herself. Size fourteen was not a hindrance, she was not a hindrance, and she inwardly smiled. Glancing around, she saw her closed restaurant with its construction underway and she felt somewhat at odds. Would she and Kyo be able to return to some of their old lives and do a grand opening? She really hoped so.

Regardless of the changes, she still was who she was, Sanna Steele: chef, daughter, and sister. Speaking of Kyo, she glanced in the evening sky. The end of the sun setting cast a ruby haze in the distance. She smiled as she felt her god sister shadow her. Something about the life of a Gargoyle seemed to fit Kyo perfectly in her opinion.

Once everything fell how it did, she felt a good change in her best friend. Her god sis had found the man in her dreams. He was teaching her everything he knew, along with what their parents knew. Custom within the Dragon world dictated that the parents approve their union and oversee it. So, that too was something new for them all to deal with, parents in the compounds and the power they both were coming into.

Both she and Kyo had sat down to talk privately with each other, testing out their mental linking bond a couple of days ago. As soon as they sat down to talk, Sanna had felt that old familiar pressure and pain in her skull with the onset of what Kyo had seen when she was talking with Ryo during their training several weeks ago. Sanna sat next to her best friend in their white meditating room, watching everything play over in their mind. Sanna was practicing an Oracle bond. Seeing into the mind of her best friend, living in her memories. Kyo had been taking on a Cursed demon with Ryo. Sanna's mind split open more, as she felt every emotion Kyo was going through while holding a demon over a ledge of a skyscraper questioning it. San could smell the demon's pungent cooking flesh in the sun while she sat in the vision.

"Ry, hurry, tell me what or who you are looking for. I . . . I don't know what I'm doing, but I see everything; hurry!" Kyo urgently demanded.

San instantly heard Ryo question Kyo about a child, a little boy from California. The more he asked, the wider Kyo's mind opened and ripped at the mental contours of the demon. The grimy stench of burning flesh tickled at her nostrils, but Kyo kept searching. Scenes of children vanishing across the nation hit her hard. Many Kyo had seen on the news. Some snatched, others sold by humans tainted with darkness, others killed in senseless murders by stray and purposeful bullets.

In every scene, both Kyo and San could taste, feel, and smell. Screams of the crying children tore at Kyo's heart. It bore into her mind until she stopped at an image in the demon's mind that begged for her attention. San and Kyo saw a young boy who looked to be no older than four or five years old. His laughter and innocent playing in a massive garden full of stone dragons kept her attention. Various trees that seemed to belong in Asia, and monks who watched in protection amazed her.

A statuesque woman with dark brown doe-shaped eyes that framed a regal yet soft walnut-kissed face walked into Kyo's vision. She kneeled down to hold her arms out to the little boy. The woman's long, wavy, parted hair, which fell around her breasts, fluttered in the wind. Her full heart-shaped lips displayed a warm, dimpled smile that puckered forward into a motherly kiss against the boy's face. A cold darkness moved through the bright baby-blue clear skies. Kyo watched as a handsome man with almond-shaped eyes that matched her own with a growing fade haircut stand before her. He was dressed as a monk but also wore a pair of jeans with workmen's boots. Curiously he also wore a ring that matched the kneeling woman's ring on her right hand. As if noticing the same darkening skies the monk quickly glanced around the garden, appearing bristled.

In that same moment, a diverse set of monks surrounded the family and both Kyo and Sanna were in awe. Monks of Asian, African, Caucasian, and Latino descent engulfed the gardens and temples shifting into various martial art warrior forms. Loud battle cries sounded around her as rings from ancient bells chimed around them all. Women dressed in the same attire stood by the rest of the monks with weapons in their hands. She listened to orders being barked out. The father of the young boy demanded both the woman and the child to head into a massive temple that appeared before them.

Kyo continued to share her vision with Sanna.

San observed then felt the enemy coming the second that the male flipped into action. His bright saffron-colored robes whipped in the stifling air. He fluidly shifted into "white crane style," a form Kyo had just learned from her father Poppa Hideo. The untraditional monk's leanly muscular frame flourished in size. His brown eyes slowly melded into a fiery amber shade. Then plumes of smoke emitted from his lush lips, displaying diamond-sharp Dragon fangs. They watched as he moved into his crane form then shifted upon his feet to stand wide legged. One arm stretched before him palm out in a dragon clutch, the other horizontal, holding a chain blade.

A battle was coming and both Kyo and Sanna could feel that the enemy wanted the child. Kyo saw the shadow of a looming male standing at the entrance of the temple. Behind him, cars parked in a grassy oval parking lot that surrounded the acres of forest and hills that looked down on a bustling city were crushed like discarded cans all over the place. Demons of every variety stood behind his broad back and a sharp roar ripped from the man's mouth. Golden-red leather ripped wings stretched wide. They knocked sleeping dragons who had not had a chance to wake up, on the ground, smashing them into pieces, killing them. Sanna could hear Kyo's cries. Her people were dying.

Kyo wanted to scream to help but instead gasped in shock, as the monstrous male stepped forward from the darkness. Wavy black shoulder-length hair rested on broad horn-lined muscular shoulders. A crisp black-and-white suit, which appeared to be expensively tailor made from Italy, adorned the male. To the untrained eye, if looking closely, you could see slots that blended into the seams of the suit, to allow wings to slide through them.

In arrogance, Kyo watched him smile her way. His eyes appeared to bore into her soul. His handsome light butter-brown skin hummed in its menacing beauty. In his powerful allure, Kyo noticed him haughtily rub his ring-adorned large hands together. Kyo stared at the strong features of a man who appeared to resemble

Marco. She knew without a doubt that it was the Cursed King, a man she had read about in Winter's missives. Confusion had Kyo bridled in anger and fear while they watched each other in a silent duel.

"Tell your Sin Eater that time precedes me. We will meet soon to finish what my daughter started; now move on, pet," *Kyo heard him croon in her mind.*

Sanna heard it as well. Sanna felt Kyo's emotions at that moment. *His dripping voice, edged in toxic sensuality, cut Kyo senseless. It left her with a jarring migraine, with the sensation of warm, trickling blood exiting her nose.*

Kyo battled with the vision, which broke her train of thought. Kyo's power tethered from her to connect with the monk, who was not a monk, yet he was. It was as if he called for Kyo's power. Power, her god sister had no idea she held. Kyo obliged to let him use it; use the power of their shared people and connect it to everyone at the temple. Sanna watched Kyo's soft Shea butter skin relax in a locked state of admiration.

Sanna felt Kyo being pulled partially from her vision, at the sound of Ryo's pressing deep voice. "Kyo! Baby, you're killing him. He's burning alive." Sanna could see that the scene before Kyo had made tears of fury fall down her plush cheeks.

Demons tore into the dragon monks. Everyone was falling to his or her deaths defending the temple, a place Darkness should not have had access to. Kyo watched as they took the little boy, whose sweet features made her spirit smile before the scene shifted yet again. No more was that sweet boy; now appearing before her hidden in dark shadows was a chilling demon. His once-brown almond eyes were dark with occasional flashes of ruby red and now held a cold, sinister feel to his once-innocent, warm spirit. The child was tainted. Twisted. Taken

by the Mad King and everyone had died in that temple
by the evil bastard's hands.

Anger made Kyo claw her nails into the demon before
her, who had been at the scene of that atrocity. At that
moment, Kyo set the demon in her hands ablaze, watch-
ing him fall from the high-rise building in nothing but
dust. Sweat coated her tanned skin. Her flyaway hair
matted against her face caused her to wipe at her nose
and take several deep breaths. Her mismatched jade
and hazel eyes stayed locked on the broad cord-tight
back of her fiancé in awareness.

"You're not the key are you?" Kyo quietly asked.

"No. The child is," Ryo replied. His eyes stayed focused
on the sun slowly setting over the Chicago skyline. Flecks
of red mixing with orange kissed and painted a beautiful
view before them.

Sanna broke from the vision in astonishment. All of
this time, everyone had been finding ways to find the
second book, when it—no, he—was in their hands. Ryo
wasn't the key, he was the book in the flesh! The child was
the key. Sanna sat speechless, studying her god sister.

Kyo held her hand to listen to Ryo's explanation in
their shared mind: *"Every extended generation the*
Dragons of my family are chosen to absorb the power
and knowledge of the book. During the first war, we
knew it would be hunted, so we found a way with our
Mystics to protect the book and create a decoy book.
Only my family knows and the Keys don't find out until
maturity. Kyo, I am his and Khauman's Protector, but
I am . . . the book. They'll come for me again when they
realize they don't have the real book. We need to get him
back from the Dark, baby, we have to, or our people,
Nephilims, will die."

Sanna was mind blown in her mental calculations.
The fact that the Mad King could sense them and had

stepped into Kyo's vision had scared them both deeply. The intel was correct; a genocide was happening all over the world. After the information Kyo had shared, Sanna felt her mind open again like a satellite. This allowed her to connect with the fading beat of humans and Nephilims around the globe and Sanna heard their cries. More like felt it.

Her vision filtered to show her Calvin and Marco in St. Louis fighting the Cursed. The fellas had stopped a man from shooting his pregnant wife and child. The man had wanted to erase his wife from reality to be with another woman, a woman who had tainted him with her Cursed bite, resulting in the man going home almost killing his wife and their one-year-old son. In her shifting revelations, she saw that child with the haunting eyes from California again, the temple, and the fallen monks; then it shifted out of the US.

She saw military soldiers battling for their lives outside of embassies and many people flooding the streets crying out for vengeance and help. Within those people who screamed for respect were demons that used the pain of some and turned innocent protests into raging mobs. Each Cursed demon used their power to twist the advocacy of innocent humans—and even some bitten Nephilim—words and tainting some humans who held corruption in their hearts into instigating a crazed hate, which spread to various nations. Those same humans spread the corruption to a few defending soldiers, soldiers whose fears became erratic. Everything resulted in bullets hitting innocents, then those corrupted innocent humans returned the favor by using grenades against them. The Mad King's presence was over it all. A war he had created, which Sanna felt it all in her dream state. She tried to stop it but couldn't.

In a blaze of smoky fog and blood, a robed man in sandals with a mane of shoulder-length thick, corded locks came to her dreams again, speaking to her and comforting her. Sadness moistened his dark oak-colored eyes. His aura rang divine, indicating that she was speaking to whom the Nephilim called the One son. He explained that she needed what was embedded in his hands. Bleeding hands that he held out to her in urgency.

Two fleshy holes rested in the palms of his hands; within the wounds lay nails. He told her she needed to balance the war, to save the innocents and Nephilim of the world. Sanna listened with her heart open, kneeling before him, her curly mane now covered in a black shroud. Before her eyes, he changed. He was no longer the iconic savior: the one and only human Sin Eater. Now he was many iconic figures, spiritual teachers, and leader's everyone around the world believed in before his thumb rested against her third eye.

Immaculate power caused her blood to sing as he whispered, *"He used my blood to create children in his own malevolent image."*

The flash of a young girl with large light brown eyes made her gasp. Her face hovered over her own and that sweet little girl's sudden tears spilled down her face turning into blood. Her rich cocoa skin began to split and harden to many scales before a reptilian clicking noise surrounded her and she melted away. The image of Marco as a young boy and the Dark Lady playing tag with daggers in each hand around San made her spin around on her heels then reach out for the child.

Sanna was confused and scared to put the pieces together at the One Teacher's words: *"He seeks to find it again through the books, but Gabriel, then his sister, the chosen first Reaper, took it and they have it hidden well. You, my chosen first protectors, reborn in this life to defend the modern world will be successful in this needed change.*

"Find what I showed you, continue to keep the books from his grasp, and keep my blood from his touch. You and my brother have always been Father's favorite as you are mine. The mouthpiece and His weapon, you both and your family make us proud. Continue to learn and stop what you can. The end is nigh, but it does not have to mean destruction of the Light. Ashe, sister, daughter. Mother of All. Ashe." The image of Khamun's loving eyes filled her then the sound of dragons and her family fighting rang in her ears as she woke up from her vision.

By now, she assumed that she would be used to these premonitions, visions, dreams, and migraines. But how could a person really be prepared to see such carnage and pain? It was hurtful but it was reality. She could just turn on the news and everything she saw was reflected there.

Society needs to come together and do what they were sent to earth to do, damn it! The sudden flicker of Kyo's nails in the setting sun drew her attention from her muddled mind. The shadow of her god sister shifted past her vision in the night sky, at the same moment of the feel of a second presence: his presence, The Reaper, her fiancé, which made her inwardly beam in love.

Sanna's mind drifted in thought about him while walking downtown Chicago. The Windy City was alive as its caress whipped at her past-shoulder-length natural curls making her draw her black trench coat together. Tonight seemed to have many people bustling around, although it was starting to turn cold. A sharp vibration from her cell phone drew her attention to its screen. It displayed intel in a broken coded language that she was still learning.

From what she learned, this was nothing she hadn't already dreamed about. Marco and Calvin were tearing up STL, working toward the mission she had sent them on. Her two light and dark sweethearts were about to head into a conflict, which would place them on an unknown path. They were going to live and walk through hell and, maybe, even bring hell to the compound after this all ended; but San felt, in it all, something good was going to come from it, finding the rest of the books and helping save the Society.

Chapter 9

(Lost Scrolls of Nephilim)

I've been witness to many human tales in my long-lived life. I've created history as ordered by the Most High. Much of my work I am proud of but even as an Arch and a Guardian I have been saddened and ashamed by some of the tales I was not allowed to intervene in and heal.

This is one: the truth of the Judas. I watch him now seeing his future at the Great Table—which was really a small meeting of the chosen Disciples at a humble home—knowing that his betrayal will be the catalyst that will change everything, including our war against the Cursed.

As our kind knows, it takes something as simple as a wind's breath of a touch to pollute a human's soul. It takes even less than that to pollute a human who already has a fractured soul from a psyche attack by others who may have been influenced or corrupted by our enemies. He was such a vessel. Such a highly prized candidate for the enemy's wicked deviations. A simple brush. A brush in the marked as he stood in support of the One son.

I was commanded not to heal, commanded not to alert the others of the taint that unlocked darkness within the once-pure male. Now I do as I've always done. Watch, even as I fight the need to protect.

Following him was a simple blink for my kind. To watch him fall into the darkness once the One son revealed that he would be betrayed by his own chosen Disciples, marked the end of the purity within the male. It marked the end of the fight he held on to as he succumbed to the lies within his psyche. He began to believe that the One son was not going to save them or the land. That the only true power, the One son held was of a wizard as a vessel to trick and deceive those around him. And in his madness he believed he could be the one to save those around the One son from the lies.

I watched, as he let the darkness eat at him. I observed as many Cursed demons came to him in various forms. They broke bread with him and fed him more lies as a means to taint him more. The final blow was the turning touch from the Dark Prince himself, with his Cursed minion and King of the top world, Caius, once known as my fallen brother Bernael. My Arch's fury blazed bright with this knowledge and truth that I was able to read from those before me. Bernael was reborn in the flesh of a human. The angel had fallen and was hunted down by me only to find refuge in the shell of a human, whose putrid soul was beyond salvation. This was sacrilege; this was a perversion and violation of the humans we were taught to guide and protect!

Yet again, they took the gift that the Most High created and darkened it. As they had stolen our brothers and sisters in the skies. Forced them to fall to create the many kingdoms of the Cursed and then mated with humans to build those Cursed Nephilim kingdoms. They continue to find ways to reproduce, which was a gift that was taken from them in the Fall. The knowledge seared in my mind as the Dark Prince stared my way with a smile. Law dictated that his hand could not touch me, but his minion, this new thing, could and I was made to leave before my existence was found out.

With this known truth, I testified to the Most High's resultant and spoke with his mouthpiece. I watched as her diamond tears fell while she pleaded to be reborn again to heal what was breaking. I listened as we were ordered to wait. Which we obeyed while the mouthpiece sat with her weapon, her mate, whose haunted eyes never left my mind.

For see, these two were a part of me, as well. My own child created from the Most High by using pieces of my spirit and that of my brother Michael, my son in spirit, the vessel of the first King of Men. His mate sat at his side in her ethereal beauty. The Most High created her for the second time. She shared both of our Arch blood due to having come from my son's rib as well as from the fire of the Holy Spirit. Legend states that they were created from the earth, fashioned from the gifts given by the Eternal Garden, and then given the breath of life from the Most High. This would be a truth but to every truth, there is fact, which I observed that day.

The sadness in her eyes changed into a righteous wrath due to her innocence being taken from one of my own brothers at the spark of her life, a menace whose own pride corrupted his divine gift of duality. The angel who was to protect the gray, but who also chose to use his power to manipulate and corrupt in his fall. His deception and act to work for the Dark Prince strengthened his goal to pollute the womb of the Most High's loved children. Which began our second war. Now they once again use this act of conception in a deed of darkness.

From this understanding and the creed to let the chess pieces shift as they may, also gave us a new gift. The right to create our own Nephilim children naturally, children who would be divine, who will work to keep the final war from coming and who will protect the descendants of the First Garden and soon the children of the One son.

Thus, I watched as a good Disciple fell to the darkness, his soul fighting against the evil and sickness. I watched while he took coins for blood. His hands stained for eternity from the treachery of the One son. Thus with this knowledge, once the coins touched his hands, it condemned him to taking his own life. His hanging body later falling to the earth and turning into a miasmic mist. As history would write, he would forever be the Betrayer. He would forever be lost to darkness never given penance for his selfish act. Nevertheless, what we see as Guardians is never what history records and his story is one of those. His act he chose. His taint accepted as a means to be an insurgent and protector for the One son. He allowed his body to be used as a means to give us truths, truths I was able to glean in that meeting between him and the Dark Prince.

Yes, some truths are never allowed to be told in history and the Betrayer will never be seen as the hero he is. Thus, as promised, what was forced to fall will rise again from madness and help change the war for us, from within. A Betrayer with his own protectors for their side but a weapon for us.

—Elder Gab'reel, Council of Powers

Chapter 10

Sanna pressed two fingers to her temples at the familiar start of her migraines. She knew she had to step back from trying to see more about the people who had come into her life so recently. Already the tension was getting to her, and she was feeling slightly nauseous. She needed to decompress, so she rolled her shoulders then shifted her mind to tracking the bright aura that woke her out of her sleep and made Khamun drop her on this lone mission.

Taking a turn down State Street, her milk chocolate pupils scanned the area while her inner scope locked in on the back of a child being briskly tugged by a handsome young yuppie couple. To the untrained eye, the couple appeared like any everyday youthful couple with a child. The guy was dressed in a pea coat trench, his arm wrapped around his savvy-dressed girlfriend or wife. The woman held up an iPad, flipping pictures while they shared a Newport cigarette. The guy held his hand around the young girl's shoulders, her vibrant auburn-reddish hair and features contrasting those of her parents' golden looks. Everything appeared peaceful but looks were always deceiving. Various hints of welts and cuts peeked through the little girl's sleeves of her coat. As the icy wind whipped her long hair to the side, Sanna saw more welts nestled against the girl's paling skin.

Pissed, Sanna's nostrils flared as a breeze hit her with an acrid, metallic, pungent smell, which coated the roof of her mouth. Smoke hit her in that same moment. It smelled of marijuana laced with something unfamiliar. Her mind computed it, letting her know it was meth. Anger bubbled within her at the people who were tainted by the Cursed. The demon within them seemed to snatch out to infect others with breaches to their hearts. Sanna moved faster to follow them. She knew she had to take them out quickly. They were touching too many people around them while leading the child down an alley connected to a major storefront. Sanna's spirit blazed to her that the child was not theirs. What they planned to do put a slight fear in Sanna.

"No fear, remember, sis. That is a weapon they will use against you, so no fear, we aren't born with it. Khamun wanted me to tell you," Kyo interjected in her mind. Sanna instantly gritted her teeth. Sanna tried to push it away but images of what they would do to that child slashed at her spirit. It was almost too much for her. Unshed tears burned at her eyes.

"San! Release it! They will feel you following," Kyo hissed into Sanna's mind, causing her to cut her eyes at her god sister and best friend. Sometimes Kyo could be bossy and overprotective but Sanna understood it. It was in her sis's DNA. The gentle tug on her arm from Kyo had led her down an adjacent alley.

"I flew over this area once. If we walk this way, we'll run into them head-on so get ready. Oh and me and Ryo, um, finally got some alone time. Just enough to share some kisses down below if you get what I'm saying, sis," Kyo nonchalantly spoke in a hushed tone.

Sanna whispered, "What!"

Kyo giggled hard, jokingly beaming. "I so knew that would distract you!" Her mismatched eyes quickly glinted in awareness before she whispered, "Wait, wait, wait. Here they come. I'll tell you later."

Sanna yanked on Kyo's arm hard to cut her eyes and stop their walk, dropping her own voice. "Kyo! You better talk right now and stop playing!"

She couldn't believe her best friend would even spill some tea like that, and not expect her to question it. What made her a little more annoyed, but not really, was that the heifer had the nerve to playfully smirk then innocently bat her eyes.

"Okay, okay I'll make it fast. It was in our five minutes. I really, really wanted to and, yeah, it just happened." Kyo's words trailed off in assessing the alleyway.

The way her Protector tilted her head to the side let Sanna know that Kyo saw a place where she could position herself.

Distracted, Kyo hurriedly continued, still murmuring. "He stroked me and I decided to stroke him, then . . . you know? Yup, it was pretty nice. I enjoyed finally being with him in person and not in my dreams. With the little time we had."

Sanna couldn't stop her bubbling happiness. She reached out to hug her laughing god sister and then quietly squealed, elated, "I know you two are ready to burst. I'll distract Take as soon as we get back so you both can have more time together."

"Thank you, sis. I didn't think I'd love someone like I love him but I do and I get it. I get how you and Khamun love each other. I feel that with Ryo," Kyo coyly whispered.

Of course, Sanna could understand totally. It felt good to have love given and returned equally. Sanna felt like a big bag of glowing joy. Her eyes softly glowed with forming tears of joy while she spoke. "I know and it's about time. Dreams seemed to have led us to our future husbands. Here they come, Kyo. I see them now."

A quick, assessing tilt of her head had Sanna adjusting her scarf around her neck nervously. She glanced around and played the game by holding up her cell to her ear talking loud appearing unassuming. She noticed the couple yank the child whose blue eyes widened with a silent "Help," the moment Sanna walked slowly toward them. Unabashed ire kept Sanna ready for battle.

Near the alley where she walked, a homeless man sat near a garbage bin, bundled up in various tattered blankets against the cold air. He coughed loud then pushed out a tattered cup with change within. The swift peek of locks drew Sanna's attention. *Always protected.* She inwardly knew who it was, which made her mentally lock in on how close the couple was.

While she spoke on her cell, she casually lifted her elbow in the air. The moment the side of the approaching male's face came close enough for her, she pivoted to slam her elbow into his head. Elbow connected with the side of his ear, jaw, and face. The sound of a loud grunt had her shaking her arm out in a turn. She quickly tucked her cell into her pocket then moved behind the guy slamming her forearm into the back of his head achieving to knock the couple off-balance.

In her peripheral she noticed that the male stumbled forward, almost falling on his face. The stunned look on his red face melted into a simple flash of malice as he barked out, his hand shoving toward her face, "You piece of trash!"

People can be bold sometimes, ran in her mind. She pivoted to move out of his way. Cowering she held up her hands in front of her face, shaking her curly mane in feigned embarrassment. Her auburn pupils widened, while her plush lips formed an O in shock. "Oh my gosh, I'm so sorry, I slipped!"

The towering guy who could have been an extra in a Gap ad stood glared at her fuming. He seemed shocked and insulted for being hit in such a manner. Snobbishly, he brushed his coat off in a hasty, disgusted manner then slowly strolled back her way. With a tug on his collar, he scrubbed the back of his knuckles against his jaw then growled low, malice glinting in his eyes, "You lying cow. You did that crap on purpose. Who are you?"

Sanna fixed her lips to give a retort but the quick feminine snarl from the right of her drew her attention. It was so jarring that it made her duck at the lightning-quick wipe of jagged nails charging toward her. Fear hit Sanna hard. She watched the couple hone in on her with widened eyes. Danger was around her, which she could almost taste. It was game time.

Assessing the situation, she noticed the deranged couple's bodies appeared to unhinge. The sound of sharp cracking and popping of bones filled the alley. Before her, the elongation and separation of jawbone and cheekbones accosted her senses. Soft pinkish-white winter-chafed skin on the pair appeared to stretch and tear, turning into a sickly grayish hue. The female's face contorted with millions of tiny puncturing needle-like teeth filling her mouth.

Callous actions had the female demon flipping her hair to the side then dropping to all fours in a resonant growl. The tall, blond-haired male gave a disjointed laugh. Each of his fingers lengthened then cracked in its contorting deformity. Amusement at the perception of cornering a simple human flickered in his demonic eyes.

From what Sanna had learned in her trainings, the wannabe yuppie before her was an Anarchy Snatcher. At his side was his Dark Gargoyle who hissed then spit yellowed streams of milky spittle. The clicking noise from the grotesque entity made Sanna's ears ring as the intense smell of venom made her stomach turn into knots.

Several cautious steps had Sanna walking backward downwind, her eyes staying on her targets. *What did I get myself into?*

Sanna licked her chapping lips. Her hand slipped to her hip to unclasp an object. A cloaked staff glinted silver in the dark. Its smooth surface clicked into place with a twist of her wrist then lengthened within her touch. Lenox's smooth voice echoed in her memories, telling her to keep her feet spaced while watching the female Gargoyle with the blond hair stalk toward her then rush her.

The instant that Sanna came face to face with the demon, she turned on the balls of her feet to swing her staff out, like a batter at base. Satisfaction hit the moment the entity encountered her staff. San moved ready to battle but inwardly cursed realizing that she couldn't remember anything from her fighting classes or warrior memories of before. Dismayed, she screamed, backing away feeling dejected. *Get it together, Sanna, you can do this!*

In that moment, the female demon turned then rubbed her back, cracking her shoulders and laughing at Sanna's screams. The demon calmly flipped her long blond hair over her shoulder then spit her acid spittle on the ground before running back her way. Elevation of her heartbeat with that of the shift of her peripheral with that of Kyo's had her seeing through her god sister's eyes. Kyo watched from above, perched on a fire escape; she quickly jumped down and sent the Dark Gargoyle flying backward with a right-sided stiff kick to its side.

"San!" Kyo yelled.

Flustered, Sanna turned red in embarrassment. Pure fear and humiliation splashed across her soft features. She didn't want to be saved again. She wanted to prove herself and show that she could protect, too, but all she could do was stand there looking like a fool.

Kyo stood partially battle bulked. Her talons shone in the moonlight. Her usually mismatched hazel and jade almond-shaped eyes were now fully green. Her incisors dropped to attacking levels and her beautiful wings curved, ready to be used as a shield or blades. Sanna stood back. She watched Kyo offer a supporting and understanding glance then commence into trailing the female demon so that she could finish tearing into her prey. Both of them went flying in the air with sharp screeches.

The moon's light cast its pale shade on the women. Wings crushed into the sides of the building. The sound of honking cars filled the alleyway and more snarls took over the alley. After a tumble of slamming bodies that silhouetted the skies, brick from the side of a building rained around Sanna. Shielding her eyes, Sanna tried to see more but could only make out the demon running from Kyo who followed right behind her.

Silence drowned out the world then the idle strand of blond hair fluttering in the wind to fall by her feet brought back a clanking noise then shriek with Kyo's voice echoing around her, "Demon bitch!"

Sanna took that as her cue to move to safety, keeping her eyes on the second demon. She noticed Khamun's form move under his blankets to look her way and she felt ever more foolish. She should be able to handle this but no, here she stood standing like a fool, feeling defeated. She dug her nails in her staff. Anger made her unhook a clear diamond and silver dagger chained to her wrist. A slow thumping pressed into her temples and tears blurred her vision but her eyes stay locked on that Anarchy Demon before her.

She felt Khamun's eyes on her again. She sensed him. He was ready to step her way but a quiet energy that made the hairs on her body stand at attention had her excited. She studied his tumbling hair, noticing the swirling tattoo against the side of neck softly light up as he stopped in his tracks. A slow, cunning smile spread across Sanna's beautiful features and her eyes shifted into an illuminating silver. Instinct caused her to drop into a low stoop. Her fist nestled to rest against the pavement.

In the other hand, the dagger she held pressed comfortably against the small of her back. "Oh you asked who I am? I'm that foot in your behind. Let's do this."

Everything she learned from her trainings as well as her past memory teachings unlocked in her mind like a flood. She leisurely rose up as if in slow motion. All fear she carried melted away and she charged headlong forward toward the growling demon.

Massive claws swiped across her way making her spin on her heels to the right of the demon. Using momentum to help her slide flat against a wall, she lunged her dagger behind her into the demon's ribs. A satisfying metallic smell wafted in the air with a high-pitched scream. Black-red blood trailed to where the demon sat crouching. Sanna used the precious time she had to lock eyes on the scared child, and then scoop her up in her arms. They moved down the alley toward a hidden Khamun. The closer they got to him, the harder Sanna's heart beat until something within her told her to duck.

Cradling the child against her, she shifted on her feet to duck in a slide. The jarring slam against her spine brought tears to her eyes. Sanna thought she felt her own blood spill down her side only to feel the little girl slump against her instead. *Is she hit? Is the little girl hit!* ran in her mind.

"Please no!" ripped from her lips.

A quick glance had Sanna's pumping heart stop briefly. Blood was everywhere. Tears slid down her cheeks and Sanna stopped where she was to lay the child down. Instinct was her teacher, telling her to bow over the girl in prayer for her not to be wounded. While her hands slid over the girl, San was rewarded with the thorny feel of a talon in the spine of the little girl's back.

Her hands started to shake with anger. Her senses flashed red while she carefully pulled the talon out. She was so sorry for the child. *This should not have happened,* played around in her mind. Sadness engulfed her while she kneeled over the unconscious child.

Her mother used to hold her whenever she was hurting and for now, that was what she felt like doing. Sanna pressed her hands over the girl's wound rocking her back and forth in her arms. Her tears splayed across the little girl's face and her body quaked with her agony in not being able to save the girl.

Sanna could feel the demon watching in amusement. Through Kyo's eyes, she saw how he noticed the way her skin illuminated as if it were warm gold. His incessant laughter was full of satisfaction, and malice fell upon her ears before he casually walked forward then ran at her. His enormous form hunkered down then tackled Sanna, causing both her and the fallen little girl to tumble backward on the concrete.

Sanna found herself pinned by the Snatcher's large form. His sour breath and ironclad grip around her neck choked her while he forced his face into her own.

"So you are the bitch our King put a hit out for. You seem weak and worthless. I'll enjoy bringing you to my Sovereign," the demon roared low against her ear.

Sanna frantically screamed in disgust. Her skin felt as if a million beetles were crawling within and on her skin. She felt her body lock down from a multitude of seizures that pressed against her. A memory from her past let her know that this entity fed on its prey's mind, toying with their worst fears. Hands reached for her, pulling at her, touching at places that no one but her Khamun had ever touched and she cried at the pain being inflicted upon her.

Moist breathe bristled against her skin. "You're so weak, and so delicious in your fear and anger. I never thought you'd be so easy to have; others were weak fools! Now give me more, pretty Oracle." The demon continued his taunting, enjoying every minute of it. "You are so frail, so useless against us. Your true self lost to you, huh? My King will enjoy this information. Let me in deeper. I like that tightness you are giving me."

Sanna's eyes ripped open at the sensation of Khmaun's burning anger close by. She had begged him not to intervene when it got too hard for her and right now she wish she hadn't. The demon's mental invasion made the pit of her stomach bottom out. She jerked forward then slashed, before clawing at the demon. A force from within her made her punch forward to slash vertically again.

The sensation of uncomfortably hot, spongy tendons embraced her fist and arm. She knew she felt the heating dagger still in her hand. Both the dagger and she lit up in eternal light. The demon tried to pull away but she only pressed her body closer to wrap her legs around its waist. The tentacle he had implanted in her mind shriveling away, breaking off into a husk. Satisfaction strengthened her resolve to press on while her incisors ripped from her gums into its battle length with the sudden need to feed.

"I'm so hungry," fluttered from her mouth, in which Sanna complied giving into that burning deprivation. Hard bone inserted into tough, sinewy flesh. Her tongue flittered then pressed against the flush of hot, thick liquid. She tasted the salty, metallic rich essence of the demon and suddenly millions of screaming voices filled her mind. The airy evanescence impression of something she could only describe tasting like cotton candy hit her palate. She knew this had to be the sins of every human, Nephilim, and other demons this monster had ever met.

This bastard was good at the game of blending in and taking what he wanted. He and his "wife" were part of an international banking and financial conglomerate. They stole money from many unknowing customers by making them sign up for predatory loans, stale stocks, and failing bonds. They stole many poor's or working poor's homes by buying their land from under them.

They were also in the designer drug game and human trafficking market, of which this little girl was going to be the next victim. They intended to turn her into their human doll by shipping her off to a client in Paris with a load of designer drugs placed upon her. The little girl's parents had been college graduates deceived into believing that they were signing up for an international job program. This program was told to pay for overflowing college debts, but in reality, the foundation stalked and recruited only to traffic the people who became a part of their company. This was madness!

Ripping her hand out of the chest cavity of the demon, Sanna's eyes shifted into night vision. Behind her lay the body of the Anarchy demon's Dark Gargoyle lying in many pieces like confetti. She saw Kyo watching attentively, wiping her bloodied nails off then resting an arm on Khamun's shoulder. Khamun stood proud holding the sleeping little girl in his arms.

She saw the thin threads of souls the demon consumed and tainted throughout its body filtering into the air. That knowledge of that with the many voices and compounding emotions of the spirits in her body made her lunge her hands into the demon's convulsing form. Tacky fleshy goo covered her.

"Now who is lying in shaking fear for the first time of its existence?" Sanna cooed, anger causing her skin to shimmer with her divine power.

"Please, I'll give you intel, anything you want, just stop this," the demon pleaded.

Sanna heard Khamun behind her.

His silky, husky voice was icy and slightly seductive when he spoke. "You will lie there and let her finish her kill. Do not plead for shit. You don't have a right to, my man. You forfeited everything the moment you allowed yourself to be created. Then you forfeited that for the second time the moment you laid a hand on her holy form. So, kick back and enjoy it."

Sanna's eyes widened at the simplicity and coldness of how Khamun delivered that response. Her skin felt saturated in his love and desire. The way he supported her gave her power in and of itself, which had her briefly looking over her shoulder at him. He stood draped in darkness with the moonlight.

His elegant, crinkled locks fell down around his shoulders. His plush lips glistened from him licking them and his mahogany rich skin seemed to emit its own shine from his power. Her eyes wanted to drink his broad Egyptian Michelangelo-carved body. To strip him down and kiss every raised scar on his abdomen, his arm, and neck, but his nod and heated stare told her to return her attention to her prey. His slick fanged smile left her breasts feeling swollen with desire in that sweet moment.

A bashful smile played across her face while she glanced at her support. She wasn't the type to find humor in gore. However, in this moment, she found herself almost laughing when she saw the demon's eyes widen once they locked on Khamun's scowling face. It also caused her to smash the demon's windpipe with her hand.

"Hey, look at me. Today is your judgment day." Her honeyed gaze forced the demon's attention. Sanna felt the monster try to fight her hold again, but whatever she had done before when she forced him down had slowed his movements. Thankfully, this allowed her time to take her diamond *kila* dagger in her hand and flicked her wrist cutting at each thread in the air connecting to the Anarchy demon. As she cut and cut, the entity let out a scream that shook the dark alley. Puddles of blood rippled when the demon screamed and he went rigid. It made Sanna cut slowly to inflict more of her own torture on the demon for retribution from its victims. Prayers spilled from her lips adding to the demon's agony while she worked.

Feet pounding against a puddle of blood alerted her to Khamun suddenly by her side crouching low. His large hand pulled her close to him by the back of her neck. He held out his wrist in offering for her. The sensuality within the act had her heady in need. Her arousal blossomed with the need to feed. It slammed harder into her in that moment of the magnetic pull of his scent and she found her incisors sinking into his spicy, sweet wrist. His moan ripped through her, covering her pulsing mound while she slashed at the threads of the demon and fed.

Each voice that had ebbed from her went into him. Shock hit her when Khamun's eyes turned black. She noticed the way he dropped down like a rabid dog to rip the demon's throat apart. Black-red blood splashed everywhere and the monster caved in like a husk before imploding into a miasmic mist, which Khamun absorbed.

The hard momentum of that absorption connected to her and almost knocked her head back. Her lover took his wrist from her mouth to place his splayed hand over her heart. A pressure filled her body to slowly flux within her like a wave. Its gentle undulation caused her head to drop back then forward against his chest before the pulse transferred into Khamun. His roar made her heart palpitate a thousand times while he expelled the sins from the demon, sending the innocent souls to the Most High.

A sedative, warming peace flowed over her body, claiming her. Her skin felt ultra-sensitive and tender.

Her nipples pressed taut against her shirt and her swollen yoni throbbed in need. She needed her Khamun in the most biblical way. Moreover, as he dropped his head forward in a slump, his locks swung forward to curtain his ruggedly sexy face. Sweat covered his thick body. His wings stroked her wings, and she knew by his tight grip that he needed her too.

"Ah, so I'll leave you both to yourself and take the little girl to the safe house. You healed her somehow, sis, so, ah yeah, bye." Kyo's amused voice interrupted her hazy thoughts.

Sanna saw Kyo pop a lollipop in her mouth then tilt her head to the side still watching in protection while glancing around the alley and above their heads. Her god sister then turned on the soles of her feet, holding the sleeping girl in her arms. San noticed that Kyo's aura funneled around the girl as a shield before she lifted them both in the night air to fly off with her golden wings expanded casting a soft flicker of light.

Warmth encompassed her. A deep rumbling "Mine," from within Khamun's throat had Sanna finding herself on her back. Her curly hair spilled onto the wet pavement with her mate deep within her. She hadn't even realized she was naked in his embrace but the swift pulsing potency of his thickness hitting home pleasingly shocked her into awareness.

Her world and that alley melted away into the familiar softness of their bed while he locked on to every nerve in her suddenly cleansed body. As the silky suction of his heated mouth made her kitty constrict around his engorged shaft, his large, rough palms trailed the curving planes of her body. Sanna's lashes delightfully closed at the feel of his lips tracing down her body, while he introduced her lotus to the different ways he knew how to savor and kiss her.

A soft, guttural sigh melted from Sanna's mouth ending in a sweet whisper of love: "Yours."

Chapter 11

Nydia was locked in a dream. The acid taste of metal lined her throat as she flinched at the feeling of her hands being bound. The odor of an abundance of fish, mixed with urine, blood, and other putrid scents assaulted her system. It made her want to scream. Links of iron held her down. Cuts on her body and around her neck seared her in pain from the dried water from outside of her moving prison, which seeped into their openings.

She couldn't move. She couldn't breathe. That inkling of fear within her wanted to dance in the darkest corners of her mind, but instinct dictated that she was born not to fear those who captured her. She was born to kill them, to place that very fear they used to gain their prisoners against them by returning it threefold over within their dark husks. Her adored prince had taken down all in his path to get to her to no avail. She was forced to watch him fall, taken down in front of her. Her precious jaguars, each one she controlled on indivisible mental tethers, lay dead at her feet while she fought; but eventually she was violated by the dark bite.

She screamed for him at that moment at the feel of the taint in her system, "Kwame!"

She screamed for him as they sequestered her then submitted her to horrendous experiments before sealing her now-corrupted body into Purgatory. She never stopped screaming his name even when she felt her soul spread with evil. She screamed while the little bit of light within her was set free by a beautiful woman whose eyes shined with hope, but whose body smelled of the Cursed. She shrieked and fought for freedom, confused by the woman who appeared before her and led her to her salvation. She praised the Most High, crying for her lost love as she shed that tainted form and was reborn fresh but marked with a dark tracer unbeknownst to her.

Her dream shifted to a new scene where she screamed at a house that she felt was hers. Her pretty room with its many stuffed animals and toys was being set ablaze by a team who swore to protect her kind as was their duty within the light but lied. She felt as if she were a young child. Tears rimmed her eyes and her soul broke by the false Protectors. They were a group corrupted by the very dark she had run from. They made her lose everything.

She shrieked in horror and loss when her attackers killed her parents. Their bodies were taken, along with her, to be tortured in front of her. Played with like dolls by an evil, crazed King. She felt herself cower in fear when that false King laughed in finding her again before submitting her to ritual experiments that turned her into what she was now: a monster. Her once pure body and spirit were locked into a vessel transformed by a Cursed demon and she screamed and screamed and screamed. The words, "As it was before, so shall it be again," cried from her soul and covered her in flickering holy light before it snuffed out.

She thrashed out, waking in agony. "Calvinnnnnnnn-nnnnnnn!"

Jerking up with a start the Medusa haphazardly glanced around her private condominium, a place she always rested her head before tracking Nephilims. Her mind and body felt on fire. The right side of her ribcage seared. Her skin pulsed and ached at the touch. The illegible writing she was born with was red and swollen where she clutched at her right side. She pushed her sweat-drenched covers from her body then emptied her stomach on her bamboo wooden floor. She knew it was a smart thing not to stay back at the Cursed fortress or near Reina due to the Mad King and his daughter's animalistic temperament. That prickly feeling she was feeling lately within her hallowed heart, after being touched by the Reaper, alerted her that something was about to happen. So she made her plans then pushed up her orders of hunting more Nephilims, especially that Oracle, and she came to her downtown condo.

Her spine was killing her, which was not abnormal for her. The sensitive protrusions of exposed bone always bothered her due to how she was created. However, that wasn't the only issue. It felt as if her skin around it had been stretched then pushed back together, only to be ripped apart again as it once was. Had she wings, she would have thought that was the problem, but it wasn't the issue at hand.

She hated this body regardless of how voluptuous and curvy she was. Pinpricking pain ripped at her backbone causing every nerve in her back and spinal protrusions to throb with each inhale she took and her tail to relase and madly whipping against her. It often hurt for her to release her spial razor tail, which is why she didn't release it often. The pain was too much, like it was now. She refused to let any tears fall. She hadn't cried ever and she was not about to start now. That was not who she was.

Pushing from her bed, Nydia stood in her naked glory, forcing her tail away. Silky mahogany syrup was what she had heard her skin called. Parts of her were flawless while other areas of her skin were covered in raised scales like that of a reptile. Nydia let the flat of her hands trace over her body, cupping her bare mound, then upward to cradle her breasts. Each breast was plump like that of a melon.

Her nipples were peaked thanks to the cool air. Down her back, the protrusions of her spinal cord curved in spikes of various sizes, stopping at the curve of her ass. It was nice being a demon.

She was a beauty, but she was also a beast. Speaking of, an Initiate lay in her bed just as naked as she was and dead. His blood covered her as she painfully walked from the bed and let her eyes adjust to the dark. Something was happening to her and it was pissing her off. Ever since the fight on that roof, when the Oracle ripped her arm from her and when that man, the one she couldn't believe she had just called out to, touched her to hit her with his Mystic magic, her nightmares had not been the same.

"I shouldn't be having these fucking dreams!" she roared to herself then pulled out a mop to clean the mess on her floor. She couldn't believe herself. She was a Cursed minion, having nightmares!

Coffee pupils glanced toward the form of the dead male in a sigh. She had hoped that his thick shaft and expert mouth would put that prickly feeling at ease. But as she rode his handsome face, her mind twisted and she saw that man from her dreams, her enemy bringing her pleasure that connected to that prickly feeling within her chest. Fury had fueled her, which resulted in her swiftly killing the Initiate at the same moment of cumming over his face. She should have let his body cook in the sun, but then, that would have put her at risk from burning as well and she had enough to deal with as it was.

"I'm going mad. That is what this is. This is insanity and the Dark Lady should end me now. I am not good for her," she hissed aloud to herself.

Annoyance caused her to fall with a plop on the bed shaking the mattress. Her broom clanked as it fell at her feet to the floor. The Initiate's body was finally evaporating into a miasmic mist, leaving her bed empty and covered in black-red blood.

Fresh turns always take long to die, she inwardly contemplated, running her hands over her semi-scaled thighs. Nydia fell backward on her bed while her mind churned. She couldn't understand that dream. She didn't remember any of those things ever happening to her, but it felt as if it was her. It had to be some taint from the Light. Otherwise, she didn't know what was going on.

Shaking her head, she pressed the heels of her palms against her eyes then mumbled to herself, "Maybe it's a Nephilim. Another thorn in my back to track, it has to be."

Propelling herself from the bed with an annoyed growl, Nydia pulled at the sheets of the bed in an angry tantrum then threw them to the floor. She had other things to worry about. Some silly dream was not one of them. While she cleaned, the sound of her cell phone drew her attention.

"What!" she snarled.

A familiar masculine voice chimed on the other side, causing her to narrow her eyes. "You know what. Meet me near West Chicago Avenue."

With that, the line went dead. This was her life. Orders and demands. Tossing her cell on her bed, she headed to her walk-in closet. Slamming her hand against a hidden panel against the frame of the closet door, her row of clothes parted, as if one was watching a curtain reveal. The many items slid to the side revealing various weapons and poisons. This was her world, her place of domain. Nydia reached to the right over her, snatching a revealing pair of black skinny jeans that were cut on the sides and fastened with various barbs of wire. Pulling out a drawer, she found an equally revealing black top that highlighted her ample bosoms. Before her, a row of glass

bottles and bowls filled with fluid had her reaching for a
flask of venom.

She calmly twisted the cap open, and then dipped
her fingers into the contents. The pleasurable feel of
her venom stacks underneath her nails plumping with
the new poisonous mix made her smile. Sealing the
deliciously rancid mixture, she turned to grab her black
Timbs then slide on her poison-tipped dagger boots.
No, heels needed later. Before her call, she was on her
way out of the house. She had picked up the faint thread
of a human with the Nephilim gene whose blood scent
matched what she needed for a fresh new Initiate for
Valac.

He needed a nanny so his bastard of a father had
explained and since she already was looking for a new
Initiate for Reina, the Medusa figured why not this human. The Medusa enjoyed chasing humans then turning
them. The ability to possess and corrupt them was so
easy and the fact that this one was human with a distant
Nephilim link made it all more fun for her. She enjoyed
the frozen looks on their faces while they looked upon
their death. Something about it all made it so sensational
for her and her lips itched to bite into the tender flesh of
this new target.

With a slap against her closet doorframe, she listened
to the doors shut and return to normal. With a serpentine
saunter toward her counter, she grabbed the keys to her
ride and assortment of personal identification cards.
Throwing her bag of weapons and clothes over her shoulder, Nydia moved to stand inside of her private elevator.
She pulled the gate down, locking it and headed out.

"Time to go." She gleefully smirked as the name *Calvin*
and the words *as it was before, so shall it be again* echoed
in her mind, causing her to scream. The bottom of her
boots slammed into the sides of her elevator as she lashed
out at the air in fury.

***

Smoke accosted her nostrils. Cackles with drunken drawls surrounded her, plucking at her annoyance. She was in a cesspool. The scent of various human dejection and depravities made her hungry to taste their blood and to add to the infection of their sins. The Medusa's nails lightly tapped the glass of spumante she cradled in her hands. Time was wasting away. She had a gig to make in time.

"Which is why I called you for this meeting, my dear Harpy," a voice crooned near her. Casually walking through the smoke fog that was the tavern, Nydia noticed the one person on this earth she hated, but admired at the same time, Fallen Elder Jacques Fur'i. If she were in the Cursed kingdom she would have stood, but since they were on human ground, she could give two shits. At his side, an attractive brunette took his cane then stepped back to speak to a gruff older man near the bar. The woman's ruddy lips parted in a fanged smile with a subtle shift under her cinnamon skin. *Succubus, more so a Dark Witch; interesting companion,* ran through the Medusa's mind.

Sipping her drink, Nydia gave a nod. "My Lord Fur'i, what is your request?"

Sitting across from her, she studied the Elder's alluring features. As was his style, Elder Jacques's bald head was baby bottom soft. The light scent of cologne meant to make ordinary female's havens wet did nothing for her, but she could appreciate the various spices within it. Cloaked around him was a long dark brown tailored trench coat, which was adorned with a fur collar. She bet it was bear. His pretentious demeanor dictated that he would kill some wild bear then sport it around his neck. The thought made her laugh while his dark brown eyes studied her, causing her to cloak her thoughts from him.

"Ah, Medusa, how I always look forward to our meetings. My son sends you his dark thoughts of course. He enjoyed the Dragon you left for him to play with; unfortunately, another will have to take her place, since she died instantly. What can you say? Children, right?" he lightheartedly addressed her. Reaching for her glass, he downed it with ease with an amused smirk.

Lord jackhole, aka Jacques Fur'I, sat before her in all his arrogance toying with her nerves. Actually, he was loving making her squirm because he knew she could not do anything about it. Thoughts of slashing his throat and dealing with it after kept her focused. "It pleases me that the young Lord enjoyed his toy. It was the same way you introduced my mistress with her first toy from you was it not?"

Nydia inwardly flinched. Why in all that was dark would she say that? She was Reina's first toy and she did not recall him introducing her to Reina at all. Silence took over. Creaking of the table before them had Nydia noticing places upon it that were rotting under the Elder's elbows. She sat, promptly put in her place while he had her feeling as if she were a lowly insect, one that needed to be stepped upon. Luckily, for her, his dark demeanor disappeared quickly before he addressed her.

"Interesting memory, one I'll think on later. Dear Nydia, as you do your bidding, do make sure to kill the woman you've chosen as my son's nanny. We will not need her services after all. She is a loose thread that should have been snipped awhile ago. Also, these are the codes to deactivate their pesky barriers." Sliding a palm-sized black book across the table, Jacques casually smiled her way.

"Once that is out of the way, have your fun," he replied, motioning with his hands. The sound of a man's gruff scream drew Nydia's attention away while she took the book. A sweet hit of the smell of blood hit her sense instantly.

"I always manage to do so, as you should recall," she heatedly replied, her body reacting to the craving of feeding.

Jacques steepled his hands together, assessing the way she sat. She knew to keep a thin line of boundaries with him because he could kill her in a blink. It was also the fact that he sat emotionless, watching her in a cool demeanor that made her skin crawl with his magnetic aura. She had to get her control back. He wasn't worth the dirt that rested under the cheap table they both sat at and she felt like telling him just that.

As she began to formulate her mind to say something to the Elder, she was stopped mid-thought. She sharply gasped the moment he phased through the table then slammed her on her back. Two fingers found their way into her pants, slipping into her moistness. Fangs scraped against the side of her neck and she glanced into the eyes of evil. To the human eye, it just appeared as if he had quickly stood up and moved to confront her, but his grip grounded her in the truth as his minions caused calamity around them.

"Give this gift to my Dark princess next time you see her. I'll be busy with my games as you are familiar with so I do not have the time. If you disappoint me, Harpy . . ." His tsk against her earlobe caused her to reflect on their rough games in bed with Reina. Laughter bubbled within at the tight grip of his painful hold and the desire to gut him burned her mind.

"Don't disrespect how I hunt. I am the Medusa. People die just by my presence, so don't confuse me with your other . . . weak minions." She said with an irritated, yet annoyed flip of her hand in the air and a roll of her reptilian eyes.

"What you need will be done. If it is not in the manner you want, you know it will be in the manner I need or want! Which is why her mark is still on my list. Okay, my Lord?" Nydia calmly drawled back.

Screams sounded around them and the Elder gave a curt nod while standing. Sometimes, being in a drunk stupor can reveal the demons that surround a person, and the longer she and the other demons stayed in the bar, the illusion that was thrown up by Jacques's Witch was quickly fading away. Especially with the spill of human blood.

"Then we are done here. You might want to go now, doll." He evaporated into air in front of her, and Nydia slowly sat up. Around her, everyone was either dead, trying to run away, or given the dark bite. The sound of thumping boots echoed outside with the loud clamor of a door falling to the ground.

"Police!"

The Medusa inwardly cursed then locked eyes on several cops who pointed guns her way. Sharply hissing, baring her fangs, the two cop's eyes briefly shifted to red, signaling her of her kind. A satisfying smile flickered across her face. One of the cops headed back to the door, letting off rounds of bullets into humans who were used as food, but who were still alive.

Nydia quickly slipped from the table, picked up a burly biker who had several fang marks in his neck and pressed an unmarked gun in his hand. Shooting around the room again, she shouted, cloaking her voice with a Cursed spell which made her sound like the man she held. Dropping him against a wall, two more bullets bore into his skull, this time from an unmarked gun Nydia had on her from a human goon she had tainted earlier in the night.

Motioning for her to exit, the second cop muffled the screams of a woman who ran from the bathroom. His bite was swiftly lethal as he snatched her. It also infected the young prostitute, which amused Nydia. Watching her fall to her side in a daze, Nydia quickly headed to the back of the club. Exiting with a kick to the steel door, she ran into the side alley. The voices of various cops alerted her that she would not be able to get to her car right away. Therefore, opting for another means of exit, she dug her nails into the brick siding of the tavern and briskly scaled it until she reached the roof.

Panting, the Medusa watched the tavern become over-run in blue, red, and white light. Annoyance caused her to shake her bladed inlaid braids before walking away to leap to a nearby building where her ride waited. "St. Louis, here I come."

Chapter 12

The name *"Kwame"* plummeted against his mind as a throbbing hit his right shoulder blade while he drove his black SUV up into his old complex in St. Louis, Missouri. The Angelic Ghanaian script that ran down his shoulder and bicep was yet again ripping him a new one, causing him pain. He had to grip the steering wheel attempting to ignore it. This was not the first time that he had heard his true name, or his soul name as they called it in Society, within his mind. Lately, he was hearing and feeling it often. Each scream giving him flashes of his old life and causing the words on his shoulder to blaze with life. But, as usual, he had to deal with the pain and ignore it as he had to do now.

It was another new day and he was back at his old digs with Marco. It seemed like only yesterday that they were all living it up and protecting STL from lower-level Cursed. Now that all changed and now he was no longer in the comfort of this city but back at the headquarters, Chicago. Thinking back, sitting and listening to Sanna comb through the book was the most awesome experience in his life these past months.

The Oracle blazed in front from him as he anchored her and Khamun fed her his strength. Calvin knew that Sanna had pulled as much of her energy as she could to help lead them correctly, due to her stunted gifts. He could see the disappointment in her because Oracle only could stay around for thirty minutes, but within those minutes, massive information was shared and they had learned a lot.

They had learned that this book was a history of the Founders, the first fallen and it blew his mind. He learned the first Sin Eater was born to protect the Lady Magdalene as she carried the child of the Messiah. That alone almost made his heart stop and had him sitting slack jawed. Shit was boss.

This unknown angel removed the One Son from his cross and in doing so, the Messiah whispered within his ear a Spirit Song, triggering their DNA, that changed him and his chosen warriors into what the enemy had become. Vampires. But unlike their evil brothers and sisters who killed and drank the souls of humans from their bodies and polluted their bodies with dark sins in order to create demons for the Dark One, they would feed from the Cursed and balance the unnatural law created by the Dark Fallen. This angel—whose name was blurred because they needed the other books to reveal it—was given a vision.

The vision showed that a second war would take place where they would need to bind the Cursed and make them impotent. Part one to the punishment for their Fall, for lying with humans to create evil Nephilim, for the conception of demons and for the implementing of pain to the Most High's children. He was told that those Chosen warriors who survived would be asked to willingly Fall and stay behind yet keep their anointed gifts, as a means to watch the Most High's children and fight the remaining evil Nephilim. As they eagerly leaned in to absorb more, the rest of the scrolling ink script disappeared and broke off as the book automatically sealed shut on its own.

As everyone sat in shock, he watched his cousin's aura dwindle, her speech wavering. San explained to Marco and him that they had to intervene with a human with a dormant Nephilim gene. She explained that the young woman had to leave STL then return to her home. In addition, that the woman would lead them to "the missing" and a clue in finding the true Key. Both men nodded their heads in understanding and acceptance of their mission. Which had them now back in St. Louis.

Marco and Calvin had been in STL raising the body count, saving innocent humans, and slamming heads together all through the week. If felt like home again while they stomped through their familiar haunts and made the enemy run for cover. Now they were back in the streets ready to do it all over again as they searched for the one Sanna demanded they find. Stepping out of their ride, both men were greeted by a text. It was around eight at night in STL and they knew demon activity was heating up.

It automatically made sense why the new team was scattered throughout the city and county of St. Louis, hunting now. Checking the cords, Calvin shook his head with a chuckle. "Hey, bro, drop this shit off and let's head across the river. Looks like some demon heads are about to roll at Pink's according to the intel I got from Dolla and Zion."

Marco slapped a hand against the hood of the SUV with a lopsided smile. "Perfect. *Exactamente* where Sanna told us we needed to be, Cal."

Whipping the ride down Natural Bridge and Kingshighway, they passed several Nephilim safe houses and churches then headed to the "Ill side." Pink's flashing sign appeared fifteen minutes later, letting them know the place was still bumping. The building appeared nonthreatening, as was the custom for places like this. Pink's was known under the circuit as a neutral zone for humans, demons, Nephilims, and other supernatural entities to visit. Rules of places like this were that no one fed, no one killed, and no one hunted. Penalty of breaking the rules was being banned via a gridline that would kill the person on the spot if they stayed on the land.

Both fellas loved how Mystic magic ran the place and how interesting it was that a non-house affiliate sect of Nephilim ran the spot. It was rumored that they could not be touched due to old laws handed down from the start of the war. That there would always be neutrals and these neutrals happened to be the only surviving Death Wraths, or Phantoms as they were called, with the infinity mark. Only the Most High or his appointed overseer could control infinity-marked Phantoms; unfortunately, no one could recall what or who the overseer was to the Phantoms and only the oldest surviving Pure Wrath could and he had disappeared eons ago.

An inside liaison-based old team member and friend of theirs was the main bartender. He was a drifter and former truck driver whom they called Dolla. Dolla had come through for them a long time ago when they first were assigned to Sanna. Scanning the place, Calvin inwardly chuckled in thought. If an establishment had the infinity mark in the land, then anyone who could read it knew the rules. In order to keep some balance, the rules had to happen as means to keep an eye on the humans in the world and the things that hunted them or their kind. That didn't mean shit didn't go down that wasn't supposed to.

Music spilled into the parking lot. Thumping bass vibrated through Calvin's blood, pumping him up. The thing about the music here was, though one might hear a song that makes them drop into a split and shake every orifice on their body, somehow the dirty, sinfulness of it was scrubbed out and left with a neutral feeling. The Prince of the Airways might have inspired much of the provocative music, but his influence was not allowed on neutral land; it was all about free will here and keeping peace.

Flashing their cards, both men walked in with smooth style. Glances from many women and even men honed in on them, during which the sensuality of poetry fused with current music blared around them. Poets spoke on the mic and dancing strippers put Olympic gymnasts to shame as they worked poles like superb artists, enticing the patrons. Tonight was "Seduc-try" night and the house was full of women, men, truck drivers, and more. Poets from around the nation flooded Pink's as they combined forces with dancers and mashed up a seductive night of poetry and enticing.

"Calvin, dog, what's real, man?" From his position behind the bar, Dolla gave a quick nod from behind his dark shades. His crossed bourbon tatted arms bulged with lean muscles, while his flashed a smile, signaling where the STL team were sitting.

Calvin reached over to give his old friend dap then glanced around. He saw their standard VIP table was ready for them where some members of the new STL team sat. Strolling their way, both he and Marco breathed in the atmosphere. This was their old stomping grounds and regulars knew exactly who they were.

Taking a seat, he leaned back listening to the music while Marco stood taking off his long black double-breasted coat. A waitress appeared at his side. Her voluptuous creamy chest lightly brushed him while she handed Marco his standard drink: Bacardi Gold in a chilled glass. His boy's gaze ran over the club at the same time as his was. This was his element, music and a crowd. He thanked the same brunette who had served Marco while she handed him a Heineken and fresh mound of caramel-coated pralines. Dolla had their back.

Music breathed life into the club, two poets on the stage forced his attention, and he easily read their auras. Slayers and Mystics.

"That's my homies from Cali. The Bad Boys. Reggie and Demetrius Darby. Guess they are doing a layover in the STL," Calvin pointed out.

"*Sí?*" Marco asked.

"Yeah, brah. They are sick with it. I learned some of my flow from them. Watch how they control the room with the lyrics, homie. They are working an old spell I taught them. Aesthetic hymns wrapped in sensual poetry."

"*Ay! Carajo wey!* You mean the Song of Solomon, Cal?" Marco mused.

Calvin's eyes softly pulsed, his dimples deepened, and he flashed a lopsided smile before answering, "Fa'sho, punk. Classic Mystic move if you have a gift to manipulate words, like they do, nah what I mean? They can hit all theses with just a few power words. Each word, vowel, syllable they manipulate act as grenades that will implode a tainted or Cursed bastard. No demon or possessed human leaves the joint, ya heard me?"

Marco chuckled lowly. He crossed his thick, muscled arms with a pleased look on his face over the slick method of attack utilized to work in their advantage. "And you developed it?"

Tossing back a couple of pralines, Calvin chewed before replying, "Yeah, your homie right here set that shit up. Was schooled by some old school records I found and shamans tapes Kali introduced me to on YouTube."

Marco gave an amused laugh. Calvin knew his boy was hitting him with jokes. Playing as if he were a newcomer and didn't know that info already. Marco respected his power. That Calvin was a master Mystic able to develop healing meds and battle psalms that could take down a tank of demons.

While the Darby Twins also known as the Bad Boys finished their set, the music changed tempo. The brother's words blended then fused, becoming heated as if they were ready to flip from seducing to hardcore screwing. Lights dimmed; Calvin's eyes adjusted with the change of the climate in the building. The intensity of the seduction in the club had him being hit with the scent of blooming lotus flowers from the women in the establishment. Steel was between his muscled legs as the music and lyrics flowed on.

The Darby Twins licked their lips with mirror grins before dropping a one-liner that had the crowd erupting in cheers. A wisp between the satin red curtains on the stage revealed a brown sugar, bourbon-hued thick-thigh female with ample, full breasts and an ass that wouldn't quit. She smoothly moved to slip down the pole from an opening in the ceiling and froze in the middle of it as the music pumped.

"Bourbon Apple Bomb/syrupy sweetness flows/from between the mental crevices associated with your Queenly gates," blended with the rhythm of the song while the woman worked her magic.

Her skin was silky and shiny from oils begging to be touched. She commanded the attention of the crowd with her gliding hands. She elegantly dropped on her back. Her graceful legs parted in allure and both of her hands caressed her body trailing downward to cup her covered yoni. Her arms constricted to press her spilling breasts while she licked her lips and flicked her tongue out over her hard cinnamon nipples. Money went flying and Calvin saw Marco's eyes flash in the darkness. Something about her had both Calvin and Marco noticing the marker in her aura. It shone bright the moment she flipped to her stomach, tossing her long jet-black hair to seemingly lock eyes on Marco.

"Maldita Sea! That shit wasn't there before; are you checking this out, Cal?" Marco muttered.

Calvin leaned forward. He took a deep swig from his bottle while intensely staring.

"You know I did, homie." Recognition had him quickly swallowing his laughter. He could tell already that Marco's world was about to be disrupted. "Whoa'na, isn't that, the waitress, ah, ah . . . Yaya? Yeah! That's her. Shit, Butter looks to be her stage name, when it should be Mrs. Butterworth's," Calvin said aloud with a huge grin. His shoulders shook up and down in laughter and he ducked from Marco's swing.

"Git'er done! That broad is smooth like butta!" a drunken trucker roared walking by with a beer in his hand. He staggered forward to step to the stage and made it rain on Yaya.

"Watch yourself, homie, don't fuck around and get popped by the bouncer, feel me?" Calvin warned. He had noticed Marco's change in his posture the moment Yaya stepped on the stage. His boy had been helping her out for over a couple of years, when she was just a clever electric cigarette–smoking waitress with a confusing but interesting laugh. Time definitely had changed.

Calvin couldn't lie to himself though. Yaya was that butta. She had a body worth slicing a punk over and a gaze that made any man's member jump for her attention. His homie had learned from her that she had just moved to STL from Cali and that she was only working here to put herself through law school. She had been working at different strip joints over the course of her life just to pay for undergrad and now law school.

Marco had told him that the idea of her doing that always ticked him off but he couldn't figure out why. It wasn't some new phenomenon, but the idea that this was how she had to survive never felt right to Marco. Calvin could already tell that now with watching her work the stage, popping her kitty in the face of a hungry demon was finally making Marco realize why. Everything in baby girl's aura stated that she was Marco's guide and that this was not where she was meant to be.

Calmly chewing his pralines, Calvin punched Marco's shoulder to distract him from his anger, and then pointed to their right. Wandering in the new leader of the STL crew came to the table and held out his hand in a warrior's clasp. Dressed in dark denim jeans with casual black boots, a black and gray button-down shirt that was rolled up to show his muscular arms, the six foot five inch brother chucked two fingers in the air in a greeting.

"Shit if it ain't this Lance Gross–looking mother trucker. Zion, sup, fam." Calvin stood laughing and pulled him into a quick shoulder hug and sat down as Zion followed suit.

"I'm taller, Calvin dude," Zion jeered, chuckled right along. Zion gave a handshake that he and Calvin had made up in Chicago as he turned to give Marco dap and the same greeting.

"Sup, my family. Good to see you two old heads finally make it back here. We've been excited about the visit for some time now. How's Sa . . . I mean, the Vessel? I spoke with my pops, but he was vague, with good reason." Zion quickly changed his language, remembering to keep all intel on lock down. "But before we get into that, I wanted you two to know that we got a lead on some rogue Houses that have gone dark. Remember that crew that killed that Nephilim family and took their daughter years ago?"

Both Calvin and Marco quickly nodded knowing all info was limited in public. "We have one of the team members who had reported them on the squad. She has some new intel to share. Intel she has been effortlessly investigating for a while now, bros. We'll talk about that some more later but let's get into this, so what up?"

Calvin gave a curt nod before relaying in code what took place and why they were there. Each word was carefully constructed to sound like they were speaking about sports, missing STL, and the drive down. Zion processed everything with a flash of a frown, his head turned slightly over Calvin's shoulder, which caused him to give a sidelong glance. A dull pain in his side began to come to life, causing him to lick his lips in the process. A shadowed dancing figure drew his attention; more like demanded his full-blown awareness.

The beat to J. Cole's "Can't Get Enough" switched on and the Bad Boys spit out another poem. This time it was performed with a third crew member from the new STL crew and Butta worked it on the stage. Several flourishing tattoos on Calvin's forearms began to flicker then sparked in Mystic currents while the hairs on his body stood at attention.

There was no ignoring what his senses were telling him: something was about to pop off. "Yo, excuse a brotha for a moment, something don't feel right. You know what that means."

Calvin calmly stood then moved through the club toward the bar. Beams pulsed to the music. The Bad Boys finished their set. More poets with dancers grew the crowd's attention and that shadow made Calvin's eye twitch. Grabbing a drink, Calvin kept his jade eyes on the individual. He instantly knew who it was, at the sound of clicking and the sight of succinct deep-set swaying curves. Pain shot over his side where his Ghanaian markings lay and a sudden throbbing at his temples marked his annoyance. That broad was doing this to fuck with him and, tonight, he planned to take both arms this time.

Chapter 13

Calvin blended into the darkness of the club. He saw his brother-in-arms Marco snuff out his Trinity then mentally check in with him: *"Time to strap up, acere. I'm securing my Guide, Cal. I know you're handling your shit. See you on the other side."*

"A'ight, homie, hit ya dome later. Don't get lost in that pretty pretty. Remember that's your Guide," Calvin joked, cutting his link before Marco could curse at him.

He took another swig of his drink then headed toward his beckoning target. She stood swaying to the music, lethal dark eyes locked on him. Her hips swayed in a slow siren's wind. Her thick thighs brushed each other, her braids flipped over her russet shoulder while Kendrick Lamar spit to some chicks about "Poetic Justice."

Cranial pain had Calvin gritting his teeth inwardly cursing. *Is this chick stalking me now? Fuck is she doing here?* Anger kept him on his pace. Sigils in the floor, walls, and structure of the land tugged at his Mystic surges reminding him to follow the law of the club. He didn't give a shit. The rules stated to never feed, never hunt, and never kill, but the rules said nothing about fucking people up with your fist.

Zion interjected his mental, cutting his inner emo party. *"Hey yo, I needed to tell you and Marco that I just found out that the girl's cousin Tweet isn't working the bar. She's back in Cali for some family emergency, so we're clear on that front."*

Marco studied the stage, his gray eyes melting into amber the longer he watched. *"Good, it's always a plan and that just worked in our favor,* familia. Sí, *Zion, keep everything low-key and ready your team,* acere. *A'ight,* retire a la persona rapido. *Move out fast. You good, Cal?"*

"Yeah, I got you locked on my right. I see you speaking to your Guide. I have something I'm working on as we speak, keep alert ya heard me?" Calvin didn't wait to get a reply.

He saw Zion rubbing his hands together, his teeth flashing with a smile that made every woman in the room cross her legs with need. Little homie slid a hand over his low wavy fade giving a signal to his other team member muttering a, "Oh yeah, here we go."

He calmly walked past the stage and clapped a hand to his heart, coughing. Another signal for the Bad Boys to kick their poetry into overdrive. Calvin had to inwardly laugh. The kid may have been a human Nephilim, a simple Slayer, but he knew that in the kid's blood flowed a power that made the baddest of demon's piss and run scared from what he had in store for them. Taking down demons was Zion's birthright. Like every Nephilim born in Society, either angel, or immortal humans like he and Zion were, they innately claimed it with the utmost respect to the Most High.

Calvin kept his pace nonthreatening while he watched his target; then Zion thumbed his nose and wiped a hand over his mouth. A battle was coming, so everything needed to be in its place. Calvin noted that Zion reinforced the platinum-steel door. He leaned against it with his arms behind him, watching the stage as a pure silver barbed bat slid down Zion's forearm to rest in his massive hand. At the bar, Dolla shifted to the side to lock down the cash register. Calvin could read the determination in his old teammate's face. Something had changed in the atmosphere. The fact that Dolla had a sword in his hand, clocking it behind his broad back, had Calvin assessing their surroundings.

With each casual long stride Calvin took, he gave an alluring smile toward gawking women whose physical forms briefly contorted revealing Cursed demons within them. Lights flickered. He glanced around the club to make sure everyone was still lost in the Bad Boys' performance, putting in a little insurance that he wouldn't be noticed once he handled his business.

His target still stood holding out both hands swaying to the music. She made note to run her stiletto nails over each arm to show him that she was back at 100 percent while she danced in front of a trucker. The guy could be Hugh Jackman's twin, except for the gray skin, twin siphon holes at his neck, and now pitch-black soulless eyes. *Stupid cunt,* Calvin thought. That guy was a goner, was stone cold dead, and there was nothing to do about it. His emissary drew first blood on neutral territory when she wasn't supposed to. Something was off.

Sweat beading around his brow, Calvin shaped a Mystic blade in his hand then reached out to snatch at his target. "You drew blood on neutral territory. You're really fucking crazy aren't you, shawty?"

Irritating clicking ebbed against his ear while his hand twisted the Medusa's arm. "I think that is the other way around, big daddy. You're fucking crazy for putting your hands on me, yet again."

The sharp jab of her elbow hitting his ribs caused Calvin to hiss sharply. He knew she hit nothing but his solid muscle but the pain was still there. "What are you doing here? We put a beating on that ass already and here you are wanting more."

Music continued to thump in beat. The loud crash, and then thud of a body behind them caused Calvin to whip the Medusa around to get a better view. Unfortunately, as he turned, the Medusa gave a soft chortle then her lips touched his own with the light brush of her tongue. Thrown off by the act, Calvin tried to grip her hard but she used the pad of her fingers to brush his jaw line. She pushed him hard at that moment, using her elbow to send a blow against his head while she hissed out, "This."

The instant impact caused him to hunker down then reach forward to pull her braids back. However, all he received was air and a couple of cuts from the blades in each strand of her hair. Glancing in front of him, he watched the Medusa jet forward in a brisk run. Ahead of them was Marco with his Guide. Marco's hand rested on the back of a woman they knew as Yaya while they spoke to one another. Yaya was blessed with having metaphoric rose-colored glasses on because she was clueless to everything going on.

The Medusa's purposeful glare of malice with the sudden scent of poison in the air had Calvin rushing forward in a tackling position. Every prayer in his mind connected with his power to propel outward and cover Marco's Guide in invisible armor. Anger had him pissed off to the highest level, which allowed him to reach out and snap the Medusa to him. His jade eyes locked on Marco and his Guide.

They quickly disappeared from the hallways. Calvin used that moment to hoist the Medusa up before him. She floated due to his Mystic gifts and he bound her hand in several bands of green Mystic power. With a sharp tug, he settled her on her feet, and then moved her into a dancing crowd. Menacing darkness ebbed through the club, and slightly darkened their surroundings.

Black currents suddenly radiated off the Medusa's skin, which connected to every demon in the room. Music that was once pure became tainted and everyone or thing associated with the Cursed came alive. *Son of a . . .* ran through his mind. Calvin held on as long as he could, as the Medusa appeared to become stronger.

"Someone changed the rules to this joint. The neutral lines are down. Time to shake 'em up and take names later," Calvin heard in his mind. It was one of the Darby twins: Reggie to be exact.

Glass flew in the air shattering. Calvin saw two twin fists smashed into a bulking demon in front of him. The shorter of the duo, Demetrius, ducked then lifted a foot in the air, slamming it right into the face of the furious, dirty, blood-covered trucker. The elder twin Reggie snatched the collar of the trucker, whose once-human hands were now sporting two twisted nailed appendages. Throwing the demon onto the floor, serrated blades appeared from his sleeves and rammed into the skull of the entity and his heart.

Calvin pivoted out the way. The Medusa let out a sharp vibrating pitch that called more demons to mist from the darkness. Lights flickered and music still thrummed. To his left a tall, thick and curvy Nutella woman with a wild mane of natural curly shoulder-length hair used mixed martial arts methods to send a stripper with brunette extensions and Kim Kardashian proportions sliding across the floor gripping her midsection. Calvin had to nod in approval as the luscious beauty dropped to one knee then sent an arsenal of ninja stars, which connected to the face of the woman who had contorted into a demon.

The Medusa screamed in his arms the moment the demon exploded into millions of pieces of miasma. They both watched the woman high-five another decadent chocolate woman with matching curves, but with a low curly natural fade, a scorpion tattoo over her right breast, and a tongue ring. That woman with cutout black gloves laughed. Her deep brown eyes glowed, and then she lifted in the air to send a sonic wave ripping from her shapely body toward a running Cursed minion. Calvin's mouth dropped open. Her long nails glittered like stone, along with her ankh tattoo on her bare waist and he smiled in knowledge; baby girl was a Gargoyle. He wondered what breed.

"Samurai and Poet. Samurai is the surviving member from the Houston crew, but she's from Georgia. She was able to escape and blend into the human population because she's a Disciple, although I'm starting to think that maybe she's of the Slayer class. Her team was seriously messed up," Zion relayed on a mind link while Calvin stepped over fallen chairs and pushed tables out of the way.

"What she saw messed with her mental so much so that she hasn't spoken in a long time until recently man and only a little. Poet, she is from Alton, a bad-ass Gargoyle that's also able to use her words as weapons against the Cursed. She found us by tracking our energy to a poetry event. She killed it that night and has been riding hard with us since her arrival. She and Samurai have become like sisters," Zion continued.

Calvin could understand. He had seen a lot in his past and present, so much so that he himself was amazed at not having gone crazy. Calvin heard Marco connect back but was instantly distracted by being rushed by a demon.

The feel of a heel pressing into his throat let Calvin know that the Medusa had gotten free. The scream that came from her alerted him that she now lay on her back courtesy of his Mystic blast. Wood crushed under his weight and the stench of demon flesh had him staring into the eyes of a human cross between a zombie and a rabid troll. Clenching his teeth, he sent his fist flying to its jaw, sending the demon backward.

His boy Dolla stepped up to the plate while Calvin stood up. Twin jagged blades were in his hands. He stooped down, reached for the end of the table, lifted it, and sent it flying with his blades toward the demon. With a simple clap of his hands, the blades and the table joined together to make a bladed wheel that sliced the burly demon in two. Dolla turned in that same moment to land a *Street Fighter*-worthy uppercut into another demon that wished to rush him at that same time.

Calvin let out an amused roar. "Damn, homie!"

Impressed, Calvin turned on his feet and moved toward the Medusa. With one look his way, she gave him a grin that stated she was ready to play and she motioned to head back toward Marco's Guide. Luckily, the Guide was gone but Marco was back in the club bringing hell into Pink's with an icy trail of dead demon corpses behind him. Calvin was proud of his brother-in-arms and he had no intention to let his own target get out of his hands. With a hard-hitting shoulder slam, Calvin pushed her off course causing her to turn in fury. Gleaming nails slashed out toward his face. Instant reaction caused him to bend his knees then lean backward to avoid the connection with her poisonous talons.

Green Mystic sparks trailed over his arms to form his blade again. With a sharp grunt, Calvin leaned forward to return the favor with his own slash toward her sinewy body. Chaos kept him close to the Medusa. He watched her spin on her heel causing her knee to connect to his face, which whipped him into action. Each spin from her had him stepping backward, blocking the hits. Oftentimes, her long, thick legs would extend with her hits causing him to duck and dive under each one, to propel a couple of punches to her ribs.

Sharp grunts from his target made him smile. Her auburn eyes appeared to darken in constrained anger.

"Agh! Why can't you stay in your place? I have work to do. Don't you realize that you're nothing to me, cockroach!" the Medusa spat.

Bladed braids whipped his way. Poison puddles lay at his feet burning a hole into the floor of the club.

Annoyed, Calvin scrunched his face up then stepped over it. "No, shawty, not really. Looks like I'm something to you, momma."

His blade changed within his large hands into his scythe swords. With the back of it, he swung out to slam the blunt of it against the Medusa's neck. Her loud curses pierced the music, giving him satisfaction.

Glass crunched under his feet. The Medusa took every hit he gave, but countered returning with her own blows. They were well matched which messed with his mental, triggering a faint mental recall in the back of his mind. It was the cartwheel side jump, which had the Medusa dropping to one knee with her poison nails clutched ready to strike, that had his attention. His emerald gaze intently remained locked on her.

"Impressed that my arm is back? I'm not about to allow your weak, imbecilic hands on them, understood?" she sneered.

"Do you ever shut the hell up, ma!" Calvin roared. He charged forward, his swords flipping before him. Her eyes widened with the insult as she tried to block his hits. Tables flung at him. Demons reached out to hold him back, but a low growl from the Medusa had them letting him go, but not before he swung his arm behind him to lop their heads off.

Pink's was a warzone. Humans who were future fodder for the Cursed ran and watched from hidden spots around the club. Bodies from demons, humans, and Nephilim alike lay in disarray over the floor, the stage, speakers, and even on ceiling beams. However, Calvin went flying backward into a wall by a Dark Witch charge that caused more damage.

The Medusa's laughter trailed over him in the process. Dust with crumbled bricks covered Calvin. Each inhale he took had him coughing while he wiped at the sweat dripping into his eyes. He was getting tired. Conserving his power was necessary since he knew this chick was going to keep going until she could fight no more.

"Some crap from Winter?" Calvin grunted in question. Shards of rock attempted to cut into the palms of his hands while he pushed himself up. Debris fell from his broad shoulder. His power shunted itself with his will while he assessed the Medusa. Currents of fading Witch magic highlighted her fingertips while she tapped her nails against her ample hip.

"Yes. A nice spell she whipped up for me. I'll have to thank her later." The Medusa's lush lips parted in a sneer. Her cocoa eyes locked on a screaming Pink's stripper; then she tilted her head to the side. Twin Cursed demons snatched at the woman who had come from behind the stage. Calvin moved to reach her, but the Medusa stepped in his way.

"No, see, if I can't get my main prize I'll definitely take a nice side piece. Although, I still intend to get my main piece," she simple stated.

"Yeah, causality of war, right? Naw, shawty, not about to let that be the case," Calvin retorted. But, it was too late. The woman was gone and the Medusa had disappeared to the back of the club. Sniffing her out was becoming easy for him strangely. She sat at the top of a stripper pole looking down at him. Her long braids fell like waves as she hoisted her body into a split then used her thighs to hold tight while she sent poison-tipped needles toward whatever object she wanted.

Electric currents flickered outward. Calvin's hand became the battery charge that lit the pole up. Screams from the Medusa made him grin as she disappeared. However, that was short-lived by the tap on his shoulder, which pissed him completely off. Today was not going to be a good day for him, he thought.

"You seriously think I didn't see that coming? So foolish," the Medusa hissed against his ear. Her silky tongue traced its surface while a sultry moan escaped her lips. "By darkness, I enjoy playing with you."

The slender throat of the Medusa filled his hands. He pulled then flipped her in front of him to hold her close. Eyes scanning the club, Calvin noticed the back of a well-dressed brother in black slacks, a pinstriped white and pink dress shirt, with black suspenders, disappearing behind the bar. The sleeves of his shirt were rolled up and the light from the club glinted off his bald head. It had felt as if he was watching the whole time in amusement, but Calvin couldn't remember ever seeing him in the locked-down club at all. It was some crazy crap going on right now.

"You move quickly. I'm not impressed, shawty, but my thing is this: why?"

Her movements made him try to keep her restrained. But it was the heel of her shoe slamming into his foot then his shin then upward against his groin that had him almost snap her in half. Her body went stiff at the pressure on her throat. Her breathing stopped and as he looked down at her, her body compressed then constricted to allow her to slide from his embrace into a tuck, and roll away from him.

Calvin was straight-up shocked by that move.

Her wink then smile reflected the satisfaction of having gotten out of his hold before she spoke. "I do as I am commanded. But you, you I hunt because something about you makes me not gut you where you stay. I intend to make you my pet so come get me, big daddy."

Jutting up, the Medusa moved to head to the back of the club, which he followed by snatching her by the nape of her neck. He lifted her and pushed her through the steel door. He was not about to make this easy for her at all. *So much for a decent night,* simmered in Calvin's mind. They had some business to get back to.

Chapter 14

Calvin was hunting. Chasing after the broad that had come after his family and who was now trying to take down another innocent Nephilim. After he body snatched her out of the club, he stopped her before she could pump poison into Marco's Guide. He made sure to carry her across the parking lot to slam her to the ground.

Cursing as she somehow contorted her body to land a foot against his face, the taste of salty blood hit his palate. His head tilted to the side. He angrily narrowed his eyes at her and spit to the ground.

Her laughter sounded around him while she slid from his touch against the asphalt. Beckoning him to follow her. Anger had him punching his fist into the pavement. He lifted up then sprinted after her. Shawty played too many games. She had almost taken everything from him. He vowed that he would end his own life in order to take hers in the name of his family.

He ran head-on, jumping fences, blending into the streets of East St. Louis while he locked in on her form in the night skyline. He held two blades in his hands and they shone bright with Mystic magic. Her laughter clouded his mind making him curse aloud.

"Oooo, did you know that I almost came at the view of you? My foot against your face felt so damn good, bastard," the Medusa crooned.

Ignoring her taunts, Calvin regarded the area to see how he could angle himself to cut her off from her chase.

He jumped over train tracks. The Mississippi River was a marker of where he was during his sprint. Honing into the grid line of the city, Calvin deciphered faint spiritual shapes in the dirt, cement, and even the murky river water, which led him to an old, ruined church.

"Bitch, come play with this dick over here since ya so enthusiastic about it, ya heard?" Calvin mocked, leading her to chase him now.

He landed with a thud over the church wall, crouching low. His fingers splayed in front of him touching the floor of the ruins. Illuminated spiritual lines flowed under each digit of his fingertips. He almost innately connected to its source, something he needed to wait on to time it just right.

With a meticulous glance, he was blown away at what he saw. The church was spectacular. He never knew a structure such as this was even built on the east side of the Mississippi and still partially intact. Ivy curled around Masonic white-gray stone brick.

Scattered pieces of trash and broken glass lay among idle bricks nestled in overgrown grass. An inlaid work of Tiffany stained glass that appeared to possibly date back to the 1920s still adorned a central atrium archway perfectly. In its beauty, he understood why. Old world Angelic script glowed against the surface of the panels, hidden under ages of dirt, moss, and debris.

Calvin quickly scaled a fallen pillar to cross a ledge that housed the glass framing. Beams of light cascaded then kissed his face while he reached a hand out then felt the spiritual lines emit from the atrium's glass panel. The closer he got, the stronger his spirit sang causing him to lean forward to gain a better view. His pressed fingertips seemed to warm the moment they caressed the slick panel's surface.

Sparks of neglected power suddenly embraced him, but the insidious clicking sound of the Medusa snatched his attention away, reminding him of his objective. She was fast but he wasn't going to trip off of that. It just meant this fight was going to be a good one.

Observing from his perched view, he watched the Medusa drop in with a laugh.

"Oh, I hate to sound cliché but, come out come out wherever you are! Did you think hiding in an old church would stop me from snatching you from limb to limb?" She sauntered.

Stomping her heeled boots, she ran her talon nail over the sides of her thighs and her tail slowly snaked out. Each sharp tip raked over the barbwire that held the minuscule fabric of her pants together.

"This is dead land." She looked around then spit on the Romanesque tiled floor. "Many innocents have died here and their blood has soaked through to the foundation. Mmm. I love the work we did and continue to do here in East St. Louis. Really, this should be murder capital of the nation." The Medusa cackled.

In Calvin's mind, the light decibel of a familiar giggle seemed to be laced within in that evil laugh and it hit his mind hard. Flashes of his dream projected across his mind causing him to pound his fist against his temple to stop it.

"Calvinnnnnnnnnnnnnnnnn!" She sucked her teeth then gave off an annoying laugh, drawing his name out to tick him off. "Really. I enjoy how you are playing with me, but I don't have time for your asinine game of hide and seek. Let's get this over and let me kill you; then we can be done so that I can slice that bitch the Dark Prince was protecting. Oh, then later I can dismember him and eat him for my Dark Queen. Yes?"

The corners of Calvin's eyes twitched in constrained anger. He watched his prey circle the middle of the church, finally standing where he wanted her.

"Oh, and I do intend to heart snatch that little whore who tore my arm off. What was her name? Oh yes, Sanna. I do intend to return that sweet favor. Then you know, let you watch me fuck her because I believe she would taste so sweet as I give her the Dark Bite and turn her into a new toy, yes? Calvinnnnnnnn! Come out and play!" the Medusa screamed making the church rattle.

Fury lit Calvin up like a beacon. He slammed his hands together and channeled all of himself into restoring the barrier of the land. Pressing his hands flat against the glass, his head dropped back then his Mystic power fluxed backward. It pumped through him with an intense force before it expelled from him to light up the church.

He watched while his power restored the line into its old self. White and blue light washed over the church. A satisfactory smile fleetingly spread across his handsome face at the sound of the Medusa screaming. Sadly, it was short-lived. The sound of a slow clap then her jaded laughter of delight sharply drew his attention.

"Pretty," she gleefully cajoled.

I can't believe this shit. That should have worked and usually would have. The hell is this? ran through his mind. He stormed forward from his hiding place. Dropping his hands, Calvin landed against the Medusa. He propelled her to the ground with his gun cocked to the right side of her head, his knee resting on her throat. Sweat glistened on her body as he realized she was still alive but lethargic. A change in her eyes made Calvin pause, perplexed by what he saw in her aura.

"What the fuck are you? Huh, shawty? What exactly are you? You are supposed to be cinder and ash right now. This is ancient land, a church built to protect the humans on this side of the river as well as act as a safe house. These are old world lines more powerful than anything I've ever encountered and you are supposed to be dead! Bitch, who or what the fuck are you and why do you know my name?"

The Medusa looked around wide-eyed as fear ground into her stomach, something she hadn't felt in a long time. The need to stay in control made her laugh but everything about this made her want to scream in terror. He was right. She should have been dead. She shouldn't be lying here. Her mind ripped open with images from her dreams settling into her dark heart and peeling at her like an onion and an orange.

Tears fell for the first time in her long-lived life and did what only she knew how to do. She swung out and attempted to slice open her attacker with her claws and tail, but fell short due to her body feeling like a ton of weights. She felt him cause her tail to descend back into her body and shift his weight on her neck, knowing that if she moved again he would snap it with ease. In that same moment, she felt that horrid liquid spill from the corner of her eyes while the gun her attacker held tapped at her temple.

"Skip me with that extra drama, momma. Get to flapping ya gums and explain this shit because right now, you are at my mercy and I very much am enjoying fucking with you as you love to do me," Calvin muttered while slowly standing. He moved away from her to circle his foe.

Pulses of power projected from his aura and he stared down in constrained anger. "Talk."

The Medusa grimaced in anger. She stared him in his emerald irises, eyes she knew better then she knew herself suddenly. Eyes she remembered fighting for her life to keep her from becoming what she was, and hatred filled her heart again as she screamed in a blocked choke.

"Where were you!" she screamed.

Calvin frowned. *The hell is she talking about?* He glared down at the woman he knew as the Medusa. The way she pushed at him in anger then dropped her hands. The retraction of her nails had his eyes narrow.

However, it was how the light in the church casted her in a silhouette under him that had clarity sucker-punching him in the gut, causing his hands to suddenly shake. He eased back giving her the space to speak her mind but he kept the rest of his weight on her to keep her in place. Her features seemed to soften before him.

Eyes that typically burned a reptilian dark brown, almost black as soot, now began to glow with light, an ethereal radiance he was all too familiar with, since he also held a bit of that power whereas his cousin held the intensity of it, as did Eldress Neffer. However, crazy as it was for him right now, before him, the bitch he knew as the Medusa also carried that torch in her eyes and he almost fell backward.

La baise est-ce! *The fuck is this?* his mind shouted.

This chick could not be an oracle and still carry the power in her. *No fucking way.* But here she lay as she pushed up and lurched toward him. Her question blazed in his mind while he blocked hit after hit. Swing after swing. Abashment kept him from blowing her brains out while her body appeared to transform before him. The molasses-toned scales along her body seemed to slosh away. More human features stood out at him with each twist of her sensual body.

The Medusa popped up in front of him.

She projected her nails forward to stab him in his heart and stomach as she ducked from his swings. Her nails slashed at his shirt while he dogged her. He could suddenly hear her mind in his own screaming out. Where was he, when they found her again and killed her papa and momma? Where was he when the very people who were supposed to protect her from the enemy plucked her and handed her right to the Mad King? Where was he!

"Where were you, Kwame!" the Medusa screeched in anger.

Calvin was mind blown. Distracted by her questions he was rewarded by being slammed into a pillar. Reflex made him reach out to snatch the Medusa, flipping her over his shoulder to throw her through a wall. Crumbling mortar lay all around them in a cloud. The bright lights of the spiritual lines pulsated with its power around them.

He couldn't see through the fog, but ticked off that he was, he found himself yelling, "Hey! What did you call me, gal?"

Nydia held a hand to her heart. She pushed forward to empty her stomach on the patch of grass around her. Flowers seemed to suddenly bloom as if awakening from a long sleep while that wretched light her attacker had washed them with saturated the land. She was going crazy. She knew she had to be.

She had just called this man Kwame, the man from her dreams. His face, once clouded, now presented itself before her in blazing clarity and her mind ripped apart with unblocked knowledge. The tracking mechanism within her surged on. It caused her to gasp with the sensation of every single Nephilim within close proximity. Horror had her screaming while crawling to her knees then cradling her head. Her ability to track never worked like this.

Her gift to find Nephilim she understood came from her light past. She knew some of it stayed intact when she was given the Bite but in order for her to use it, she always had to rely on the touch of Reina or a hit of her blood. When her mind or senses opened, it gave her the knowledge of where to find her prey. Even though it only resulted in a hazy vision of where the Nephilim lived or the area they lived with their scent. Then from there she was able to locate them anywhere. Now, it was different, now she could feel the life force of them all. She knew innately if she wanted to pinpoint just one, all she had to do was hone in on the heartbeat of one, and she would see them clearly as day. This was pure insanity.

"No! No, no, no. What did you do to me? Huh? What in all that is hell did you do to me, son of a bitch!" Nydia shrieked. Her anger had her pushing up to propel poison blades at Calvin. She observed him evading each blade as his jade eyes wavered in plain perplexity. This was a torture worse than anything she had ever experienced at the hands of her kind. A supreme cruelty only her kind were known for and she couldn't help but be impressed.

"I hit you with Mystic power, shawty, you know that. You were supposed to be dead and . . . and now you sit here in front of me a different person, calling me a name no one knew except one person." Calvin paced before her, seemingly just as affected as she was. "And you are asking me what the fuck I did? You must think I'm crazy, wodie."

Something in the tone of his voice pissed her off to no end. It made her lunge at him again just because fighting him seemed to make her aware that her body was no longer in pain. Each punch she threw did not reverberate back in blinding, yet pleasurable, pain. No, this time, she fought in harmony and bliss. Pain free, tears fell again; this time they were of relief.

Which caused her to lash out: "You violated me! Y . . . you did! You used your repulsive white light and . . . and you tainted me! Bastard!"

Calvin stepped to the side and hooked his arm around the Medusa's waist. Her spinal protrusions, sharply pressed to his body, made him quickly flip her to pin her against a pillar. Water from the nearby fountain glowed with renewed life. She struggled the moment she saw him lean to the side, cupping his hands to gather some. Water sharply splashed over her. He callously poured the contents over her face then wiped her face clean with his large palm.

All the while, the Medusa hissed and fixed her mouth to spit on him.

"Whoa'na, chill all the way out. I'm doing what I'm trained to do, shawty, and you keep igging me. Clearly, some other spell has been linked into your DNA, it has been triggered, so tell me why, and how you know that name. A'ight? Then we figure this shit out because, one, you stand on holy ground. Two, I just washed you with holy water and nothing has happened. And three, I'm feeling really generous tonight so I will not haul off and blow your brains out as we stand." With a flash of his dimpled smile, Calvin yet again tapped her temple with his gun.

Nydia hissed at the bastard who held her pinned down. Her eyes darkened and she twisted her body against him. He was Kwame. The man from Africa, from Ghana, her warrior prince who battled until he was taken down in front of her and she was snatched away in front him. He was Calvin, the Mystic Slayer who kept her intrigued and made her body heady for his closeness and, now, made her once-dead heart beat and pump with life. *Oh, God, he smells good,* flickered in her mind. Once again trying to formulate the words to tell him what he asked, the hardness from his body made her kitty yearn. Made her own body feel foreign as if she now was one of the many flowers awakening in bloom and she felt sickened then elated.

"I know your name from your team's loud, filthy mouths. They are so very chatty," she spat out, trying to remain in control.

Calvin's hand quickly gripped her throat. He growled dangerously low while leaning in close against her ear. "Thought I wasn't crazy. You are fucking playing games with me, time for you to die."

Fear jettisoned within her causing her to croak out, "Wait! Please, you are Kwame and in your first life, you were born in Ghana. You were fighting to protect me and we both were taken down from the Cursed! That's all I know, my mind confuses me right now."

Calvin's mouth dropped open in blatant confusion. She saw him step back. He let her go, but his warrior instinct blazed in the massive build of his body, which resulted in her staring down the barrel of his gun again.

"Say the Lord's Prayer, then the Arch's code," he commanded.

This bastard, almost slipped from her lips. She glanced at the man she wanted to taste more than fight until he fell at her feet, in disbelief. She couldn't believe him. How would she even be able to go there? Was he insane? Damn two screws short of a basket case? As her mind ticked off like a checklist full of rants and insults, Nydia suddenly pulsed with knowledge. Her heart blazed, causing fear to burn in her throat while she spoke out what he asked.

She shouldn't know these things. Her kind was not able to quote those verses and here she was on holy land with the words pouring from her lips as her soul blazed. Her soul. She felt that metaphysical piece of her that she had believed was gone slap her with understanding and peace. Her cinnamon eyes glowed golden then she stepped forward.

This man was hers. She knew she had to make him understand that. Therefore, she repeated what he asked and she spoke in the words of the Firsts. Then to prove herself again, she stripped off her top and weapons. Each item fell while she walked forward, standing before him in need. She watched his hand quiver in disorientation, and then she saw her opportunity.

Jetting forward, she pushed into his blind spot to disarm him. Swiftly, she forced him backward making him fall onto the ground to straddle him. Her lips pressed to his angry ones. She melded her body against his. Then she whispered into his aura as he grunted trying to fight her off. His body bucked under her as if she were riding a bull. The feel of his slamming and sudden need gave her exactly what she wanted at the moment, especially the moment he gripped her ass, easily ripping off the barbwire that held her pants together in the process.

Pleasure sparked between the pair as their auras collided and blazed like an atomic bomb. Anger, fury, and confusion seemed to fuel them both.

Calvin palmed her plush rear, separating, kneading her until her wetness drenched his shirt. Her unique sweet scent knocked his head back. The pinching protrusions of her back melted into her skin. The flickers of his Mystic currents coating her slick skin to leave her with a smooth curve of her non-scaled back. He needed to be inside her now. All instinct whispered, *mine,* though it sickened him to the core. Her scent, her taste, the feel of her soft mouth made his soul say in authority, *wife.*

The audacity of it all had him flipping her on her back while he felt her push at his jeans. His mind barked out, *get away,* but his body and soul moaned, *mate.* Soon all he could do was comply while her hand circled his hardening shaft pulling him out. He watched in conflicted disgust mixed with lust the moment his manhood sprung out then thickened in length and width in her hold. The way she touched him to stroke him had his eyes wanting to close in bliss as he felt his tip weep in need.

Craving had him sliding down her body. Her skin became soft like silk. He encircled his tongue around her sweet cocoa nipples. Each bud saluted him in their taut erection and he pushed her leather bra to the side in greed. His soul name spilled from her lips. It hit him in his gut when that spark from her caused him to slip between her tender thighs and lap at a nectar so sweet, so sublime, so familiar to his dreams that he knew there was no return.

Eden was between her thighs. He found himself lacing the tip of his tongue around her swelling bud. Damn, he was humbled at the way she moved her hips against him. Enthralled at the way she pleaded for his seduction. Calvin couldn't help but comply with the use of his thickened his tongue, slipping between her silky petals. She tasted of caramel and sweet cream. Hits of his dreams played across his mind, slapping him and cracking open his third eye. He worked his mouth, pressed his glowing fingers against her at the feeling of her arching against him.

Each long digit opened her wider while he played with the ribbons of her delicious yoni. Mystic currents spread into her, using his gift to hit her many erogenous zones. The loving feel of her hands ran over the waves of his scalp trigged his groan. Sensation of his side burning with each mental resonance had him savor her on his taste buds. Calvin could feel the rhythmic beating of drums playing around them, which made them both reach and grip for the other intently. Its drumming gave him the craving to go deeper in which he obliged. Sliding against her slick skin to lean up, glossy-eyed, Calvin pulled the Medusa unto his alter, filling her with his widening scepter. Woman had become his first hit of crack.

His soul name filled the area around him and he heard the Medusa rapturously cry out. Her thick thighs sharply wrapped around his waist and her name ripped from his lips at the ecstasy, "Fatima!"

He rode her hard, as unknown tears spilled down his face. His body radiated with his power and his nails scored down her back. More spinal protrusions sunk back within her flesh, along with her scales. This left her body smooth and left him looking down at a woman, who was an oracle and no longer his primary enemy.

He watched her arch against the ground, her braids splayed out in a blanket under them. His hips sharply pumped upward, circling within her allowing her to slide up to his tip then slam back down to the hilt. The sensual sounds of their bodies mating played in sync with the song of the drums of Africa. As their sensual dance began, Calvin took a handful of her pooling breast to suckle then lapped around its smooth surface. Notes of their past unraveled as if in Braille.

He had fought for her. Fought to save her when he was chained and shackled. Taken to a foreign land where he continued to look for her, constantly escaping his masters until he found a safe place to call his own. Even then, she haunted his dreams with her sweet melodic laughter and the many games they used to play.

He remembered she loved to weave baskets and whenever she would visit, she had a new gift to present to his mother. He loved this woman. This woman was his soul and though he did take a wife eventually later in life this woman always stayed a part of him. After his second wife was murdered by the Cursed, he knew that he would never again take a woman. It wasn't possible regardless of how many women had tried to get him to marry them. Not until he found his true wife, Fatima, and made her his again.

Her incessant heady cries of pleasure brought Calvin back to reality at the feel of him emptying himself hard within her. He filled her with Mystic power and decades of locked away pain and desire within her womb. The abrupt release caused her body to lift in the air and glow with a power he was familiar seeing, the power of a gifted oracle. He was transfixed and didn't know where to go from here.

Nydia held the man from her dreams to her body as if he was the most precious thing in the world to her. A part of her screamed in anger at it all, but enjoyed the sex between them. Even as the awakened side to her gave praise to the lovemaking that just occurred, she found herself opening up for the first time ever and accepting a man's seed within her body. This male was not just any man but a man who strangely whispered into her hallowed chest and made it call him her husband.

The heated burn in her side distracted her for a second. It ached badly and it got worse as he lifted her with an erotic grunt then a hard thrust that made her smile and cum again. This man had filled her up in a way she never had before. She felt no empty dull inclination after sleeping with this man. No, this time she felt a pleasure that embedded itself within every molecule, fiber, vestibule of her body and baptized her in bliss. She felt full and she never wanted it . . . no, she never wanted him to stop.

Calvin sat on his knees gripping the woman he had just been ready to kill. Their heated kiss turned into a sensual tango while she rested on his lap, her hands cupping his face. He wanted to say he loved this woman aloud, but reality hit him hard, causing him to push her off his lap in scrambled revulsion. His face contorted in fury, bewilderment, love, lust, and need.

"Naw. Yo, we didn't just smash. We did not just bump and grind!" he found himself saying astonished.

Searching for his weapons, Calvin pulled up his pants trying to keep his distance. He watched the woman he knew as the Medusa sluggishly push up on her arms to glare at him over her delicate shoulder. Her mini-twisted micro braids spilled down her face, curtaining half of her features while tears shone in her eyes.

"No, we didn't just smash as you say! We just . . . damn it. I think we just made love. Something I never in my existence knew I was capable of doing, boy!" she brokenly stated.

Resting her hands over her face, Calvin watched the change in her eyes the moment he stumbled backward. Sweat coated his deep mocha skin, trailing down the flat yet thick plains of his abs before disbelief had him falling to his knees in a groan. He didn't feel good. His breathing was slowly becoming harder and everything was becoming dizzy. His massive hand, a hand that just only prior too had touched and stroked the Medusa's body until she felt alive in a heat she could not explain, he heard her mind whisper, quickly found his gun in his and cocked it.

"Don't fucking ever call me boy, a'ight!" Calvin bellowed; his speech sputtered, wavering in and out as if in a daze.

He felt the shock of his actions hit her in her gut inflicting pain before she quickly shifted to stand in front of him, gradually drop to his side in a low crouch. The familiar ticking sound within her throat despondently returned and she glared at him in hurt. The glint of hatred shifted and widened with sudden awareness. *Shit, her poisoned nails, and razor adornments in her hair!* he heard her shout in his mind.

"Knew you were playing me, shawty." Calvin gritted his teeth.

He pushed his gun toward her. He knew this was too good to be true. He knew this had to be some elaborate test and he failed horribly. She had pumped him with venom while they screwed. He just knew she had. He had let her get into his mind and successfully take him down with her body. He was convinced she had planned this out. He still wasn't sure how she was able to stand on holy land, but he for fucking sure knew something here wasn't right and he wasn't about to play this twisted game anymore.

"I forgot. I forgot about the poison. I wasn't thinking. Calvin, damn it. I didn't do this on purpose," she pressed. She seemed to plead as if she was truly concerned. He could see paranoia race through her while he pushed her away from him in a feeble attempt to keep her at a distance.

Mystic rule 101: when captured, use all your gifts to your advantage, rung in his mind. A weak chant spilled from his lips, which caused him to double over emptying his stomach.

The rancid stench of poison hit her nostrils as it exited his body. Nydia viewed him pull out a vial then spit a yellow substance into it, which she knew was the rest of the poison. She felt dumbstruck and in awe at the power in him. But, she knew she had to go. There was no way that she would stick around to meet a bullet from him.

Darting around the church garden yard, she threw on her clothes. Something within her tickled the back of her mind making her notice his cell phone lying haphazardly in a pile of garden grass. Swiftly, she grabbed it. She searched for what she needed, and then threw it back where she had found it.

She then took that time to jet to the mason brick wall of the church. She quickly climbed its exterior. Then she glanced back over her shoulder at the man who had cracked open her mind and produced a living heat within her empty chest in confusion. She had to figure this out. She knew if she stayed around any longer, that that man's own confusion would be the death of her.

As if on cue she ducked from his bullets while he cursed, "Shit was nothing but an elaborate mind fuck, nah what I mean? Right? Guess what, there won't be another time."

Cruel laughter bubbled out from the darkest corner of her being. She knew there were no gentle words that she could give him. She was just as furiously disturbed at it all as he was. So she let her hurt and the hate he spewed at her fuel her. The Medusa she was slowly bloomed into life and she hissed in spite of falling into playing the game.

"Oh, there will be another time, Calvinnnn, believe me there will. I'll be stalking you later, sweetie. Your dick was oh so sweet. Muah."

With that, she turned to run faster than she ever had in her life. She had to get away now before she compromised herself more in this madness. As she ran the reverberating booming of his voice trailed behind her. "This ain't even what ya want, shawty. Show me love; show me evil but stay in your lane. I'm from an era and time where sometimes we move too fast for you to understand what I'm saying. Ya heard me?"

Her mind blazed with knowledge as hurt, fury, and burning desire sent her over the edge. *No, this bastard did not!* She wanted to turn around and make his whole existence turn into chaos but she did not have the time. She needed to feed. Needed to hide until his taint washed off and she needed to kill. She had lost her Nephilim target. The Medusa knew that she would hear about her weakness later, but as she ran, she was suddenly blindsided hard.

Darkness slowly swallowed her and the memories of what had just happened in the ruins in East St. Louis continued to play within her unconscious mind.

Chapter 15

"*C'est si bon,* my man. It wasn't hard to get her here. After picking up Amara and Miya, gaining that intel then taking Amara to Uncle Bishop's grave everything else was straight, man." Nydia held her breath listening to the world drum back to life around her. Cottonmouth made it severely difficult for her to swallow and the bastard who knocked her out but who also filled her body in affection drew her attention while his molasses deep voice ebbed on, "San is looking over what we found. Yo, look who's awake."

An incessant piercing snap of fingers sounded near her ear causing her stomach to tighten in nauseating cramps while her ears rang in agony. "Sleep is for the wicked and you slept enough. Wake your ass up."

Watery gloss covered her vision. Her head lolled around seeking out the jagged, deep voice that stirred something in her chest akin to fear. The shape of a dark masculine figure slowly came into the view of her sluggishly opening eyes. Shock caused her to jump backward from her space being threatened by the man she once called the Attacker but who she now knew as the Reaper. Awareness had her struggling to glance around to find out where she was at before realizing that she was tied down to a chair.

"Where am I?" she angrily screamed at the man who stood wide-legged, arms crossed over his broad chest with black locks that spilled over each shoulder. The bastard studied her in amusement and she wanted to spit on him. Past him, she noticed she was in a massive holding area. One that held several chairs, a table, and a large, flat TV monitor. Disbelief mixed with fury caused her nails to lengthen and she struggled to cut at the binds around her wrists but that only resulted in each nail breaking.

"The more you struggle, the tighter your binds become. We figured you'd like that shit so, yeah, welcome back to Chicago, Medusa. Been a long time coming." The Reaper dispassionately clapped his hands together then moved around the room. From the far back of the room, he disappeared in a wall of darkness, only to come back with a thick manila folder. Never in a day of her life had she ever thought she'd be the one snared in the trap of the Light but here she was. The more she thought about it, the faster her chest thumped in rage.

"I know you are wondering how you got here. I'm sure you'll remember your meeting with my Mystic, Calvin, right? You really messed my brother up with your . . . confrontation."

Recollection caused Nydia to spit out in anger at the memory of what had happened between her and Calvin. "Oh yes, I remember my meeting with Callllvinnnn. Did he tell you how we both fucked on holy land and I made his seed gush with just a touch?"

Malicious laughter fused with panic flowed from within while she tried to struggle. An invisible force caused a tightness at her throat bringing about a terror within to break her resolve. Memories from her past accosted her senses and she felt sick all over again.

The Reaper strolled to stop then crouch in front of her. His amber eyes appeared to glow like that of embers. His head tilted to the side while she noticed that a note of pity then edged anger glimmered then disappeared. She watched him tap the side of his solid jaw before speaking again. "Holy land . . . turn on the barrier."

White light washed over everything in the room. Concrete walls and floors became radiant in pale energy. The smell of holy water, something humans are not able to detect but the Cursed could, choked her throat causing her to bow forward to empty her stomach. Water fell down the corner of her eyes. Only then did the Reaper nod his head. It shocked her when he reached up to wipe at her face as he stood. Everything around her went back to normal while the Reaper turned his back to her.

"Calvin was right," he said.

Nydia watched the Reaper turn around, holding that thick folder again before addressing her. "Medusa. Let's get to the point of the matter. You are here on charges of the atrocities you have committed to my people and the human population. Unfortunately, death is too good of a sentence for you, so truth will be your punishment."

Pushing in her chair, Nydia gritted her teeth pulling again. Flashes from being chained then taken by the Cursed on a massive wooden boat jabbed at her dome causing her to scream out, "You think I could care what you do to me! Torture is my ecstasy! Death means nothing!"

The low rumble of the Reaper's laughter sent chills down her sensitive spine. Chills she had only experienced in the face of the Dark Lord and Prince of Darkness.

"No, death by my hands always means something, which in fact you fear!" Jet-black wings erupted from the Reaper's broad back.

The air around her became thick and a trickle of piss would have run down her thighs in embarrassment, but she was better than that.

His voice drowned out even her own angry hissing as he continued, "Medusa, Protector to the Dark Lady. It's time you woke up. The bindings were supposed to do that, which I see they are, so let's get into the rest of this. Something your Cursed King hasn't told you or your Mis-

tress is this: your name is Nydia Randal. You were one of
the many first daughters of the Nephilim who were taken
by the Cursed and created to be weapons of madness. You
became a success for their side."

Nydia had to laugh. How they got her name was something but the rest was comical to her. "Yeah, right. Let's
keep this going; how did you get me knocked out anyway?
Poison runs in my blood."

Her captor shook his head. His thick lips formed a
lopsided smile then he nodded his head again. Heavyset
thumping of boots sounded in the chamber. Calvin
stepped out of the wall of darkness before her, holding
a neon yellow syringe. She studied the way his muscled
body tensed in her presence. The way his eyes glanced
briefly at her before looking away. He was still living in
what they had shared and she intended to use that to her
advantage.

"Poison runs in your blood, shawty. But each time we
ran into your work, I've taken some of you and created
my own venom that I knew would disrupt your chemistry. Mystic power combined with what you create gave
me this. Fucked, ain't it, wodie?" Calvin chuckled holding
up a murky, glowing vial.

If she could flick him off or flick her hair at him, she
would have, so she resorted to using her words as weapons. "Actually it's not. What is fucked is how you had me
on my back, legs over your shoulders as you drove your
manhood in and out of me. Now that was fucked. Do you
intend to do it again? Come, my pussy is open and ready,
come show them what you really are about, Callllvinnnn."

Nydia attempted to open her bound legs in a taunt.
She watched, then cringed, the moment Calvin's irises
darkened then sparked emerald green. His fists tightened
at his sides. The jean hoodie jacket he wore, with the
black crew shirt, stretched as his muscles doubled in size.

Laughter made her smile in glee. The hard slap of a pair of women's hands around her skull caused her to scream.

"What was past will become present. What was lost will be found again," was sung in Sanskrit to her. Static sparked from red-tipped fingers that dug into her temple. The beautiful brown sugar-toned face of a young woman came into her vision. Her kohl-lined deep oak eyes lit up with her power. Her black, brown highlighted hair spilled in waves over her as Nydia's third eye ripped open.

"Big bro, now," the woman said. Nydia tried to look away from her, but the woman's pooling dark eyes held her in a trance, along with her glowing henna-lined hands.

Soft, spicy musk filled her nose, and then the familiar touch of the man she had recently shared her body with threw her over the edge of an abyss. His emotions, his thoughts, taste, sight, and sound became hers in his vision. She watched a Nephilim woman share her story with Calvin and the Gray Prince back in STL in perplexity.

Calvin watched the one he was told was a partial mute from a traumatizing event that went down with her old house shift on her feet before him. Her pain was palpable and he felt for her deeply. The scars with that one were deep, so much so that it read through her aura as she locked eyes with him then licked her lips attempting to work her never-used throat muscles.

Silence took over the STL crew while the Samurai tried to formulate her words. The whole ordeal put Calvin on edge in sympathy for the girl, so he stood and reached out to her. He rested his hand on her shoulder. The girl was practically shaking with the memories and it reminded him of how San used to look whenever she had her migraines. Fuck, it was also that same hunted look in the Medusa's eyes when they had their ordeal at the church; what the hell was going on?

"It's all good, shawty. Soldat forte, come sit and we listen." He guided Sam to the couch. The pain from her was working his heart because while he sat her down, it was if she were a kid again and not the twenty-one-year-old she was right now.

"Twenty-one years ago back in Houston, Sam's father was taken out by his own team members in front of her. They were given a hit and were told to watch and protect a young Nephilim. A girl who was possibly going to be an oracle. Sam's father as captain set everything in order and hit up the house."

"They were tainted and he didn't know. I tried to tell him. I was six but I knew. Tried to tell him that I saw the demons in their auras but Dad was focused on saving that little girl and her family, protecting her because we needed living oracles," Samurai quietly whispered; her wavy, thick ebon strains of hair spilled over her brown sugar soft face and she fisted her hands on her lap.

Zion opened his mouth to continue for her, but she held her hand up and shook her head. *"I can tell it, Zi,"* she quietly interjected.

"A'ight, let me know when you need to break. I got you, sis," Zion protectively responded and Calvin was quietly impressed again. The kid was trained well.

"Dad always had me go with him, trained me from the womb. After my mom died in battle . . . anyway I always was with him. I helped be their ears, so this was nothing different. Like, but it was, you know? That whole night was off. First clue was I heard one of them call their boss, told them that they would get the target as long as they got the stuff. Found out that they were junkies and that's how the demons got to them."

Both Calvin and Marco glanced at each other. Only way a Guardian team would be addicted to drugs was if they weren't full-blooded Guardians at all but humans with an active Nephilim gene. Although Calvin himself was an immortal, a human with a dominantly active gene, even he couldn't get addicted to drugs. However, if you were a human with a slight gift, like a psychic, then it was fair game.

The gene was strong enough to combat every impurity that a human body was exposed to, which, for many, was their downfall. Humans who had a little extra boost often confused their not being able to be sick with that of being immune to other vices. The Dark knew this and loved to use it against gifted humans to make them succumb easily.

Calvin knew what was up before she could even finish. Shit, they used the oldest game play in the book. Use the weak links in the team to start the pollution and get whatever intel they needed from them, then snatch 'em up like taking candy from a baby.

"You all were a human team, mamacita?" Calvin heard Marco solemnly question, interrupting his thoughts.

"Yes, it was only my daddy, me, and my aunt who weren't. We are Immortals. Houston was stretched thin with teams back then and Daddy always felt our area needed protection so he started up a rogue team. He recruited whom he could find at the time. But, it was the humans with a touch of our blood in them who stepped forward, blinded Prophets. They were good people, too, and Daddy didn't think the humans who knew of us and who had strong enough abilities would be affected. So my daddy trained them just enough to be deeply aware of being tainted; but he was blind from what I saw. It was too late."

"Dios." Marco leaned back in his chair and ran a solitary hand over his waves. "Doesn't take much to get to a human if you want to, but those with slight active Nephilim DNA strains, it takes time. Which means the

Dark had been working on your team for a while, mami, so you have an idea who brought the taint in?"

Samurai gave a sad sigh. "No, but I noticed how quickly they were becoming different, a little moodier. Anyway, we got word from Chicago that an oracle may have been born. I remember hearing Daddy talk about it and making plans, then, when we got to the house, they ambushed my daddy. I was in the car but I went inside because something told me to and I saw they had him gagged and bound. He was trying his best to get free to protect the oracle and her family but it didn't help. They shot him like an animal, right in the head, no remorse, and laughed about it. Then they kicked his fallen body. They beat the girl's parents and . . . the father saw me and he told me in my mind to stay back."

The pain and images of her as a child flashed in Calvin's mind. He saw her hiding near the back of a Santa Fe-style ranch house, her little hands pressed against glass panels of the sliding doors, peering through an open crack of sheer curtains. Her little face was streaked with tears as she watched her family be tortured and later her father gunned down. Seven rounds had to be pumped into the man to keep him down before they aimed for his head. Shit was sickening to his soul as he watched the girl's memories in his own mind.

Samurai's voice melted into his cognizance and he glanced at her, wanting to hug her tight and protect her. "He told me that if his daughter made it out, tell her that they loved her deeply and protected her as best as they could. He gave me some codes I later learned were for her legacy vault.

"He also told me of some friends to go to who would help me since I had no one and he made me run and hide. So, I found my godparents though the man's friends and they kept me hidden, training me until I was old enough

to find out what happened to the traitors," she somberly muttered.

Tears rimmed Samurai's soft face while her fists clenched against her lap. The memories were vibrant and strong, as if they had just happened.

It made every team member in the house on edge as she continued in a soft, strained voice, "I hunted them like they hunted down my father and the oracle girl, seeking out information. Then I met up with Zi in Chicago."

"Shawty, you were strong and did what you had to do to survive those fuckers," Calvin explained in concern.

He watched her use the heel of her palm to wipe away her tears, nodding. "Yeah. I guess. That girl, she fought hard. She grabbed blades from the kitchen and took down seasoned members until they hit her with Cursed spells and restrained her."

Pausing, she then continued, "I found out later that the rest were wiped out. Made to be nothing but food for the Cursed. Guess I got my retribution, huh?"

"No doubt you did, shawty." Calvin shifted to sit by her side and wrap his arm around her. She reminded him of San and Kali in so many ways. Living this life wasn't easy. Once you lost a parent or parents your whole world changed. He would know that better than anyone would.

Marco moved forward in his chair. "Mamacita, what was the family's name? We have the records of a female oracle going missing after a House went rogue but we need to know if the same girl."

Samurai looked up at Marco then at Calvin. Her toffee eyes seemed to light up with the connection of those past painful memories. In that same moment, the hairs on Calvin's arms stood at attention. Something major was about to pop off.

"Yeah, Nydia Fatima Randal: her parents were Gavin Randal and Thema Ozigboi Randal." Awareness dawned on Calvin the moment the Samurai muttered those words.

Calving blinked a couple of times in shock. This had to be a joke. Someone was busting jokes on him and playing him dirty, yet again. That's what had to be going on. Otherwise, shit just got real and everything that just went down hours before was officially confirming everything for him. The voices around him buzzed during the conversation and Marco's concerned tone ebbed through in broken spurts.

"Gavin Randal, latent Slayer gene, aged twenty-nine and Thema Ozigboi Randal, dormant gene, aged twenty-seven but . . . ahh, precioso." Marco flashed a dimpled smile while reading through the records that rested on his massive, muscular thigh. "Senora had ties to the African Ghana Nephilim nation. Both met in college in Houston, Gavin was an electrician for CenterPoint Energy Co. and Thema was an advocacy lawyer. Any of that ring a bell for you, mamacita? Any pictures that you may have seen, any small detail that we can used to get an image of Nydia, Calvin will get whatever you see."

Sweat began to bead around Calvin's temples. Not because he had depleted his power but due to the reality of the story hitting him. He had to keep his game face on. A small part of him, that natural ancient law that had them at war with the Cursed, made him want to dispute everything here but the memories and the truth of it all ran true as it flashed across his visual. Everything in the Samurai's traumatized mind was clear and covered in truth and he had to take it face value, regardless of his mind saying this was fabricated BS.

"Ah yeah, she looked to be around eight, pretty, she had braids and . . ." Sam detailed.

The more she spoke, the more vivid the scene was for Calvin. It was as if he were walking and breathing her past. He saw the little girl, Nydia, in her room hiding. He later saw her running, finding blades in the kitchen and using them as if they were warrior blades in a manner very familiar to him. Calvin swallowed hard the moment he locked on to the little girl. All fear seemed to be gone from the child as she defended herself and her family. Her little ponytails flew in the air and she moved like the wind. Shit!

Remove the scales that run over parts of the Medusa's body. Remove the protruding spinal nodes, the poison nails, with everything that makes her the killer she is now. Then de-age her. Then you got the younger doppelganger of the Medusa. *Dumbstruck, Calvin shook his head. This was a problem compounding on to a problem.*

Another issue for him was that he was staring at a little girl who reminded him of the young girl he met in his own past when he was a child in Africa. A girl with beautiful, big, round eyes, an adoring smile and long braids, who was introduced to him for the Promising: his tribe's tribute to marking an arranged marriage to the Jaguar clan's own royal daughter, Fatima.

Calvin felt his Adam's apple bob up and down in trying to swallow. Anger hit him hard when he saw the rogue team snatch her by her head then lift her in the air by her throat, throwing the child across her house. Her screams and cries bore into his mind. Feeling helpless, he pushed from the couch pacing back and forth. Tears almost stung his eyes, as it hit home to a memory of his own past in the twenties and thirties. He could still feel the burning cord around his throat while he paced.

"Show me, acere," was all Marco hesitantly asked.

How could he show his brother this shit? The cruelty and inhumanity of it all? As he linked with Marco to show what Samurai saw, young Nydia's eyes seemed to burn holes into his mind before her high-pitched scream shot him across the compound. The pitched scream was so strong that it flung him backward into a supporting brick wall. Pain ricocheted through him at the separate memories from Samurai and the memories of Nydia's own soul.

Tears fell down his face. He saw Nydia as Fatima, locked away in darkness. Her body confined, and constrained. Many thousands, no, millions of hands pulled at her as the wailing of agony engulfed her. He felt that he was stuck, almost as if he could be in the burning cells of hell but not so much. This place was stagnant and overcrowded. It choked him with the drowning, enclosed feel.

He smelled and felt the decay of ancient lives mixing with vibrant fading younger beings all around him and it made his heart constrict and pump in claustrophobia. He tried to run but ended up nowhere and everywhere, bodies upon bodies on him, through him and in him. However, through it all, he saw Fatima, her soul light blinking bright for him but flickering and getting weaker and darker. He reached out for her, and felt a pain like a thousand needles and slashes all through her. Tears fell down her face and before he could get to her, tendrils of curling threads of light wrapped around her.

A woman's hand peeled open the darkness as if it were a womb ready for birth and that hand that controlled the tendrils of light reached in and pulled out Fatima. As the wall closed around him, he screamed for her. Silence surrounded him before he heard a voice. A voice so soothing and purifying as the waters of the Nile that it blanketed him in comfort: "Your freedom and rebirth is here. I'll hide you and take you where I pray they do not find you, child."

That voice made him scratch to get any peek of her. The moment he did, the face that met his own caused his mouth drop in shock and spiral backward in the void of the vision. He swore he was staring at Marco, and Khamun, but in the form of a beautiful woman with sad eyes.

His name being screamed in his mental ripped him back to reality, away from the vision he was sharing, in a holding cell in Chicago. *"Calvin!"*

"See that truth, shawty," Calvin muttered, stepping back to drop on the floor before the Medusa who sat staring in shock in her chair while Kali held her head.

He sat with both hands pressed against his skull. Flashes of everything that went down suddenly drowned him. She had tasted good. Her harsh skin had seemed to melt against his body with each rise and fall of her riding body and his impaling thrust. The flicker of her tongue against his lips and hard nipples made him hard again. His mouth watered in the sudden desire to know what her wetness taste like. Then the soft whispered silky moan from her echoed in his mind making him swear that could smell her unique light, flowery, and spicy scent.

"Ugh! Get out of my mind, wodie. This here ain't what ya want and you for damn sure ain't want I want, babe. Never should have fucked with you. Should have taken three bullets to your temple and gave you eternal peace, shit!" He growled more so to himself than at the images playing back in his mind.

"But you liked it because my tightness is one in a million," he heard the Medusa callously taunt.

This broad was right; his heart and soul wanted to debate with his screaming, irate mind. His tattoos lit up in swirling magnificence making him remember that the woman he hated was also that little girl taken in Houston. And that, she was also his long-lost love and soul mate, Fatima. Damn, it sucked to be him.

Chapter 16

Sanna quietly observed from the far end of the room. From her understanding, they had brought the woman she had learned was named Nydia, but who was also the number one most wanted woman in the Nephilim world, to a holding cell built under Chicago's bustling city. High security was what Khamun had explained it to be and she couldn't fault him for securing everyone's safety. But, she could be pissed at the way he was handling the woman. Her eyes narrowed in frustration while she watched the man she loved work. This was her first time seeing him like this in his element. This was the first time she was slightly scared of what her man could do to the enemy.

Nydia struggled in her chair. The woman continued her fight, refusing to believe everything that was shown. Nothing was enough. Khamun tightened the bindings around the Medusa's body while Calvin paced in annoyance.

"You seriously think that propaganda would change me? Did you think it would give you all a little boost? Oh please. Come at me a different route." The moment those spiteful words flew from the Medusa's lips, the moment her spit landed on Khamun's face, was the moment Sanna pushed up from her chair and broke through the gripping hands of Lenox, Marco, Ryo, and Amit.

Kyo flanked her, as was custom since she was her Protector. Sanna burst into the room heading straight toward the Medusa. Khamun's voice instantly entered her mind, but fury at the chick spitting on her man and the hours of torment going on had tugged on her last nerve. Glancing at Khamun, she immediately told him that they would talk later.

"Yes, I think that everything you just experienced these past two days has definitely changed you. You are a frighten child resorting to the defense mechanism of a number one bitch and I'm done on it. You know our side doesn't lie. So let me make sure you understand the gravity of what is really being asked of you," Sanna hissed.

Reaching out, Sanna slapped the taste from the Medusa's mouth. She pulled the snapping woman up by her bindings to stare deep into her eyes. The quick suction of air from the Medusa had the woman gasping. Sanna ripped through the woman's core replaying everything until it caused her to almost black out. Before that could happen, Sanna leaned to whisper against the Medusa's ear.

"Before you truly wake up, you will experience your death again. From our side this will not come, but from the people you truly call your champions. Then you will know. Then you will be saved, and then you will know where your allegiance really lies and what to do. If not, that moment you open your mouth to betray us will be the moment your soul will depart your body and feed my Sin Eater without him ever touching you. With this brand, I promise you," Sanna hissed.

Light filled the room. The sound of a woman's screams then thump of her body behind Sanna had her turn the Medusa to face the woman. Red unruly hair covered the floor. The Dark Lady's number one Witch sat on her knees bowing forward, rocking back and forth while clutching her skull. She whipped her head up to stare their way, her usually coffee and cream–colored skin paled to white in fear.

"Tell her, Winter. All truths are now!" Sanna demanded. Her hair flew around her face. The floor was no longer under the Witch's feet as she hovered in the air.

She watched Winter's confused stare before nodding quickly. "Ny . . . Nydia, you are . . . you were created from a Dragon, fused together with a mighty warrior. I wasn't Cursed then but the Queen explained it to me like something from Frankenstein. Centuries ago, during the first war, the Mad King was able to take a small amount of blood from the One son . . . from the teacher."

Winter slowly stood, smoothing her hands over her clothes and wild red hair before continuing, "Our Queen bound us to our Mistress to protect her, which we have done. We forgot our Light and embraced the dark to survive the horrors. Now you are awaking, as have I. This means that Reina is next in her awaking, too, sis. If you choose to walk this path, you will be protecting her still by making sure the Cursed never have her—"

"Because that is not her purpose. She does not belong to the Dark, nor will she ever. Do you understand? Like you tell those you've hunted then later killed, Nydia Randal, the Medusa, they stole your rightful place in life. You now have the choice to finally pick where you will go. Do so wisely," Sanna interrupted.

She whispered a Mystic verse for Nydia to repeat at the right time then she dropped the Medusa on the floor. The room around the women darkened then opened up near the entrance of a CTA transit tunnel. Light spilled everywhere causing her to notice that both Nydia and Winter hovered away from the Light. Nydia stared incredulously at her then Winter.

"You both are able to move through the Light as can Reina but she does not know it. You two use this to your advantage with our side. The moment you don't, you two will be null and void. The woman you took in STL is beyond our means of saving so she is yours through right. Take her. All things happen for a reason so use it," Sanna contemptuously explained, then paused with an annoyed exhale. "We're done here. I have shit to handle."

She never cursed a day in her life. But she was so ticked off at what had gone down that cursing was what felt right in the moment; besides, it was time to handle another issue. Walking away, during which a nearby transit train blazed by, she headed back into the holding cell to look at her teammates.

Amit stood next to Lenox showing the lines on his arms swirling then disappearing. His handsome, nutty-toned face glanced her way, and his thick brows frowned in concern.

"Amit. You take Kyo and you both trail the Medusa." Amit hastily headed to the door with Kyo at her command. While she agitatedly spoke both of her hands flurried around in front of her. "Track her and watch her every move. Khamun . . ."

Before she could say anymore, Khamun strolled her way, gently gripped her arm, and used a Transition spell to move them to the privacy of his manor.

"What was that, Sanna?" Khamun growled at her.

She could feel his anger; though she cared, she didn't have time for it. He was a bully to that woman. How he handled his captive bothered her to no end. Which was why she was trying to get her thoughts together, before she blasted the man she loved.

Moving out his touch, she shifted to his side to stare up into his fiery eyes. It was time for their first fight. "I should ask you the same thing. What was that Reaper! So you snatch at women and treat them like dirt. That was a woman who was awakening to her traumas. How dare you—"

"Hold up! Back that shit up," Khamun retaliated. Both hands flew up in front of him. He stepped back in disbelief to stare at her as if she were sprouting two heads. "Why are you coming at me like this? I'm doing my job. What I have done since the day this House was formed. That woman you are fucking defending is a killer, baby. A killer who is programmed not to talk, not to react to the slightest pains and then some. Everything you saw her do. You used your power to overstep my role and possibly just place everyone in Society at risk because you were on some woman bullshit! This is not how that works, Sanna," Khamun yelled.

He turned his back to her, running his large hands through his locks and then pulled off his tank in agitation. Old battle scars marred his back, abs, and arms. The moment he turned to glare at her, it caused her to stop her study of the plains of his hard body, including the slick dip of his Adonis cut disappearing into his jeans.

"So tell me how it works because that crap in there was not okay. We are better than that and I did not overstep a damn thing!" The moment she flung a curse word at him, Sanna swallowed hard. Khamun's head tilted to the side, locks spilling around his face; he strolled forward walking her backward against a nearby wall.

"Say that shit again. You didn't do a what?" he growled low.

"I . . . I didn't do a damn thing, Khamun. See this is the same shit like before Adam! You act a donkey ready for whatever. She is not going to betray us—" she stammered.

Khamun's hand fisted the shirt he still held in his hand, and cut her off. "How do you know? Just because you went Oracle, seeing shit, doesn't mean that it'll be etched in stone. That's rule one of the order, baby. You know your visions are skewed . . . and who the hell did you call me?"

Sanna was heated. She stared up at the man she trusted more in the world, feeling their wills collide. "I called you Khamun! And you did not have to go there. That was straight up a low blow. I'm not calling you out on the fact that you don't know your full power potential am I!"

Pent-up frustration had Sanna breathing hard and red faced. Her cocoa eyes blazed white before realizing what she had thrown back at him in defense. Inwardly taking a mental step back, she tried to angle her argument differently. "Baby, just listen. You didn't—"

A deep rumble had Khamun yelling without raising his voice. "Hell no, San! I get what you are saying. You said the shit just right, but truly hear me now. We both may be still learning but I know what the fuck I'm doing. Yes, with you in the fold, things have been changing for the better. We weren't bad before, ma, but we've just gotten better. We operate in the Gray. That means the light is our armor as we exact righteous wrath. It is these things that will make Society's stomach churn at what we have to do, but we do it, why? Because no one else is!"

Rumbling under her feet made Sanna reach behind her to brace herself while Khamun's voice escalated. "Fair exchange is no robbery, especially against the Cursed. We do not harm good but we will dismember evil, as is our right. As is my right as a Sin Eater, as is your right as Oracle. Feel me? We need to stay ahead of the game because for generations, Society has been sleeping, we will not get soft and forget our right to fight against the Dark. Okay?"

"I have my role too, Khamun. I am not ever going to take over your place. You are my world but I stand at your side as equal and what went on in there was crazy. You know it!" Sanna excessively pleaded.

Annoyance glared in Khamun's eyes while he spoke. "My job . . . I was doing it, San! Do I have to break it down to you like you don't get it? Bitch didn't think twice before opening you up like a book. Do you think she wouldn't do so again? Huh?"

Frustrated, Sanna bit her lower lip. He was right. There was no way around that. Every word he spit out at her in trying to help her understand was right. She didn't know why it bothered her so much to see the Medusa tied up like that but it did.

"I guess, but I still didn't like it." She sighed. "I still feel it's a better way for you handle business, because after all of that, you worked yourself up to a point where you need to feed, Khamun."

She watched the man shrug his shoulders, throwing his shirt behind him to watch her. "Then I would have hunted and fed, but besides that, I have you. You didn't like what you saw because we were working on her soul. Rebuilding it, opening it up. On the surface, you saw the little girl she was in that chair and it bothered you. That's your heart, baby, but what I saw under that was a demon who would kill us all before we could finish interrogating her."

Sanna dropped her head in surrender. The fight in her was already slowly melting away with his closeness but her stubborn mind had her mouth opening to pop off again. "Okay, damn it. I see your point but . . ."

A swift scoop of Khamun's lips had Sanna being lifted against the wall. Hard plains of muscles caused her to body to react in brazen lust the moment Khamun's hand fisted in her hair to roughly tug to expose her neck. The slick flat of his tongue with that of the sensual scraping of his fangs and teeth against her jugular had Sanna splashing waterfalls between her thighs.

His simple, rough, "Shut up, you need to feed," had her complying, knowing the fight was over.

She understood what he was saying. She could tell he got what she was saying but right now, they needed to meet in the middle. Which she knew was going on once the sound of tearing fabric sounded in their chamber. An aching of her gums alerted her of her incisors dropping. Her hand slapped against his bicep, which jumped under her touch at the anticipation of her bite. His heart was in her hands and his fingers were now deep within the syrupy wetness of her confines. Viper swift insertion of her bite was her penetration of his armor.

The man was incredible. Her fingertips ran over the sides of his hips, hooking into the belt buckle of his jeans. As soon as her siphon intensified and his ruddy essence pumped down her throat, the buckle to his jeans loosened allowing his member to break free and spring forward against her covered stomach. This was rough; this wasn't pretty. While he stripped her naked, he removed her mouth from his neck to turn her around then pressed her against the wall. His rough hand took an ample grip of her ass, lifting her onto the tips of her toes. In the heated moment of it all, Sanna still felt his love, need, and respect he had for her.

She had never experienced him like this. Yet again, she was a pupil under his eager tutelage. Once his shaft pierce her slippery folds from behind, his name ripped from her throat. The man was Pharaoh. Long fingertips stroked her swollen bud, collecting her moisture to keep his caresses going. Fangs from his lips tickled then cut a thin line from behind her ear to her collarbone causing Sanna to hit octaves she never knew she could in that moment. Satin tough wings wrapped to hold her while her own fought to reach with the dip of her reach against his body.

Poetry was in the motion. They mated as if they were in the Garden of Eden. The slick sounds of their body colliding together kept her wet. Her name rolled from his lips, his hand griped her plush breasts and the floor with the wall seemed to melt away.

Her throaty gasp rewarded her with him turning her around again to passionately claim her with his own bite. As he drank, Khamun picked her up, gripped the side of her thigh, and then pushed up deep into her, releasing her throat at the same time. His length was so good that it felt as if he had hit her spine, which caused her to arch into him. The low slurp of him sucking her aching nipple and fleshy breast into his mouth made her yoni constrict desperately around his shaft milking him.

"I get you. I feel you understand what I was saying so this fight is over. Now tell me something," Khamun drawled against her ear.

The man smelled so good, so intoxicating that she wanted to just lick his body until she got her feel of his taste. He still didn't bite her and by the Most High she so wanted him to. No she needed him, just like she needed more of his essence and touch.

"What?" She almost couldn't breathe out. His staff plumped inside of her, stopping its stroke to just thump against her bud like a heartbeat before surging back into her.

"Who the fuck is Adam and curse for me again. I like that shit, it was sexy," he murmured.

Sanna's mind wheeled with the pleasure he was serving. She had no idea what he was talking about but whatever it was, she wanted the answer herself. Just as long as he didn't stop the dance he was giving her.

She fought to formulate the answer but all she got out was, "Ahhh, I don't know, man. Adam is you! Oh my gosh!"

A pleasure-filled cry ripped from them both the moment he hit that million-dollar stroke. Water formed in her eyes then his grip tightened. Khamun's slick skin appeared like fresh Nutella in the jar. Every tattoo on his body, including his wings, illuminated in front of her, telling her to clamp her mouth on his neck. Her tongue dipped out to trace the veins that bulged from his neck, arms, and then hand. Sucking on each finger, she glanced into his eyes, and then she felt his legs crumble. Falling on top of him, she giggled then slowly groaned at the feel of both of his hands gripping her lush rear.

"Yeah? Then you must be Eve," he crooned against her mental.

His touch guided her, telling her to ride him so she did. She made her hips roll, then the walls of her plum breathe in and out while popping against him. She guided his hands to hold her sensitive breasts, and then she was rewarded yet again by him flipping her on her back, one leg strewn over his shoulder, the other hitched over the crook of his arm. Every part of her creamed in newfound pleasure. His shaft felt as if it had grown even more, causing her to growl low.

Tears spilled and Khamun kissed each one away before inviting his tongue to dance with hers. His head shifted to suck on her tongue then nibble on her lips. His low moans of "sorry" as if he was hurting her melted away the moment his locks brushed over her heady mouth, and then when his lips connected with her swollen pearl. The King of Babel was his name once he sang the Song of Solomon against her folds. Lovemaking after a fight was definitely damn good.

Chapter 17

The bitch had to be out of her mind if she thought for one second that she would submit to her will. She knew her place. She knew her life and all of that jazz she just went through had to be some crap. Ever since the fight with the Oracle and the delicious confusing night with the man from her nightmares, Calvin, she felt as if she was off. More like tainted and for the first time since laying eyes on the Reaper, she was scared. Her kind invented fear and this was not accepted in her mind. Pushing up from where she still sat, the Medusa glared at Winter.

"This whole time you've been playing us for fools? Oh, okay, Winter. You know what time it is then," she yelled at the woman she felt close to as if a sister.

Winter's sapphire eyes illuminated the room. She sat kneeling; her crinkled red hair spilled over her face, and some of it stuck to her from wetness of water dripping from the tunnel. "You need to accept the truth at hand. I'm ready to die for my role in this. I helped as the Dark Queen commanded me. Her law will always be first for me on the Cursed side. However, for now, do what the hell you have to do, Nydia. I helped you and our Mistress; if you desire to kill me then bring it. Fight you I will, but for now we need to go."

Each jewel around Winter's collar and ring resting on her middle finger glowed. A waning pulsing wave hit Nydia in that instant, causing her own metal collar to light up before they were swallowed into its void.

Everything was replaying in slow motion for Nydia. St. Louis was clearly a fail for her and she knew she had to think of a way to not be skinned alive yet again. Her trip to St. Louis was like a drugged haze to her now that she was back home.

Ever since the conversation she had with her enemy, everything seemed to muddle into nothingness except the intensity of his manhood within her. She still felt as if he was pulsating within her when she walked and that made her nervous. It also made her skin flush with fear. She couldn't remember a thing but snatches of the meeting and she was known for her long memory. One hint of her sexual play gone wrong from her Mistress could mean the end of her, the demotion of her life to that in the bowels of hell. She couldn't risk that regardless of the fact of her brief captivity with the light and Winter's betrayal. Something had changed within her once-cold, empty chest. However, she still had every intention to reveal to her Mistress and the Mad King what had just happened.

The Cursed Great Hall was overflowing with Cursed minions. She felt as if all eyes were on her. Tension in the room had her square her shoulders while slowly sashaying into Reina's personal public chambers. Since her appearance was always for her Mistress and Mad King's pleasure, she wore a black hooded robe.

The sides were split open, held together by barb threads. The comforting heaviness of her prize kept her level while she dragged it with her into the opulent white chambers. Nydia was ready for the big reveal but a flash of a frown hit her pretty features as she focused on what was before her. What awaited her shouldn't have surprised her, but it annoyed her nonetheless.

"Oh, you brought me a present, my pet!" Nydia heard Princess Reina cajole.

She immediately dropped to stoop in submission in front of the Royal Princess. Both of her knees painfully dug into the hard stone floor. Her reptilian eyes shifted then focused to gaze upon the voluptuous, alluring frame of the Dark Lady reclining in her usual regal seat. A loincloth-clad male servant settled against her Mistress's shoulder to offer his neck for her to drink from him. Nydia couldn't help to notice Reina's plush lips, which were coated in blood-red ruby-dusted lipstick. The Princess loved her lipsticks. Each one was crafted specifically for her to inflict pain on others through the shards of poison dipped gems or metals blended within the blooming pigment. Vanity was a luxury here and Reina embodied it well. Her beautiful black yet auburn tresses fell in waves over her smooth saffron-golden shoulders. Her silver-white dress revealed shapely legs and dainty feet that were currently being rubbed by the Mad King himself, while her razor-sharp ruby-dipped nails sparkled in the faceted kiss of candlelight around her.

The Mad King's malevolent gaze fell upon Nydia. It felt as if he knew all of her secrets especially the ones she was intent upon sharing. King Caius sat dressed in clean-cut black suit that was tailored to his broad shoulders and thick yet lean muscular shape. If one wasn't accustomed to his presence, they would think he was in a casual mood as he sat in a chair that was the duplicate of his throne.

Yet, Nydia knew this man and she knew the game well. He was by far not calm, as was apparent due to his reddening irises, and lengthening incisors. Nydia quickly averted her gaze from his. Pride with that of her rank had her keep her posture upward to display her own power and command.

Nydia felt exposed. She felt vulnerable, something she was not accustomed to feeling. She hated it and she wanted it torn from her so that she could be invisible.

Maybe she deserved whatever punishment was about to come her way because she was weak.

Yes, maybe this was what she needed as a way to remove these feeble emotions growing within her thanks to that Oracle. Nydia was supposed to be an unemotional being, an entity to be feared, not this sniveling weak thing. Her world was off-kilter and it pissed her off. She clutched her fist tight, tugging on the barb chain that savagely tore into the neck of her latest captive. She blamed Calvin.

A light brush against her mind caused Nydia to sharply glance up. She noticed Winter resting on her side against an opulent antique rug. Her bare, softly muscled arms rested on the arm of the Dark Princess chair and her cheek lay near her cupped hands. She seemed to be smiling at Nydia, yet her face stayed cold and unfeeling.

Her crinkled hair was now dyed a vibrant red, instead of the dark red it was before, that accented her smoky café-au-lait hazelnut-toned skin. It also made her sapphire bright eyes glow and accented the plump swell of her creamy breasts. She was covered in an icy royal-blue split dress and black skintight leather leggings that displayed her lethal curves. There was an unspoken secret in her aura. Nydia quietly made note of it. Bitch was about to go down.

The collar around Nydia's throat seemed to constrict, letting her know that her Mistress demanded her attention, cutting off her seething thoughts. Resting her eyes on her Mistress, Reina dramatically motioned for Nydia to stand and speak. Inwardly smirking, she thought this was her time.

"Mistress, I brought for you a treat from my mission in St. Louis. I hope she pleases the Royal house," Nydia cautiously relayed. Her eyes locked on Reina to let her know that this new toy had information useful to their cause.

"Ah, your mission, dear Stalker; do tell us what you found in this one," the King quizzically responded.

With a flick of her wrist, Nydia tugged and forced her captive closer to the Royals then spoke calmly. "I foresaw that there was a missive in St. Louis, one I was told to eradicate in order to protect Lord Brandon de Valc-Fur'i and aid in our cause."

"Yes, this message I was also given a chance to see from Lord Jacques. Now how did that turn out for you, my dear weapon?"

The cool tone in the King's interjecting voice seemed to grate her nerves. He kept rushing her. She had more to share with her mission but the heated flash of a quiet voice from within told her that he saw more then she understood. So she gathered that she had to be careful in the relay of her choice of words.

"I found that Lord Brandon still had a surviving relative, Aiyanna Braves. That the California Cursed kingdoms did not eradicate all of his blood after our esteemed King took down the enemy's temple. From this, I knew that the link needed to be taken care of, that I had to clean their mess," she explained. A tension grew in Nydia's stomach. It was so sharp that it had her digging her nails within her palms drawing blood while she waited for the King's affirmation.

He waved a slovenly hand in the air, and then pushed his daughter's feet from his lap to lean forward. A dark delight burned in his eyes. His Latin heritage seemed to become more handsome the longer he stared at her.

The rich deepness of his voice suddenly had her skin crawling as he cajoled, "Do continue."

"My hit was distracted due to our enemy infiltrating the club I found her at. It appears that our enemy is furious for our victory over killing their precious Oracle." She hoped that knowledge would keep the Mad King at bay but one never knew with him.

Nydia made ready to tell him that the Oracle was still
alive, but a burning sensation in her throat caused her
to stop and notice the King's posture. When that piece
of intel was stated, she saw a flash of fury in the King's
eyes point at his daughter and her. His stare was a dark,
mincing, abysmal, evil glare, one she was accustom to as
a dark entity, but as fast as it appeared was as fast as it
had disappeared. The look that was in its place was one of
appreciation in their battle.

Hurriedly licking her chapped lips, she continued with
that note of caution blaring in her mind. "In that fight, I
was able the mark her with my nails an—"

"And then you lost her!" the King interrupted then
roared.

Nydia hastily returned to kneel in obedience, but found
herself lifted to her toes dangling by the large grip of the
King's massive hand. She knew not to fight, but everything in her wanted him dead. The satisfaction of seeing
his death was so intense that it made her body bloom in
ecstasy as she tried to speak.

"My King, I . . ." she struggled to croak out. She really
wanted to tell the rest of her intel but could not. The
burning continued, reminding her of when she was
bound in the chair.

"*Sí?* You . . . you . . . what? You came to us thinking
I would not smell the taint of failure on you. Nydia, *mi
amor,* I've raised you near my daughter. I chose you
specifically for her and enjoyed bringing you into the fold.
How sweet and fresh you were, but do not think I don't
smell the taint of a liar. We live in the house of lies. Do
you enjoy how I torture you? How it arouses me?"

In that moment, she realized it wasn't a reminder of
being held in that chair with the Light but the power of
the Mad King's grip. The King let his eyes roam over her
body, which caused the flicker of disgust to coat Nydia's

mouth. He dropped his head, and then let his lips brush over the top of her soft breasts before running the flatness of his tongue scrap over the ridges of her scales, then over spots of smooth coffee skin.

"I think you do," he sinisterly murmured. "For your failure, I think I shall remind you of where you came from, *niña*."

That simple word, *niña*, meaning "little girl," sparked a queasy anger in her and triggered a faint memory from her dark dreams.

His spiteful laugh tore into her as confusion hit her hard. *"Where did she come from?"* echoed in her mind and her eyes widened.

The Oracle said this would happen! Helplessly, the Mad King walked her backward then flipped her face forward against the chamber's walls.

Painted handprints shifted along the surface with that of the outlines of many faces. They reached for her. Pulled for her and she knew innately that this was a punishment worse than a flogging, flaying, and beating. The sensation of the Mad King pressing her face into the malleable surface of the moving wall tore at a rising panic she had never felt before. This was true fear. This was fear she had inflicted on her many victims over the years and now it was her turn.

"Sí, mi pequeña mascota, mi niña preferida. Su miedo huele muy dulce, luchar más para mí." the Mad King cajoled against the curve of her ear and it translated within her being as, *Yes, my little pet, my favorite little girl. Your fear smells so sweet, struggle more for me.*

She wanted to tell him to fuck himself. To go and impale himself on the nearest sword for calling her "girl," but soon her defensive thoughts were quickly casted away with a brush against her from behind. A panicked scream ripped from her lips as thousands of hands scraped and pawed at her. Voices of millions sounded in the chamber emitting from the surface she was pressed against.

The wall softened into a pliable, gritty surface, almost like dried flesh and clay. A rotting scent made her gag the farther she sunk into the wall. She tried to push backward, almost pleading. Nydia felt half of her face sink into the madness of what was the Wall of Purgatory, causing her to begin to fight. The King seemed to love it as he pressed his girth into her backside. In that moment, she knew that she would give him anything if he would not place her into the wall again.

Her screams intensified then her mind spilt wide open. *Again?* She didn't understand; she never been in the wall. She had only witnessed the pain that it caused. Yet now, the more her breath was snatched from her, the more she fought, it slowly became clear that was a lie. She began living her nightmares again and the King's maddening laughs only drove her into the darkness of insanity.

Her mind opened to her like an ancient tome revealing truths she had suppressed for generations upon generations as she lived it again in the present. The Cursed locked her into the wall after they had caught her the first time and gave her their bite. She felt the sickening pain of it spread slowly through her body, changing her pure soul once they locked her in this hell. She could only watch, seeing the generations go by of her not being reborn but being tainted until the day they brought her out.

She remembered being pulled from the wall by a cloaked woman to escape and be reborn but later found again due to that taint of the bite having latched on to her soul like a tracer. She traumatically saw her child self being thrown into that wall again to later be ripped from it by the Mad King and another male: Jacques. She then was forced into the body of a freshly turned Gargoyle. Her body instantly burned in that moment.

A strange embryonic-like liquid covered her flesh, causing her tendons to crack, rip apart, and then fuse again. She felt that searing fusion with the Dark Gargoyle as her fleshy shell sloshed off, turning her into what she was today. She remembered that she had pleaded to be given death but that enigmatic laugh of the Mad King washed over her as he looked down at his newest and only surviving creation: her.

Tears formed in her eyes for the first time of what she perceived was her long-lived life. Their iridescent wetness almost fell as she saw herself being changed into a Cursed demon. The humiliation, anger, and grief washed over her. She saw her light almost extinguish until a low, healing song touched her spirit. It wrapped her in a soothing balm making her forget everything, until now. She had changed into pure evil, but now she was slowly awakening.

Her survival instincts cloaked the budding knowledge then she yelled, "I put a tracer in the girl because I saw other relatives. Relatives we must kill. Relatives that we can maybe also bring in to strengthen our side, *my King!*"

The Mad King was lost in his sick game. His maddening obsession with her body and this torture had him yanking her back. A frozen malice flashed across his chiseled features. Impeccable evil revealed his monstrous serrated teeth, ready to strike her neck at the same time of fondling her bare orifice.

Nydia closed her eyes. She recognized in that moment that the very people she felt was her family were now her enemies. Clarity explained that their blood would flow by her hands. It gave her hope in knowing that she would die protecting herself and her Mistress from this evil. She would die in satisfaction of having gutted the King open to feast on his rancid entrails. She wanted this retribution and she would have it by working with the Light. This was her vow.

Blades clicked in her arm bracelets ready to insert themselves into the King, before Reina's scream broke the Medusa from her dark intent. "She is mine, Popi! You will not taste her!"

A slap then hiss sounded in the chambers. Nydia found herself pulled from the wall, and then thrown across the floor like a ragdoll. Momentum from it had her instantly push up to her knees to crouch low while watching Reina confront her father who stood grinning from ear to ear. Blood coated Reina's nails. Her Mistress hoisted herself forward with a blade protruding from her asp bracelet pointing at the King's devoid heart.

"*Mi hija,* my child." Sharp-nailed fingers snatched Reina by her throat squeezing before the Kings lips fell over hers in a sick kiss. Nydia watched Reina's body stay erect. Her venom-tipped blade inched upward toward her father's heart. In her silent struggle, the King dropped her to the floor in malicious pride, glaring down at her crumpled form.

"I'm sure the spilling of my blood would amuse you both, *sí? Pero,* today is not that day, however. I did enjoy our time together and you are correct, my daughter. I bestowed her upon you, so she is yours to taste only because it amuses me. Now tell me, Nydia, what does this whore on her knees you brought to us have to share?"

Nydia almost gave Reina a thousand blessings, but she remembered where she was and who she was. Such ideas were unnatural for her to think, which caused her to flex her fingers while standing. To show her submissiveness Nydia kept her head bowed. She pushed her loose braids over her shoulder then ran her hands over her sweat-soaked skin. Glancing toward her owners, standing erect in defiance, the guttural clicking resonated softly from her lips.

She returned to the dark game she always played. The Medusa spoke, "My King, she can tell us where my prey went because her marker is lost to me while in the air. Which I believe she is in, since I cannot track her. This one will tell us what we need to know; besides, as you can see, she is very ripe with sins. Ready to be drunk and turned to fill your taste, my liege."

The King bellowed with laughter. He seemed very pleased with that as he circled the crying woman who held the side of her neck. Pleading for her life, the stripper's naked, voluptuous body shook in fear, pain, and disbelief. Her hands shifted to cover her face and body, ineffectively attempting to block any attacks that may come her way.

"She is a beauty. I see she likes to dance for money and spread her legs for the enjoyment of others while pumping her system and others with chemicals befitting a pharmaceutical lab. Delicious catch, my dear Medusa. You please me," the King replied. His bulky hand ran down the shaking woman's back. Lust brightened his caramel eyes in gluttonous resolve. "Daughter, you will bring her to my chambers. Then you will play with her for my enjoyment before we ready for the event."

Nydia noticed Reina's sharp jerk. A swift blaze of hatred sparkled in her silver-rimmed eyes before the look and the rings disappeared. Rigidly addressing her father, Reina's voice dripped in veiled contempt. "Of course, Father. I do enjoy new toys."

The King brushed his tan blazer off and called for his attendants. Twin golden-etched chamber doors inlaid with black-red blood and swirling trapped spirits opened to let him pass.

Casually glancing over his shoulder to run his eyes over both Nydia's and Reina's bodies he paused, buttoned his cuffs, then coolly addressed them again. "Do not take your time, daughter. After we are done, Medusa you will take whatever information you can get out of your captive, and go from there. You disappoint me again and you will spend time in the wall with your pets and your former friends, understood? We do not have time for any errors. The gala is coming up. Nephilim Light Houses are turning dark by our hand. Any failures or weakness will result in immediate death, which I do not have time for. Understood?"

Nydia scornfully bristled then snapped her aching spine back to stand erect. Her face smoothly hardened in resigned anger before she genuflected in prostration. "Yes, my King, I only live to serve you and my Mistress."

"Good, be sure to remember it. I have begun the war; do not fuck it up, my dear," King Caius smoothly commanded. With that, the King left. His aura told everyone that they were dismissed. Nydia watched Reina briskly follow, the folds of her dress sweeping against the marble floor.

Relief at having dodged a bullet caused Nydia to inwardly wince the moment she felt Reina's lips press against her own.

"And the book? The Oracle bitch?" Reina inquired.

Falling into her usual role, Nydia reached upward and brushed Reina's silky hair over her shoulders to kiss her cheek at the corner of her lush mouth. "I saw that if we get her blood with that of Brandon's that we may be able to read the contents then locate the Dragons around the world, without your father knowing my Mistress."

Admiration caused Reina's plush lips to part in a slow smile. An elegant hand played with the ends of her hair. Nydia took in Reina's mental musings while she walked back to her seat next to an observing Winter. "And then I will be Queen and the Oracle will truly be dead."

Nydia bowed her head in resignation. The game dictated that she play the servant, which she did. She sat at her Mistress's feet next to Winter. Reina brushed her fingers through her braids in thought. "We will continue this later; for now father waits. Nydia, do be careful because I will not be able to save you from the wall next time."

Swift as a breeze, Reina stood motioning to her private attendants then exited the chambers. Nydia was finally left alone to her confusing, jumbled feelings, ready to crumble to her weakening resolve when she heard, "Nydia, come with me so that I can restore your energy and talk about your truth and purpose."

The truth? What truth? Her purpose? She had no purpose. Her purpose was to protect Reina and be her lapdog. Her purpose was forever to be a slave in hell. Fury made her lash out at the voice near her ear, at the hand resting on her shoulder and at the blurred body near her side. Everything seemed to flood her senses and hit her in a flash making her see nothing but red.

Tears flooded her eyes. She squeezed the throat of her target. Her thighs clamped tight to constrict the airway of her prey while she sat atop their chest. She growled then muttered low to her enemy before she realized who it was. Winter lay calmly under her grip, softly smiling with knowledge that lit up the Witch's features.

"Told you we would fight. So now that that is out the way, you finally are now ready to reclaim your rightful destiny, flower. Moreover, you understand my role. I do all for Reina. Now come, we have work to do, insurgent Fatima," she simply stated in her mind.

Nydia blinked at the name. She slowly stood taking the hand of the woman she always called a comrade and staggered to Winter's healing chambers. Yes, Winter's word added to the burning sensation in her chest. But, it was the reality that they hadn't lied, that maybe there was more to her life and that Calvin could be hers. Thinking of his cell phone number so that she could text him intel, Nydia knew her ties had changed and that her Cursed family was now her enemy.

Chapter 18

"Gentlemen and Ladies of the city of Chicago please raise your glasses and let us toast your presence here. On behalf of my father, I would like to again welcome you all to the seventy-fifth fall annual M'ylce Masquerade Ball and Charity Gala hosted by Primus-Grete Tech formally Primus-Grete, Inc. My father and I raise our glasses to our many supporters and new faces who have devoted their time to partner with us to bring change and growth to the Chicagoland area."

Thousands of hands clapped in response to the soft and delectable words pouring from her lips and Reina beamed. The many people here were either politicians, business moguls of every kind, high society, or newcomers interested in bartering away whatever they had to be part of this world. This pleased the Cursed to no end. The endless supply of greedy humans always built up their numbers and tonight was no different.

Reina had watched her father make a quick exit to play with some humans. Therefore, it was her obligation to continue hosting the gracious event and keep the Southern Cursed houses and international councils fed with fresh blood and human souls ripe for the corruption. Her night was busy but she knew it would be a profitable one. After their prior meeting, her father, the Mad King, had hastily reminded them of the ultimate goal of collecting humans like cattle and hording them on their side. The Cursed needed large numbers for the final battle against the enemy and this time they would win just as they had almost done when her father had taken down the One Son.

The sweet taste of her red champagne slid down her throat as everyone mimicked her move. Her silver stare roamed over the masses watching some humans who sipped their wine quickly grip their neck, or arm, or some other places where their fresh Cursed Bite throbbed then spread quickly through their systems. Varied individuals' irises instantly dilated, while their bodies slowly became tainted with darkness due to their drinks. This was the way of Cava rose M'ylce champagne, freshly made from demons and possessed humans blood with that of white champagne to give it its pink tone, disguising it as a sparkling rose wine.

Reina savored hers and waved her hand. "Celebrate and raise those donation numbers; remember we aim to feed the homeless and provide community service to children and families in need."

The lies she thread spilled from her lips and she had to laugh. Her father's company did do what she just delivered but, of course, it was a façade. Whatever appeared good only helped them counter it with multiple levels of pain. Such as buying out families homes on the South Side and West Side. Forcing many to foreclose on property some have owned for many years. The numbers of homeless they helped, the more they multiplied by causing homelessness. Those they helped receive medical care, the more they gave cancer or the worst of the STDs in order to raise the level of open souls for the darkness. It was twisted and delightful.

As the music played, Reina adjusted her golden waterfall jeweled mask and moved to speak with many dignitaries. She laughed while addressing a member of the Southern Cursed council. The weakling had the gall to try to explain why their numbers were not up to par.

"M'lady Princess, you must forgive us. As you understand the South is heavy in religion and breaking through
the barriers is just not as easy as it seems but we did
manage to pollute a major pastor in Atlanta and already
our counts are slowly rising."

"Lord Johnson, I almost thought I would have to gut
you alive where you stand for the insulting failure you
have become," she coolly stated.

Reina surveyed the icy blue stare of the older male
in front of her widen. He was handsome in his age. To
others he would seem to be forty years old, tall with broad
shoulders, blond hair, and a smile that reminded her of
Brad Pitt. His body was just as built. But it was the way
those blue eyes widened in shock at her that made this
interesting for her.

"M'lady? Ma'am?" Nathan stammered.

"You heard me clearly, Nathan. You stand in front of
me in a tone that reeks of superiority and you wag your
finger at me as if I am but a child. You also expect me to
accept that your numbers are low because you all can't
behave like the top-level demons you are and wreak hell
on the South? Tsk, tsk. Oh, but I should be happy that you
effectively turned a well-known pastor to our side?"

Reina gave another soft laugh. She rested her hand on
his forearm then stepped closer. Both of their personal
bodyguards stood watch just in case something went
wrong. The exciting sensation of that possibility happening made Reina's nipples tighten and her bud throb with
the anticipation.

"You forget to use the natural history of strife saturated
in the very blood we purposely spilled years ago, generations ago to create a culture of hate and fear in the South."
As she spoke, her voice softened as it were silk wrapping
around a throat.

She then leaned forward to whisper in her subject's ear, "I should rip your throat out now. Feed from you and fuck you at the same time as my guard feasts on your innards, but . . . I won't."

With a soft laugh, Reina pressed her soft lips against the elder's cheek then stepped back. "I won't because you amuse me and clearly you've been overstressed, yes? So stressed that you forgot that you were speaking to King Caius Primus-M'ylce's only daughter. I, born from his dead seed, something none of you elders have ever done and can never do. I, who was raised as his second in line. Silly rabbit. You so foolishly believe that I would accept that feeble excuse? That I am injudicious?"

Madness crept into her pupils. She stood delicately sipping from her flute glass assessing the now-fuming Lord from beneath her lashes. Toying with him, she continued to speak meekly with a lethal tinge of fury. "Hmm, you are forgiven for your slight impairment and I applaud you for getting into the church. Oh wait, yes, my father seeded the church with darkness at its very birth! You did nothing innovative! Hmm, excuse me. I often forget my manners. Lord Johnson, what a wonderful insurgent skill you use. Please let us discuss this more at a later date. Enjoy this night! It is a wonderful delight that the Southern districts are here. A toast to you, good sir."

Lord Nathan Johnson inwardly fumed. "Princess, I meant no offense to you," he mumbled in restrained pauses.

The ruddy hue of his tanned skin marked his body in splotches. The darkening of his iris let Reina know he was ready to kill her, which she enjoyed.

"Of course you didn't. Drink up, dear; it is never good to let your drink get warm, not this kind. It was just a slight miscalculation of course."

The male lifted his glass and downed his drink quickly. As they conversed, he was clueless to the area emptying around them, leaving only a few of the lord's house members and her. He also was blinded by the fact that as Reina hugged him, she had nicked his flesh with her asp ring and given him the kiss of death. By the time the night was over, he would be nothing but ash.

"Yes, you are diligent in your understanding," Nathan bolstered.

"As are you; please continue your night." Turning to leave Reina paused, stopping her retreat. "Oh and Lord Nathan?"

"Princess? How may I be of service?" the Cursed Lord bowed before her, his irises fading due to the poison flowing through him.

The sting of a blade hitting air then meeting the side of a throat made everyone gasp. Reina turned on her heels and worked her blade across the hard tendon of flesh and bone. She smirked with sensual release as those blue eyes stared in confusion and hate before the body burst in plumes of blood and ash covering her guards who suddenly flanked her.

"To the house of Johnson and your new Lord soon to take his place, let me make myself clear."

Reina coolly walked around her guard and pointed her blade at the various family members who looked on. "I am a Royal! At any goddamned time, I can dismantle your kingdoms. Insult to me and my family will not be permissible. Ignorance and imbecilic behavior as well as actions will not be permitted!"

Her voice rose with authority while she walked around her subjects. She watched the males' fangs lengthen in desire and women watch on in respect. "You do not question me. I question you! You all will get your numbers up ASAP. The Southern houses will act in accordance to the governing laws as dictated and you will not forget that we are the Cursed! Humans and the Nephilim are our cattle; you will do everything in your imbecilic minds to govern the darkness. Do I make myself clear? Who the hell am I?"

"Our Princess. Princess Reina A'archy, daughter to the royal lineage of M'ylce. Our Dark Lady and Primus Anarchy Snatcher."

The words from the house of Johnson fueled her pumping blood causing her to drop her head forward with a scoff. She pulled back with a bloody open-mouth sneer, smoothed her hair back, and nodded, shielding her blade while walking away.

"Please enjoy your night and congratulations to your new heir."

Heading back out to the party, Reina noticed Winter slowly walking next to her returning father and her stomach quickly soured. She hated when she could tell that her father touched one of her pets. She had no power over stopping him from touching Winter because she had belonged to her mother but nonetheless it angered her. Duty kept her from seeking Winter out.

It was strange for her. Only Nydia and Winter were able to silence the madness that crept into her mind and she never could understand why but, right now, the madness was a comfort. The heated stare from her father made her hustle through the dance floor searching for someone to distract her. Her wish was answered in the guise of a handsome human who stood in a black-and-white suit.

His smile drew her in. The broad build of his shoulders and body made her plum clutch in need. His blood made her hunger ravenously as she slowly walked his way. She knew he wanted her, could tell by the way his eyes held her. She did not even have to drop her gaze to see if he was hard. His aura fed her that truth. He stepped forward and asked her to dance. The roaring in her ears in need of his blood blocked out her ever hearing his name and the moment his hands swallowed her waist made her mark him as hers. Tonight she didn't need any new pets, but damn if he didn't almost make her want to turn him herself.

She swayed to the music in his arms; his spicy musk and brushing girth of his bulge made her feel intoxicated. Why was she so drawn to this human? No, she wasn't drawn, she just wanted to be away from her father's stares. *Lie.* She was drawn to his scent of incredible. She needed him now.

Her mind was a confused jumble, but she was far from falling into lust. Her lips found his earlobe. Her tongue teased the sensitive area of his neck, which caused her to lightly groan as his voice dripped over her like molasses. This brother was fine as she heard some of her pets describe men such as him. His arms seemed to almost crush her and she liked that a lot.

She never had a man fit her body like this except for Jacques and she did not want to think of him. Every time she did, she knew he was near. Sure enough, with a sudden glance up and around the dance floor there stood that bald bastard with an amused look upon himself. She instantly wanted him within her and it pissed her off. It made her want to cast this guy off and go fuck Jacques like a wildcat but it was the woman who stood behind him who drew her attention and made her return her attention to the man holding her.

A rising anxiety caused her to glance back to where Jacques stood again but she was immediately greeted with nothing but the handsome man in front of her. Who was that woman and where did she go? Reina frowned then shuddered in confusion. It should have been like cold water over her libido. Instead, it was the opposite.

Everything in her whispered that she wanted and craved this male she held so she continued her dance and focused her gaze into his toffee irises. His skin was like caramelized honey, brown and syrupy. She wanted a taste. She let him whip him around in a slow, seductive tango, and she noticed the tattoos that were scrolling over his neck, slightly hidden by his collar.

She tried to ask him his name, but all she got was his seductive smile. His thick lips spread for her, asking for a kiss as his thin moustache and trimmed patch of hair on his chin accented the chiseled cut of his handsome face. Her chest hurt and she felt strange in this man's arms. Quién coño es esto? *Who the fuck is this?*

Her hands slid over his wavy low-cut hair and his hold tightened again making her glance over his shoulder again. He was so tall, like a giant, built like a warrior and she swore if he wasn't human that he had the traits of a Nephilim, which would not be good for any of them here tonight. *There it is again, that strange feeling.* She needed to step away from this *culo,* but the moment they whirled around the dance floor, she swore she saw her again. That familiar face. A woman who had her drawn but also seemed have her stuck in this male's arms.

The music ended cutting off the connection as rounds of applause sounded. She pressed a hand to her chest then looked up at her dance partner. He gave her another seductive smile then walked away. That act alone made her tilt her head to the side and glance after him. Men were attracted to her. Drawn to her like moths to a flame. No one left her! No one! Well her plaything did escape her but he did not count.

This was not acceptable or tolerated! She found herself following him as he walked away. People stopped her, her own father's Councilmen and she almost decapitated them in that moment of scoping the crowd for the male.

Where was he? He was so tall that he shouldn't have been able to blend in. *Hijo de puta!*

Music played on. People danced, ate, or were eaten. It appeared every minute someone came to distract her from finding the human and, each time, she tried to get away only to be locked into a boring conversation. The ache between her legs was talking to her and the hunger in her stomach was furious. She wanted to be eaten. She wanted to feel his girth between her lips. Never had she craved like this, and it made her want to kill off half of the population in Chicago.

"You seem in a rut, my dear," an amused male voice whispered against her ear.

Goddammit! She did not have time for this. Of course, he would find a way toward her. "Hello, Lord Jacques."

"Princess. It is good to see you and a shock that your Harpy is nowhere near. Who was that human you found yourself looking for?"

"My next meal, if you'll excuse me. I have a man to suck and eat." Rushing past him, she huffed.

She did not have time for his banter today, which was shocking for her. She usually always was interested in spitting blades with him but right now a human had her high and that was not something she could accept.

"Of course. Maybe later, if I'm still around and not checking on my old property, you and I can pick up where we left off. Enjoy your dinner," Jacques cajoled.

"I hate your laugh!" Reina spewed out and disappeared, her hunt underway as more people swarmed around her.

Hours later, nails scraped the wide span of a broad, muscular back before sinking their stiletto length into taut flesh, cutting deeply. Erratic heated moans lifted and filled the looming corridor of the intricate hallway. Sharp tears of fabric and the repeated pounding of flesh slipping in and out of each other rent the air with both the sweet and spicy scent of a male and a woman. The sharp intake of breaths becoming continued pants stopped with a loud release and a final grunt marked the end of the intimate display. Red splashed then dripped in tendrils into an ominous pool. Music seemingly made its gleaming surface vibrate with its tune. Its warm, sweet velvet liquid slowly seeped over the creamy tan marbled floor and flowed toward a pair of spiked golden-toned open-toed Louboutin Pigalili stilettos.

"M'lady? Princess?"

A deep voice resonated near her as she held her dinner between her fanged clenched mouth. It was like this for her every time she fed. She'd zone out and lose her awareness, which was why she always kept her protector near at all cost. The loud thump of a heavy mass reverberated down the hall of the hotel where she resided, making her look down at the crumpled male at her feet.

Delicately stepping upon the chest of the corpse in front of her, she huffed and lifted her golden draped trail attached to her golden dress. It showed off her sculpted soft thighs and long glistening legs. The dampness between her lush thighs made her drop into a crouch on the body to retrieve a handkerchief and move to a clear spot as she wiped his seed and her juices from between her. A simple black card fell and floated in the blood near the body, making her narrow her eyes to read the silver inlaid script: *Mikael Lawson {Atlanta, GA}*.

"Take him and feed him to the dogs. They'll enjoy his flesh as much as his polluted soul. Then put him in the wall."

The mention of that holding cell, a place humans called Purgatory, made her own supple flesh crawl. Her skin felt it was crawling as she threw the white cloth she held over the body and studied him. The sound of her protection gargoyles taking the body away, their mouths suddenly dripping in hunger from the meal she had gifted them with, instantly irritated her. A disgusted huff formed in her throat as she watched her demonic pets drop to their knees and lap at the blood, cleansing the area from any evidence of anything going on.

Something in the way the blood pooled made her lost in its glossy surface. The pulsing beat of her dark husk of a heart made her stumble forward and move down the hallway away from the party her father had demanded she oversee. Music thumped over her, instantly adding to the forming headache she was having and shifting vision plaguing her senses. *What was in that bastard's blood?*

A click of additional heels made her look up and she gave a quick smile.

"My pet, Medusa?" Reina languidly asked. The image before her hazy stare made her blink, once, then twice at the curvaceous body walking her way and stood in a fear that unexpectedly had her gripping the side of the walls.

Nydia? She found herself screaming in her mind. The fact that her pet was mingling with other Cursed representatives at the ballroom was forgotten on her as the indescribable body inched closer. A dipping undulating of the marble floor and walls around her made her footing unstable and hard for her to pull out her blades and she couldn't understand any of this. She was trained beyond the usages of blades; and whatever that was coming from her instantly washed in clearing white light drowned her nose in sweet lilac and honeysuckle and made her swing out against the affront.

"This game you are playing will not be allowed, Nydia!" she screamed in crazed confusion.

The moment she swung forward, that body dropped into a low crouch to come forward. A hand covered in matching gold rings and a filigree braided chain jeweled glove, slammed over her face, covering her mouth and nose to drop her in a slow backward fall. With that hand, the mirror of her own features followed and her eyes widened at that familiar face. It smiled lovingly at her before shifting into a contorted darkness with soul-tearing pupils that reminded her of the Reaper, the Sin Eater: her cousin.

The simple word *"No,"* softly tore into her mind. She fell backward by that hand that pushed her to the ground then straddled her.

"Momma," Reina sputtered out, paralyzed in her mind and that face bowed her moving head then her hand to kiss her temple. The sound of the blades that came out too late falling to the marble floor clattered in sad disarray.

"Remember your place. Remember you are mine, not your father's, but mine, and His. Remember what you did and what you promised. As was before, shall be again," the woman said.

With those simple words, Reina seemed to watch from the side of her body as her mother tore her heart from her body, covering its decrepit husk with threads of entwining white light, making it turn red and plump with life.

The instant it pulsed with a beat, a charge hit her and set her flying into darkness and light. Reina saw everything that happened with that male was nothing but her mind twisting her reality. None of it had happened and all of it triggered by her dead mother. Fury made her reach out to her mother in one last failed attempt, but the final image was of black wings ripping from her mother's back. She locked in on those piercing orbs of knowledge and truth, pupils of a Sin Eater, which left her paralyzed in shock. Fear made Reina scream and fight for a life she never knew she had to a right in claiming. All the while, those threads of light cut through the light and covered her in a blanket, sending Reina into the deepest recesses of her mind.

The smell of the sweetest of blood, no, wine hit Reina's awareness and made her open her eyes. She gasped as she tried to talk but all she could do was watch, as she felt locked into a body that wasn't her current form. Hands reached up into her visual and Reina almost screamed again. She was no longer herself, she was now a he and she was no longer in the present but in the past.

Chapter 19

(Lost Scrolls of Nephilim)

I am the scorn. The deceiver. The vilified. Number two in the line of people who brought a plight to the human race. Titles of hatred I wear due to my own weak resolve. Thirty pieces of silver were my reward for my betrayal. My name remembered with those who brought shame unto the human race. Nevertheless, before that, I was just a man. A devoted disciple, gifted with extended knowledge of protecting the coinage of the One Son until I was made tainted by that silver's promise.

Before that, I was just an innocent businessman. My tribulations were as any other, yet it was the teachings I heard from other men and women, scholars who were called Disciples that changed my life. I was drawn to them instantly and it was that meeting with the One Son, a man who instantly felt like family, a brother who made me accept my place as a fellow Disciple. He welcomed me.

In his tutelage, I learned that several of his scholars were legends in the flesh and that my wife and children carried the same gifts, which was why they accompanied me and why I instantly felt safe with them. I gave up my old home to travel and learn with these fellow Disciples. Absorbing the teachings as if it were bread and water. I was at peace with being the treasurer to the One Son and assisting in his healing help to those lost by the hands of the enemy.

My travels were wondrous and I saw breathing myths. Men and women who were called Dragons from the far East, some from Egypt, as well. Trusted protectors, whom the One Son entrusted with his Word and who assisted in preserving his Word. Those were peaceful times until we came home. Whispers of Nephilim, a word used in tandem with demons, began following us.

Traitors, liars, killers, also followed us. Danger surrounded us at every turn and it became hard to protect our families. Those Disciples with divine gifts, including my children and wife, who passed the gifts to them, had to go into hiding and I became scared. It was indoctrinated in us all to never to allow such fear into our hearts because the enemy whom we fought, the ones who tainted the good name of Nephilims, could creep in and twist our psyche. I wish I had listened.

I recall being ordered to meet the chief priests of the land before the grand Supper. My wife and children had gone to her family and I was left in our home. Like everyone in the towns and cities we traveled through, the One Son was wanted as were we and we vowed to keep our families safe. As did the One Son and the Angels who followed him as Disciples, as well.

We prepared for any dangers that may have come our way and we sent many families into hiding. Everywhere I went I saw demons watching us in the flesh of humans who gave way to their sins. Every night I prayed for the nation's safety with that of my children until it came to the day of the Supper. I remember sitting in my home thinking of my family as I readied for the night gathering. I should have gone with them, for it was that night when the chief priests invaded my home. Three men came into my modest home. These men dressed in opulent attire stifled me with their power. I knew as I stared into their pupils that they were pure evil, but I was forced to stay where I sat.

"You are a follower of the treacherous Messiah?" was asked of me by a man whose face I recalled. He was the Iberian Roman general and soon to be King Caius Grete. He was as was told by the locals. As tall as a giant with dark, long hair that curled around his neck. Eyes dark as soot but a face as handsome as sin. One glance from him and my soul was open to fear and it was if he knew and fed from it. A madness seemed to choke at me due to his look and I tried to remember the faces of his partners. It was hours that I sat locked in my home with them. I fought them and tried to make them leave but to no reprieve. Those two silent men, who seemed to guide General Grete, eventually threatened my safety.

The hood fell back from one and I almost tumbled backward. He was divine. His features golden and perfect, eyes of many hues, a smile of sunlight and I knew that he was related to the One Son yet he wasn't. My heart quaked and whispered to me, as this man calmly spoke in a voice that felt like silk. His hand brushed my own and I felt sinful lust and engulfing hatred at that moment. I never felt such before and it burned me great. This man was a fallen Angel. The ruler of hell.

I was instantly condemned. The third cloaked figure poured us cups full of a dark wine that stunk of sweetness and sulfur. It was then that the devil himself handed me the cups as General Grete coaxed me into the drink.

"Thirty pieces of silver will be your reward if you tell us where your Messiah is. If you tell us, your family will go free."

This for me was my moment of failure when darkness crept into my heart. Fear tore at me, but I still fought. I fought until the third cloaked figure dropped his hood and stared into my soul. His head was bald and he shone with an odd power of his own. He wore a branding on his wrist in the shape of two twisted interlocked S's and he simple stated, "You want to do this and you will do this to keep your brothers safe. You know we will never harm thee. Thus is your birthright."

I was drowning and I felt my world turn apart. It was then that I heard myself pledge myself to General Grete. I kissed his rings and I felt a nick, no a bite, on my wrist. The General looked down at me with blood around his lips: my blood. My vision then was overcome by sinewy rotting wings as the two men he came with disappeared like dark mists.

Coldness with that of a sudden sickness took me over and my path was set.

I still tasted that sickening wine they gave me coating my mouth like oil. I tasted it at the Supper. I tasted it when I found myself betraying my divine brothers and I tasted it when those cold coins lay in my hands. That taste. That acidic, vile, sulfuric taste.

It followed me to my wife's family home where I saw them slaughtered. Demons hovered over them, their very souls ripped from them as the mark of General Grete lay branded into their skulls. This was my punishment and I understood that it was time for me to meet them for my deception. That silver. My faith. My life. All torn from me.

It was suddenly easy to allow the rope to wrap around my neck. It was easy then to fall for my sins as I asked for forgiveness again. The One Son had known this would happen, but he did not stop me. I finally understood why. I had to learn to see Him in my soul, fight as I had and fall all the same. I started a humble man and died a legend. I betrayed and I vowed that I would set it right. I prayed with my last breath that I would set it right.

Chapter 20

The sound of "Life is a Highway" incessantly rang near his side. Accompanying it was the irritating clicking of typing that followed right behind it. Khamun stopped his pacing to glance at his boy Calvin while he tapped at his cell, cursing and scowling at it. His boy had serious frown lines etched in his forehead and around his mouth. As of late, since capturing the Medusa a week ago, Calvin's cell had been buzzing or ringing nonstop with intel from the Medusa. From what he shared with Khamun, other times it was annoying texts such as:

> Calvinnnnnnnnnnn! I need you to trust me. I'm on your side, ingrate! Pay attention when I'm sharing info with you! When will we screw again? Calvinnnnnnnnnnn!

Khamun could only laugh. From the anguished look in his boy's emerald irises, Khamun could tell already that Calvin was in the trenches of a reluctant forming rekindling romance, regardless of how fucked up it began in this life. Calvin sat with both legs stretched out on the table near the TV. Across from him were Ryo, Take, and Dare who were watching a basketball game but fighting over which basketball game to watch. The crap was hilarious, because it was over old games that had passed awhile ago and some off-the-wall bet.

"Take and Ryo, man, your asses are so foul, bros. I won that bet on the court that you both didn't know that teeth are called canines right?" Dare griped.

"No, that was your imagination, dude." Ryo chuckled.

"Man, shut up, but I wasn't wrong either. We have dentine, damn," Take grumbled, scowling, brushing off his black jersey. His partially shaved hair on both sides of his head was pulled back into a ponytail and his jade eyes were glowing like flames.

"Man, no one is thinking about this shit; turn the game on," Ryo retorted giving Take dap while they both laughed.

Dare's chocolate gold-rimmed eyes lit up as he let out a deep laugh. He shook his fitted-hat-wearing head and crossed his muscled arms over his chest. Ryo headed to the kitchen.

His shoulders shook wittily before continuing, "Yeah, man, but teeth are also called canines! Ante up, brahs, ante up. No point in being salty. I get the right to the TV. I let you sit back to eye hustle my twin, so go back to that shit so I can watch this game."

"Just disrespectful, man," Ryo said, chuckling while strolling to the couch with a bowl of popcorn.

"But guess what? Dare is right. Take should be focusing on choppin' it up on you know who." He plopped on the couch and started singing Miguel's "Adorn," teasing Take about Amara. Every young guy busted out in laughter as Take caused Amit's popcorn to fly out of his bowl.

"This shit," Take growled.

"It's just jokes!" Ryo countered in jest.

Listening to the new kids in his House reminded Khamun of his relationship with his brothers, Marco, Calvin, and Lenox. It felt like good to have the male banter in the room. In the security room, Kali clicked on her keyboard showing Amara as well as Miya the prayer lines that made up both Chicago's city grid and STL on the security board. A map of Atlanta's massive grid instantly popped up while Amara pointed out different places she'd said had high levels of Cursed or demonic activities.

"See, if you throw a Mystic spell over a prayer grid like the ones I'm showing you, if you tailor it just right, you can blow up a whole neighborhood or army of Cursed, if strong enough. Let me show you," Kali explained. She typed into her keyboard, pulling up a Mystic spell, and went into teaching Amara and Miya Mystic skills.

"Oh, so, um, a random question: when you made the Medusa see her past, then linked it with Calvin, what type of power was that?" Amara casually asked.

Kali gave a lighthearted giggle then pointed to the screen on the monitor. "It was all still Mystic power, cuz. Like I was explaining, everything on our side, is on their side, so if it helps, think of me as a White Light Witch, who had psychic abilities."

Being who Amara was, she let out a slow, "Ohhhh, so, why are you scared to fly planes; can't you just create a spell that helps with that? And teach me how to see the past of my ancestors. I want to sit in a café in Harlem and listen to Langston Hughes. By touching Calvin, he should be able to help ground me and take me back then for a bit right?"

Kali stared slack jawed at her cousin. Khamun himself couldn't help but to stare too. She just spit out some wisdom, all wrapped up in common confusion of what it is to be Nephilim. There were limitations to everything in life, power was one of those, but the idea of being able to go back in time with just the whisper of a Mystic spell was damn interesting. Maybe one day Kali could find such a spell because it could definably help in this war against the Cursed.

Behind him, Dr. Eammon sat with a laptop speaking with his son Zion and Kyo's parents on Skype about additional intel that was pouring in from STL. Through the whole conversation, Zion would have to repeat himself multiple times to his father, as Kyo's dad Hideo watched via his Web cam in Boston with the same quizzical look Khamun had. Worry was etched across Dr. Eammon's face, but Khamun could tell that Zion felt confined in what he could do since he was in STL.

As they continued their conversation and Pop Hideo signed off, Sanna's mother Tamar regally strolled into the rec room of the compound with Sanna. Nestled between his beloved's hands was a filigree-carved silver box that Calvin and Amara had dug up from Bishop Steele's grave. San's mother was dressed in a cream pencil skirt and a white blouse with a hat that accented her short, wavy chin-level bob. Both women spoke quietly to each other as they moved to sit down at a table.

Dr. Eammon abruptly ended his conversation with his son, then moved to pace around the room before noticing Tamar. His hands were behind his back. His brow furrowed lost in thought, resulting in Khamun watching the Elder closely. Tamar lightly sashayed to the Elder, reaching out to take his hand. A smile spread across her butterscotch feathers as she held the hand of Dr. Eammon Toure in love.

The Elder's broad, muscularly lean frame stood intimately close to San's mother, almost respectfully shadowing her in a manner that felt very much like a gentleman. A comforting grin, which held a hint of seduction, played across his magnificent face and it made Khamun think of his own love for Sanna. Quietly studying the Elder, it appeared as if his hand fit perfectly around San's mother's and Tamar bashfully gazed up into his handsome face. Her fingers adoringly reached up to remove his frameless glasses to clean them, calming the Elder instantly.

Khamun admired how they looked together. Dr. Eammon's almost regal attributes and welcoming aura was comforting on a mentoring level. His strong jaw, duo lines in his cheeks that almost could be called dimples appeared when he smiled at Tamar. The Elder's salt-and-pepper spiky low afro and crisp-cut goatee melded nicely with his mahogany skin.

Khamun noticed the way he stared into San's mother's eyes made Sanna smile. The Elder exhibited the strong stature of a loving man that Tamar needed as much as Eammon needed her, which marked Dr. Eammon as a man who could have been of royal blood in his past life. Khamun was inspired. He hoped he looked that same way in the presence of the woman he loved: Sanna.

Coming back to reality, closely observing the tense Elder, Khamun realized that for a while, slow change had been occurring in the male. Over these past couple of weeks, he had learned the Dr. Eammon had gone on a much-needed hiatus from his job at the hospital. From there, he had been spending a lot of time at the compound talking with Sanna, Dare, and now Amara with Zion on call.

There was something odd going on with the man, more and more every day. Some days it felt as if Dr. Eammon was forgetting everything. On other days if felt as if he knew more than what he was letting on. It was strange to Khamun, which caused him to assess the Elder's aura. Twin interweaving lines of color twisted to fuse around each other, brightening in magnitude. The shape of a phantom shadow, with its hand on the Elder's shoulder drew in Khamun's interest.

"Is . . . is that my box? The box I found years ago?" Dr. Eammon gloomily questioned.

Khamun noticed Sanna's curious gaze. Her cinnamon pupils warmed in kind then she pulled out a chair and patted its surface.

"This is your box? Amara and Calvin found this box at our father's grave. Would you like to see what is inside with me?" San gently asked.

Dr. Eammon hesitantly moved toward the table as if unsure if he should approach. It was crazy to Khamun how the man had just been an assuring, strong Elder but now seemed to be a frail, confused stranger. Something was going on. Khamun could taste it, and from the look of it, Sanna felt the same. His beloved gently glanced his way and told him to keep silent and let it play out for what it is, without saying a word. The strong, refreshing scent of ancient Mystics' spells filled the room, stopping everyone in their tracks to focus on Sanna and Dr. Eammon.

"Eammon has been acting this way for a week or so now, sweetie. He's been having dreams about us . . . Dreams about things that only your father knew of," Tamar softly explained.

Sanna glanced toward her mother then stood to hug her gently. "Let's open the box then, to see if we can find some answers."

Tears fell down Sanna soft cheeks the moment her hands touched the box. Khamun watched her urgently flip the box over, finding a hidden lock on it. The sound of a click then the pop of a latch allowed it to open. Stepping forward, the musty scent of age filled the compound and Khamun stood near Sanna's side peering into it. Inside rested what appeared to be a gossamer-wrapped book; next to it was a glass vial holding rusted misshapen pieces of metal. He watched as Sanna carefully removed each item, setting them on the table.

Dr. Eammon reached out to brush his fingers over its covered surface before gripping it. Light crackled across his dark eyes, snapping his head back in a gasp. "My book."

Khamun cocked an eyebrow, ready to question what the hell was going on, before Sanna's gentle voice spoke up. Taking both of his shaking bulky hands, Sanna tilted her head in question coaxing him to spill his secrets.

"Who are you, good sir? It's okay, you can open your mind now, you are safe here. You are safe with us. Ahh!"

Sanna's screams put the fear of God into Khamun; instinct had him reaching to pull them apart, but the power of Oracle had him locked in place. His wings unfurled to wrap around her as both Amara and Dare stepped forward to anchor her gift. Roughly, like that of a seizure ripped through Dr. Eammon; the power charge was so strong that it also snapped his head back with force. The sound of monks singing on the bluffs of Alton, Illinois, surrounding the grave of Bishop Steele, ripped across Khamun's psyche before the sounds of his teammates brought him back to reality.

His heartbeat drummed in his ear. His vision waivered then returned to normal to see Dr. Eammon slumped over.

"Sweetheart? Baby? Eammon! Please, wake up! Sanna, baby, are you okay? Darius? Amara! Khamun, do something," Tamar frantically yelled.

She stood shaking Dr. Eammon then moving to touch her children. Khamun observed unsure what to do. Feeling drained from his own power being spent and out of being needed, he slowly pushed up to rest his hand against Sanna's cheek.

A spark between them, a sharp current caught his attention the moment he touched her and the sound of her sharp gasp, with that of everyone else, had Khamun standing up. "San?"

Her coughing then abrupt thrust of her arms around his neck had him rocking her in relief. "I'm okay, Khamun, I'm okay."

"The nails, the gauze, we'll need it when we go against Caius. Look at it," Dr. Eammon sputtered.

Khamun turned Sanna on his lap to see, but his eyes kept going back and from Dr. Eammon to the gossamer sheet on his lap.

"Baby, do you know what you have? Look," Khamun incredulously asked.

He rested a hand on her cheek and drew her attention back to the sheet. On its sheer surface lay what appeared to be the faded imprint of a man. A man whose features were clear and exceedingly defined, a man who Khamun knew, had come to Sanna in her dreams and told her that she and her family would heal the Society. A man known as the One Son. In the glass stopper, multiple ancient metal pieces clicked in vibrating power. Upon what appeared to be an iron surface were red flecks that illuminated in radiance to flicker new again.

"It can't be," she whispered.

"Baby, but it is. I feel it in my DNA. This is legit." Khamun's own eyes burned amber; tears of astonishment ran down his handsome burnish face. Two tears fell in sync down Sanna's illuminating cheeks.

"The shroud of the One Son and the Nails of Nazareth," Calvin uttered. His hulking form cast a shadow over Sanna to reach out then touch the glass vial.

Astounded, Calvin gently picked up the glass. "I found this back in the day. Died keeping it hidden because if you use the nails as bullets, that's KOS to Lucifer and the Cursed King. Damn, I had forgotten all about it until now. Man look'eah, how did Uncle Bishop get this?"

"That's a good question; and how do you know what we need to use it for, Dr. Eammon?" Khamun cautiously asked.

Elder Eammon gently gripped Tamar's hand, casting a puzzled glance at everyone. It was as if you could see the wheels coming alive in his brain while he tried to remember something of importance. That something he shared next would forever change everyone's lives in that room.

"You've all earned the right to know that it was given to me by Archangel Gabriel. On my travels, I came across two elders; one was Gabriel. The other gave me a gift hidden in a 1930s record player. He told me that a close friend of his had died protecting it and he had taken it to continue in that protection. I had to protect it and learn its history, so I did. This and my children were the reason why Caius came after me, just like he sent the Cursed after you, Calvin. He knew once we got our hands on the Shroud but mainly the Nails that we would tip the scales and be able to snuff him out," he carefully explained.

Calvin sat with a frown before slapping his thigh in laughter. "That dude was my homie Mike. Man was always wildin' out back then. Good dude, glad he held me down, just like Nox did taking those bussas out."

Dr. Eammon slightly chuckled then continued, "So when I died, Gabriel knew that I wanted the box and my book of Mystic spells, which held my whole life with that of the binding spell I place on my family, hidden. So what better place than the grave. Make it appear that it burned at my death, and then hide it in my grave.

"No one would ever know until my children awakened. Not until my Vessel, who was chosen for me when he lay in a coma dying during my death, was later awakened by the Oracle finding the box," Eammon carefully explained.

Everyone in the room became silent, until Darren's baffled, "Fuck outta here? Pops?" and the sound of rushed feet with the slamming of doors that disrupted the peace in the compound.

Kyo hustled in appearing tattered and disheveled. Specks of blood that singed into dust covered her fingertips. Her incisors dropped low. "We have a problem everyone. The Mad King has declared war. He is sending an arsenal toward the Nephilim city hall."

"Demons have the city going mental! From everyday
people in their enclaves, to politicians, which isn't new, to . . .
I don't know what. My stomach is clenching in sickness,
bruv, and I smell, taste, and feel Cursed all around. See,
these blood tats are moving like crazy, blood!" Amit
rushed out in a disarrayed pant. He stumbled in behind
Kyo, his hair matted, his dark eyes rimmed in fatigue, and
his various blades falling as he pushed off his hoodie. The
sleeves of his jean jacket were rolled up and he flashed
his cinnamon toned forearms, where the dark lines of his
veins moved and curled into designs.

Lenox calmly moved to lock down the doors, having
come back with the duo. Khamun couldn't help to think
of the Cursed women who were drawn to his best friend.
He silently hoped his boy had a high kill count at the gala.
Tonight he wore dark denim jeans with black leather
work boots. A black mid-length double-breasted casual
coat adorned his broad shoulders, which also showed his
white turtleneck. His black leather–gloved hands held
out a set of key cards with a jingling key as he glanced at
the team. His icy blue eyes darkened with his anxiety and
glowed in the chamber hallway.

"The new blood is right, Khamun. The Medusa, Nydia, did the Oracle's bidding. Calvin and Kali's Mystic
cloaking spells, which carried yours and Marco's blood,
worked wonders. The Medusa was able to pull us into
the Gala and we were able to learn more intel," Lenox
exasperatedly explained. He strolled toward the kitchen
to grab an apple; seeing that there was none there, he
growled in exhaustion.

Kyo stepped forward. She was dressed in dark jeans
that accented the sensual curves of her body. Her ample
breasts heaved up and down behind her dark green tank
while running a hand through her asymmetrical bob.
She bit down on her plump lower lip then pulled off

her leather jacket, showing off the tattoo on her back that indicated where her dragon wings would exit and revealing the SIG Sauer semiautomatic resting against the small of her back.

Impatient, Kyo cut in to explain what was going on, her shimmering green fingernail-tipped hands moving a mile a minute. "San was right; that chick is on our side. We learned that the Cursed have spies in the Light Nephilim Houses thanks to giving them the bite, of course, you all knew that, but now those Houses are disappearing. Some were at the party. Anyway, the Cursed King gave a nice speech. Told us that tonight they would take out the Light. I swear it was crazy in there.

"When we went to follow the Dark Lady, we saw the Key, Ryo! The Medusa told us that he is guarded and so-called raised by the Cursed King's right hand. Anyway, Nydia was on point. When Reina was alone, after feeding on some guy in another part of the building, she cornered her using a cloaking spell Winter made. She then whispered a Mystic spell she said San had told her to use at the right time. In that moment, Nydia turned into someone the Dark Lady kept calling 'Mom' and the rest was history. Nydia woke Reina up, I think," Kyo explained. Her almond-shaped eyes were wide in emotion.

"Right, for now the seed is planted in her mind as the Oracle wanted. Reina will wake up to her mother's original spell. As for the Key, Amit took us through the connecting underground of the Cursed. We couldn't go too far but it was enough for now. He took the same routes when he escaped. When we get the opportunity, we will go back and try to extract the child. As for now, we need to call an intercom emergency town meeting. Shit! They are already at the council for the introduction of new houses and dignitaries!" Lenox cursed. He slammed his fist down on the counter next to him as awareness dawning on him.

Khamun knew that if the people of Society were not warned, or if they were not evacuated from the town hall, the end would be now. With everything that just had happened, handling a war was in the forefront.

He and his House were supposed to go to introduce San; now things were about to be different. "We need to go; we have a war to stop."

Chapter 21

Chaos was ripping through the streets of Chicago, forcing the remaining Houses to seek out the Nephilim Council. Through the mist of the growing dysfunction, San's mind continued to be disoriented from what had happened at the compound. Her father Bishop Steele was back. He had quickly explained before they all left that everything happened by accident.

He had found a record of the history of Spirit Bindings when visiting New Orleans. She learned ultimately that it was the start of him learning advanced Mystic spells. Various spells and history of Nephilim Mystics he found, he collected for his book, which was what they had found in the box, for his children and for Calvin. Her father at that time had no idea that by sacrificing his soul then attaching it to his family it would create a ripple effect, one where his Vessel was born at the same time of his life, although unknowingly due to the spell making them forget. History was written for both men, destined for them to be a part of a greater plan due to souls not being bound by time. Once upon a time, a young Eammon Toure would become sick as an infant where his heart would stop before his mother's Mystic touch revived him. From that day, baby Eammon would be a new child. All of it occurred because of a spell placed upon Sanna when she was seven because the Cursed were slowly taking notice of the power she had. Her mind was frozen in disbelief over it all. She wanted to think on it and ask so many questions, but Chicago, as well as STL, from the reports being given down there, was coming apart at the seams. This was why Sanna now stood in awe.

"Welcome to the World Nephilim Council Center, also known as Council Town Hall, baby," Sanna heard Khamun whisper near her side. His comforting palm rested against the small of her back while he stood so close that they felt like two puzzle pieces.

Ever since coming to Chicago, Sanna had no idea that this building was directly smacked in the middle of downtown Chicago. International and national flags were nestled outside of its immaculate structure. Various marble Gargoyles, some actual stone, others the real breathing entities, sat in quiet watch, protecting every human, or Nephilim, who entered its secured holding. Inside, the view of the Hall was like something from the history books. Rows of alabaster entwined with sandstone columns were inlaid with hieroglyphs, and many other languages. They stood erect as statue soldiers lining the majestic hall ready for war.

Various pieces of art, paintings, books, and murals rested on marble walls. Colorful banners reflecting many cultures and Houses, as well as statues of individuals she could only guess were Nephilims of the past, kept drawing her attention. Exotic plants and flowers surrounded an atrium with a misting waterfall. A flowing, bubbling stream, covered with glass, ran down the floor of the building and to the entrance, mesmerizing her. Outside opulent gardens cloaked the surrounding area. Sanna felt like she stepped into the lush emerald bamboo forest in the movie *Crouching Tiger, Hidden Dragon,* before stepping onto warm, heated sand that swirled around smooth rocks.

All around her was a fusion of cultures that blended in harmony and she could not believe that she was in what was once Cleopatra's library and lighthouse. Men and women of every race walked past her dressed in various regal attire. Others were dressed in black uniforms and silver military caps. To her, they seemed to reflect the image of US Marines, but in the body of Angels. Their various-hued wings lay flat against their spine and as they walked by, each one saluted and caused her to look around at the people who came into her life to protect her, and who now were her family.

While they walked through the building, various soldiers who opened a majestic carved steel-wooden door saluted Khamun. Light cascaded over them to reveal millions of filled opera boxes and floor seating. Tension filled the air. People coughed, grumbled disgust, and some flashed red, sickly eyes Sanna's way. Grimacing she gripped Khamun's hand, her soul hissing in disappointment because she knew instantly that those people could not be trusted, that they were tainted Cursed spies. The sound of a woman's voice immediately drew Sanna's attention due to the pain in the voice.

"My children and I are without electricity. The Cursed burned down our block, we barely have any food, and all the Council can say is that you have services that help with such situations?" Sanna heard a woman respond desperately, "What services? The services are broken! They are failing and we are going without! I was told that my application was denied, but if I were two steps away from being homeless, then I would qualify for aid? What has happened to our community! We need help and not just people who give aid to rich people who don't deserve those services!"

"Ahem," sounded behind Sanna, causing her to jump then turn. Lenox gave her a respectful nod, speaking low. "Follow me and I will escort you to the private boxes."

"Pay attention to everything because Khamun is now playing the game of a Royal. Check out this surprise," Lenox suggested.

Sanna swore the corners of his mouth twitched in amusement as they all settled into the box. She wondered what was going on.

"Please stand for the Royal House of T'em," the deep bass of an attendant announced. Gasps instantly surrounded them. Sanna's mouth dropped in surprise. Her fiancé had finally done it. He had done what she knew he always felt he wasn't ready to do. He had taken his place as his father's heir and declared it to a society that was hell-bent upon shunning all he did. Marco's gloating chuckle sounded behind her. Khamun continued to stand, waiting for his right to address the Council once the woman who pleaded with the Council continued.

"Once the news came back of the war going on, Khamun placed the signed paperwork in that Kali had ready. We knew in order to continue to have some pull with the Council that we had no other choice. So, now we're legit, but legally rogue; welcome to a new day, Oracle," Lenox explained to her.

He stood proudly next to her chair, as did Marco and Calvin, who were Khamun's adherents.

"Forgive me for interrupting you, dear mother. I only do so in respect to the testimony that you have just shared. I wish to cast my support in your cause and words. My council, I must press to you all, she is right. The Cursed have depleted us all, but what is worse is that they deplete our innocent population, both Nephilim and human alike. Right now the Cursed have begun the war. They are coming this way, and you all have been lulled into a slumber by your own people, some who have become Cursed themselves, and sat ignorant, ready to be slaughtered like sheep. It's beyond time that we woke up and—"

"Lying Swine!" erupted from the crowd.

Sanna abruptly glanced around the crowd to see where it came from. Saturated hatred hit her the moment she locked her gaze on a male sitting in a box close to the main floor. Red glinted over the rims of black shades. Brown crisply cut hair adorned the jaw of a sharply handsome male. Olive skin appeared to be gray in a sickly hue as fangs dripped from a pair of plush lips. Sanna knew by the way that the male kept shifting in his seat, then rubbing his inner thigh that she was staring at a Cursed Phantom insurgent.

"That *chulo* is Lord Gregory Ryan de Mer'ce," Marco grumbled next to her, "and next to him is his Shirley Temple–curl wearing sister. Chick washes her ass in bullshit."

"They hate Khamun?" she wearily asked quietly needing to know because the way the male's nails appeared to lengthen then turn black had her anxious.

"Hate is an understatement, *mami*. They want Khamun's birthright," Marco coolly replied. He leaned forward to run a hand over his growing hair, then growled low, "Hey, understand who the fuck you're talking to, bastard!"

An incessant slamming of a gauntlet echoed in the chambers. Council members and Society socialites began to grumble in protest. Nephilim citizens glanced up to Khamun's box, with hope, and years of pain shining in their eyes.

"Prince Khamun, you must remember your place! Royal or not, there is a time and place for that, and this is not the time. It was Ms. Hughes's time, not yours," a short, balding, and husky Elder chastised.

Each time he slammed his gauntlet down, the redder his face became until even his eyes turned red. Sanna gasped. They were surrounded by turncoats.

Sanna noticed Khamun furrow his brow in resigned anger, concern, stress, and exhaustion over everything. She knew he carried the weight of the world on his shoulders and it hurt her to be helpless in not being able to take that stress from him. The shift of emotions in the Council chamber caused her to stand to support her man. Her palm gently cradled the side of his scruffy goatee-covered jaw. His ropy soft locks brushed the back of her hand and she let their auras connect and soothe each other while he spoke.

"It's time, baby. Don't worry about protecting me or them ostracizing me like they did you and your team. It's time they knew the truth because evil is in the ranks, helping bring an end to your world, baby," Sanna coaxed.

Sanna closed her eyes the moment Khamun's large palm reached up to cradle her face. His touch always seemed to quiet the fears and worries within her. A rosy hue flushed against her golden skin the moment he moistened his lips with his tongue then turned to address the Council. She watched him drop his head as if thinking. His hands rested behind his back, and then he glanced up to turn his father's way, who sat next to other High Elders. Sanna swore she saw his father give a slight nod then rest his finger against his temple in wait.

"For years, we and other Guardian Houses have been working, doing our duty to keep you all alive. Protect the innocent as more and more Houses disappeared, fell to poverty, sickness, homelessness, or worse, lost to the Cursed."

A low, sarcastic chuckle rippled to Khamun while he paced back and forth ignoring the muted rumbles of anger, boo's, hisses, jeers and hate of the elite below. "The meek have suffered enough. You all have lost your minds and I'm going to remind you of it all."

"Prince Khamun! That is enough! Sit down and respect your elders and this council!" the floor speaker spat.

Khamun just laughed, and then held his hand out. He glanced at his family. Every handsome and broad male stood, moving to head to the lower level. Amit muttered to them that the Cursed were on the ground in droves while gripping his arm.

Sanna could feel them as well. She studied the man she had learned was her father's Vessel as he led her mother below to safer quarters. The moment Khamun's eyes settled on her, Sanna felt her body hum and knew this was the time.

Slowly standing she laid a hand in his as he pulled her to his side. Kyo and Ryo appeared behind them as their Gargoyle Protectors, their bodies slowly shifting to reveal the mystic legends that they were. Marco moved to the other side of Khamun, and then Calvin moved to her left. Lenox positioned himself by Marco.

"*Dios,* old head is sweating worse than a virgin in a strip club," Marco quipped.

"Disrespectful, spoiled pup! Your House will obey our rules and—" The Elder literally broke his gauntlet in anger.

"Dearly beloved!" Khamun dispassionately interjected, his voice dripping with authority and anger. "Avenge not yourselves, but rather give place unto wrath: for it is written, 'Vengeance is mine; I will repay, saith the Lord.'"

"Romans 12:9," she heard Darren and Take mutter then nod in respect.

Wings the color of midnight and steel erupted from Khamun's back. Incisors dropped from his lips and he growled low, "Your history has been manipulated and hidden to support the Cursed. That day is done. Truth is before you in the eyes of those before you all. I am the bringer of Death. The fabled Attacker. The Reaper."

Everyone gasped. Whispers of, "He's the Attacker? He can't be," fluttered in the crowd.

At that same time, Sanna pushed back her lace lilac hood, which was attached to her dress, her eyes scanning the crowd. The air in the room seemed to thicken with an electric charge causing lights to flicker off and on, and she felt her pulse quicken with the closeness her family. An eerie sensation had San immediately dig her nails into her palms. A tall, butterscotch-hued man walked, no, more like strolled as if he was a king, around the main floor, heading into his own box. He was dressed in black slacks, a black vest, and a white shirt that made Sanna think that he shared the same tailor as Lenox, except that Lenox's look was better.

She knew that bald man. She knew that shifty smile hidden behind a well-groomed goatee and perfect smile. Why she knew him was irritating her, but watching him had her full of caution. As she stared, she observed him briefly turn and stare directly into her eyes, so she assumed. That brazen stare made her jump back in fear mixed with anger and something more. Something more that produced a dangerous knowing in her soul before she was forced to pull her attention back to her surroundings.

"The Cursed are coming to bring their war. Many of you have seen it and experienced it. I also lived through it and was saved by Khamun and his House. Many of you would shun me because of my background because I was a mere human sought after by the Cursed. However, I stand here today because the House of Templar saved my life. You must believe him! He speaks the truth, his is the last Sin Eater, the Angel of Death reincarnate, and he will help us save ourselves from the Cursed!" Sanna pleaded.

"Sacrilege lies from a youngling who knows nothing of our world. There are no more Sin Eaters. The Prince is just a brat who has come up with a theatric means to distract us from our lives! Who are you to address us, child?" the Elder hissed then bore his eyes on her. His stare alone made Sanna sick to her stomach at the smell of taint in the air. But, his words of disrespect had her digging her nails into Khamun's own clutched one, in anger.

"Who am I? You disrespectful puppet! I am your salvation! I am the Mouthpiece for the Most High!" Anger had Sanna breathing hard as her hair flung around and the room became white in her power. "You Cursed bastard! *I am the Oracle!* And Khamun is his weapon. The Living Sin Eater!"

Silence marred the chambers. Not even a pin drop could be heard before, "Go 'head and pop a Advil because ya gonna to die today. Whoo!" offhandedly sounded behind her from Calvin.

Khamun simply glanced toward her brothers and brothers-in-arms before muttering, "Lock the doors, all of them."

He regally lifted her into his arms, stood on the edge of the opera box, then snarled.

Ah, how he loved the electrifying tension and chaos that currently was forming among the elite and Houses of Nephilim Society while he strolled into the atrium. It wasn't often that he came to these preliminaries, but today he felt a little intrigued. His work in St. Louis had turned toward his favor. He had played his role well, tipping both sides of the Nephilim races to continue the battle between the Light and the Cursed. His job never seemed to stop.

Ever since the Garden, he had been devising ways to serve both sides yet also serve himself, and today was no different. Jacques Samael Fur'i strolled through a set of silk black curtains and sat calmly in his secluded opera box. He idly glanced at his smart phone. Brandon, his adopted son, flashed across the screen. His son was shown taking down his newest Cursed nanny within his mansion. The boy feasted from the demon's body with a sinister scowl that made Jacques proud. Brandon's tiny dragon fangs tore at flesh but did not break the bone as he played.

Jacques held out his hand to his Phantom attendant and felt his typical tinted glass rest in his palm. The show was about to begin and he was very curious as to how his antics were going to play out to the clueless sheep in society. Taking a sip from his glass, sweet demon blood coated his tongue and he licked his lips while his incisors fought to descend. He felt electrified.

However, a sensation within the building made him glance around anxiously. A familiar taste was forming in his mouth. One that he hadn't savored since his days in the Garden, which had him wondering exactly what is was that had him feeling this way. He let his gaze slowly comb the audience. He glimpsed a couple of his Cursed insurgents, including the weakling, the Dark Lady's second Pet, Gregory Ryan de Mer'ce.

He was such a fool. Jacques enjoyed pointing out the ingrate's flaws every time. The Mer'ce House sat directly under his box in their private section. He believed it ironic that no one in Society ever realized the open declaration of deceit. Nevertheless that was not his concern. His involvement with that House was still hidden and it would stay that way for as long as he wanted. Licking his lips, Jacques continued his scanning, briefly pausing on the riffraff Royal House. It was fascinating.

Jacques turned in his chair to watch as the rebel prince and his vagabond team address the clueless Council. He had noticed the silhouette of feminine forms moving around in the box upon entering the arena. He had to guess that the prince must be up to something new. News traveled about the uproar the prince had caused the

Council at previous meetings. How he had annoyingly brought up issues about the Cursed.

His bothersome insurgent Gregory Ryan had reported to the Cursed about the ordeal and it made Jacques smile to see the worm so disturbed by the simple prince. However, now there was something new, yet again, going on with that group. He hated being out of the loop on anything he could destroy. Frowning, he watched the curtains part allowing his eyes to gain a glimpse as his manhood instantly swelled. She was here.

Staring in awe, transfixed on everything that was going on, anger saturated the air. That pure, unabashed anger aroused his hunger for the blood of those around him, both good and bad. They had unveiled the plan of the Cursed King. Had revealed who they really were, and all he could do watch her in her opulent beauty.

It was as if he was back in the Garden when he had first seen her. Naked. Unashamed. Sexually stunted, and oh so naïve.

He had taught her so much. Had her eating the apple of Knowledge from his bare hands when she was his in those moments. His tree of life her downfall. Then later her forever-changed fruit, her mate's downfall. Destiny was blowing full circle. He was blessed to be in her presence again and she would be his again for only a moment.

Jacques cleared his throat then adjusted his black diamond cufflinks against his black-and-white button-down dress shirt. Grinning wide he casually smoothed a hand over his black slacks, stood, then stepped farther back into his box, waiting to secretly disappear. "Now this is interesting."

Chapter 22

Screams sounded in the Council room. Calvin slipped behind the seating areas, locking down every exit as he could with his power. Blood scent prickled his nose, upsetting him in the process. There were a number of Nephilim who were turned or in the process of turning Cursed, which was sickening.

Khamun's booming voice immediately shook pillars. "Blood is now on your hands, Angels. Society is being attacked. Pillaged, and violated. Civilians are being tracked by the Society insignias on their post boxes, or address signs, or auras. Taken down out of their homes to be turned! Made to be erased!"

His fist fisted tightly at his sides and he continued, "Yet unabashed you sit and worry about mundane issues such as my house being supported by our own blood. You shun people because they come from humans, from the gargoyle culture, or were born on the wrong side, but carry more light in their hearts than any of you. Guardian Houses are disappearing and you all sit here as if it's nothing? This is the mighty Society of people who were born from the major five chosen, Arch?"

A deep, sarcastic laugh sounded then paused as if more knowledge just hit him and the speech continued. "I think not. This is a Society laced in Darkness, so it's time you all truly met your Maker."

Calvin lifted himself up to sit on top of a pillar. He watched Khamun slam his fist down on the railing of their house box. His muscles strained alerting Calvin that he was trying to hold back his power. Mini shuffles began and a chair flew toward Houses of Nephilim that now stood aligned with the Region Prince Khamun.

The commanding rumble of the Region King in everyone's mind drew united Nephilim's attention. "Move everyone to the exiting tunnels now! Bishop . . . I mean, Eammon, my friend, move my family; that means you all through my private tunnels."

Dr. Eammon gave a curt nod, immediately motioning for Tamar and Eldress Neffer to follow him behind a hidden passageway.

Amit was standing near the King's side; his eyes were the cover of polished black marble, his swirling tattoo now inched up toward his neck, and his hand shook while gripping his gun. "The Cursed King is here," was all he said. In that moment, doors rumbled, shook, then bowed forward, groaning in pain.

Calvin glared over his shoulder. Sparks of green currents ran over his dress shirt-covered arms while cautiously stepping over heart-snatched Nephilims. Nephilims who were Cursed traitors. The red curls of a woman spilled over the floor before him and Calvin shook his head. Gregory Mer'cer's sister. Frost covered her plump lips while her once-blue eyes were now vacant black orbs. Marco's kill.

Pounding continued around Calvin causing him to remember to connect to his team, *"I didn't get to tell you all but when I found the Nails, it was five of them. Their history hit me and I learned that the touch of a Mystic woman, a disciple would be needed to charge them. Kali, we need you to charge the nails, shawty, since you are the most skilled one; no disrespect baby girl, but, San, you can't do it yet. You still need to learn that level and you're not a disciple, you're more. So we need Kali."*

"*None taken and five? I thought it was four,*" San quickly asked him. She stood over a dying Council Elder, the one who had insulted his house. Blood covered her hand; the misting ejection of the man's soul sped to Khamun, who held Sanna's wrist, quickly feeding to regain strength.

"*Okay, what do I need to do to charge them?*" Kali asked in a pant. She sent a Nephilim flying with a slam of her Sanskrit-carved hammer, impaling him with her Mystic current. Henna from her hands returned to her, to cover her brown sugar skin as sweat sprinkled her brow.

"*Use what you know and the rest will hit you once you touch the nails, little sis. The fifth nail was saved for the One Son's heart. San, you have to keep that charged part with you. Put it in your Kila blade because you will anchor it. From the scroll I had, each piece will multiply for as long as we need. They will kill the Fallen, fam. They'll kill the strongest Cursed and the heart nail will end the Prince of hell. Y'all understand now why I died and will die again? We need to protect that fa'sho.*"

Sanna's eyes widened. Khamun bowed his head in respect, then placed his fist over his heart to salute Calvin. "*Bro, I have the shroud protected on me; my baby will protect what you asked her to. We got you in this. Thank you for your sacrifice, fam; this war isn't just about Society but it's about all of us. Retribution will be had. Let's get ready because my uncle is coming.*"

Marco's low growl: "*Punta won't be expecting this one.*"

Kali moved like the wind in front of Calvin. She held her hands out toward Sanna. Her eyes locked on Amara and Dare before cocking her head to the side. "*I need our two resident batteries, please.*"

Everyone moved around her including the High King, just in case they were being watched.

"I never thought I'd see those again, my children," High King Omri astonishingly whispered.

Currents of red henna covered everyone before undulating in and out then causing the nails to jolt in power. Calvin watched her furrow her brow briefly before a slow smile crept across her face. The fragile metal softly vibrated, illuminating then multiplying into many pieces, reforming, and shifting into red-tinted silver filigree-scribed bullets. Mystic verses etched the surface as they illuminated in purity. With the sound of the cork popping, the scent of bliss hit everyone, causing tears to fall in remembrance of why they existed.

Calvin watched each metal piece fall into his sister's hand.

"Here, everyone take as many as you can. I was able to form them into what we needed in the moment, which was, ta-da, bullets. My King, here's yours." Kali cautiously held out several bullets.

Calvin noticed the flicker of sadness in his eyes while he stared at the bullets before taking them with a bow.

"My thanks; now spread out. The war is here!" he yelled, backing away to sit in his throne waiting. "I take my place as Region King, High Elder of the North American Councils. Taint was allowed in and I expel it in holy righteousness. We stand today as the children of the Most High, and you all stand in the rightful armor of your ancestors as Sin Eaters and Disciples, as it should have been. Prepare for anything but don't expect less, my children."

Moving fast, Calvin glanced around, seeing the hall empty out. Bodies lay in calamity over chairs, tables, and the Council stage. A pricking sensation caused his heart to beat fast at the sound of more banging.

"Happy birthday," suddenly echoed in his mind.

Nydia was near. The countdown had started and mid-night was approaching. So far, he had stayed out of major fights but the stark realization that the war was now had his skin sparking.

The soft sound of Sanna's voice drew his attention and made everyone, including him, stop mid-step.

"Don't you all feel that?" she worriedly asked.

He noticed Khamun's amber eyes narrow then darken. His finger hooked around his tight collar and loosened it then pulled off his jacket.

"How is this happening? How can they step on blessed land?" Calvin heard Amara whisper.

She stood near San, taking off her rings and earrings. Kneeling down to whisper a spell that changed her clothes into jeans, multicolored pink Nike high-top shoes and a pink tank, she glanced up at her big sister, clearly nervous about her first fight.

Khamun gripped San by her waist and muttered to her, "I can send you back to the comp—"

"No! I'm standing by my family. We all need each other so I'm staying," she demanded, leaning up to kiss his lips.

Calvin watched Sanna turn to smile in love at her little sister, their hands touching and glowing.

The pounding and vibration of the building drew everyone's attention. Calvin changed his own outfit, opting for his standard Timbs, jeans, and beater. He pulled on his hooded leather and jean jacket, felt for his usual weapons and threw out several healing spells that worked on impact of a lethal injury around his family. Sweat trickled on the edges of his temple and the sharp jolt and hit of replenishing energy made him turn to look over his shoulder.

"I got you, cousin," Dare replied. His toffee dark skin seemed to illuminate with his power, casting a dark rich golden hue and he smiled placing his iPod ear buds in his ears.

Calvin reached out quickly to give his cousin a familial hug. Popping his ear buds in, twin silver guns appeared in his hands, and he waited for the coming.

"Wait!" San's voice echoed around everyone in the midst of them all changing clothes and the sounds of remaining Houses, who stood ready for war, suddenly murmured, "What is going on?"

"One sec, everyone, I have to ask. So, the second Elder San's father met in his travels gave her family protection. Keeping everyone hidden all this time, huh? Gifting her pops the nails of Nazareth, which Calvin died hiding to help us in this cause." Khamun studied his father's quiet form.

His fingers ticked off everything that led them all here while he spoke. "We learned in the books that the mythic crown the One Son wore, which was in reality bruises he obtained from being beaten, will always be hidden with the One Son for the true Armageddon. The fact that you said that it's been a long time since you've seen the nails means you're not a Nephilim that was reborn many times. Pops, who are you?"

"What do you see? Do you know who you and San are, my son?" King Omri countered.

"I see the Archangel Gabriel standing before me. A man I had understood to be my father, but who is much more than that: a legend in the flesh. Your aura gives you away, as does those arm tats and your true age, Pops. I also see the truth of my and Sanna's past. Something she unlocked in me recently. Thank you for what you did for us, what you and Michael both did," Khamun quietly responded.

Dr. Eammon, formally Bishop Steele in a past life, walked forward.

In his hand was a sword he laid over his shoulder. He stood at the High King's side indicating his place as the King's right hand, which was shocking to Calvin but respected. "It was my honor. We will talk later, but right now we all fight! Son, I am and I have never been so proud of my son then I am now," the King proudly stated.

Shouts from the soldiers who protected the entryway of the Town Hall ceased. Doors that bowed outward, ready to break, finally burst open as bodies of the soldiers flew into the Council meeting atrium. The hulking shadow of the Cursed King spilled across the floor. Dust cleared and Calvin did a double take. Glancing at Marco, then at the man before him, his shook his head then chuckled.

"Yeah, I know, acere, I am my father's seed; get over it," Marco griped.

Several rounds sounded from his gun, and then he ran forward, flanked by Ryo, who lifted in the air in his full Gargoyle state. Acting as his Protector, Ryo snatched demons, crushing them with his hands. Plumes of smoke mixed with fire turned demons into ash with just a blow from Ryo's mouth. Game time was on. Calvin glanced at his family, searing them in his mind, and then set his watch. His birthday was counting down and he had a fight to win.

"You kill my children for sport and you think that I will not do so in kind? Fair exchange is no robbery correct, brother? Ah, it's good to be home. Warriors, finish the rest but kill what should have been dead the moment I ripped him from his mother's womb!" Caius bellowed.

Damn, ran through Calvin's mind. Demons plummeted through the various doors. Nephilim warriors pulled back, bracing for impact of battle.

"Fair exchange was lost to you in the first war the moment you all chose to follow our brother Luc. You have no authority here," King Omri evenly stated, standing to meet the Cursed King head-on.

Calvin dropped down to touch the floor and tap on the spiritual grid to no effect. He inwardly cursed then chose a different route by creating a Mystic net and throwing it on teams of Cursed warriors. The smell of cooking flesh hit his nose the moment it touched them. A smile spread across his face then he pulled out his twin scythe blades, forward flipping to land on the floor in front of him.

"Grid is down here but I found out why!" Kali yelled in everyone's mind.

Calvin could feel his little sister running near the second level. Her power spread out causing him to see her flip over the shoulders of a hulking monstrous demon, big enough to be a rhino but stuck in the body of a man. Gashes appeared on the demon's body, his blonde hair with that of his brain in Kali's hand.

"I checked the monitors; the Cursed Lady used her blood and, get this, the Medusa's to shut the grid down like they did back in STL with San's land. But, check it again, it wasn't on purpose, it was a warning to us. The Cursed King had his Dark Witches and Warlocks kill our people, those missing Houses to break the barrier. I'm working to get it back up as we speak, over and out," Kali rushed out.

Calvin gritted his teeth pissed off. After all this, the Medusa was back and helping to bring the house down? Fuck a warning. She helped bring the barrier down, hell naw. Two human cops with peeling skin, disjointed limbs, and demonic teeth stood in front of him. Calvin quietly exhaled ready for battle. Cracking his neck, he flipped his blades in his hand and lunged forward. One shifted in his blind side to appear behind him. Leaning backward, knees bent, a swipe of nails narrowly missed his throat twice from both demons. Carnage flew everywhere. Calvin bounced back up to see how his scythe blades sliced off both arms of his prey. He then swung upward to circle and decapitate their heads. Writhing bodies twitched in front of him then exploded via a Mystic current from him. Chuckling, he patted his own shoulder then wiped the blade off.

Jogging across the room, his soul alerted him of the woman he had learned was his destiny. Anger flickered in his eyes while he watched her do her work. She called demons to her, pointing to take down Nephilim. Glee shined in her eyes as blood rained in the air. To the right of her was the Dark Lady who lassoed a woman by her neck, pulled her toward her, and then reached into her mouth latching on the woman's tongue. She yanked back in a harsh force, tearing it out in glee.

The sound of crushing loud barks drew in Calvin's attention. Her luscious body was draped in a white skintight body suit. Whoever documented that the Dark couldn't wear white knew nothing about the art of deception. Her cat suit was covered in interweaving filigree, Cursed magic placed there by the Witches of their kingdom Calvin could tell. His eyes skimmed over the words, noticing Winter's work, which let him know that it was created to protect her as she fought. Around her tussle of mahogany curls, which were pulled back into a ponytail that fell over her shoulder, was her familiar hood, this one the color of ruby blood.

Around her fists hands were barbed golden chains, each one connecting to her jeweled hand gloves, and connecting to four snarling beasts. Hellhounds. Each dog was white as the cat suit the princess wore. Their beady red eyes were hungry for Nephilim bodies. He could feel the Dark Lady's eager to let them feed.

"Popi is playing his game, don't you feel it, my pet? It's starting and I cannot wait to get my hands around that Oracle bitch's throat," Calvin heard her say to Nydia.

Calvin fumed. *There is no turning a bitch into a housewife,* ran in his mind. He was definitely ready to tackle them both on before being thrown backward by a Dark

Witch current. Coughing hard, his head lolled against the floor. The sound of the hellhounds being let loose drew in his attention.

Before Calvin was Amara running for her life. Each hound flanked her. He needed to get to her fast. Calvin struggled to get up but instead just stood in astonished. Miya flew near Amara swiping at the dogs. Shurikens flew from her hands, then bullets from her gun. Her golden eyes illuminated in their power then she threw a Dragon spell at a demon that tried to get in her way. Miya's diamond-sharp nails cut at flesh, digging deeply, before being struck down by a Dark Gargoyle. A scuffle went down in that moment. Both entities scrapped hard but it was Amara who made him know that she wasn't just going to go down without a fight.

A sharp scream belted from Amara's mouth. Her curly shoulder-length hair lifted in the air as static surrounded her. Her hand reached forward, fisted in the air, and pulled back with the sensation of her tugging on a tether. Calvin pushed up slowly, watching in shock. Time immediately slowed to the rhythm of her heart.

An ear-pounding thump, thump, seemed to wash her face in a sensation of calm as the objects in the air froze and then reversed. Calvin observed each bullet, each star that flew back toward her. He could tell she was assessing each object as Nox had trained her. She knew where they needed to go and with each blink of her long lashes, her eyes locked on the demonic dogs, then the bullets and stars reversed to hit their mark: the dogs.

Amara let out a heavy gasp, and then time sped back up. A force ricocheted from her in a pulse, which pushed the demonic dogs backward, sending them flying then bursting into splattered goo. Calvin saw her standing mouth gaped open in shock before she turned to glance at her best friend who stood just as shocked.

Both girls turned in unison then let out a high-pitched squeal while jumping up and down in unison. "That was crayyyyyyyyzeeee!"

"Sweet stuff, peanut, now take ya asses down through the tunnels." Calvin chuckled. He pushed up watching them turn then disappear in a wall of white light.

Calvin stood up brushing himself off, only to be hit with another blast. Flying across the floor he now lay in a pool of demon blood, almost choking on it as he gripped his sides. His lungs felt afire. His ribs threatened to break under the pressure of a pillar and the decaying body of a demon lay near him, blocking his view. Everything was messed up but he tried to keep his cool and listen to what was going on below him in the main council room. The Cursed King was playing his games. As soon as he had entered, he let everyone in the room know who he was.

"Stop moving. They will notice."

A clicking near his ear made his nails scrape at the pillar he had hit. Iodine and dry blood with the light new hint of fruit and honeysuckle made his jaw clench. His power sparked with the familiar scent and closeness of the person above him.

"You don't want my fucking help, bay'bee. You're doing this to destroy me," he growled.

He pushed again to let his power levitate the pillar to the side. The touch of the woman he had learned was his soul mate rested against his chest. Her usually patchy, scaled skin was now a flawless smooth mocha brown. Her eyes were still reptilian in coloring and look, but the rest of her took the last remaining piece of his breath away.

"Let me help. Here!" she grunted pushing the pillar with him. Calvin could see his aura connecting with hers and their power blending seamlessly. It felt invigorating, sensual, and intense. It scared him shitless.

He rolled to the side then felt her hand move away from his. As he pushed himself up to stand and wipe blood away from his mouth, thumbing his nose, he stared down to glance at her. Her smooth skin was now gone and she was back to what he always knew her as. The Medusa.

Her serrated tongue jetted out in constrained anxiousness. She pushed her razor braids out of her face in constrained frustration while looking around. He watched her hastily move to step back in order to look for anyone. When she saw none, she whirled around on him, her reptilian eyes narrowing at him.

"I told you. I'm on your side. I'm playing the game so this is not my fault! You all were supposed to get the warnings in time. Reina doesn't know she did it. We did it last night while she sleepwalked. Winter told me that she has been doing this for a while now since Winter and I woke up, so chill! I'm not the enemy, okay? I hate the Cursed as much as you and I meant my vow," was hissed in his mind.

Calvin's emerald eyes flashed in their brilliance. He snatched her wrist holding it tight before pausing. *"Hold up. How'd the fuck you get in my head like that? Huh?"*

He was dumbfounded and blinded by fear he shouldn't have had. For the first time in his life, he felt afraid, afraid of himself and at the whispers, his heart was voicing. He knew now that they were mated as one. What they shared wasn't just a random lay. This was a marking. He had spiritually marked her and she him.

Exasperation had him clutching his head to look at her in disbelief with a loud, annoyed groan. "Ah fuck me! *Beaucoup crasseux!*"

"Exactly! Now you get it, so pay attention please, big daddy. I need to stay near my mistress and keep her protected. You all have no idea what she has done. I . . . you need to help her or she will be that soul forever loss

because of you all, just like what happened to me!" Nydia pleaded.

She stood to the side of his view, using darkness to hide her from the flood of demons who were taking over the hall.

He could feel that his words had hit her hard and his mind could only reflect on that scared little girl who was ripped from her safety. The same girl who was his Fatima and who was ripped away in the same way. The hairs on his body rose and he heard the familiar ticking of his eternal clock. Calvin's gaze searched around for his cousins, then back at Nydia. Sacrifice was what he did and he now knew it was time to do it again.

"I'll do whatever. Just don't play me dirty," he quietly muttered with his eyes locked on her in reassurance then brief authority.

The look of love that flickered in her reptilian gave off a light brown cadence. She was beautiful perfection to him regardless of her exotic looks.

"Winter threw the fire. She used it as a cloaking for us all but as a means to keep the Cursed King clueless about what we are really going to do," the Medusa explained.

"And what are you really gonna do, shawty? Nydia?" he apprehensively questioned.

The appreciation she gave him with just a look from her eyes made him harden in that moment. He threw his own caution to the wind and stepped forward to snatch her by the back of her neck cutting off her reply. He covered her mouth in a heated claiming that was long overdue. Immediately, he was rewarded with the feel of her body melting against him in that rough embrace. The toughness of her softened and her lush thigh wrapped around the hardness of his ass. Her nails scraped over his jacket and the moment their tongue touched, it was an explosion.

He saw her soul spark to life in a blue white flame that covered them both. Her panting became erratic. Her own fear made her push at him, but he continued needing to recall that taste. The taste of the woman he had lost centuries ago and he felt it, making him pull back in a throaty groan.

"We're finally getting our lives back. I'll play my part while trying to distract her but I need you to trust me okay?" Nydia whispered against his ear.

Calvin gave a slow nod. Both hands rested against her small waist, he exhaled low, "Fatima. I'll do whatever."

"Then don't die on me." The sound of his Glock going off near his head made him look over his shoulder. The slumped body of a watching Dark Warlock left a black-red streak on the wall behind them caused them to let each other go. She held his gun in her hands with a sparkle of amusement in her eyes.

"Don't harm my family, protect them as your own and I'll hold you down, a'ight, bay'bee?" Calvin demanded.

Her sudden laughter was like music to his ears. He hadn't heard it in a long time and it made him take her hand to study each elegant and lethal finger. Her skin was soft again, scales gone. Who stood in front of him was nothing but a human-looking woman before him. A woman with power like his own and she nodded her head in acceptance. Around her kohl-lined eyes lay the markings of her tribe. Markings he recalled labeled her as a Royal oracle of her tribe. The brow-lining dots kissed her temples then ran down the side of her neck disappearing under her halter top. The marital insignias, he now recalled were what was on his own body, lay in the same spot as his own, over her ribcage. All this time, she was in front of him. The Most High definitely didn't play. Maybe this meant a new change.

"I'll take whatever I can, Calvin. I intend to prove myself to you, I mean it. Follow me; the Mad King has a plan."

Follow her he did. They moved toward the fight. His brothers and sisters were surrounding demons. He could see the Dark Lady enjoying herself, laughing while she flung Nephilim soldiers away from them like rag dolls. Bitch was still going to get hers, regardless of the fact that she was a sleeper spy. Everyone had to get his or her karma in order to get on the right track and he knew the Dark Lady's day was coming.

Chapter 23

The body of a Dark Gargoyle flew over Nydia's head, causing her to hunker down into a sliding duck. Ricocheting of flying bullets soon followed after with that of a reloading of a gun near her head. To the right of her, she saw Calvin taking down several demons, their bodies lighting up with his Mystic currents then exploding into miasmic mist. The inky fluid of their tainted souls lifted into the air to seek out the pull of the Reaper while he landed blows against the Mad King's skull.

In front of the King's reaching hands was that of a handsome Nubian male. His salt-and-pepper locks swung in the air, matching the Reaper's. His brown skin lit up in a cascading copper glow. Mighty wings sliced forward to cut into the Mad King. That angry warrior immediately found his face held by her Master, then rammed against the force of the Mad King's knee. Nydia knew she was staring at an Original one, an actual Archangel.

The town hall shook from the battle by the three angels she was watching. Several Nephilim came jetting her way. Like it or not, she knew they had to die. She was still who she was and no matter who or what got in her way, she was going to end their life.

Blades slashed toward her. Their weakness was her strength. Quick jabs had her able to twist her attacker by his arm. A prick of her poison nails had him collapsing on the floor. She had to play as if they were dead. If one of the Light Nephilim played to rough then it was lights outs for them permanently, which happened to be case for the one approaching her from behind. Dropping into a backward cartwheel, she propelled herself over the Nephilim woman's shoulder. Her hands reached out to cradle the warrior's head and twist to snap her neck. Landing into a low crouch, she pushed her braids out of her face to see that they also had made their mark.

"You might want to get up and continue to play the game, Medusa," quickly jarred her thoughts.

A pair of icy blue eyes sourly stared down at her, making her ready to fight again, but the attack of another demon saved it for another day. She watched the man she knew as Nox casually walk past her to send his large fists into a demon's ribcage. She spun up quickly to tackle another warrior. She knew her Mistress might be calculating her every move, so she made sure it lined up with her being Cursed.

Winter came to her side in that moment. The Witch gave Nydia a quick nod then moved to fight with Lenox. One punch from his fist into her stomach sent the Witch flying backward, with him following after her. The way they fought had Nydia thinking of her and Calvin, causing her to inwardly laugh. Hastily moving, she scoped a large area to see she was no longer in the Town Hall meeting chambers. Standing in a large atrium, Calvin's shape drew her attention and had her following him. He kept glancing down at her watch, which made her question what was going on.

"Why do you keep looking at your watch, Calvin?" she breathlessly asked into his mind.

"No reason, shawty, just my birthday is coming up soon. It's all good; handle your business and keep the demons from tracking me," she heard him reply before he disappeared behind a wall.

She ran, scaled a wall, and then brought blades down into a demon's back. Glancing behind her, she saw Reina pinned against a nearby wall by her brother. He whispered something to her that had the Princess screaming in a fit. Old instinct had her running to reach out to pull him off her.

She stood face to face with the Gray Prince. A sharp malicious edge of coldness caused her to shiver before she too was thrown backward against the wall. Her blades swiped at him to no avail. Blows she sent his way did nothing but hit solid muscle.

One comment from him had her staring in compliance before he eventually let her go: *"Nydia. Let me remind you of a little something, mami. As you are in my presence, you are still bound to me by the laws of lineage. As is my right as the still-living Prince of the Cursed, you are my pet as well. Don't worry about me killing my own sister. Apparently, it's not her time, so step back off me so I can help my family. Nod your head if you compute what I'm saying."*

She had no choice but to obey his command because he was right, but best believe she was going to show her ass. Once he let her go, she sent the flat of her boot into his back, heel connecting to the back of his head. He swiftly turned. His hand grabbed her ankle twisting it as he snarled. His once-hazel eyes were now swallowed by silvery gray. Where he touched, her ankle felt frost bitten in the moment.

"Tend to your mistress. You get one pass, punta, after which you will get no more from me. ¿Comprende? You have to prove your trust with me. Now back off," he growled in her mind.

Frustrated, she threw her hands up then let him walk off. She noticed the Dark Lady sat stoic before coming back to her reality to address her by holding her hand out.

"I see the Oracle. Let's go," Reina simply replied, all emotion disappearing from her gray eyes.

"As you wish, Mistress," Nydia muttered.

Taking Reina's hand, thunder shook around them in that moment of standing. As both women moved to run over thrown pillars, dust clouded their vision and the Mad King was slammed into the Council's stand. Laughter bubbled from within her, causing her to notice her Mistress's own glee. Sharply turning left, a large Dragon paw landed in front of them.

Ahead of them, Nydia saw Calvin snatch the Oracle down a passage. Cherry blossom tattooed skin drew her attention, then Nydia pulled back to cover Reina from Dragon flames. The one named Kyo blocked their way but Reina was too swift for both Nydia and Kyo. Inwardly cursing, she saw Reina slip pass, snatch at the back of the Oracle's head then disappear.

"Let me pass!" Nydia screamed at Kyo.

Anger blazed in the Dragon's mismatched eyes, but her dedication was to her own best friend. After a moment's pause, frustration caused the Dragon to return to her human state then let Nydia pass. The both of them ran through a dark passage that turned out to be a subway passage.

Lights from a CTA train whipped by. Its loud screeching had Nydia pressed against a wall. Darkness caused Nydia to adjust her vision. Before her, an Elder woman with red locks twirled a staff in her hand, taking down a Dark Warlock who could have been Trinidad James's twin.

Her staff lit up in the same color of her golden eyes, covering the whole tunnel area with her power. The moment her staff touched the railway, electricity washed through, to cleanse the tunnel way from demons. Pushing her burgundy locks out of her eyes, the Eldress noticed Nydia. Another elder woman in a cream pencil shirt with a short bob held a gun in her hand. Two bullets whizzed past Nydia to take out demons behind her.

Nydia sharply turned in shock, staring back into the mismatched eyes of the Oracle's Protector. "If you're going to be a part of this team, then you need to act like it. We all are letting you pass to handle your Mistress. Keep her from my sis, and we'll keep your back clear."

Respect flickered in Nydia's gaze before she took her window of chance to pass through the tunnel.

The sound of screams rent the air leading them on. Several Nephilim warriors fought off Reina, but Reina was too slick for their advances. Chains from her wrist bracelets wrapped around the necks of Nephilim warriors, decapitating them instantly. Their blood covered her bare hands, which she licked clean in satisfaction. The Oracle stopped her running to watch in anger. Invisible hands held Nydia back into the shadows, giving her no choice but to watch what was about to go down.

She watched the Oracle pull her hair back into a wild bun. Her hands opened then closed into twin fists before she stepped forward to handle business.

"I'm about sick of you coming at me as if you think I won't fight you. You might be insane but you are not crazy. I mean clearly you don't have any sense, but what you need to start understanding is that, one, you are lucky that I am being ordained to protect you. Second, that does not mean that you are not about to get an old-fashioned STL arse whooping, Reina. I know you dreamt about it," the Oracle spat out.

Sanna rushed forward, sending her Nike-covered feet toward Reina's stomach. Reina instantly grabbed the Oracle's ankle, twisting it then lifting her own leg up to kick the woman's waist causing her stumble backward. Nydia watched Sanna glance around as if searching for something to hit Reina with. She dropped down then picked up a broken metal silver rod that lay on a boulder at her feet. Once the rod was in her hands, the Oracle stepped back waiting, twirling it between her fingers, her honey eyes narrowing waiting on Reina's next move.

The sudden bristling feel of power sizzled in the train tunnels. Its intensity caused the hairs on every woman's arms to stand on end. Nydia's own nipples hardened and her breath came out in spurts from the thickness in the air.

In that moment, Sanna turned then lifted a hand in the air. The Witch fire that flew at her was instantly caught in her hand as if it were a baseball. Inky sparks of electricity tried to latch around her hand. Nydia was familiar with how a witch current felt. Its charge was always mucky with a slimy, watery feel. Quickly squeezing it, Sanna seemed to cleanse that sooty fireball then threw it hard, back toward its Warlock owner.

Nydia's head whipped around to see where it hit. She observed a male, with sandy brown locks, wearing a jean jacket with a hoodie attached to it, try to duck out of its way unsuccessfully. The sound of a prayer flowed around them. Reina closed her ears. She screamed aloud. The Oracle pointed at the Warlock and ripped his sins out. Nydia watched him fall to his knees, head back, mouth wide, screams rending the tunnel. Each sin wrapped around the Oracle's hand before she let go and let them flow like ash in the wind.

A rumbling sounded around them before the bulking forms of the Reaper, the Archangel, and the Mad King came tumbling down into the tunnels. Other Nephilim Elders, dressed in different-colored robes that she knew represented the regions they came from, flanked behind the battling warriors. Cement cracked, and then groaned to open up in a massive dark hole. The earth spit up more demons to fill the tunnel then attack. Metal sword hitting metal pipes clanged. Then Nydia felt herself suddenly released. She saw Reina take that chance to attack the Oracle. Nails slashed at the Oracle's face. The Oracle ducked, kicked, and then sent her pipe against Reina's head.

Running forward, Nydia saw Reina crumbled on the ground before she flung herself up with supernatural force then lunged toward the Oracle. Both women fell backward in the blow. Reina pinned the Oracle down then reared back bearing her fangs to bite down on the Oracle's neck. A sickening scream instantly echoed in the tunnel.

Screeching of another CTA train zoomed back drowning it out. Shock paralyzed Nydia in that same moment. Kyo, in her partial Dragon form, flew in the air. Her nails lashed down Reina's back slicing her open but Reina's power flung the demon backward. Nydia tried to step forward, but it was the Oracle's own power that sent Reina screaming backward into the Mad King himself.

Reina erratically shrieked, "What did you do to me!" repeatedly.

The Mad King turned his attention to the Oracle walking her way, but it was Calvin who stood in the way. Several rounds from a gun went off from Calvin's Glock. Kyo slammed her body into the Mad King. A male dragon, one Nydia remembered to be Ryo, covered Khamun as they both laid in on the Mad King. Blades pierced him but didn't stop him as he flung everyone out of the way but Calvin.

Nydia felt her stomach drop, in that moment. She saw the Oracle stand, eyes wide in power. Charges of light flung past Calvin's shoulders to send the Mad King into another tunnel. Calvin turned his gun on Reina blocking the Oracle, but it was too late.

Nydia watched them both go head to head. She yelled into Calvin's mind to stop but he would not listen. Her own false attempts at fighting him resulted in only fueling his anger. Nydia saw Reina snatch at him to disrespect him at every chance she could get before it was too late. A scream ripped from Nydia's throat as she flew forward. "Nooo!"

Then the sound of hissing bullets hitting flesh burned her ears before silence filled the tunnels with that of an eerie chiming of an old grandfather clock.

Ding. Ding. Bam!

The sound of a clock signaling midnight mirrored the end of his Light. The feel of the bullet that pierced his lung didn't hurt so bad. What hurt was the feel of the woman he had just gained back in this lifetime lying in a slump over his body. The scent of her sweet smell with a hint of that Cursed taint in her system made him cough up blood in anger. He had succeeded in protecting his family but failed in protecting his heart again.

This wasn't fair. This wasn't life.

Razor-inlaid braids fell around his face. The feel of a delicate hand in his own made him grunt in trying to stay alive but the slowing beat of his heart muttered that this was the end. Iridescent light washed over his senses making him look up at the ceiling. He prayed his family survived this battle because he knew now that since his love was Cursed her soul would never be with his own.

I'm sorry, Fatima.

He lay gasping for breath, his 'Nam dog tags pressed into his face. Calvin's mind shifted into rewind.

He had stepped into the line of death to protect his cousin Sanna who stood with demon ash raining around her from just her touch. He had seen Reina commit the ultimate sin of feeding from his loved one. He knew he had promised Nydia that he would protect her but the moment she laid hands on his fam he was done. That promise was instantly broken and he was not about to let that bitch kill his blood. He knew he had to get to her by any means necessary. The sound of Reina's wails intensified around him. Nephilim logic let him know it had to be due to her feeling the effects of San's blood in her system.

In that moment, he found himself locking eyes on Nydia who stood watching from afar rubbing at her collared neck. Everything was on rewind for him. He heard a demon approach him trying to stop him from what he knew he needed to do.

"What are you going to do, boy?" echoed behind him then he snapped.

His burnished rich skin sparked with his Mystic power and he called on the power of his ancestors and past lives to help him in this moment. The flip of his scythe had the sound of a demon's head rolling next to his feet. The image of the Cursed King lifting an Elder in the air and ripping him in two to throw the pieces toward Khamun made Calvin go off the deep end.

Boots crunched over pebble, broken glass, and stone. His fisted hands stayed near his side. He blocked Sanna from being hit by the Dark Lady. Nydia rushed to his side but he saw nothing but red as her blows came his way.

He focused on the Dark Lady and his arm lifted in the air to block Nydia's hits. In an erect stance, he twisted his arm up and down, dropping into a low crouch to duck under Nydia's kicks then slash of her razor tail. He heard her in his mind screaming for him to stop, to stay back, to not do what was blazing in his eyes. But all he could hear was the drums of his ancestors and the need to protect those he loved.

A whirling sound of Nydia's blade almost connecting against his chest made him step back then send a punch into her solar plexus. *"Step off, Nydia!"*

He saw her out the corner of her eye. She held her waist then chest, tears spilling down her eyes, pleading in his mind, *"Please, she'll kill you."*

"I'm prepared for whatever, cher." Love was his guidance, and the pain Nydia washed over him was almost hindering, but he pushed on.

Chanting, he called on a Mystic cage to hold Nydia back. He stepped to the Dark Princess who sat half covered in a loose bricks. Insanity in her eyes had Calvin standing his ground, keeping Sanna behind him. The pleas from Sanna's own voice couldn't stop him from what he knew he had to do. The fact that she shot charges at the Cursed King, then even at Reina made him proud in this moment.

The soft tug at his shoulder from Sanna had him quickly turn to hold her back, staring into her pleading eyes. "You are the Oracle, you are needed here. I'm not. Let me protect you, baby girl. This is what family does."

His cousin's tears fell like rain, which made him hold her tight one last time, before facing the enemy. Calvin watched the Dark Lady push herself up from the ground in a supernatural force to pull out her blade to go head to head with him. She jumped over his head in a quick leap to fall behind him land a hard blow into his back. He quickly sideswiped her by hitting her with a roundhouse kick, followed with a jolt of Mystic light.

His blow caused her to drop into a low crouch, pulling out twin blades in both hands. He saw that they were carved into the same asp that wrapped around her hands. Her fangs glinted in the light. Angling his body for the fight, he swore he saw a hint of white wings peeking from her cloak before she plunged both hands forward to slice into him.

The adrenaline boost Sanna had given him with just a touch kept Calvin going, not noticing that blood was saturating his stomach. He let his elbow connect to the side of her face. He heard Nydia screaming behind him. A slight lightheadedness made him stumble slightly, but he ignored it to land another hit to the Dark Lady's face.

"Hey, wodie, you think you're a bad bitch, but watch this." Calvin stepped forward to overtake her space.

A sharp pain at his side caused him to hold his stomach. He quickly realized that he must have been hit, so he used a Mystic spell to hold himself together to continue his fight. He reached behind him then pulled out his twin scythes to slash at Reina, cutting her arms. Sending her flying backward into a wall, that exertion of his power had him spent. Sweat fell down his face. The cage that held Nydia up gradually weakened. He needed to get to his Qua gum, but his world was suddenly tilting.

He felt himself stumble backward. Felt the warm feel of liquid leaking from his side, due to his continued blood loss. The holding spells weren't lasting and he was slowly deteriorating.

Shit, he was only human, in a sense, wisped in his mind.

His hand reached behind him to brace himself, leaving behind a bloody handprint on the tunnel wall near him.

The sound of a gun made Calvin glance to where Reina had fell. He watched her push back up pointing a silencer his way. "Looks like I am a bad bitch, homie."

A scream propelled him backward; light pooled over his body. As he fell to the floor, he saw the quick flash of the Medusa running in front of him. His heart suddenly sparked with his power and he threw it her way in the form of a Mystic cloak to protect her as the bullet hit his chest. The cries from his sister in his Bluetooth made his soul weep. He could feel and hear the roars from his brothers, as well as warriors who were aligned to his house. He had met his destiny in one shot.

In his arms flew Nydia. She jettisoned in front of him, trying to block him from the hits, slashing at charging demons. Her nails became blades. She was the Jaguar princess he remembered in their shared past, Fatima. He watched her take down two burly males with glowing black eyes, ripping then shredding them like meat. Nydia quickly turned to lock eyes on Reina and she frantically held her hands out. More bullets rained from behind Nydia toward the Oracle and in front of Nydia as she turned to cover him.

The sound of bullets hitting his flesh echoed into the tunnel while another train went by.

Ding. Ding. Bam!

"Calvin!" he heard her scream.

He saw the confused look on the Dark Lady's face while that bullet took him down. He didn't realize that Nydia too had been hit until he felt her heated body cool.

"Nydia!" he roared, choking on his own blood. Pain tore through him. Her blood mingling with his own made his nostrils flare in agony.

Her quiet voice softly ebbed against his ear. "We've loved each other before our love was darkened and torn from each other. I saw you die many times, and mourn me in every life. This time, it's my turn to do something for us. I'd rather be the one; there's no saving me, but, please, let the Reaper destroy whatever is left. Please don't let me die with a chance of being reborn back on their side."

As the bell chimed, he couldn't say anymore. Blood clouded his throat then spilled from the corner of his mouth. His eyes glazed over and he glanced at the ceiling mouthing Nydia's true name one last time before turning his head to take one last look at his cousin and his family.

Chapter 24

The taste of blood was in his mouth. He could smell the burning singe of Witch fire eating at his pants and shirt making him quickly pat them to put out the fire. His ears were ringing from the force and his eyes were slightly blurry from leaving a crater into a nearby wall. Bitch had come up on his blind side. Khamun spit out grit from the dust and residue of crumbled rock that made it into his mouth. War was here and it was wreaking havoc on the Nephilim community that protected the council hall.

"Khamun! Can you hear me? I can't link because you're too far away," sounded in his Bluetooth. A searing burning from the dust around him ate at his lungs. *"Khamun!"*

A rock lay on his stomach, holding him down. The weight of the world was compounding him. His mind was ticking going over everything in slow replay. The Cursed King was succeeding.

He had wiped out a large number of Nephilim who were here for the general council meeting. Several High Elders were strung across pillars, hanging as if decorative pieces of artwork. His father and Dr. Eammon were going head to head with the Cursed King, holding him off. They worked at draining him of his energy as best as they could without the help of any Nephilim teams. He was impressed. Now it was up to him, Sanna, and their House to finish this thing.

The sound of ringing made his mind focus on Calvin. His boy was on his last leg. He could feel it and he was working with the enemy and taking down massive demons that seemed to be drawn to him. Khmaun could taste Sanna's fear immediately and it fueled him to fight harder. *Our kind is not born with fear, baby.*

With a grunt, Khamun sunk his nails into the gravel under him and pushed up. *"Yeah, I'm here and I'm good. Just was winded by Winter. Lenox, handle that. I don't have time to be distracted by her bullshit."*

"I'm already on it, man. Over and out," Lenox quickly responded.

The sound of metal making contact with each other had Khamun turning to see where the fight was originating. Teams of Nephilim, men and women, Houses of fighters who stood behind him and his own House were going head to head. The sound of grenades shaking the great hall, automatic guns, swords, and other weapons made Khamun feel as if he were in WWII and 'Nam. That brought his mind back to Calvin.

"Hey, Cal. Where you at?" Khamun tapped his Bluetooth and stood up. A hand from a fellow Nephilim royal helped him crawl out of the hole he lay in.

"I'm here, taking down these punks. Nydia is on our side; just keeping her covered and making sure she still looks like she's on their side, ya feel me?"

Time was of the essence. He quickly thanked the gruff buzz-cut brown haired guy who was covered in demon blood and gave him dap. The guy sported a rugged beard. His almost-violet eyes gleamed with power and the fangs he sported made Khamun nod in utmost respect. He was a warrior-class angel like himself but the scales that ran over his shoulders marked him Gargoyle as well and that blew Khamun away because he never heard of a Gargoyle and non-Gargoyles actually mating. Yes, they may fall in love but it was usually short-lived, never producing offspring, he was told as a child. From the male's tags on his fatigues, he could read that he was from the Atlanta house. A rogue team who had just recently came up to seek an alliance with his House.

"Thanks, man, much respect," Khamun quickly replied moving to a darker area of the room he now was in.

"Not a problem, brother. Watch your back. We have you covered above, below and around you," two bandaged, glove-covered fingers lifted in the air signaling where his team members were flanked.

Taking in the intel, Khamun rushed out the crumbling tunnel. Gunshots rang in Khaumun's ears. *"Just checking, man. Make sure you keep your back flanked, a'ight? Hello? Calvin? Bro! Hello?"*

A whizzing of bullets zipped past him. The slight sparking of the land's grid let him know Kali had handled her business. However, the fact that Calvin wasn't answering him was pushing on his nerves. He stood facing the devil's chosen leader, his uncle Caius. His father and future father-in-law both were under a wall of bricks due to being thrown there by the King. However, now, the feeling that his brother-in-arms had just possibly been hurt had Khamun shifting back and forth.

"Good look with that grid, Kali?"

Kali's voice chimed in. He connected with her quickly and could see her sitting around monitors with Amara, Dare, Take, and Miya around her. Amit was running back and forth, jetting out of the control room, and coming back covered in black-red blood. Gray charges of light sparked from his forearm and fist, something Khamun wasn't expecting.

"We keep getting blasted by demons," Kali quickly replied. *"Amit, Take, and Dare have us covered. We are on our way down. Something happened to Calvin, Khamun. Something happened."*

"*I feel it too, little sis, I'm trying to get to him but . . .*"

"*I know. Keep prayers up. I'm out; watch your back please,*" Kali's desolately requested. Her voice was choked with tears. Khamun knew whatever it was that happened with Calvin was life changing.

Khamun quickly took to the air, taking down demons with a glance from his eyes. He fed quick and discharged what he could. Demons ran from his touch whenever he was near. His fangs ripped into the flesh of many. Their essence filled his mouth, but a reprieve that they would not get and a lifelong punishing prison trapped in the body many of his enemies had taken over was his judgment.

The sound of the Cursed King's reverberating voice echoed from under the rumble of the tunnel. "Your Oracle is saucy, I give you all that. Once I have her, I intend to teach her exactly how a woman should behave when her man is fighting, *¿comprende?*"

I'll kill you first, ran through Khamun's eyes.

If he thought that Khamun would allow him the satisfaction of the day to get near San, then the fucker was shitting gold. Khamun's eyes flashed dark as oil in that moment. There was no chance that was going down. None. Not in any lifetime. Moving as fast as he could, he froze as words hit his peripheral. The knowledge of his past lives, and the lives of all Nephilim, contained in the book he had only just found, slammed into him hard. Voices echoed around him.

"*Understand and use the knowledge. King is yours to take down, not mine. Be strong, son,*" his father encouraged.

His skull throbbed, almost ripping in half and he saw Sanna's face within that moment smiling at him. He understood her pain in that moment. He had to kick-start the awakening again. He had to charge the books.

Determinedly glancing around, he remembered the mural in his home. It had pointed him to a flaming sword, one that was in the arms of the statue before him. He had never noticed it here, sequestered in this quiet hall, but today was not time for questions. Sprinting forward, he lifted in the air, his wings allowing him to fly up in an arch, back to the council room.

A statue stared him right in the face, staring at him in authority. Its black marble arm held sword out to him, which Khamun respectfully took. The Archangel Uriel appeared to kneel before him. His white robes turned black and Khamun saw his beating heart spilt into many sections. Sections that burned brightest in a vibrant color matched his aura. He also saw the silhouette of a woman with wings that matched Khamun's. She felt familiar and her face blazed before in awareness then the body of Uriel merged into hers before disappearing. The creator of the Sin Eaters.

He was blown away. Taking the sword, he felt his power blaze bright then light aflame. The council hall seemed to vibrate with his power and he heard Sanna's roar in his mind. She was ablaze and he could see it without even seeing her. She shouted her command to him, which ticked him off. He had other plans for his uncle, but now he was being told something else. He had a choice to make.

The chaotic power from the Cursed King quickly shunted out the resonance he had kick-started. Darkness crept over the council hall, eating at the remaining light that fought against it. The groaning sounds of what he could decipher as trapped souls reached out to him in pained, devoid suffering. Everywhere he moved was as if Khamun had triggered a live mine. His wings pressed against him to shield him from falling bodies, blood, organs, and debris.

Ryo's voice tapped his mind. He glanced up and saw the Dragon bulked into his true dragon form. He held a hybrid of a man and a demon by the throat walking him backward. His diamond-hard nails shredded at the monster's face peeling it off before dropping his head to rip its throat out with his own mouth. Ryo's tattoos seemed to swirl lifting with words Khamun couldn't unlock. Yet, while he dropped the demon and pointed his Glock at other entities in the reaching dark, rounds sounded around them both and he held his arm out, holding a blade in his free hand.

Ryo chucked his head back to usher Khamun on. *"I don't know what you did, dude, but I'm amped. But check it, hurry, the King is coming. I have you covered."*

"Thank you, bro," he quickly yelled. Entering the tunnel, Khamun stopped. Calvin stood near a floating Sanna. His brother was translucent but solid as rock. Khamun knew Calvin was no more, but even beyond the grave Cal was going to fight for his family. Calvin kept San behind him and away from the King. A smile played across his brother's face the moment his twin scythes flipped back and forth.

"So you want my fam, huh? Gotta go through me, patna, before I let that one happen because this right here is divine; you can't touch her," Calvin taunted. Mystic magic flowed from his fingers. Statues that adorned the secret tunnels came alive to rush the approaching Cursed King in a running tackle to hold him down to the ground.

Khamun moved fast holding his blazing sword. Face to face with his uncle, his blade almost made contact with the Cursed King, but was immediately halted by a dark current blast from the King, sending him falling into a heap.

Marble broke and cracked.

The Cursed King roared and lifted from the ground in full demonic Fallen form. His menacing wings systematically broke down statues that continued to reach out for him. Other of his Cursed kind came forward and helped battle those statues that still clamored to trap the King.

"Don't even think that I would allow you all to take me down so easily. The blade of Uriel can't touch me, pup!" his uncle hissed.

The Cursed King rested in a one-kneed crouch surrounded by demons. He glared at Khamun with blood-red eyes. Wiping at his mouth, his uncle disinterestedly brushed off his jacket then spoke. "Maldita Sea. Blasted! You're like a roach. Give me what is mine! Your Society is now extinct, thanks to me, accept it, and hand me the Oracle, boy!"

In that moment, Ryo landed hits against the jaded King. Blade fighting sticks appeared in the Dragon's hands. He leaped in the air to slam them into the King's shoulders, penetrating his shoulder blades. Blood flew in the air, splattering like paint against the walls. The King roared pissed but also distracted.

Khamun's eyes glanced at Sanna. She no longer was floating but standing near Kyo, both women watching with blades in their hands. Sanna's beauty, even in this moment, fed him and reminded him of his purpose to protect his family. Sweat ran into his eyes, making him wipe it away with the back of his hand then push his spilling locks back. He flipped his wrist to turn the flaming blade in his hand. His other hand rested on the Glock that held the blessed bullets within their chamber.

"Miss me with that crap, Uncle! You know what I want? I want to peel your flesh from your body and crack your chest open, that's what I want," Khamun crooned.

The clang of his spinal blade with its serrated edges hitting the Cursed King's own red-tinged sword drew everyone's eyes their way. Sweat rained down his massive body. Khamun's arms strained from the weight of the Cursed King's blows making him clenched his jaw in his adrenaline rush.

His forearm made contact with Khamun's face. The blow as like a pile of bricks had fallen onto him and he found himself on his back. Pain reared his head and the Cursed King's blade made contact with his shoulder going clean through and connecting to the floor. Caius held a finger up, wagging it in his face as he looked down at him.

Kneeling down to grip on to Khamun's locks, the Cursed King forced his face toward Sanna before growling low then pointing her way. "Mira, wait right there. I want you watch this, nephew."

Sanna lifted in the air and flew toward him. Her eyes widened and she screamed. However, it was a second scream that made him smile. Her beautiful *kila* blade rang in the air then made contact with the King's broad chest. Black oily blood coated them both. His uncle's grip loosened causing Sanna to fall backward to her knees. Khaumn proudly watched her scramble up and move to the side.

Khamun knew he had to use this open window fast. Fisting his hand around the blade in his own shoulder, he pulled hard. A roar ripped from his mouth and he turned to the side to see the King standing back up again, Sanna's blade now at his feet, Khamun hustled placing a healing spell, created by Calvin, over his wound cauterizing it. Blood pooled around his hands. He remembered the spells and history he had learned in his books. Spelling out different runes, he clapped his hand against the floor underneath him and he went flying in the air ramming the Cursed King backward.

Khamun surged his fist forward. The back of it made contact with the evil King's face. As he felt the force of the punch against his uncle's face, Khamun was shocked at how much Marco didn't look like the King. They shared the same eyes and jaw line as well as the same cinnamon skin, but the rest reflected the appearance of the woman in his dreams: his aunt. Something within caused Khamun to glance around, noticing the bodies of both Calvin and the Medusa. Strangely, Calvin's spirit still cloaked Sanna helping Kyo fight off demons that came Sanna's way.

Fury fueled him and made him drop into the Reaper. An ominous smile crept across his face. "Psst, let me tell you something."

A force of power from Khamun sent the King backward deep into then through a wall in front of Ryo. His dragon let out a roar, wrapped his tail around the Cursed King, and then slammed into an open pipe in the ground. Dragon flames mixed with that of Khamun's own ominous power covering the evil King in a blanket of divine flames. The charred scent of fire left everyone transfixed and in awe. Khamun stood in his full Sin Eater form. His eyes were black, his skin shimmering with his flaming aura, which connected with his sword and lit it with celestial fire.

"Death is upon you. I am what goes bump in the night. I am your last breath. I am the last thing you see. I am at your birth and I am at your end. Your sins are mine, Uncle, and your fallen soul will burn with the devil's," Khamun icily taunted.

Sanna felt the close blow of a blade near her neck, then the sideswipe and a punching slap. She ducked low, spinning on the balls of her feet and punched forward then upward. The blunt of her knuckles made contact with a stomach and then a face. A feminine grunt sounded and the sound of a body hitting brick had Sanna stepping backward. Trying to regain her equilibrium, she looked down and saw Reina lying before her. Her rich mahogany mane was neatly pulled back into a ponytail, the end of it spilling like velvet ink next to her.

Even after taking down her cousin, the harlot had the nerve to still come after her? Lessons were about to be taught. Sanna licked her lips and clutched her fists. Instinct roared for her to protect herself from assault. Logic screamed death was not going to happen to her today.

Rushing forward Sanna sent her Nike-covered feet toward Reina's stomach. Reina instantly grabbed her ankle twisting it and lifting her own legs up to kick Reina's waist causing her stumble backward. Sanna glanced around her to look for something to hit the crazy chick. She dropped down and picked up a broken metal silver rod that lay on a boulder at her feet.

She slammed it hard against Reina, pinning her down back where she has sat in shock. Heated power shifted the steel pole in Sanna's hands, turning it into a chained invisible platinum collar. Sanna clamped it down around Reina's throat then dropped close enough to the woman's face to catch the slowly budding sparks of awakening in her eyes.

Sanna could feel the bristle of power sizzling around them both. It caused the hairs on her arms to stand on end. Her body tensed and her breath came out in spurts. Sanna turned and lifted a hand in the air. Several blessed bullets made from the nails flew into Reina's shoulder, thigh, and hand.

The searing slice of pain at Sanna's neck paralyzed her in the moment stopping her in her tracks. She couldn't believe this was happening. The pulse of her life suddenly was beating away, each drop at a time. Before her in piles of bodies lay her family, just as she had saw in her dreams, fighting with many other Nephilim warriors.

Reina had killed her cousin. Reina had stood there and shot him with no remorse. No iota of respect to the ounce of Light that coursed in her blood. She sat and let that bullet also penetrate the woman who was once her Medusa but who now lay over her cousin in human form as Nydia. Tears spilled down her cheeks as she held the back of his neck. The grave sound of chiming continued.

"You killed them. You killed my family!" Sanna forced out. Anger was blinding her. The whispers of the Most High's commands guided her.

Reina lay in utter shock. Blood spilled from her wounds. Her hands were cut from digging them on the floor, which was littered with broken glass and other sharp objects. The scent of silver was in the air from the Nazareth bullets having gone off. The Cursed King's blood was over her body and Sanna slapped a bloody handprint against Reina's face, pushing her cheek into the ground.

"I said, you killed my family. Calvin; even your own precious pet! What do you have to say? Reina." Sanna spit out between her teeth.

"I . . . Nydia. Nydia! You killed . . . I killed . . ." Reina slowly stammered.

Sanna narrowed her eyes, watching the Dark Lady closely. The sparks of light in the woman were almost gone, but with knowledge, there is always power and those sparks started to brighten. "Exactly. You betrayed family again. You allowed your father to manipulate you, yet again in this life. Are you grasping at what I'm saying?"

Reina hissed out, trying to slash at her but Sanna sent a surging fist near the side of Reina's face before slapping her hard. Wrapping a hand around the woman's collared throat, Sanna's honey eyes blazed as if they were fire. Pain swallowed Sanna's spirit, making the emotions she was feeling raw in anguish. The sudden power of the ancestors from all Nephilim ripped through San's body and she felt herself snatch Reina's life force. The sounds of heightened screams made tears fall faster down her caramel skin, her voice becoming ominous in its seriousness.

A cold calmness settled over her and she solemnly muttered into her enemy's mind, *"Feel my blood within you. Feel it connect with the nails of Nazareth. Do you feel it restoring and cleansing what was tainted? Showing you the truth of who you really are? You are not his child. Your brother is not his. He betrayed him all and now you will do the same. Remember your promise; remember who you are!"*

The room darkened. Everyone stopped their fight, then silence filled the chamber. The click and sharp sizzle of the grid being pulled online made every remaining demon run.

"Grid is back on. Sanna do it!" Kali yelled in her earpiece.

With a simple, smooth fluid motion, Sanna slammed her fist back into Reina. Pillars, walls of art, floor panels, and the eyes of every Light Nephilim in the room lit up with the power that she sparked into the grid. She wanted this over, right now. Reina's screams echoed in her mind as light swallowed the woman, then sent her back to her Cursed Kingdom.

Khamun drew her attention the moment he dropped to one knee her way in reverence then stood to position himself over a burning Cursed King. Everything erupted in that moment. Sanna connected with Khamun's and Ryo's fires. She listened to the Fallen angel scream then pull himself from the wall in flames. What were once cuts that lined his chiseled face were now exposed flesh. His all-black tailored-cut Italian suit was shredded, covered in fresh and dried blood, instantly blazing in flames. The bulked strain of his muscles caused his suit to fall to the ground then he lifted a hand and blasted Khamun with his power.

"Your efforts are nothing! I am Caius, Fallen Vessel of Bernael. I will continue to reign!" the Cursed King raged.

The deplorable sound of bones crunched in Khamun's body with the clutch of the King's fist made Sanna's stomach lurch. She stepped forward to help but the drowning yell from his voice in her mind, telling her to stop, kept her in her place. Sanna moved away from a pinned Reina to quietly rush to Calvin and Nydia's unprotected bodies. Khamun stayed lifted in the air, contorted in pain. His attempt to show no pain slowly broke the longer the King held his grip on him. Ryo fought to get to Khamun but he too was quickly hit in his throat, and then slammed backward into weakening wall.

Sanna screamed. She wanted to go head to head with the King but her dreams kept playing over in her mind and flooded into this reality. The Cursed King stood on the dead bodies of Nephilims who fought against him. The floor was a sea of their blood with that of the Cursed who hadn't dissolved into mist yet. Pieces of body parts haphazardly lay mangled in different areas of the room and captives were hanging by their arms in chains. She felt helpless in the moment, fighting with herself to help Khamun, but it was Marco who stepped forward that made the breath catch in her throat.

Twisting Khamun until another snap of bone echoed in the room, the Cursed King snarled out, "You come any closer and your cousin is dead, *hijo. Any* of you come forward and his blood will spill. Now, where was I?"

A deep, devoid laugh erupted from Marco. He calmly walked forward. The sound of Khamun's scream ripped through Sanna's heart.

"You think that's going to stop me from taking you down, *Padre?* Waited a long time to decapitate you with my own hands; aren't you ready for that too?" Marco cajoled.

Sanna watched in shock. Marco's icy aura made the King lock on to him as if in a trace. His outstretched hand slowly relaxed the longer he stared into his son's silver iced eyes causing Khamun to almost gradually fall to the floor.

"*Sí,* it's beyond time that we had that father-son reunion," the Mad King muttered in amusement.

"Indeed." Marco hunkered down and ran forward. Twin blades appeared at his wrists.

The King seemed to wait for the hit then moved his hand in front of him, using Khamun's body as his shield.

Sanna's screamed out, "No!" but the battle continued.

Marco made smooth, calculated moves to dodge every blow the King made Khamun's body maneuver. He turned to move into the Mad King's blind spot, landing a blow to his father's face with a spiraling air kick.

Sanna could instantly see that Marco has assessed every weakness the King had and she honed in on to them herself.

When the King was using his power, he left his back open and the side of his body where his arm was outstretched. It took Marco only a few distracting moves to push his blades longer and slide up to jab a silver blessed blade into the Cursed King's ribcage. That act resulted in the King bringing his fist down into Marco's skull and planting his foot into his chest.

The ringing of a gun from behind the Cursed King caused him jerk forward with the impact. He released his grip upon Khamun and fell on to his knees. The Cursed King pulled at the blade that was lodged in his ribcage throwing it at Marco and sending him flying into several watching demons. He rubbed at his throat, a thin line of blood forming from where he wasn't even aware of Marco cutting him.

The King roared. All around him shook. A static charge of heat emitted around the room and dead Nephilim began lifting from the ground, their skin grayed and peeling off.

"Did you all see that? I need backup; our Prince needs backup. Do everything you can to keep his and our Oracle's backs clear as they handle business. Take the demon's heads, blow out their hearts, and line it with locus tracers. Nox out!"

The clamoring noise of the battle ensuing in the great hall spilled into the street of the Nephilim stronghold as teams tried to keep the enemy from destroying whole building. Sanna watched every soldier still fighting, including Elders, Council Elders, and dignitaries, break apart and head after the roaming corpses. The sound of Khamun's laughter brought her attention back to her beloved. His locks fell over his face in a crinkled mess. He used his fists to push himself up to slowly stand in a predatory state. Flames covered his body, healing the bones that were once broken.

Tilting his head to the side, he raised a finger in front of him and tsked. "I've been feeding and now your ass is under a pile of shit. This healing right here isn't nothing but a thing. What about you?"

Rocks, broken beams, and then rubble began to groan then shake. A loud burst and a roar from the King had him escaping from his cage. Lifting in the air to fall in a low crouch on top of the mound, the Cursed King growled and held his hand up motioning for Khamun to come to him. "You have effectively gotten on my nerves!"

Charging toward the King, Khamun ducked under his enemy's massive arms then swung his sword. Metal made contact and hit his back, pulling out two daggers to pierce the Cursed King's sides. Caius glanced around thinking nothing of the wounds as he too ran forward toward Khamun again to attack, slicing at Khamun's chest. A satisfied smile flashed across his face and he licked the blood he collected from Khamun's wounds with his jagged nails.

"*Delicioso*," the Cursed King taunted.

Khamun gave a warrior's cry then met the King head to head. The decision Khamun had to make was instantly chosen. Sanna could read the judgment and animosity in her beloved's dark eyes. He turned the Dark Lord's own sword on him then sliced from the side of the neck and downward through his chest. The glorious sound of the bastard's blood falling on the land made him step back then grab the King by the face staring into his crazed eyes as he gagged on his own blood.

Sanna could tell that Khamun knew that would not be enough for something created by the devil himself, but he decided to have fun anyway. She watched Khamun rip the King's jaw, letting it hang and watching it mend itself. Pushing the King onto his face, he walked away, saturated in blood with a fanged smile on his face.

"You and yours have been trialed and judged. Do you have anything to say before your sentence?" Khamun grumbled.

They all watched as the Cursed King stood, madness still fueling him making his broad shoulders shake in laughter. "Until we meet again?"

Before he could mist off, Sanna gasped then smiled.

Khamun turned quick as a cobra and snatched the Cursed King by his leathery wings ripping them from his back. Khamun yanked hard to pull the Cursed King against him then grabbed him by his throat. With one motion, he punched his fist through the King's spine. It exited through his broad, scorched chest. Groans of a thousand souls wailed around them. Hands seemed to reach out begging for help, for release. Khamun's wings stood erect from the force of it all. His head dropped forward, fangs extended, and then he tore at the Mad King's neck. The sins he drank were too much for him at that moment and Sanna could tell.

"Wound him; he'll meet his death soon, Khamun," she hastily commanded him. Khamun had fed from too many and this could be too much she feared, so she had to act fast before he became sick physically.

His grip on the King grew tighter and as he began to shake. "I got this."

The wails of many souls surrounded them all causing a tornado of debris, blocks of marble, brick, and other items. Khamun's growl echoed in her heart. She connected to him to give him her all. Fire erupted then she watched Khamun's sinisterly grin. "Burn . . . in . . . hell!"

With a rip of his hand, the King hollered. Demonic hands reached for his contorting body, pulling him to the gates of hell down the midnight-dark tunnel. White light washed over everything sealing the tunnel. A lump caught in Sanna's throat. Reality instantly hit her. Calvin.

Kneeling over Calvin's and Nydia's lifeless bodies, she glanced up to see her cousin's soul watching her. He stood in his warrior attire from Africa. War paint covered his toned body. His weapons were in both hands, covered in sizzling demon blood. Near his side, stood Nydia, a woman who took Sanna's breath away.

She laid a hand against Calvin's arm watching Sanna in a regal queenly state. Matching tattoo glowed in power. Her long braids were no longer lined in blades, but now lined in conch shells. Polished maple-brown skin decorated in warrior paint replaced reptile scales. Nestled between each fingers were demon blood-covered bladed claws with that of a sword in her left hand. Tears lined Sanna's eyes. The feel of Khamun behind her let her know that he saw them too. They had protected everyone. Nydia had shown her worth. The quick sound of guns cocking made Sanna looked up.

Lenox stood wide-legged, icy blue eyes glinting with anger with two barrels pressed against the skull of their emissary's red hair. "This is the third time I was present at his death. I'll always have his back. Back away, witch."

Winter held her hands up, tears falling. "Please, Lenox, is she really . . . is she gone?"

Sanna couldn't say anything. Her heart was torn apart. Her cousin had died. Nydia lay over his body, their hands entwined. The pulse of their hearts was no more; the tether of their souls was fading from her. Sanna gently moved Nydia by Calvin's side, keeping their hands together.

Winter whispered again, visibly in pain, "Is . . ."

Frustration bubbled up in Sanna, which had her taking it out on Winter. "Yes! Now it is your duty to remind your mistress of what she owes us and when she awakens, you know what the hell to do. Get out of our faces. Go!" Sanna covered her eyes with both hands.

Tears spilled through her fingertips, lighting up both bodies in her hurt. The trembling touch of Winter's hand on Sanna's shoulder had her sending a mental flash of orders. At that same moment, Lenox's protecting presence shadowed them as Kali's screams echoed in the chamber.

Kali ran and fell over Calvin's body, her cries of pain cutting through everyone. Winter's sad sapphire eyes locked with Sanna before disappearing.

Khamun's loving touch and words gave Sanna's strength in the moment. She watched him go to one knee to pick up his fallen brother. "We give him honor."

Sanna sat choked up. All she could see was her dead cousin before she quietly requested, "Please, take her with us too. She sacrificed herself for them both."

Khamun solemnly nodded picking the Medusa up, then sending them all back to the Council chambers. Once there, Khamun laid them side by side on a wide marble table, respectfully keeping their hands together.

Kali's pleas continued. "He made it past his birthday. This can't happen. Please do something please, please."

Her painful words hit Sanna repeatedly. The sound of the chiming clock echoed again, again, and her third eye opened. Voices of the Elders in her present and past flooded her mind. Her dreams with the knowledge of the books caused the language of the First Chosen Fallen to spill from her lips causing her body to shake. Everything she had experienced played in rewind. The spirits she saw, the books, the sacrifices made, and she locked eyes with Khamun.

Water from the fountain of Eden rained over everyone, drenching them in its healing balm. Rays of beams from the rising sun caressed broken glass, cascading flickers of light within the hall. Khamun dropped to his knees. Tears rimmed his bloodshot eyes. He studied the body of his fallen brother and the woman at Calvin's side as they lay as if in a deep sleep. His spinal blade rested against his back, ebbing with its power to rapidly connect with his aura then swirl 'round his muscle-tensed arms.

Sanna could see he was scanning for something. His head would occasionally look around pausing on the spirits of Calvin and Nydia. His hands moved around, reaching out as though putting something invisible together and into him before glancing up. Back in command, Khamun pointed at everyone in the room, directing everyone to stand at Cardinal points. Exhaustion had him running both hands down his face, and wearily pulled his locks into a ponytail.

Battle worn, blood from his wounds slid down his taut arms and sides dripped to the floor. His eyes settled on Sanna before he fisted his hands then whispered, "Blood to blood. Brother to brother. Sister to sister. Mother to father. The Light is our binding and let no man or demon tear us asunder."

Sanna felt their spiritual connection strum like a guitar string, causing her to feel as if she were bathing in bliss. Knowledge from anon ominously spilled from her lips and she bowed forward, her dripping wet mane falling into her angelic face. "What was broken shall now be healed."

"As so it is said, so shall it be. From the Most High blessings will fall," Khamun earnestly stated.

Both knew what was being asked from them. The hope of the Nephilim race lay in their hands; their rebirth was on the cusp of this war. Hands entwined, San glanced at everyone.

Both she and Khamun signaled to their Dragons. As Sanna watched her sister Amara hand her the Shroud of the One son, she, her brother, Take, and Kyo gently covered Calvin and Nydia's resting bodies in respect as his family.

Sanna placed a hand over the lovers' entwined hands. Her fangs ripped from her gums. The sound of Khamun hiss let her know that he was also ready for the next step. Khamun's beautiful mahogany flesh glowed copper, matching that of his watching father. His amber eyes simmered like heated embers and his body bulked more. The future was now and the healing was just beginning. On cue, both she and Khamun dug their fangs into Calvin's and Nydia's bodies. Ryo and Kyo opened their majestic mouths then roared covering the bodies in flames.

Light washed over everyone in the room as the wings of the Sin Eater and the Oracle expanded. The sound of drums ebbed in the great hall. The ancient soul song from the First Chosen connected with everyone's spirits syncing them to it as the world fell to silence and a moment of peace was felt around the world.

> *And the world will lift up in peace.*
> *The fallen will end up redeemed.*
> *All that was lost will live on and heal.*
> *And the children of the Chosen will succeed.*
> *All that fell will be cleansed.*
> *And love will conquer all pain.*

Chapter 25

The silence in her mind was deafening. No longer was she captive to the confusing muddle that only she could hear. No one understood how truly intense her madness was. She operated on fear, something she never realized until now. It was also something her community of killers never caught on due to her mirrored condition of her father. However, now here she was lost again in her mind, but this time, in peace.

The kingdom was in an uproar with the loss of numbers on their side. They had lost many souls in that battle and found out many truths of certainty. One truth was that the legend long ago forgotten had been reborn. The mouthpiece of he who shall not be named was alive with that of his divine weapon, the Reaper. This sparked the return of the Sin Eaters.

There was no making her theirs. With the Reaper's return, their side was now worried that other Sin Eaters would come into light again. For if that happened, the scales would tip and a balance would come about. A balance they did not want, so they had to stop the repopulation and find the other books.

"We start the end of days now! Bring me the book!"

She heard her father roar and his sickening madness rubbed at something within her. He didn't care that she had just lost her Protector, not that she believed he would. He didn't care that his son, the dark prince, was alive on their side. Correction, he cared. He took out his revenge on her body for not taking out her brother those many years ago, but how could she have? He was the other half of her, her darkling mirror, her best friend. Nydia. Marco. Winter.

See, these were things she couldn't remember in the time the darkness muddled her mind, no, when her mother's murder muddled her mind. She felt the eyes of her ex-lover and true Elder in her kingdom on her: Jacques. He watched her in quiet reserve. She knew that look. Understood exactly what was going on in his mind.

The man never should have let her touch him because now things were different. He did nothing but sit back and cause chaos among both sides, and now she knew it. He got joy out his power. Joy out of playing the middle and she guessed she would have to at one time or another. However, what he was doing was foul in both societies. The fact that he did nothing when the Mad King went out of his way to kill his Queen, the fact that he practically put the gun in Reina's small hands . . .

She could remember her mother showing her and Marco something she had hidden. She had taken them deep within the underground city that was the Cursed kingdom and she have felt a slight shift in the atmosphere where they stood. She remembered hearing Marco saying the land felt different, that this was not home. She then remembered hearing her mother say it was part of their true home, where their father could never step foot but they could. It was curious back then and it was curious now. She wondered . . .

"Reina! I want her head do you hear me? She may be in her full bloom but I will still have that Oracle bitch."

Locked in her daze, she quietly nodded in silence and she watched her father's crazed eyes gleam in satisfaction. He stood bloodied, burned, and battered. Bullets were lodged into his flesh that none of the Witches or Warlock medics could pull out. He was still cut and bleeding from the fight with the Sin Eater and Oracle. His torso held an open, gaping wound. His charred chest held the claw marks of the Sin Eater's soul snatch and his neck held the Oracle's bite mark, which was currently eating at his flesh. Her father was a walking zombie in a sense. His once-mighty wings were now stubs of torn flesh, true representation of his Fallen identity.

However, through it all, he didn't care. He didn't care about all the blood that was on their hands. He didn't care that she had just killed her best friend and her lover. All he saw was traitors as he walked around in unhinged torn pieces of flesh. As if he wasn't a failure.

"Daddy is going to be mad," she muttered to herself. Her father had the child Brandon in front of him, screaming about the book, and needing the blood of the One Son.

"It's not for yews! No, no, no! It's mine!" Brandon screamed in a tirade.

A swift swipe, then the shout of Jacques had Reina watching in shock. Blood coated the floor. The child's body lay depleted of life, his soot-black eyes turning cold with death. She had sat observing, listening to the ramblings of her father. The voices in her mind were calm but that touch of madness she had changed. It made her different, and ready to lash out on her enemy when that child fell to his death. But, a problem arose the moment the King stood behind her, decaying before them, although his Warlock was fixing it as they all sat. She felt him dig his nails into her flesh, cutting at the skin of her own neck while he spoke.

"Fool! He was the key to reading the book!" Jacques yelled, his hands gripping his chair.

"The child is nothing. We have the book and my daughter will rectify the losses. She will regain our numbers, as we all will. The Princess will step into her rightful power with her new responsibility as the leader of the Horsemen," her father countered.

Reina was shocked, pleased, and pissed. She knew this was another ploy to keep her by his side, so that she wouldn't stray to play her games of power within the kingdom. He knew what she wanted. She wanted Jacques's position. She wanted the crown and he was making sure she would not have it by sacrificing her to be the punching bag for the true King. Lucifer.

Her mind screamed, and betrayal flowed into her. She felt her eyes go silver as the air around them chilled. This was new. This was what she wanted. This was what the Mad King was afraid of.

"She will be my grand warrior. I took you from your weak mother. Then ended her tainted existence as my false queen and now you will wear that mantle and fight as a true Dark Ark." He cooed in pride in his soulless eyes.

He bared his fangs then shouted, "Bring in the demons."

Tension had her ridged. She knew what was coming. He was going to infuse her with the demons like he did Nydia. She remembered that pain Nydia went through. She remembered the wall, too, and she knew as he watched her and undressed her with his sick eyes that he wanted her in his bed next.

Al igual que el infierno. Like hell would he ever touch her.

She knew she wasn't his daughter anymore just flesh and as she sat in stupor, the words from the Oracle rang in her mind. She would be her mother's retribution. Everything happened fast. The moment the King dropped his head to give her the royal kiss on her lips, his hands on her thighs, she watched him step back and hold his hands out in celebration.

"We will win this; we will be victorious in bringing hell on earth!" he yelled.

Reina smiled and stood with him, as the Warlocks and Witches made their way to her. She saw her own Witch Winter, the hatred in her sapphire eyes blazed bright and she knew her Witch was on her side. That confirmation had something from within her snap. As if on cue, she pushed back to walk around the King.

"No. I want your crown, *Papi*," Reina coldly whispered.

Her blade was at his throat then she slashed deep. The chains from her wrist wrapped around his throat cutting at the rest of his charred flesh. Her father's dark red blood spilled as his eyes widen in satisfaction, and fury. Her head bowed forward. Her then mouth lapped at all that he spelled from him. Then pleasure of her wings slashing out and ripping forward to impale him from behind made her gleefully smile. The Dark Lady then unhinged her asp ring, revealing the Nail of Nazareth, given to her and blessed by both the Oracle and Sin Eater.

"A final gift from the ones you tried to destroy, *Papi*, and a kiss from Mommy." She gave him a kiss as old as time: the kiss of Judas.

Sinisterly smiling, she saw everyone in the room try to fight to get to her and end her life. Jacques was held down by Winter, who locked him in chains of iron while she sat straddled on his lap. His head was in her arms ready to snap it at the signal. Everyone knew not to move toward the Elder or he would be done and that would bring nothing but war from the true King.

Reina plunged the nail into his heart and she almost came at the sound of his pain. All of the sins she knew were replaying for him, slicing through him. All the torment of the world was turning in on him. His weak shell was done. He was not a true Elder, not like Jacques. Jacques would be hard to kill, but shockingly her father was simple and easy to take down. She laughed then dropped his body. She snickered as she took a blade from the wall and stood on his throat, the blade pointing at him.

"This is for Marco and for you tainting me to become the Betrayer. Thirty slashes equals the thirty pieces of silver you gave me!" she shrieked.

She knew as he stared into her maddened eyes who she truly was, and he laughed in pleasure before she beheaded him. She dropped down on his chest. Ripped out his husk of a heart, and then used the nail to stab it again. Underneath her, she held on as the body groaned, bulked, and then exploded into black-red visceral goo. Every drop of the King fused again then turned into glowing white ash before his voice could be heard in the fires of hell. He was no more. He was officially truly Lucifer's and she smiled.

Tilting her head to the side in satisfaction, Reina flipped her hair over shoulder then slowly stood. Covered in the blood of her father, she walked to the throne, and then took her place as Queen.

Winter climbed off Jacques. She unlocked him to saunter next to her side. Jacques smugly sat back, adjust his cuffs, and then stood with a slow clap.

"Touché, but you know I can't accept what just occurred, baby girl. No, not acceptable," Jacques pleasantly stated.

She watched him walk off, his fury blazing. It was time to insert her power, but she found herself inwardly laughing before muttering, "*Sí,* you better run; you know your time is next, lover."

Demons, Dark Nephilims, and the High Cursed councils moved to prepare for the next phase, unaware that soon, those plans would be their end. Retribution was now hers. She intended to play it the only the way she could. Eye for a delicious eye. Reina's mind became clear while she listened to the message given to her by the Oracle.

"Yes, my daughter, you honored me, but your suffering is not over. They have you. Protect your mind." The comforting voice of her mother washed over her. Light blanketed her senses, and then was ripped apart in swallowing darkness. She was not where she believed she should be. She was not free. The quickening of her heartbeat, the sudden sulfuric taste in her mouth and smothering pressure on her chest, made her try to lash out but she couldn't. Hands snatched at her hair, clawed and cut into her skin. Endless darkness took over her vision and she knew instantly the moment the sound of a banshee's wail and millions upon millions of sobs, pleas, anger, pain, and soul-rendering sadness bore into her sense.

"No, I'm free. I'm free. I got out! Damn it, I got out!"

"Yes, you are now free from the madness and now you must be free of this prison. I'll guide you, my daughter," her mother said.

Confusion made her scream. She turned in the muddled ink-black thick mass that ripped at her. Anger and the flash of her being pulled into the darkness at the battlefield by her father slipped into her awareness. She saw herself falling to her knees in front of him, and her successfully attacking him, killing him, only to be pulled off by Jacques. The scene made her eyes close in defeat. She had achieved the first steps of being her mother's sleeper agent with Nydia and Winter. Helping the Light all along but never knowing it. Nydia had gotten away in time; she and Winter didn't. Now the attack on her father had her locked away with only the images of her true purpose playing in her mind.

Sadness made her lash out. It had her snap the necks of the demons locked in her prison with her. Caused her to feed from them and rip their evil away as her mother's light cloaked her with that of the essence of Nydia's light.

They helped her rip forward moving like a hurricane. Her madness was her weapon.

She used it to empty out a space to move. Ice trails followed where she walked, and evil shrank away as her touch. The wall of Purgatory groaned and swelled. She heard the voice of her captors; asked if anyone saw where she now rested. Demons, helpmates to Jacques hissed and roared a no. The familiar laughter of her dead father echoed around her before the screams of those demons tore at her skull and the scent of their blood permeated the wall.

They were dead. The only one who knew where she was held was the appointed leader of all that was evil on Earth.

No one will ever find me.

Cries of pain and sorrow assaulted her, while the wall bowed forward pushing and clawing to get away from the woman it held. Reina's wings ripped from her back to slice at its evil and feed the good captives within. Wisps of ice decorated the hand-printed wall. Her power froze its surface as black-red blood slowly wept from its wall in light frost. The wall had her. However, she now held it in her control with the knowing feeling that one day she would be freed. She gave a slight jerk as the sound of her mother's voice suddenly echoed in her mind and the face of a woman she once called pet flickered then faded into the darkness.

Epilogue

Six months later, in a hidden location in St. Louis, Missouri . . .

The sound of keys clicking from the rapid typing of a young woman, dressed in casual jeans and a simple red shirt, sitting in front of a computer fills an old university library full of books from around the world. Her mendi-covered hands and gold-painted tipped fingers spark with electricity. She flips her ponytail over her shoulder then glances around giving orders. A small band of people, three young men, walk around in a hustle, with cell phones to their ears, while a tall young male with markings on his arms speaks to individuals on large monitors in a wall. In the middle of this flurry, a woman with thick loose-coiled hair upon her shoulders and glowing amber eyes stands surrounded by cameras, and lights.

Her caramel-toned skin glows in an ethereal luminescence. She rolls her shoulders, her lush, plump lips moving while she speaks to herself as if reciting. In her left hand is a blade, which appears to resemble that of silver and liquid diamond, fused together; she places it on a matching chain and it lies between her bosom. On her jean-clad thigh, she nestles a silver gun, once carried by her lover, a man who awakened her and brought out her true destiny. Determination sparkles in her eyes. She gives a warm smile at a woman with a short, asymmetrical bob haircut and matching outfit. The tips of her hair are the color of her mismatched jade eyes. Her nails sparkled, reflecting the lights around them and she stands to the left of the woman. On her wrists are two silver axe bracelets that match the woman's next to her. They stand strong as warriors as they address the screen.

"Start transmission.

"Sometimes life doesn't always tie up in a perfect ribbon. A lesson I have taken with me on the start of my journey in learning and growing into my destiny. The battle against the dark, the Cursed, has given us many wins, but we lost so much more. The Darkness, those individuals I've just only began to understand, the Cursed, have found a way to even make what I thought was our triumph against them into their success.

"From our battle, a fraction has occurred between the Light Nephilim, who were in support of the wrong old ways. This fraction is with those who finally woke up and saw the taint that was spreading in the Council and bourgeois Light Nephilim Society. Those of us who know the truth, who recall the true ways, are at attack. We are at attack for standing up against the wrongs done in Society. So much has occurred in a small gap of time because of it and I now realize how deeply rooted the Cursed hands are in destroying all that is Light.

"Our battle made us lose my cousin and his true heart. My power was too unskilled to bring them back fully though they have changed. I had no idea that the Shroud was capable of resurrection, but it was me, not being fully in my birthright that caused it to malfunction. For now, we work with the blessing we were given from it, their deep, healing sleep.

"They are hidden away in safety from both sides of the Light and Dark, who have put a bounty on our heads for going against the grain. They act as additional sources of power that guide us all. I watch their dreams. I see how one's true gift as a first-level oracle mends itself with my cousin's Mystic healing gift, giving the remaining ragtag rebels and me clues on how to fix what has gone so wrong.

"Yet, everything is still so wrong.

"I did not expect this separation to occur. It was not planned for the House of Dusk to truly turn into an underground movement. However, it has with the arrest of my love, the Sin Eater reborn, High Prince Khamun with that of his right and left hand, the Gray Prince Marco and Templar Knight Lenox. Everything was turned against us in the end. Those surviving Council members and Nephilim Dignitaries, who were already against us, formed a strong alliance. A Shadow Council bent on preserving the pure blood of the Nephilim race and cast out all Gargoyle races with those of us who carry the human gene. We thought the battle would expose them and wipe that evil out but like festering cancer, it only spread. With help from within, we have learned that a Shadow Light Council, who are nothing but puppets for an enemy worse than we had previously battled is contesting High King Omari and High Queen Neffer's rights. This must be stopped.

"The Snake. The creator of the original sin. He and I will come face to face and his acts will be handled. He took my love and part of my family. He secretly claimed the open seat to hell and now is going after the seat to heaven on earth.

"I know his plan because it worked once before, and because of that, he has already failed. He cannot have me and even though he has put a bounty on my head, and is using old world laws to try to strip the royals of their power, he will not succeed. He forgets that I am no longer blocked. With the ending battle, my memory of who and what I am has been restored and yes, I must continue training.

"With studying the books of our history and unlocking the second book, I dedicate myself to helping our people. I must continue seeking out the knowledge and resources I need to prune out the darkness in the light. I am the Oracle. My words are not dripped in lies, as the Shadow Council will have you believe.

"This is truth! This is real talk!

"My power comes from the One and his son. I am the mortar in the foundation, the hope in the teachings, and the true final component to the spiritual Trinity. I am His mouthpiece. I was there when the One Son, the true Sin Eater, sacrificed himself and became the teacher, the symbolic father to the first angel-made Sin Eaters.

"Because of that, I know the secret to ending the snake that crept into Paradise. Balance will return and innocents everywhere will be protected from harm; this is my word and destiny. So it is back to the basics. I now seek out my new teacher, a man who helped us bring down the Cursed.

"It is him that we need to help us revive an enemy and her other protector. Like all games in chess, we need the opponent's pieces to continue this never-ending battle and this time we will use the upper hand we have in better use.

"In these words, is my vow to all humans and Nephilims around the world. With my Protector and the rest of the surviving House of Dusk at my side, the journal of the first Sin Eater will lead me to the lost Archangel, and he will lead me to specific knowledge that I need to strengthen our goal. It will also lead me into awakening the Sin Eater and oracle DNA in all that carry the spark. However, first, my objective, my primary vendetta, is against the Shadow Council and the new leaders of the Cursed will begin with fair exchange and an eye for an eye. Their blood will flow.

"The game has changed and Gray's network is now up. This is a call to all rebels who live in the gray and who battle against the Dark. The Light has fallen and it is up to us to shake the system. We are the true children of the Light. All nations, all creeds, we stand against those who chose to oppress us. We will prevail as true children of the Light.

"When the Light and Dark are at war, sometimes the Gray can be the only salvation. This is what we were born and trained to do. Protect the innocent as all cost. That includes ourselves. So I will say it again: it is back to the basics.

"We will do what the Shadow Council won't. Nephilim of every rank, guard the innocent but stand with your fellow Immortals, Slayers, and Gargoyles. Pick up the mantel of Warrior, as you once were when the Houses were founded. This fight is for us all. It will not be easy and a bounty is on those who stand against the new Council.

"As the Cursed would say, 'What is lost is what is taken and what you lose is what we take."

"It is time we give that back to them. We are the Gray and fair exchange is no robbery. Balance is our mantle and we will heal what was broken, no matter how long it may take.

"I am the rebel and a Sin Eater. I am the House of Dusk. I am the Oracle."

"This is my journey and my entry into our own chronicles. Stand with me."

"End transmission."

The Oracle walks away and stands over the sleeping bodies of her beloved cousin and his long-lost love, peeking into their dreams as the Shroud glows like a cloak, healing, and changing the pair's bodies. She leans down and whispers her thanks for giving her more clues to her mission, and she lets her power encompass them, hiding them from the world until it is time for them to awake.

The sound of a doorbell ringing loudly interrupted the Medusa from flipping through the pages of a leather-bound book given to her long ago by a beautiful woman she had met as a child. She always found herself reading it, discovering new stories written in it about a rogue Nephilim team, around this same time. Now, the pages had her mind filled in confusion with hope and happiness. She minimized her Internet browser, which displayed news pictures of Chicago's many deaths after the fiery pruning of the Nephilim and humans by the Cursed. One click, she turned off her laptop as Miguel crooned "Adorn." A knock at her door drew her attention.

"Sweetheart, your father said get to the main house; you have a visitor. I hope it's not about that car accident you got into while going to the courthouse. Messing up your father's car like that over a kitten in the road," a lilting, accented voice said.

"Ain't this a biscuit! Momma, you know how I am about cats," she said.

"Yes, I do flower, now do as I said and get to the door. I have food on the stove about to burn!"

The soft-decibel laugh of her mother seemed to give her a healing balm she always needed. Slowly pushing off her bed, she gingerly headed to the living room at the main house. Familiar aches down her back kept her pace in control. The weather was blazing in Houston today, the heat advisory warned everyone to stay in, but for her family this meant a barbeque, especially since she was celebrating her twenty-eighth birthday. This life was a blessing and her mind traveled back to the trapped woman in the wall of her book.

She wondered if the woman would be saved because something about the chick made her heart go out to her in sadness as did her many dreams. The sound of the doorbell going off again had her rushing to the main house.

"Hello, can I help you?" she asked shielding her dilating eyes from the sun. Eyes her friends used to tease her about for looking reptilian. The brief whiff of male hit her hard, making her step forward in desire.

"Yes, ma'am, are you Nydia Randal? I'm the owner of the car you hit downtown at the courthouse. I wanted to get your insurance information together since I'm only in town visiting, shawty."

She gawked at the strange accent; a fusion of New York meets New Orleans triggered something familiar in her mind. Eyes the color of jade grass glanced down at her, studying her with a knowing understanding she didn't get. Brotha was fine. Chocolate with deep-set waves in his fade that formed a faux hawk. She swore she saw different swirling tribal designs cut into it, but she had to be wrong because it was nothing there. Rugged laced-up black boots with dark jeans that fit him like a man should be fit, not sagging but not tight, covered his long, muscle-thick legs and thighs. He wore a simple black vest, dark gray button-down shirt with rolled up sleeves and a black beater peeking from under the unbuttoned gray shirt.

She licked her lips and glanced up at the man who was around the same height as her father. A pair of pearly fangs flashed at her in a smile. Fangs that marked him a Guardian Nephilim. His presence, his height, build, and electric flash in his pupils had her stepping backward and opening the door wider. She stared hard, noticing a jet-black business card that had the words: Templar & Co. International. Nephilim always recognized each other in subtle ways, by the Society House crests on their doors, or in small differences in their auras. In this case, it was that smile and the name of the company that triggered something deeply within her.

This man had just called her out. The quickening of her heart made her nervously push her long braids over her shoulder. She anxiously moved to the side, opening the door wider to watch him smoothly step in. There seemed to be a quiet knowing in his jade eyes that had her muttering, "Call me Fatima."

And she heard him croon, *"C'est si bon,* bae'bay. I'm Calvin. Happy birthday, Fatima."

Humans:

Nephilim: A race of individuals who are born from the pairing of an angel and human. They can be Light or Dark. Their subsets are: humans with recessive traits (Prophets), Latent, Immortals, or rare full-blooded (Archangels). Very few have fangs and wings.

Vessels: Humans or Nephilim who carry the blood of the Ancient Archangels, but are hidden. They are usually protected by Gargoyles.

Guides: Also known as Chosen. Humans who are being watched by Guardians.

Prophets: Humans who have the gift of mystics or seers but are not immortals, who also help Guardians and angels who do not know their history. They are the keepers of the history of Eternity.

Latent Nephilim: Humans who gain their gifts later in life, or have a partially active Nephilim gene. (They are usually Prophets or Disciples.)

Nephilim:

Archangels: These are the combat guardians. They are meant to only intervene in their chosen lives if they are in danger and they hunt the Cursed and demons. They have disappeared over time. (It is speculated that they are Elders, and may be pure blood.)

Sin Eaters: A lost sect of Archangels chosen to take on the traits of the Angel of Death i.e. Reaper. They are able to drain the sins and darkness from humans and demons. They feed on the Cursed and neutralize sins and evils, by either killing the host or demon, or by returning the sins to the Light, which, with demons, kills them. In later generations, these angels become Nephilim, half human/angel. Sin Eaters are marked by their fangs and aggressive personalities. The Reaper is a Throne-class Sin Eater.

Guardians: Nephilim Angels who only watch over their chosen. They do not get involved in combat, and they record who to watch. They are able to detect tainted humans and Phantoms.

Guardian Disciples: They can be strong Immortals who take on the role of Guardians. They are Guardian Disciples. They only watch and record. This happens if a region is limited in Guardian Angels.

Oracles: Lower-level angels also known as intercessors or Virtue Angels. Their power is determined by levels. Some are gifted with sight. Some can move through the past, present, and future in their visions. They hold the history of everything. They carry out the Most High's orders by hearing his commands. Some can heal/restore energy and can read people's souls. They have the power to read truths. If powerful enough, they can unlock a blocked angel or Nephilim's mind. They do not have any other powers.

The Oracle: Also known as a Throne Angel. Is a being that is gifted like an intercessor, but has the power of all Nephilims. He or she is a powerhouse, and only one is born a lifetime when called. Can directly speak with the Most High.

Oracle Intercessor Levels:

First level: Throne. They can do everything oracles, mystics, and slayers can do, but the only differences is they can directly speak to the Most High, receive direct orders, and are the breathing Holy Spirit with the power of the divine. To have a Throne-born always means a war or something major is going to happen, which is why Thrones are so rare.

Second level: Dominion (their job is to regulate the duties of the other Angels and ensure that God's wishes are carried out).

Third level: Virtues. Stronger gifts, also known as Guardian oracles.

Fourth level: Seers/Mystics. They help guardians by recording the history of all the angels and human chosens, and locate other immortals or angels born outside of the Nephilim society. **Note**: They do not call this level Oracles because it is lowly ranked, but they are related. This means someone in his or her line is an Oracle or will be. This is why they are frequently targeted by the Cursed.

Triad: Also known as the Trinity, when linked with the Oracle. Hidden weapon of God long forgotten and only known by the eldest blood. They are able to detect and possess the Dark, making them do anything they want. Only one triad is born a generation and the gift usually dies out in the bloodline. The Dark does not have an equivalent so they tip the scales, which is why the Dark always seeks to kill any Triads if found. Triads cannot be turned.

Mystics: Also called Light Witches. Same as seers but are able to use scripture, chants, et cetera as white magic, and channel white magic.

Immortals: Also called Disciples and Slayers. These are the long-lived humans (50,000 years). They stop aging at twenty-five years and age four years a decade after that.

Immortals Disciples: These Immortals are those who just have the gift of sight or white magic. They help the Nephilim Mystics' powers as anchors amplifying their powers.

Slayers: These are the Immortal humans who help with the fight against the Cursed. They have some of the strength of angels.

Gargoyles: Also known as Protectors. These are the human-like hybrids of demons and humans. There are also other hybrids of them, such as Dragons. They are ostracized in the Light community and are used as killing pets. They are loyal to Vessels and Sin Eaters. They have super speed, hearing, smell, taste, and psychic sense. Some can fly and all have nails hard as diamonds. Some make a clicking sound and have poisonous nails or fangs. Gargoyles turn into stone at sunlight. They hibernate until the sun sets. Some are able to cut their hibernation in half, if there is a strong link with their Vessel or Sin Eater.

Infinity Phantoms: Nephilim angels who keep the balance of neutrality. They can play whatever side they want, which makes them unpredictable. But the majority are good unless made to be Cursed Phantoms.

House Garrisons: A House made up of hunters, Stalkers, et cetera, who watch and protect high-ranking Society members if they do not have a gargoyle. Not every House is able to afford or have an H.G.

Dignitary Council: Members of a Royal House. Able to apply at twenty-five years old.

Dark Nephilim/Cursed:

Cursed Initiates: Also known as Cursed Chosen. Individuals the Cursed snatch or plan to turn.

Fallen: Also known as the Ancient ones or Shroud-Eaters. Only Fallen Elders. No new bloods have been born after they were Cursed. They cannot create or reproduce.

Anarchy Snatchers: Also known as Stalkers. They are comprised of many different sublevels of fallen, such as Stalkers. Anarchy Snatchers are combat Dark Guardians. They are meant to cause chaos and death to many humans and Light Nephilims. They feed off of the souls and blood of humans and can turn light angels into cursed through a venom bite and soul-polluting infusion. Historically they are the demons labeled Vampires.

Anarchy Stalkers: They only stalk their prey and they hunt those humans who have potential to lose their souls, turning them into Dark Immortals.

Dark Immortals/Hunters: These are the long-lived humans, as well as the sublevel races. They can be created only by the Anarchy levels or born evil.

Seers or Witches/Warlocks: They help stalkers by recording the history of all the dark angels, and human chosens. They locate other Light Nephilim. They can also use Dark Magic and heal.

Hunters: These are the Dark Immortal humans who help with the fight against the light. They have some of the gifts of the demons and strength but only have the half-life of a demon. They stop aging after twenty-five then begin to age rapidly after four decades.

Dark Gargoyles: Also called Demons and have many sublevels of their race, such as Dark Dragons. They are the human-like hybrids of demons and humans. They are ostracized in the cursed community and are used as killing pets; they have not gained a soul. They are flesh-eating maniacs. They do not change into human form and smell of putrid sulfur and acid. They do turn into a soft stone if they touch hallowed land. Gargoyles are extremely fast, some can fly, and are lithe and flexible.

Demon Dragons: Can no longer hold the pure and honorable shape of a Dragon. In their human form, their nails seem to be dipped in black ink, as their scales line varied spots on their skin. Some have protruding spinal columns. Others have varied nodules on their skin that will later turn into serpent horns. Dark Gargoyle Dragons can never stay hidden as spies for long; that telltale sign of a persistent cough, which spews black blood, always gives them away. They can no longer walk in the light as well (allergic to direct sunlight).

Phantoms: Light Societal Members who think they have more to gain on the Dark's side. Insurgents for the Cursed. Their skin has a soft glow to it from their spirits taking over their human body. Their eyes are opaque or really light, which is why many wear sunglasses or contacts.

Terms:

Trinity/Trinities: Society's term for a cigarillo that has ancient spices and herbs from China, India, and Egypt blended to calm or heal. It boosts the immune system and grants additional speed. Very helpful in calming agitated Gargoyles. It is not addictive but it is still frowned upon in high Nephilim Society.

Qua Gum: Energy gum; a quick energy restorative like Red Bull.

Hemorush: Process of giving a person some of their blood to help the individual who was bitten create blood faster in order to replenish them.

Sustaining Mixture: Hemorush, water, proteins, and herbs. A drink that tastes like cod-liver oil and cooked grease. Helps slow down the Cursed bite.

Psylin: To heal a human who is bitten, with a touch or counter bite.

Slayer Runes: Also known as Protection spells. These are markers left behind for other Guardians to know that a tracking or battle went down. They can see what Protection scriptures are used, what weapons, and then some.

Locus Tracer: A tracking system injected into a demon's and Dark Nephilim's bloodstream for Slayers to track. It also slows demons down until they die from poison.

The Priming or Evolution: When a Nephilim comes into their maturity usually between sixteen and seventeen years of age. Those coming into their power, if human, are known by their glowing skin; only other Nephilims and the Dark can detect it. If a late priming occurs, some may not survive it.

Transition: To teleport from one region to another. It uses a lot of energy so it is only used for short distances. Angels can carry up to three people in flight, but can move a small group through transition spells.

Denotation: A vision that is sent as a warning. Usually a jumbled premonition. Anyone can have them, but usually they are given to non-seers and Prophets.

Mating Attraction: If a female is near a male who matches her pheromone, they will automatically mind lock. If the mind syncs perfectly, then a female knows she has found a strong potential mate. If not a good match, i.e. threat, the woman either attacks, or calls a protector to defend her. If it were just a normal incompatibility then she would shun him.

Craving: When a male goes into heat for his mate.

Marking Bite: The releasing of pheromones through the fangs that is injected into the intended mate. This only happens during the Craving and when an intended mate has opened their mental barriers for the union. This bite signals a marriage of sorts and it is a sweet, tart flavor for some. Residue of it can be in the saliva.

Oil of Ruth: A mixture of spikenard, myrrh, cinnamon, and olive oil. It helps with aches, pains, and is used in lessening the pain of cramps. It is also used on the marriage night with a virgin.

ORDER FORM
URBAN BOOKS, LLC
78 E. Industry Ct
Deer Park, NY 11729

Name: (please print):_____

Address: _____

City/State: _____

Zip: _____

QTY	TITLES	PRICE
	16 On The Block	$14.95
	A Girl From Flint	$14.95
	A Pimp's Life	$14.95
	Baltimore Chronicles	$14.95
	Baltimore Chronicles 2	$14.95
	Betrayal	$14.95
	Black Diamond	$14.95
	Black Diamond 2	$14.95
	Black Friday	$14.95
	Both Sides Of The Fence	$14.95
	Both Sides Of The Fence 2	$14.95
	California Connection	$14.95

Shipping and handling-add $3.50 for 1st book, then $1.75 for each additional book.

Please send a check payable to:

Urban Books, LLC

Please allow 4-6 weeks for delivery

ORDER FORM
URBAN BOOKS, LLC
78 E. Industry Ct
Deer Park, NY 11729

Name:(please print):_____

Address: _____

City/State: _____

Zip: _____

QTY	TITLES	PRICE
	California Connection 2	$14.95
	Cheesecake And Teardrops	$14.95
	Congratulations	$14.95
	Crazy In Love	$14.95
	Cyber Case	$14.95
	Denim Diaries	$14.95
	Diary Of A Mad First Lady	$14.95
	Diary Of A Stalker	$14.95
	Diary Of A Street Diva	$14.95
	Diary Of A Young Girl	$14.95
	Dirty Money	$14.95
	Dirty To The Grave	$14.95

Shipping and handling-add $3.50 for 1st book, then $1.75 for each additional book.
Please send a check payable to:
Urban Books, LLC
Please allow 4-6 weeks for delivery

ORDER FORM
URBAN BOOKS, LLC
78 E. Industry Ct
Deer Park, NY 11729

Name:(please print):_____

Address: _____

City/State: _____

Zip: _____

QTY	TITLES	PRICE
	Gunz And Roses	$14.95
	Happily Ever Now	$14.95
	Hell Has No Fury	$14.95
	Hush	$14.95
	If It Isn't love	$14.95
	Kiss Kiss Bang Bang	$14.95
	Last Breath	$14.95
	Little Black Girl Lost	$14.95
	Little Black Girl Lost 2	$14.95
	Little Black Girl Lost 3	$14.95
	Little Black Girl Lost 4	$14.95
	Little Black Girl Lost 5	$14.95

Shipping and handling-add $3.50 for 1st book, then $1.75 for each additional book.
Please send a check payable to:
Urban Books, LLC
Please allow 4-6 weeks for delivery

ORDER FORM
URBAN BOOKS, LLC
78 E. Industry Ct
Deer Park, NY 11729

Name: (please print): _____

Address: _____

City/State: _____

Zip: _____

QTY	TITLES	PRICE
	Loving Dasia	$14.95
	Material Girl	$14.95
	Moth To A Flame	$14.95
	Mr. High Maintenance	$14.95
	My Little Secret	$14.95
	Naughty	$14.95
	Naughty 2	$14.95
	Naughty 3	$14.95
	Queen Bee	$14.95
	Say It Ain't So	$14.95
	Snapped	$14.95
	Snow White	$14.95

Shipping and handling-add $3.50 for 1st book, then $1.75 for each additional book.

Please send a check payable to:

Urban Books, LLC

Please allow 4-6 weeks for delivery